PRAISE FOR
NOVELS OF T...

BL...

"Not only was this book ju... readable as *Shadow Kin*—... with it and spun its own story all the w... continuing the grander symphony that is slowly becoming the Half-Light City story.... Smart, funny, dangerous, addictive, and seductive in its languorous sexuality, I can think of no better book to recommend to anyone to read this summer. I loved every single page except the last one, and that's only because it meant the story was done. For now, at least." — seattlepi.com

"*Blood Kin* was one of those books that I really didn't want to put down, as it hit all of my buttons for an entertaining story. It had the intrigue and danger of a spy novel, intense action scenes, and a romance that evolved organically over the course of the story.... Whether this is your first visit to Half-Light City or you're already a fan, *Blood Kin* expertly weaves the events from *Shadow Kin* throughout this sequel in a way that entices new readers without boring old ones. I am really looking forward to continuing this enthralling ride." —All Things Urban Fantasy

"*Blood Kin* had everything I love about urban fantasies: kick-butt action, fantastic characters, romance that makes the heart beat fast, and a plot that was fast-paced all the way through. Even more so the villains are meaner, stronger, and downright fantastic—I never knew what they were going to do next. You don't want to miss out on this series." —Seeing Night Book Reviews

continued . . .

"An exciting thriller . . . fast-paced and well written."
—Genre Go Round Reviews

SHADOW KIN

"M. J. Scott's *Shadow Kin* is a steampunky romantic fantasy with vampires that doesn't miss its mark."
—#1 *New York Times* bestselling author Patricia Briggs

"*Shadow Kin* is an entertaining novel. Lily and Simon are sympathetic characters who feel the weight of past actions and secrets as they respond to their attraction for each other." —*New York Times* bestselling author Anne Bishop

"M. J. Scott weaves a fantastic tale of love, betrayal, hope, and sacrifice against a world broken by darkness and light, where the only chance for survival rests within the strength of a woman made of shadow and the faith of a man made of light." —National bestselling author Devon Monk

"Had me hooked from the very first page."
—*New York Times* bestselling author Keri Arthur

"Exciting and rife with political intrigue and magic, *Shadow Kin* is hard to put down right from the start. Magic, faeries, vampires, werewolves, and Templar knights all come together to create an intriguing story with a unique take on all these fantasy tropes. . . . The lore and history of Scott's world is well fleshed out and the action scenes are exhilarating and fast." —*Romantic Times*

"A fabulous tale." —Genre Go Round Reviews

Also by M. J. Scott

Shadow Kin
Blood Kin

IRON KIN

A NOVEL OF THE HALF-LIGHT CITY

M. J. SCOTT

A ROC BOOK

ROC
Published by the Penguin Group
Penguin Group (USA) Inc., 375 Hudson Street,
New York, New York 10014, USA

USA | Canada | UK | Ireland | Australia | New Zealand | India | South Africa | China

Penguin Books Ltd., Registered Offices: 80 Strand, London WC2R 0RL, England
For more information about the Penguin Group visit penguin.com.

First published by Roc, an imprint of New American Library,
a division of Penguin Group (USA) Inc.

First Printing, April 2013

 REGISTERED TRADEMARK—MARCA REGISTRADA

ISBN 978-0-451-46505-4

Printed in the United States of America
10 9 8 7 6 5 4 3 2 1

PUBLISHER'S NOTE
This is a work of fiction. Names, characters, places, and incidents either are the
product of the author's imagination or are used fictitiously, and any resemblance
to actual persons, living or dead, business establishments, events, or locales is
entirely coincidental.

The publisher does not have any control over and does not assume any
responsibility for author or third-party Web sites or their content.

ALWAYS LEARNING   PEARSON

For Chris, Carolyn, Freya, Keri and Robyn.

For many years of laughter, commiserations, chocolate, celebrations and wise words. Lulus rock!

ACKNOWLEDGMENTS

Writing this book has spanned a year of broken ankles, new feline additions (welcoming the fuzzy girl to the ranks of writer companion cats), and many other unexpected twists and turns. So once again, there are many people to thank.

My patient and excellent editor Jessica Wade, who, as usual, made the book better and made this writer happy by not thinking the book was terrible.

My agent, the lovely Miriam Kriss, who is always supportive and full of good advice, no matter what has happened.

The wonderful team at Roc, including the ever brilliant art department, who keep coming up with covers of jaw-dropping beauty (with bonus glowing daggers), who help turn my words into a real live book (never going to get old), and send it out into the world.

All the lovely readers, who've been telling me that they like it here in Half-Light, which means the world to me.

And last, but never least, to my always-there family and friends who have carted me around, picked me up, brushed me down, cheered me on and gotten me through. You're awesome.

To see too far
To know too much
Some want to look
Yet cannot see
Some would hide from sight
It's better not to know
Because the future burns

Chapter One

FEN

My head hurt like a bastard.

Nothing terribly unusual in that, but the fact that my wrist also throbbed like a Beast had chewed on it was disconcerting. If I'd drunk enough to set devils driving spikes into my brain and yet had still had to tighten the iron around my wrist, then the visions must have fought me yet again. Hard.

They were getting worse.

I lay for a moment, breathing cautiously, trying to remember. But the images of last night were hazy and blurred together with those of the past weeks. Each new day, harder than the last. Right now, I wanted to will myself back to sleep. And the oblivion it brought.

But just as I was savoring the thought, I remembered the ball.

The oh-so-respectable human ball I had promised to escort Regina to.

Shal e'tan mei.

The muttered curse made my head pound harder. Couldn't I just stay here in bed?

No. Veil's buggering eyes. There was no way to do that without risking seeing that shadowed look that all too often haunted Reggie's blue eyes since Holly had rescued her from Summerdale. I'd do many things to avoid seeing that expression. Reggie was still too quiet and a little too thin and the ball had been one of the few things that had seemed to genuinely engage her interest these past few weeks.

So I wasn't going to disappoint her. Or Holly. A gentleman doesn't let down his best friends—the closest thing I had to family—after all. And even though, in the eyes of most people who would be attending tonight's shindig, I was very far from a gentleman, I liked to think I still knew how to behave.

I opened one eye and the headache redoubled its relentless jig inside my skull. Somewhere in my room was a vial of the foul-tasting hangover cure Madame Figg sold to her patrons. I didn't know where she got it or who made it for her, but it worked if you could stomach the taste.

Tonight it was going to have to work its hideous magic quickly. The crack of sky showing through my crookedly drawn curtains was dark. I'd overslept. Not even started the day and already it was going to hell. I needed all the help I could get.

Five minutes later—once my stomach had apparently determined it wasn't going to violently reject the hangover cure and the jig-dancing devils had quietened—I decided I might live.

After a quick bath, a shave, and several mugs of strong tea, I even looked vaguely alive. But my wrist still throbbed where the iron chain pressed against it. Madame Figg's miraculous cure-all was no help there. Each link felt like a razor peeling my skin away with acid-bathed teeth, even though to the naked eye there was nothing to see other than ever-deepening bruises.

Despite the pain I couldn't risk taking the chain off. Without the iron, the visions would knock me flatter than the hangover.

I gritted my teeth and untwisted the links, laying them flat against my skin before tightening the clasp. My hand shook a little as I slid a gold and jade hoop through my ear. Human men didn't usually wear earrings, and doing so would, no doubt, earn me some dubious looks at the ball. But given that I had little chance of fitting in anyway, I might as well look like myself.

I drank more tea as I dressed. I couldn't afford to start in on the brandy. Not yet. Not until the ball was well under way. Escorting Reggie, making sure that she felt safe and no one hassled her, meant I needed my wits about me. I would allow myself a glass or two of whatever the DuCaines were serving, but nothing stronger until my duties were done.

Which was going to make the whole thing even less bearable.

I bared my teeth at my reflection and moved to set the mug down on my dresser. The chain bumped against the wood and the pain flared bright, making the room swirl around me. I sucked in a breath, cursing my clumsiness.

I was pushing too hard. Every night, out in the taverns and brothels of the border boroughs, loosening the chain a little and letting the visions rise, trying to see if I could glean anything useful.

I'd never loosened my control over the visions to such a degree and for such a lengthy period before. Every night, no matter how tightly I wrapped the chain around my wrist, it became harder to lock them away again, to push them back to the point where I had some peace and could function like a normal person. Every night it took more alcohol to offset the pain of iron and visions denied.

I didn't know how much longer I could keep going. Not whilst keeping my sanity.

Too bad my options were limited. I could stop looking. But that might mean missing some useful snatch of the future. Something that might keep me alive. And if I confessed the truth to the human healers, then . . . what exactly? They could give me something stronger to fight the pain? Opium or worse? Something to knock me out and render me useless.

Humans didn't have the Sight. They wouldn't know how to help me. The problem was that my Sight had two possible sources. My Fae father. My Beast Kind grandmother. Going to either branch of my very estranged family for help was something I wasn't yet desperate enough to try. Both sides would try and use me, try and tie me down. I'd spent most of my life staying out of their way. Keeping my freedom. I wasn't ready to give that up.

There had to be another way. But damned if I knew what it was.

*   *   *

When my carriage door flew open, I knew my night was about to go to hell.

The thick stink of Beast rolled into the hackney as my visitor scrambled in, tugged the door shut, and seated himself opposite me, all while holding a gun at the ready. My hand drifted down to the gun concealed beneath my coat as I studied my unwelcome guest.

"I thought I made it clear last time that I wasn't going to do this anymore?" I said, keeping my voice coolly polite.

Willem Krueger shrugged and smiled, revealing teeth a little too white and pointed. "It doesn't matter what you think. It matters what my Alpha wants."

"He's not *my* Alpha," I said in the same cool tone. I was a true City mongrel—part Fae, part Beast, and part human. I didn't let any of them claim me, least of all the Beasts. My grandmother was one of the *immuable*, the unchanging.

Beasts who only knew human form.

They were often gifted with the Sight, as though the gods wished to compensate for their lack of access to the wolf side. My grandmother had been particularly blessed, one of the strongest seers in generations. The *immuable* are usually treasured by their packs, their powers invaluable, but my grandmother had defied her father to marry a human and had been cast out. Left to fend for herself, without the security and tight-knit obligations of the pack. She'd survived but she'd never forgiven.

But minor details like history and tradition seldom stopped Martin Krueger from making use of any tool he could.

"He's *my* Alpha," Willem said. "And he wants to see you."

I bit back a curse. The Lady definitely had it in for me. "When?"

"Tonight."

I gestured down at my frock coat. "I have a prior engagement."

"Martin doesn't care."

I knew that all too well. Martin had been calling on me—or rather sending his bully boys to fetch me—from time to time since I'd been a teenager. Usually what he wanted was innocuous enough. Glimpses of things that I saw no problem in sharing.

But now things were different. So far, I'd managed to walk the tightrope and maintain the illusion that I was a neutral party. Nobody in the border boroughs or the Night World yet knew that I was feeding information to the humans through Holly where I could. They still just saw Fen, the feckless fortune-teller, drinking and whoring around. Business as usual.

I couldn't keep up the pretense much longer and now, staring at Willem's hostile expression, I wondered if the game was finally up. Had Martin found me out? If so, I should just shoot Willem and have done with it. Putting myself in the clutches of a pissed-off Beast wouldn't be good for my health.

Martin had a short fuse. My ribs still remembered the last time he'd been unhappy with me. That had been just before Lord Lucius—undisputed lord of the Blood Court—whose disappearance had stirred the current tensions in the City to a boiling point, had vanished. That time I hadn't seen what Martin had wanted me to see and I'd paid the price.

I'd managed to avoid him since then, but apparently tonight my luck had run out. Still, the fact that he'd sent only Willem rather than a whole squad of *guerriers* suggested that maybe my secret was still safe after all.

Regardless, I didn't want to face down Martin tonight. Not while I was feeling like the blighted depths of the seven hells. "I'm due at a ball thrown by the DuCaines. They're not the sort of people you disappoint."

"Neither is our Alpha." Willem sounded casual but he shifted a little on the seat. Afraid to tangle with the sunmage and the Templar, was he?

"Your Alpha," I corrected. "Maybe not, but Simon DuCaine's invitation was polite. Perhaps Martin could learn from him." Simon DuCaine was a sunmage, a gifted healer. He was innately courteous but that didn't mean he was to be underestimated. Even Martin wasn't thickheaded enough to aggravate one of the most powerful mages in the City. Or was he?

Willem bared his teeth again. There wasn't the faintest trace of humor in his expression. "You can come voluntarily or I can drag you there."

I thought of Reggie and Holly, waiting for me to show up. I had no doubt Willem would do exactly as he threatened. I couldn't match the strength of a Beast. But I could outthink one. There might be something useful to be gained from a visit to Holt's End. The Kruegers, like all the packs, were embroiled in all sorts of things, none of them good. Not quite on the level of the Roussellines, who were the closest to the Blood lords, or the Favreaus, who wanted to be, but no Beast pack in the City was entirely free of the Blood and their games these days. I might be able to learn something.

"How about a compromise? I'll be done at the ball by two. Surely Martin can wait a few hours." The Beast Kind, like the Blood, lived largely nocturnally.

As Willem's expression turned grim, I drew the gun. "Let me phrase it another way. You can tell Martin that I'll see him later or I can put a hole in you." I was gambling that Willem wouldn't actually shoot me. If Martin really wanted to see me, then Willem needed me alive. The sound of the hackney moving over the cobbles echoed loudly as we stared at each other.

Finally Willem blinked. "Fine. Three. No later or we will come to fetch you. You won't enjoy it."

I nodded. "I'll be there. Now, get out of my carriage." I pointed to the door with the tip of my gun. Willem snarled but pushed the door open and swung himself out. We weren't going terribly fast, not enough to worry a Beast at least. I reached out and pulled the door closed before taking a deep breath, trying to take the edge off the adrenaline rush. Teasing a savage dog is never a good idea. My gamble had paid off for now. But it could still backfire later on.

Wanting to be sure Willem had actually gone, I stuck my head out the window of the hackney. Only to yank it back suddenly as a horn sounded and an autocab came careening past us, making the horses swerve wildly.

I caught a momentary glimpse of a woman in a dark cloak in the back of the 'cab, staring at me in shock—eyes big against pale skin—before the 'cab had pulled ahead and I was left with the sound of the hackney driver's curses ringing in my ears.

Muttering a few curses of my own under my breath, I settled myself back in the seat, trying to slow my pulse down. An ultimatum and a near decapitation. And the night had only just begun.

* * *

Sometimes even I can't see the future. If anyone had asked me as little as a month ago where I would be tonight, there would have been no chance I would have picked my current location.

Standing in the middle of a grand society ball, of all things. Surrounded by humans in their pretty dresses and suits, pretending the world was perfectly all right.

Little did they know.

I swallowed more champagne, watching the smiling people swirl around me and wishing I had brandy. But it was still far too early for that. Not with Martin and the Kruegers to deal with later on.

The champagne did little to ease the pain in my wrist and here, surrounded by so many people, even doubled iron didn't stop the visions.

Everyone was ghosted by the images of the futures that rose around them, so many that they blurred and mingled and, thank the Lady, made it difficult to get a clear picture of anything. Other than an omnipresent sense of darkness.

Darkness and flames, pressing around me so tightly I could smell smoke in the air. It made my stomach clench and my heart race with the suppressed urge to tell them all to flee.

My hand tightened around the delicate crystal glass. I focused on trying to feel the etched patterns in its surface, to connect to something real. To remind myself that the panic and doom I felt didn't belong to this moment. This place.

It helped somewhat. Which was good, because here I was and here I had to stay since I was stupid enough to be a man of my word when it came to two particular people in my life.

Across this grand ballroom stood one of my best friends, Holly Evendale and her lover, Guy DuCaine, smiling and looking like they were having a perfectly splendid time. Guy in evening clothes looked only slightly less intimidating than he did in his Templar mail, looming tall beside Holly, his pale blond head bent toward her. As usual, the visions clustered strongly around them and I saw the gleam of gold on their hands where no rings yet existed in reality. They hadn't made any announcements, but I was near certain they were getting married. If we didn't all die in whatever darkness was bending the futures to fire and pain.

Next to them stood Simon, Guy's brother, and Lily, his fiancée, all four of them listening intently as an elegant woman wearing a deep green dress, her fading blond hair piled in an elaborate coil, spoke. Stones the same color as her dress winked from her hair. Simon and Guy's mother, Hilary DuCaine. She was the one throwing this particular folly. An extravagant celebration to herald the start of the treaty season.

Treaty season. A very frivolous name for a very serious time. Every five years the four races—humans, Blood, Beasts, and Fae—gathered to renegotiate the treaty they had forged centuries ago. The treaty that was the only reason the City was still standing and, quite likely, the only reason that the humans had survived here. The negotiations were vital. They determined the shifting lines of territories, punished violations, and maintained the balance between the races with a new law here or an adjustment of the rations of iron and silver allocated to the races who used them for protection and industry.

Crazy humans to celebrate the start of what could be the City's downfall. But celebrate they did, which meant the DuCaine brothers were called to the social duties that came with their family's place in the City. Where Simon and Guy went, so did Lily and Holly. And where Holly went, so did Reggie. Which, right now, meant that I was dragged along as well.

So here I was, watching over her, even though so far Reggie seemed perfectly at ease and in demand as a partner.

She was out on the parquet floor in the center of the ballroom right now, circling with some human scion, her pretty pale blue dress just one in a sea of pretty dresses. Which left me with not much to do other than drink champagne and tighten the chain around my wrist to try and stave off the visions swimming at the edges of my sight like ghosts.

Ghosts with teeth.

A thousand competing futures, all shouting for attention. Swirling together to funnel my sight toward the larger fate of the City. Different from when I was among fewer people, getting glimpses of individual futures. There were flashes of those here. The odd pleasant flash . . . a woman with a child or a man winning at cards, but mostly it was a haze of that unrelenting sense of doom. Sharper with each passing moment.

The end of the night couldn't come fast enough. I drained my glass and gestured for another. Reggie and Holly would frown disapprovingly if they spotted me, but that was all the more reason to drink fast.

I raised the fresh glass to my lips, felt the prickly fizz of bubbles across my tongue as I let my gaze go unfocused. Sometimes that helped . . . not looking directly at anyone. Sometimes it didn't. Tonight, it seemed, was going to be one of those times. The visions still hovered around me insistently.

Buggering Veil's eyes.

I squeezed my eyes shut for a few seconds, denying them. I didn't want to look, didn't want to know what fate might await us all. Whatever happened in the City, it would be the people on the edges of society who felt the brunt of it.

As hard it was to be Blood or Beast Kind or even a human in the City, those of us who were half-breeds were the ones who were truly screwed. Betwixt and between and not really wanted by anyone. Mongrels indeed. Though some of the females I'd bedded in the past would've probably used "bastard" instead. Which was also true. My father never married my mother. The Fae don't marry whores after all.

I looked across again at Holly and Lily. They knew better than anyone how I felt. Holly's father, recently dead at Guy's hand, was a true prick of a Fae lordling if ever there was one. He'd used and discarded her mother and tried to force Holly into betraying Simon to further a plot against the Veiled Queen. He was the reason for the shadows in Reggie's eyes. If he hadn't already been dead, I would've cheerfully cut his throat myself.

Lily was something different altogether. A wraith. Half Fae, half unknown. Reviled by the Fae for her ability to turn incorporeal and move through any substance at will, she'd been sold not long after she'd been born to Lucius, the late unlamented Lord of the Blood Court, who'd used her as an assassin, a tool of fear and blood to enforce obedience to his will. The fact that she'd moved from that world to this one after meeting Simon was probably the one thing stranger than my being at this ball.

But if either Holly or Lily was uncomfortable being here,

they didn't show it. Holly wore a deep bronze dress that was a little more conservative than those she'd worn when spying on the Night World amidst the theater halls and Blood Assemblies they frequented. Tonight her hair was glamoured to match the dress, and her eyes, happy as she looked up at Guy, glowed nearly the same shade. Lily, pale and redheaded, wore something soft and simple in a pale green that made her look innocent. If I'd had to guess, I'd have said that Reggie, who worked as a modiste, had picked a design for her that was intended to make people see something sweet and unthreatening rather than the trained killer she was.

It worked, to a degree. Lily was smiling, like the others. Her gray eyes were watchful, and I would've bet good coin that she could describe all the exit points to the room and likely had picked out anyone who was armed amongst the crowd. Holly probably had a good idea of that as well, plus she probably knew some interesting secrets about some of the starched shirts surrounding her. Since I'd known her, Holly had owned the modiste salon where Reggie worked. But that was only for appearances' sake—her real talent lay in using her considerable skills in charms and subterfuge to spy for whoever paid the highest price.

But right now both Holly and Lily looked as if there were nothing more pressing in their lives than dancing and drinking under the elaborate chandeliers. I frowned as I swallowed more champagne. Enough alcohol and maybe I could look relaxed as well.

Reggie reappeared at my side. "Haven't you had enough?"

"Not by half," I muttered. I avoided meeting her gaze. Eye contact always made the visions worse when they slipped my control. I still caught glimpses anyway. As always, Reggie was surrounded by colors and textures—a sign of her vocation as a modiste—and images of dancing people dressed in beautiful clothes. There were Fae faces amongst them now, more than there had been before she had been held in Summerdale. Some danced, but some watched. The images had an unsettling mistiness. As though the fates weren't sure of what they showed. But that was probably just due to the general uncertainty I felt right now.

Reggie flipped her fan toward me. "You're meant to be dancing with me, not propping up the bar."

I glanced at the nearly full dance card dangling from her wrist. "Doesn't look to me like you're lacking partners."

"I saved one for you," she said coaxingly.

I wondered if she'd done so in collaboration with Holly. A "let's distract Fen to cheer him up" ploy. True, I wasn't averse to dancing now and then, but tonight I wasn't in the mood. "Ask me later."

Reggie tossed her head, her silver and blue filigree earrings bouncing. "Who says I'll still have any unfilled dances later?"

"Then that will be my loss." I rubbed at my wrist absently, wishing the champagne would at least do *something* to ease the iron's bite.

"It's hurting tonight, isn't it?" Reggie said in a softer tone. Eyes the same shade as her dress filled with worry. "Can't you take it off?"

"Not here." Not unless I wanted to cause a scene by screaming. I forced a smile. "I'm fine, love. Go and have fun."

"The idea is for you to have some too."

I just raised an eyebrow. She frowned, snapped her fan shut, then sighed and turned away. I watched her thread her way back across the ballroom to Holly and Lily.

Simon and Guy had moved out of my line of sight, leaving just the women, still talking animatedly. Beside Holly stood a girl I didn't recognize. Her back was half turned to me, so all I could really see was the pale pink sweep of her dress and dark—reddish perhaps—curls falling down to hide the line of her face and neck. Both Holly and Lily were smiling at her—perhaps she worked at St. Giles Hospital, where Simon was Master Healer?

Reggie reached the group and obviously reported my recalcitrant behavior. Holly craned her neck to frown at me over the unknown girl's shoulder. I tipped my glass to her, then turned back to the bar before she could send me any further indicators of her concern. The starched white linen covering the polished wood offered no reproval, at least. No answers to any of my problems either.

When I turned to look again, the girl in the pink dress had disappeared, leaving just Lily and Holly and Reggie clustered together. As I watched, a young buck in immaculate evening dress came up to Reggie and bowed. There. She had a partner. She was safe. No need to feel guilty.

"Don't you like to dance?"

The voice came from my side, low for a female and somewhat amused. I turned my head. It was the girl in the pink dress. Tilted green-gray eyes watched me with interest and she smiled, revealing a dimple in her left cheek that only added to her prettiness.

I tipped my head, taking her in. The pink dress floated over sleek curves, to curl around her feet in a sea of flounces. Her hair was unadorned, apart from a single bar of pale pink pearls that matched those at her ears. Lovely. Lovely enough to distract me for a while at least. I smiled at her. "I don't generally dance, no."

Her smile widened—there was something vaguely familiar about that smile and the dimple. "Oh good. I hate it too."

I blinked. Not what I expected a well-brought-up human female to say.

The girl turned to the barman and asked for champagne. Another blink. I would have thought her a little young to be drinking champagne. "Why are you at a ball if you don't like dancing?"

She wrinkled her nose, sipped champagne, swallowed, and then sighed. "My mother requested my presence." She flexed the hand not holding the champagne glass. She wore long gloves of an even paler pink than her dress . . . a pink that almost wasn't. Her skin, bared between the top of the glove just below her elbows and the floating ruffled sleeve halfway down her arm, was faded gold, not pale white. And there were muscles under that skin, smooth curves revealed with the movement of her hand. *Where had she got those?*

"My mother has a way of talking people into things."

"My sympathies," I said. "I know a few people like that." I cranked up my own smile a little.

A bored young thing at a ball. A bored, young, slightly unconventional thing. Perhaps my night wasn't going to be a complete waste of time after all.

She laughed, then offered the gloved hand. "You're Fen, aren't you? I'm Saskia. Saskia DuCaine."

I almost choked. Saskia *DuCaine*? This was Simon and Guy's little sister? I took her hand gingerly and shook it, then released it as quickly as I could without being rude. The kid leather slipped over my skin softly, warm from her body as our fingers slid away from each other. I tucked my hand into my pocket before I could reach for hers again. That would be a very bad idea.

This particular bored young unconventional thing was not for the likes of me. For starters, her brothers were a sunmage and a Templar, respectively. I was fond of my head being unfried and attached to my neck. True, both Simon and Guy had chosen women who weren't exactly the type that heirs of a powerful human family were expected to fall in love with, but I wasn't stupid enough to think that the DuCaine daughters would enjoy the same leeway.

"Pleased to meet you," I said, after a moment of gathering my wits. "I know your brothers."

"I know."

Her tone held more than a hint of eye roll. My brain clutched for something else to talk about. "Did Holly send you over?"

She shook her head, setting long dark curls bouncing. They gleamed red under the light of the massive chandeliers. Now that I knew who she was, I could see the resemblance to her brothers in the dimples and the smile. The dark hair was her own, though—both her brothers being blond—and the angled grayish green eyes made her face more exotic than either of theirs.

"No, I wanted to meet you."

Definitely trouble. I fought the urge to move backward. Retreat would be futile with the bar at my back anyway. "Why?"

"Because everyone else in my family has."

"Not everyone," I said. "I haven't met your sister . . . Hannah, isn't it? Or your mother, other than in the receiving line earlier." I hoped it would stay that way. Mothers didn't approve of me. I didn't resent them for it. After all, I rarely approved of me either.

"Well, now you've met one more of us." She took another sip of her champagne and studied me over the rim of the flute. "You look concerned."

"Did I mention I know your brothers?"

"So?"

"I'm not the sort of man your brothers want you talking to."

That got me a dimple flash and another nose wrinkle. "My brothers don't tell me what to do." Her head tilted and her smile widened. "Or rather, they try to, but I ignore them."

I ignored my desire to smile back at her. No good could come of it. "Really?" Not many people found Simon and Guy ignorable. "How do they like that?"

"Not very well. They seem to think I'm still sixteen."

"How old are you?" She obviously wasn't sixteen or she wouldn't be at the ball. It wasn't a debutante sort of affair.

"I'm twenty-three." She shook her head. "If they had their way, I'd still live at home. Hypocrites, both of them. They were both Templar novices at seventeen."

"It's different for boys."

"You sound like my mother."

"Sometimes mothers make sense," I said, more because it seemed the right thing to say than because it was anything I believed. What did I know of mothers? Mine was hardly a stellar example of maternity, but Saskia didn't need to know that. Better she thought me boring and left me alone and I didn't find myself being hunted down by Simon and Guy.

I looked past Saskia to see if I could spot Holly. She was still standing where she had been earlier and she raised an eyebrow at me as I caught her eye. I lifted my hand to wave at her, our long-standing "come save me" signal.

The movement made my coat sleeve fall back and for a moment my chain flashed into view.

Saskia's smile died. "Why do you have an iron chain around your wrist?"

I smoothed my sleeve, hiding the chain from her sight. "How do you know it's iron?"

"I can tell."

"From one look?" I doubted it. It was only a glimpse, after all, and one dark metal chain looked much like another.

"I'm a metalmage . . . an apprentice, at least. It's iron." She looked confused. "But you're half Fae, aren't you? Like Holly? That must hurt."

I'd known that, somewhere in the back of my mind. Holly must have told me. I tried to reconcile the young woman in front of me with my mental image of metalmages—which consisted largely of forges and flames and grime. It didn't work. "Some of us aren't affected by iron. Like Holly."

"Holly's immunity is pretty rare. Are you saying you have it too?" It was her turn to sound disbelieving.

The lie stuck on the tip of my tongue, caught there, perhaps, by the pain in my wrist where the chain bit. Luckily I was saved from answering by Holly's arrival.

She looked from me to Saskia and back, eyes narrowing as they met mine. I kept my face carefully bland. After all, I was innocent in this particular situation. Saskia had sought me out, not the other way around.

"I see you two have met," Holly said.

Saskia nodded. "Fen was just telling me how the iron around his wrist doesn't hurt him."

Holly's eyes widened, her famous composure, for once, disturbed. "Was he now?" One hand strayed up to toy with the chain at her neck. Worried, then. "Saskia, your mother asked me to fetch you. The speeches will be starting soon."

I knew that tone well enough to get the "you stay right here, Fen" intent. I was being warned away from Saskia, which I had to admit stung a little. For one thing, did Holly really think I was stupid enough to mess around with a well-connected human and, for another, if she did, did she really think I wasn't good enough for her future sister-in-law?

I watched the two of them leave, my wrist throbbing and the taste of champagne sour in my mouth. I turned back to the barman. Fuck restraint and fuck Martin Krueger. I needed a proper drink.

Chapter Two

SASKIA

The half-healed burn on my right hand itched under the leather of my glove. I resisted the urge to pull it off and scratch.

Young ladies don't scratch in public. It's impolite.

My mother had drummed that, amongst many other rules of correct behavior, into my head from the time I was big enough to appear in anything even vaguely resembling a public place.

Of course, I was hardly a polite young lady despite her best efforts. I had stopped being a polite young lady when my powers came in, but Mother did her best to ignore that and I did my best to pretend she was right when I was with her. It was easier that way, even if sometimes the pretense itched worse than the burn on my hand did. Itched and scratched and made me feel like I couldn't breathe, as though I was wearing a too tight corset. Which I often was, around my mother.

Still, I could never quite banish her voice telling me exactly how I was falling short of her standards at times like these.

I tried to think of something else as I listened with half an ear to whatever it was the always dull Anthony Killington was pontificating on to his circle of admirers. The trouble with trying to think of something else at this point was that the only other things my mind kept returning to were the amused dark green eyes of the mysterious Fen and the iron chain wrapped around his wrist.

It only proved my point. He wasn't the sort of man polite young ladies thought of. No, they would have the sense to give him a wide berth, to feel that hint of otherness about him and distance themselves. Men like him didn't keep you safe from danger. Men like him attracted it. The same atmosphere that surrounded Holly and Lily—that same sense of potential for . . . mayhem? Danger?—hells, *freedom*—surrounded him like burning spice. Exotic. Enticing.

I wanted to let it surround me too.

But Fen wasn't the right path for that. No, if I wanted to be finally allowed to *do* something and not be kept wrapped in cotton wool by my brothers, then my best chance was the Guild of Metalmages and mastery of my powers.

My hand itched again. The Guild. I couldn't wait to get back there. Back to the power and fire and the place where I was valued for myself, not for some idea of who I should be. Back where the metal sang and everything seemed simple. Where no one looked at me with that polite face that said, "Oh, Saskia, she's a little . . . odd." At the Guild, those without powers were the odd ones.

Tomorrow Master Aquinas would be choosing the students who would be part of the Guild's treaty delegation. Choosing me, if all my hard work had paid off.

One more night.

But first I had to get through this hideous ball.

The first ball of treaty season, thrown by my mother, as usual. Short of actually setting myself on fire, there was no way I would be able to leave until early morning. Not whilst Hilary was keeping her eagle eye on me. If I tried to slip out any earlier, I'd have to deal with weeks of lectures on my shortcomings. A few hours of pain now were worth avoiding that. Which was why I was standing in uncomfortable shoes, in an uncomfortable dress, pretending to enjoy myself while my hand itched and Anthony Killington droned on about his latest victory in banking in a voice that buzzed like a very dull bee.

Across the room, my mother smiled approvingly and

tipped her head in Anthony's direction, urging me closer. I resisted the desire to stick out my tongue in response. Surely one definite and one imminent engagement were enough? My brothers were settling down, hopefully ensuring the family line for another generation. Couldn't my mother let that distract her from trying to match me up as well?

Apparently not, if I read the gleam in Hilary's eyes correctly.

Perhaps because of the women Simon and Guy had chosen, my mother's determination to marry me and, in a few years or so once she turned twenty, Hannah, off to suitable—for which one could read *human*—men seemed to have intensified.

Well, she was just going to have to wait for any form of marital triumph when it came to me. I was only four years into my studies at the Guild. Marriage, if it ever did tempt me, would come after I became a Master.

Anthony changed the topic of conversation to currency valuation and the impact of the silver stockpiles. The itch intensified. It was warm in the ballroom, the candles in the chandeliers and the press of bodies heating the air to an unpleasant closeness. My hands were damp in my gloves, sweat stinging the burn. My fingers flexed unwittingly to ease the pain.

If I'd been sensible I would have asked Simon to heal it for me, but if I ran to my brother every time I had a minor scrape or burn at the Guild, I'd spend all my time traveling to and from St. Giles.

Hardly conducive to clinching the race for the top spot in my class and securing my inclusion in the delegation.

Beside which, I'd have to put up with Simon teasing me about a metalmage burning herself each and every time I asked for help. He knew as well as I did that, while metalmages can't be burned by metal being worked with their power or fire they have called, we are perfectly susceptible to the whims of other sources of heat. But he was also my older brother and therefore duty bound to tease me when he could.

Determined to ignore my hand, I excused myself from the group of Killington hangers-on and made my way slowly through the crowd, trying to look like I had a destination in mind. My attention was only half on the endless parade of couples whirling around the room while I looked for a place to hide away for a few minutes. I didn't understand how they could all be so cavalier. Acting as if they didn't have a care in the world and as though the looming treaty negotiations were nothing to be worried about.

Denial seemed to be in fashion amongst my mother's set. And she kept up the charade as well, moving amongst her guests, laughing and smiling and making sure everybody was having a good time, though in reality she knew more than most about the trouble that lurked in the heart of the City.

I caught sight of her across the ballroom, smiling determinedly. Trouble indeed. She only had to look at the women standing beside her sons to be reminded of that.

I didn't know exactly what the trouble was. Guy and Simon both turned stony-faced and closemouthed when I asked. Yet here was Simon with Lily, a former Night World assassin and Guy had risked a trip to the Veiled Court to help Holly—a relative stranger at the time, not to mention half Fae—rescue her mother. Lord Lucius had disappeared around the time Simon had met Lily and there were all sorts of rumors flying about the Veiled World being in an uproar since Guy and Holly had been there. Whatever trouble was driving the undercurrents of unease swirling through the City, my brothers were at the center of it.

And totally determined to keep me ignorant in their knuckleheaded belief that it would keep me safe.

Stop me ending up dead like our sister Edwina.

But just as my mother was wrong in her belief that I was her perfect lady of a daughter apart from that whole unfortunate metalmage issue, Simon and Guy were wrong if they thought they could keep their secrets and keep me from helping them if I could.

I just had to find a way in to the truth.

Tomorrow, I reminded myself. Tomorrow I would have a ticket to the negotiations and they would have no excuse to keep me ignorant any longer.

I could make it through tonight—behave myself—to get to tomorrow. But even as I thought it, I found myself turning back to look across the room to where Fen had been, seeking another glimpse of dark hair and wild green eyes.

There. I spotted him just in time to see my brothers coming up on either side of him. My fingers tightened around my fan. What were they doing? My hand stung as I watched, wishing I could hear what they were saying. But for that I would need one of Holly's charms. Instead, I just had to stand and observe as the three of them made their way across the ballroom to one of the doors. Damn. Where were they going?

I wanted to know, to follow, but any chance of escape was thwarted when Anthony Killington appeared before me, bowing low, and I remembered I had promised him the next dance.

FEN

The door shut behind me with a quiet click. I stayed where I was, close to the exit, as Guy walked over and lifted a decanter from a tray on a table near the window. "Brandy?"

I nodded agreement. I assumed that whatever was kept in the decanters here, in what looked like someone's private study, was probably a step or two up from the liquor they were serving downstairs. And what they were serving downstairs was more than a few steps up from what Madame Figg served.

While Guy poured, I waited, still aware that Simon stood behind me, near the door. I'd never been in the DuCaine town house before. Too risky.

"I thought we'd agreed not to talk tonight," I said. Letting Reggie and Holly talk me into this was one thing, but being seen going off with Guy and Simon was another altogether.

"It's all right," Simon said. "You're glamoured."

Holly's work, I presumed. Well, that was risky too. "There are people who can see through glamours." I examined the room, looking for wards. The drapes pulled tight across the window were dark red brocade and the furniture was deep brown, both wood and leather. A fire burned in the grate despite the mild night, faintly sweet smoke mingling with the smell of the gaslights. On the walls hung portraits of Hilary and Garret DuCaine and their children. The whole place reeked of elegance and wealth. The wards were elegant too, subtle shimmering layers of magic that would take a lot of work to break. I let myself relax a little.

Guy filled one glass, then put the decanter down and picked up another to fill a second glass with the whiskey he preferred. "Simon?" He looked past me to his brother.

"No," Simon said. "I'm working later."

Behind me a tingle of magic prickled my neck. Simon giving the wards another boost. Nervous, was he?

Apparently I was going to need that brandy Guy was holding out to me. I walked over and took the glass, feeling the weight of good crystal in my hand. Probably not good form to bolt the whole drink at a gulp.

I sipped it instead, watching the DuCaines warily. "I take it you didn't ask me here just to share your family's excellent brandy," I said. "So talk."

Guy looked at Simon, one of those inscrutable Templar looks he was good at. Apparently Simon had no problem interpreting it. He shrugged, then pointed to the chairs near the fireplace as Guy tipped his own glass and half drained it. Maybe I could have bolted mine after all.

I chose the chair closest to the door, mostly to watch Guy squirm when he couldn't take the most obvious defensive position.

"The negotiations start next week," Simon said, once all three of us were settled.

"Just as well, when your mother has gone to all this trouble with this ball," I said.

"This ball might be one of the few pleasant things associated with the negotiations," Simon said.

"This is hardly news," I said. "Your point?" They wouldn't risk dragging me in here for no good reason. I wondered exactly what Simon had to say that had him dancing around the subject like one of those silly girls who came to the Swallow and took several nights to screw up their courage enough to sit down at my table and pay to hear their fortunes.

"Do you have somewhere more important to be?" Guy asked, tilting his glass slowly so that the whiskey glowed red in the firelight.

I looked away quickly before the color could spark the

visions to renewed strength. That happened sometimes. The insistent fog of futures had mostly dissipated here in the study, away from the crowds, but Simon and Guy had always been hard to be around. The futures swirled around them like moths circling a lamp. Men with destinies.

Destinies that, at this point, seemed as full of blood and fire as everybody else's. I didn't know whether I was seeing true or still picking up the overflow from what I was seeing from the masses below. Either way I wanted to close my eyes until I didn't have to see any more.

"As a matter of fact, I do have another appointment this evening," I said.

"Anyone we know?" Guy asked, head tilting like his glass. His eyes, paler than his brother's, were suddenly coldly intent.

"I doubt it. She doesn't move in these circles." I lied glibly. No need to bring the Kruegers up at this point. If I learned anything useful about them, I would pass it on, of course, but until then what the DuCaines didn't know wouldn't hurt them. I didn't have the patience for hashing over whether or not I should risk a trip to Beast territory tonight.

Guy relaxed, mouth twitching. "I should have known."

"Don't tell Holly. She wants me looking after Regina."

"Reggie's doing very well," Simon said. "Holly hovering over her isn't going to help her."

I tipped my glass in his direction. "I'll let you tell Holly that. If you dare."

"I've said as much to Lily."

Braver man than I. I didn't understand how or why, but Holly and Lily were friends. Or friendly, at least. A wraith befriending a half-Fae former spy. A dangerous combination. "Oh yes? What did she say?"

"That fussing made Holly feel better and that Reggie would put her foot down when she wanted to. And that we should stay out of it."

We all sat silently for a moment, none of us wanting to contemplate crossing Lily.

Guy roused himself first, setting his glass down and leaning forward. "You won't have to stay here until the end of the ball anyway," he said. "Holly and I are staying here tonight and Mother has invited Reggie to sleep here as well."

"Good," I said with a nod. "Which brings us back to the topic at hand. Why am I here?"

"We want you to be part of the human delegation," Guy said bluntly.

Brandy burned my throat as I coughed. "Me? Why?" I'd known they wanted to use my visions to their advantage, but I'd never expected this. It wasn't completely unheard of—or against the rules—for members of other races to be included in a delegation, but it was unusual. Including someone like me, who didn't even strictly belong to any race, would be even more unusual. Not that that would stop Simon and Guy from doing something if they decided it was right.

"We need every advantage we can muster, Fen," Simon said. "Anything you see might help us."

I swallowed as I regained my breath. "No."

"Why not?" Guy asked. His voice had deepened, cooled. Not a good sign.

But still, was he seriously asking why not? Why not put myself in the very center of whatever it was that was coming? A healthy sense of self-preservation for a start. Feeding information to the DuCaines under the table was one thing. Being an acknowledged member of the humans' side of the fight was another altogether. "We agreed that we would keep our association . . . quiet."

Guy tilted his head at me. "We all knew that you would be discovered at some point."

"Hasn't happened yet." I was stalling. Truly, I hadn't wanted to think about what would happen if someone ferreted out the truth of what I was up to. I'd been telling myself no one would. Apparently I'd been happy to believe me. *Fool.*

"I don't think I would be particularly helpful," I said. I gestured toward the wall closest to the ballroom. "In crowds, my sight is less than reliable." I wasn't going to mention the pain. Not just yet. Not if I could talk my way out of this without giving myself away.

"Don't you care about what happens?"

"I care about what happens to me," I said. "And mine."

Guy's eyebrows lifted. "If 'mine' includes Holly, then she'll be at the negotiations."

Of course she would be. She'd thrown in her lot with Guy's,

for better or worse. And her skills as a spy and someone familiar with the players of the Night World would no doubt prove an asset to the humans. But just because she'd lost her head, that didn't mean I had to volunteer to lose mine.

But what would she and Reggie think of me if I didn't?

The brandy suddenly soured in my mouth.

I put down my nearly empty glass, then rose. "I need time to think about this. Now, if you'll excuse me, gentlemen, I promised Reggie a dance."

For a moment I didn't think they were going to let me go, but neither moved as I crossed the room. I kept my pace slow and steady, not giving in to my urge to run from the building. I didn't think I had heard the last of this particular request, but for now at least I was still free.

The night air was cool as I stepped out through the double front doors several hours later and crossed the marble portico, feeling the weight of the visions ease like a change in weather. I let out a breath of relief. There was still a thunder in my head and flames flickering at the edges of my vision— after almost five hours surrounded by hundreds of people it would take a while for the visions to retreat—but it was easier to bear.

The second and third brandies I'd downed after leaving Simon and Guy helped somewhat . . . just enough to make the world feel a bit detached, as though I was part of the mist dampening the cool night air.

I sucked in a few more breaths, clearing my head. I still had Martin to deal with, after all. I checked my watch. I had paid the driver of the hackney to return for me at two thirty. I was about to discover if I'd thrown my money away.

The semicircular drive that curved around the front of the house was empty except for one thing.

Saskia DuCaine.

She stood on the bottom step, watching the front gates. A dark cloak hid the pink dress, but her hair was uncovered and gleamed in the misty light. I could only see the side of her face, as she was half turned toward the house, or the warmth from the gas lamps that hung from wrought-metal poles and chains fastened to the marble portico above her perhaps.

I hesitated, debating whether I should attempt to remain unseen. Moving closer would only bring the visions back, plus she wasn't the type of girl who loitered with men in the dark. I was surprised there wasn't a servant waiting with her now. Perhaps she was sneaking away too. It was early for her to be leaving her own family's party, but who was I to judge when I was making a break for it myself? The thought of her giving her family the slip made me like her even more than I did already.

I squelched the sentiment hard, but it refused to vanish. *Stupid, Fen.* Even Holly had warned me off this girl. A warning that right at this moment, the brandy seemed disinclined to heed.

After all, it said, *it was only gentlemanly not to leave her standing out here unaccompanied at such an hour. It's not safe out here.* Of course, I didn't imagine that Saskia Du-Caine was headed off to a rendezvous with a pack alpha, or anybody else for that matter. Well-bred human girls didn't do that sort of thing. No, she was probably trying to make her curfew at the Guild. If the Guild had a curfew. A safe destination, the Guild of Metalmages. Much like the drive of this house was, most likely, perfectly safe. Still, the stupid side of me set free by the alcohol latched on to the excuse to walk to where she stood.

"Miss DuCaine," I said politely as I reached her side.

She jumped a little, then made a noise of apology as she turned to see who had spoken. A smile curved her lips briefly. "Technically the correct form of address is Prentice DuCaine."

"I stand corrected." I swept a bow, not sure why I felt the urge. "Prentice DuCaine. What are you doing out here all by yourself?"

I waited for the visions to crowd me, but it seemed that the iron was enough to deal with just one person and the air around her stayed almost clear. Flames flickered over her head but they were fainter. Much fainter. And really, flames around a metalmage were to be expected.

I was tempted to push, to look again and see what was to be seen now that her futures weren't tangled and blurred by those of everybody else in the ballroom, but I stopped myself.

"Waiting for my 'cab," she said. "It's late."

"Likewise my hackney," I said. "Perhaps something is slowing their travels."

"I hope not," she said, frowning. "I have to be up early."

Whereas I was unlikely to see my bed before dawn. A timely reminder that we were from two very different worlds. I took another breath of that cooling, calming night air. "I'm sure they won't be long."

She raised an eyebrow at me. "Exactly how sure?"

I mirrored her eyebrow lift. "I can't see them turning the corner down the street, if that's what you're asking."

"Pity." She scratched idly at the back of her hand, then made an exasperated face and tugged off her gloves with impatient movements. Once her hands were freed, she shook them, flexing the fingers slowly before stretching her arms out before her. "Sainted earth, that's better."

A red weal marred the skin on the back of her right hand. A burn?

"Did you hurt yourself?" I didn't reach to touch her. One didn't take the hand of nice young ladies alone in the dark.

"It's nothing. I was just a little careless." She made a fist, then dropped her hand to her side. "It will be fine tomorrow."

Looking at the angry red mark, I wasn't so sure of that. Burns hurt—I knew that much. I thought of all the time she must have spent tonight with men's hands pressing on the burn through her gloves as she danced. She'd either numbed it up with something or she was tougher than she looked. Something made me suspect the latter. "You should get Simon to look at it."

She flicked her fingers in a gesture of dismissal. "We have healers at the Guild."

"Then you should get one of them to look at it."

The exasperated look returned to her face. "You sound like my brothers."

I wasn't sure if that was insult or compliment but before I could ask, a 'cab chugged through the gate and came to a steaming, heaving halt before us. I stepped down and reached to open the rear door.

"Prentice DuCaine," I said and, unthinking, stretched out my hand to help her into the cab.

As her fingers touched mine, the thunder in my head

disappeared, the flames flicking at my vision snuffed like candles. Stunned, I stepped back, releasing her hand, but before I could speak, the 'cab took off and she was gone.

"Did Saskia leave?" It was Holly.

I started, eyes still staring at the gate where the 'cab had turned and rumbled out of view. Had I imagined it? That sudden respite from the visions?

They were back now, back as soon as I had let go of Saskia's hand, rising around me like shredded ghosts once more. I reached for my wrist to press the iron closer.

"Fen?" Holly's voice sounded concerned.

I shook myself, trying to break the trance. There was no logical explanation for the touch of Saskia's hand stopping my visions. I must have imagined it. "Yes. She left in a 'cab just now."

"And you?" She tilted her head, eyes shining bronze gold in the gaslight, matching her dress. The unusual color didn't distract from the worry they held.

I shrugged. "Reggie said she was staying the night here with you."

"She is." Her tone suggested that wasn't the point.

"She had plenty of partners in there."

"You said you'd stay."

"I—" I turned back to the gate, my palm tingling with the remembered sensation of Saskia's skin. "I have somewhere I need to be."

"Fen, you're not going to do something stupid, are you?" Her voice held more than a hint of censure.

My hand clenched, sensation fleeing. I turned back to Holly. "Such as?" I asked silkily.

She jerked her head toward the gate. "She's not one of us, Fen. You can't toy with someone like her."

"Guy is hardly one of us," I pointed out.

"I'm not toying with Guy."

"You were when you first started."

"It's different."

"How?"

"She's human. She's grown up with all this." Holly gestured at the pillars that supported the domed portico. At the expensively intricate gas lamps and impeccably manicured topiary standing in enameled pots at their feet. It was a long way from the back alleys of the border boroughs, from the sweaty, stuffy attic rooms above the brothel where our mothers had worked, from hunger and learning survival the hard way. A long way from the childhood Holly and Reggie and I had shared.

"Too good for a gutter rat like me?" I couldn't quite keep the anger from my tone. Holly was supposed to be on my side. Had always *been* on my side before now. Until Guy had come along.

"I think she could hurt you," Holly said softly, stopping my anger in its tracks. She was worried about me, not about what I was going to do. Or maybe a little of both.

"What makes you think I'm even interested?"

Holly laughed. "I know you, Fen."

"Do you?" I tilted my head at her. We'd shared that childhood and had kept each other safe in the years since then, but she was leaving our world now. Joining Guy's. Keeping secrets.

She looked hurt and I regretted my temper. "Sorry." I took a deep breath and pressed my fingers into the base of my skull where brandy and the visions had joined forces to make my head ache like hellfire.

Holly's gaze followed my hand, narrowing as if she wanted to see through my shirt to the chain beneath. "It's bad, isn't it?"

I shrugged.

"You have to do something about it, Fen. You can't just drink yourself unconscious every night."

"Why not? You don't seem to approve of my other choice of distractions."

"Screwing the entire female population of the border boroughs won't help either," she said tartly. "You need to learn to control your visions."

"And would you recommend I go groveling to one of the packs or to the Veiled Court for that? Just whose slave should I become, Holly?"

She looked away, mouth twisted. "You're going to kill yourself."

"Then I'll die free."

"Don't even say that." She blinked rapidly, hugging herself, and I cursed under my breath. Holly had lost everyone except for Guy and Reggie and me. I didn't want to be her next loss.

But nor was I willing to find the type of cure she recommended. My mother had been a whore, selling her body in lieu of any other talents; her life, after my appearance, governed by the demands of Madame Figg and the threat of being cast out into the streets. If I was going to sell myself, then it would be on my own terms and I would be the one to profit from it.

A clatter of wheels and hooves announced the hackney, saving me from having to figure out what the hell to say next. As it pulled up in front of me, the driver looking unrepentant about being so tardy, I touched Holly's cheek. "I have to go. I'm late."

"Is it worth telling you to be careful?"

I flashed her a meant-to-be-reassuring grin. "Maybe not, but do it anyway."

For a moment an answering smile chased away the worry in her eyes before it stole back and her face turned serious again. "Be careful," she said fiercely.

I nodded, not promising anything, and climbed into the hackney.

Twenty minutes later the hackney drew to a halt. I pushed the leather blind back and peered out. Orpheus Station. Holt's End, as agreed. Hackneys wouldn't go any deeper into Beast territory; there was only so much well-trained horses would put up with. Most of them would handle a few Beasts, but being completely surrounded by the stink of predators was too much to ask. The Beasts had their own horses, of course, and Lady alone knew what sort of magic they worked on them to keep them under control, but my driver was human and I couldn't expect him to work miracles.

I checked my watch again. Five minutes before the bells would ring three and Willem would come looking for me. Just about enough time if I hurried.

I didn't want to leave the relative safety of the hackney, where the visions had fled, leaving me in peace for the first time all night. But I had little choice. I checked the position of my gun on my hip and the knives beside it and in my boot, then opened the door.

The cabbie wasted no time in urging his horses back toward Mickleskin. I watched him go, then turned in the opposite direction, walking quickly through the night and trying to look not worth messing with. The streets were busy, as they always are in Night World boroughs when the moon is high, but for once my luck held and no one challenged me.

I reached the north side of the high stone wall that surrounded the Krueger Pack House with a few seconds to spare. Willem leaned against the wood and metal gate, near the guardhouse, eyes scanning the street. He pushed away from the wall as I approached.

"You're on time," he said. "Wise man."

"Worried about me? How thoughtful."

"Worried that I was going to have to waste the rest of the night hunting you down," he retorted. "I have better things to do. Let's go, half-breed. The Alpha is waiting." He gestured me forward and I obeyed, not liking him walking behind me but unable to do anything about it.

I stood back when Willem pushed open the front door, but once again he jerked his chin, waiting for me to go first. I did but I dawdled, trying to delay the inevitable as I stepped across the threshold.

The pack house smelled like Beasts. Sweat. Fur. Musk. Earth.

Danger.

The scent made the hairs on the back of my neck rise, as did the sight of gleaming eyes in the darkness. Beasts change unbidden under the full moon but also shift at will. And they are dangerous on two legs, four legs, or in their hybrid forms.

I kept my eyes on Willem's back and acted like nothing was bothering me. There might be worse places to appear nervous or weak than a pack house after moonrise, but right now I couldn't think of one.

The visions stayed under control, which made me think that most of the Beasts must be out in the night. A small mercy at least.

Willem led me down the hall, his boot heels tapping along the floorboards like a drummer beating someone to the gallows. I resisted the urge to loosen my tie. It wasn't a rope and if anyone was going to hang this evening, it wouldn't be me.

Mercifully, the next turn of the corridor landed us in front of a familiar door. Solid oak carved with snarling wolf heads, it led to Martin's reception room. One of my least favorite places in the City. This was where I ended up whenever Martin got the yen to know the future. Tonight was going to be the last time.

Willem opened the door without any sort of announcement. Obviously we were expected.

I crossed the threshold and stopped as close to the door as possible. As always, the room was lit with lanterns rather than gaslights. Their flames flickered rapidly, making the shadows move uneasily. The walls and carpets were a deep dark red, combining to evoke a sensation of the room pressing unpleasantly close around its occupants. Carved wooden screens stood in the corners and along the walls. You could never be sure just what might be lurking behind them, waiting to spill your blood onto the carpets where it wouldn't show.

Smoke from the lanterns and heavily spiced incense mingled in the air with the Beast smell. It made the atmosphere even more claustrophobic. Other than anyone who might be hidden behind the screens, the room was largely empty. Four Beasts stood in a semicircle behind the desk at its heart. *Guerriers* protecting their Alpha.

The man sitting behind the desk studied me as I studied him. The *guerriers* all stared at me too, eyes focused with predatory intent.

I was flattered that they thought it would take four—five if you counted Willem—Beasts to take me down. In reality it would probably only require one. Which Martin well knew. Which meant his display of force was a threat and that he was in no mood to be trifled with.

I wondered if anything in particular was raising his hackles or whether he was just infected with the general jitteriness of the Night World right now. Because he was nervous—that much was clear, even though his expression remained impassive as he beckoned me forward.

I narrowed my eyes. What did Martin Krueger have to be nervous about? It was a pity I couldn't loosen the chain and see what I could see, but there wasn't any time for that.

Martin's face—black hair pulled back from deeply tanned skin that made his green eyes seem very bright— was still as I walked toward him. Yet there was something in the way he held himself that confirmed my instinct. He was definitely uneasy. In Beast form, his hackles would have been rising.

My stomach began its own nervous dance. What exactly was going on here?

Martin's expression offered no clues. As always, the sight of him made my gut twist with anger. I might be only one-eighth Beast but pack blood runs strong. Looking at Martin, I saw echoes of my own face. My coloring was all Krueger, even if my eyes were a stranger shade of green than any human or Beast ever sported and I lacked the bulky muscles of a Beast. Set amongst the men standing here, I looked like a younger brother; one who had some growing to do but who was still undoubtedly blood. No wonder Martin thought he could call me at will like an unruly child. Perhaps it was time to disabuse him of that notion once and for all.

"Martin," I said, bowing shallowly. No submissive acknowledgment of his superiority, just the minimum respect I could get away with. "You wanted to see me?"

"I wanted to see you several hours ago."

"As I told Willem, I was otherwise engaged." I stood my ground. No submission.

"Consorting with the humans. You think they're going to take you in, a mongrel child like you?" His tone was scornful.

"No," I said bluntly. "No more than I think you or my father's family would acknowledge me. What do you want?"

He looked stony, then gestured at the others. "Leave us. Except Willem."

The *guerriers* vanished, melting away at the too fast, too graceful pace that always made me see the wolves inside the men far too clearly. I stayed on alert, waiting to see what would happen next.

Martin rose from his desk, came around it. The gun and dagger at my hip suddenly felt too far away. I was fast but not as fast as a Beast.

"What's this about?" I repeated, putting the edge of a growl into my voice. I was outside his pack, outside his authority. I wasn't going to roll over and show my belly.

Martin halted, a few feet away from me. "I need some information."

That much I knew already. "Information about what?" I

wasn't promising anything. I moved my left hand to my hip, nearer my gun.

"About Simon DuCaine."

Buggering Veil's eyes. I was the belle of the ball this evening. Everyone wanted to dance with me.

"What makes you think I have any information about Simon DuCaine?" I asked, trying to sound bored.

"Come now, Fen. Your little friend . . . the one who does the dresses, amongst other things"—his voice dropped, lower, edged with a threat—"she is keeping company with his brother. The Templar. And, in the past, it has tended to be true that where the dressmaker goes, there you are."

I cocked my head. "The only things I know about Simon DuCaine are that he's a healer and that he's a brave man when it comes to choosing a woman." A little threat of my own, reminding Martin just who he would be messing with if he went after Simon. The thought of incurring the anger of a wraith was enough to give any sensible man pause. And make him run fast in the opposite direction. Not that I'd ever known Martin to be particularly sensible. "And that his brother is, indeed, involved with my friend. Touchy man, Guy DuCaine. Both of them are, actually."

"There's more to the story than that."

"So you say. But I'm telling you what I know."

"You're telling me you haven't seen anything about him?"

I shook my head, "I've seen things. I see things about many people. But nothing that would be of interest to you."

"Be sensible, Fen. We can help each other out."

"I don't need your help, Martin."

"Oh no?" He closed the gap between us with one swift stride. His hand grabbed my forearm, wrenching it up. He pushed my shirt back with the other hand, baring the chain. "I'd say you're in trouble, boy." He studied the skin around my wrist, which was bruised and angry-looking. "Iron won't help you much longer. You need to learn to control the visions. I can help with that."

"If you had a seer, Martin, you wouldn't need me now, would you?" I knew better than to struggle against his grip. A Beast was stronger than any half-breed. "Yet here I am. Which means you don't have anyone who can help me."

"There are other packs," he snarled.

"Have you forged an alliance then?" For another pack to lend Martin a seer would take a very close bond, beyond the ever-shifting temporary alignment of interests that wove a web between the packs. And exact a very high price in return favors. Martin would need to be getting desperate to do that. "Risky times to trust anybody, these."

His lip curled again, but his hand left my arm. I shoved my sleeve back down.

"Don't make this difficult, boy," Martin said.

"Believe me, I don't want to."

"Good. Then you will tell me what you know about Simon DuCaine."

I fought the urge to reach for the gun at my hip. Two Beasts. I might shoot one of them at least before they got to me. Maybe. Even if the Lady favored me and I got them both, I wouldn't get past the *guerriers* waiting outside the door.

"I'm telling you I haven't seen anything."

Martin leaned closer. "Then I suggest you take that chain off your wrist and look again."

I stared at him. "It doesn't work that way. I need to be close to someone."

"You're close to me. There's trouble in the City, boy, and I believe that Simon DuCaine is tangled in it. If you look, you'll see him."

Fuck. He was probably right about that. "I can't guarantee I'll see anything."

"I suggest you try very hard."

There was no way out that I could see. Gritting my teeth, I opened the clasp on the chain and unwrapped it from my wrist. The room suddenly blurred around me, the visions pouring in with a force that made my head whirl greasily, pain and nausea rushing through me.

I bent over, trying not to retch. It felt like my head was trying to tear itself in two. I didn't know how much more pain I could take. Saskia's face flashed into my head, her and the weird moment of stillness I'd experienced at the touch of her hand. Maybe if—I pushed the thought away. No time to think about what might be. I had to deal with the pain now. I drew in a long breath, my head still screaming in protest.

"What do you see?"

"Right at this moment," I managed to say, "your very fine carpet."

Martin wrenched me upright. "Hurts, does it? Still think you don't need my help?"

"I'm not an *immuable*, Martin. I'm a mongrel, remember?" One who was going to stay far away from anything that resembled a leash.

"If you don't want my help, it's on your head." The grip of the huge hand on the back of my neck tightened, sharp nails pricking at my skin. "But I will know what you see. So look, boy. Look hard."

I didn't see any alternative. I didn't have to tell him everything I saw of course, but I wasn't getting out of here until I told him *something*. Something that would make it worth his while to keep me alive. After all, he lacked a seer and if I wasn't going to fulfill that role for him, he had no reason not to indulge the anger that smoked his voice.

Martin was not the delicate type. He would hurt me or kill me with no compunction. The images that flickered at the edges of my peripheral vision, the ones rising in response to Martin's proximity were littered with bodies and blood.

For now they didn't contain anyone I knew, but that could change.

I swallowed hard, fighting the nausea, and opened myself to the visions. It felt like stepping off a cliff and falling into a nightmare. The room went away and I stood alone in darkness, watching the flickering show that only I could see. Images danced around me, almost too fast to interpret. Some were faded and indistinct but some flared almost too bright to bear. Flames searing bright across the City turning the moonlight to smoky orange. A broken sword lying on marble tiles. The face of Ignatius Grey snarling in triumph, eyes blazing as red as the blood that stained his mouth. A crumpled pile of white fabric. Ash falling over cobblestones. But no Simon. Not this time.

Thank the Lady.

I tried to find the Ignatius image again. If I couldn't offer Martin the insights into Simon that he sought, then perhaps knowledge of the Blood would be an acceptable substitute. Ignatius Grey was currently the Blood lord most likely to retake control of the Blood Court. The Blood had been embroiled in deadly politics since Lord Lucius had vanished. As far as I knew, Ignatius was allied with the Roussellines, one of the packs who had backed Lucius. Perhaps Martin could use some leverage to better the position of the Kruegers there.

I let my mind focus on Ignatius, remembering the last time I had seen him. At one of the Blood Assemblies, feeling sweat trickle down my back in the overcrowded, overheated room, trying not to breathe in the smell of blood and smoke and fear too deeply. Ignatius had passed just a few feet away from me, moving amidst a pack of his supporters as they walked toward the stairs that led to the private chambers above. He had scanned the room with arrogant brown eyes, the very image of a man well satisfied with himself and his place in the world. He exuded an air of casual cruelty, of belief that whatever he wanted should be reality, that made the crowds part to let him through. Even now the memory made my spine crawl.

I had told Martin that I needed to be near someone to see their future but that wasn't strictly true. It was easier that way, but sometimes, if I caught a glimpse of someone in a vision, I could follow that glimpse and expand upon it.

I didn't do it often. Hells, I did as little as possible with my power. Each time I used it, it grew stronger and the pain of resisting grew worse. The deepest I cared to go was the surface skimming I did to tell fortunes to foolish women and men. That had once been bearable, but lately even taking such quick glimpses was growing chancy, requiring more and more brandy to dull the pain.

I'd let myself go deeper over the last few weeks as I'd sought information for Simon and Guy while I was out skulking around the edges of the Night World, and I was paying the price for it in my constant headaches.

Tonight, despite the fact I'd already strained the limits of my tolerance by going to the DuCaines' ball, it seemed I would have to risk delving even further into the depths of my abilities.

Ignatius, I thought fiercely. *Show me Ignatius.*

The images swirled around me, flickering like leaves in a storm wind. I searched them desperately, trying to find that arrogant face amongst the whirlwind. Other Blood came to me. The stark beauty of Adeline Louis and the cruel face of the late unlamented Lord Lucius. Not what I wanted to see at all.

And then, finally, another glimpse of Ignatius. I reached out my hand and grabbed at the image, drawing it closer in my mind.

Ignatius.

The images multiplied around, rising like a swarm of bees. Full of blood and horror. Ignatius standing over corpses, Ignatius feeding, fangs buried deep in the neck of a weeping woman. Ignatius laughing as someone was killed in front of him. Ignatius seated in a vast hall, in a chair that had to be called a throne while Beast and Fae knelt before him.

What the hell?

I wrenched myself out of the vision, nerves screaming with the sharp pain of my resistance. *Fae kneeling to the Blood.*

No.

Not possible. If that were a possible future, the City was in far worse trouble than I had suspected.

My heart pounded in my ears as the room reeled around me. I tasted bile and brandy in my throat and swallowed it back with an effort.

"What did you see?" Martin's voice was eager in my ear. "What is it?"

I swallowed again, not sure I could speak without my voice shaking. "I didn't see Simon DuCaine." Fire rolled through my head, searing. Gods. I wanted the pain to stop. If I survived this night, I was going to see Saskia, find out if the effect of her touch had just been a coincidence.

Martin growled. "I don't believe you, boy."

I opened my eyes as the sick burning feeling in my head receded. Turned my head and stared at him. "I'm telling the truth."

Chapter Three

The morning came too soon. The hall maid knocked at my door at precisely half past six as I had requested. I'd had only a few hours' sleep and they'd been uneasy, with the memory of that last touch of Fen's hand on mine mixing with images of my brothers fighting and the City in uproar in my dreams.

In truth, it was a relief to be awake, even though my body tried to persuade me to stay where I was. Ignoring the siren song of more sleep, I climbed out of bed, groped for my robe, and stumbled the short distance across the room to the door. The steaming tea tray set neatly on the floor outside was a welcome sight. Even better, the smell wafting up from the china pot it held spoke of coffee, not tea. Thank fire.

I gulped down coffee in between bites of bread and jam. Not my usual breakfast, but nerves kindled sparks in my stomach as I'd known they would. I could eat more after the ceremony. Hopefully I would have something to celebrate by then.

After breakfast I dressed carefully, donning the best of my apprentice tunics, the one I kept for official occasions. Its earthy red was unmarred by burns or scald marks or chemical stains and it smelled like the soap used by the laundry instead of the faint scent of smoke and fire that usually permeated my clothes. With my hair braided behind my head and a clean black skirt, I looked respectable. Adult. Trustworthy.

Nervous, I realized, studying the pale reflection in the mirror. I pinched my cheeks, not wanting to bother with cosmetics or glamours. There were enough opportunities to play with feminine things in my mother's world, particularly now with Holly joining the family. Having the services of a very talented modiste at hand was useful. I frowned down at the boxy tunic. Maybe Holly or Reggie could make one that would be slightly more flattering.

And that was an odd thought. Normally I was happy for the comfort of my Guild clothes and the familiar sense of focus and anonymity they provided. I obviously had had far too little sleep.

With a last nervous poke at the pins holding my braids in place, I forced myself to turn away from the mirror and leave the room. I wasn't the only one hurrying through the halls early this morning. Almost every student in the Guild was heading in the same direction as I was, toward the Ore Hall, where the Guild Master would be announcing the members of the delegation.

There were plenty of Master mages and journeymen making their way too. Everyone, it seemed, was curious to see who would be selected. Even if only a few of us could realistically expect to be chosen. The Guild didn't officially rank apprentices, but after four years of study and sweat and sheer bloody hard work, I knew that I stood very high—if not first—amongst my classmates. Surely I had done enough? Surely they would pick me?

My hands curled into fists as I pictured it.

My name. My hard work. My place earned and nothing my interfering family could do to stop it. A place in the delegation meant not only freedom and being able to contribute to something important but a chance to mingle with the Fae smiths who would accompany the Veiled Queen. To be known to them.

Which was the very first step to one day perhaps being able to study with them. The Fae did things with metals that no human metalmage could hope to emulate and they guarded their secrets closely, but if I wanted to become a true Master. . . to maybe one day find the alloy that could replace iron and free the humans from some of the tyrannies of the treaty restrictions . . . then learning what I could from the Fae would be essential.

They only ever worked with the brightest and the best of the human metalmages.

I needed to be the best. I needed to be chosen today. I didn't want a life shaping iron or metals to the whims of the Guild of Mechanizers or other customers. I wanted to help change the City for the better.

I forced myself to relax, to look unconcerned, as I reached the doors to the Ore Hall. As I passed through, Master Columbine spoke my name, looming up at my side like a sentinel crow in her Master's robes of black and gold. "Saskia, a word if you please." She was shorter than me, the top of her black bun just level with my shoulder, but size didn't equal power. Master Columbine was one of the strongest mages at the Guild, able to make gold dance to her will. Normally I would be happy if she singled me out for attention, but not this morning.

I tried not to let my flash of frustration show on my face. If I was too slow, I would lose my chance at a seat near the front of the hall. I wanted to be nearby when my name was called. "As you wish, Master," I said and let her draw me over to the side of the foyer.

"Master Aquinas would like to see you, afterward," Master Columbine said. Her bright blue eyes had a look I couldn't quite decipher.

"Of course," I said automatically, then pressed my lips together, hiding a grin. Of course he would want to see me. He would want to see all the delegates. I had done it. Elation made me giddy, rushing through my veins like brandy.

I ducked my head toward Master Columbine. "Was there anything else, Master?"

She sighed and flapped her hands toward the front of the hall. "No. Go on. I won't keep you any longer."

I hurried off, working my way through the throng. The first few rows had filled up with the Masters, but I spotted an empty seat in the fourth row, off to the side. Not ideal, but it would do. I took my seat just as the Guild Master entered the hall, silence spreading before him as he walked down the center aisle, heading for the ornate bronze lectern at the front of the room.

Like Master Columbine, he wore black and gold, though in his case, his chains of office were so elaborate, a complicated intertwining network of gold medallions and looping chains of every possible kind of metal, that it was more gold than black, as though he were clothed in metal. Indeed, the chains shifted and flowed more easily than they should have, the enchantments that bound them and powered the Master's bonds singing softly through the air. The spark of power within each medallion made it gleam, so that to a mage's eyes, the Master was surrounded by a glow of authority, an echo of the molten earth fires from which the metals we worked came.

Master Aquinas was not overly tall but he bore the gold decorations easily, despite their weight. He, like me, was a mage whose affinity was for iron and he seemed to echo the strength of that metal as he laid the leather-bound book he carried on the lectern, set his shoulders, and waited for the silence to be total before beginning to speak.

I listened to his words with only half an ear, impatient for him to get to the important part. We all knew that the negotiations were important, perhaps more important than ever, given the current unrest in the Night World and elsewhere. What we wanted to know was who would get to take part in them. Aquinas spoke for several minutes before he finally finished the formalities and opened the book.

"These are the Guild delegates," he said and began to read the names. Masters first, then journeymen. I held my breath as he read out the tenth journeyman. There was a soft buzz of voices now, whispered reactions to each name, but it died away as Master Aquinas paused and looked out over the room with a frown before he turned back to the book.

"And finally, the students who have been chosen to serve the delegates." Master Aquinas paused again and I fought to keep my hands calmly in my lap. "First year. Carlisle Abernathy." He held up a hand for silence when there was another buzz of noise. "Second year. Marcus Trent. Third year. Rebecca Covington." He took a breath and I felt mine freeze in my throat. "Fourth year." He paused and looked out over the crowd. Not at me. "Sara Ledbetter."

I didn't hear him speak the fifth name over the roar of shock in my ears. Merely sat frozen, trying not to show dismay on my face as the naming drew to a close and, eventually, everyone started to depart the hall. It was almost empty when there was a light touch on my shoulder and I looked up to see Master Columbine.

"Saskia, you have an appointment with Master Aquinas. No dawdling."

There seemed to be no polite response that I could conjure. I merely nodded, managed to stand, and headed toward the exit, moving automatically.

The time spent cooling my heels in the Master's antechamber did nothing to cool the rage burning in my heart. Hell's fire and blighted earth.

Simon and Guy had done this. I knew it.

Somehow they had convinced Master Aquinas to keep me out of the delegation. I didn't know how they'd done it. I wasn't aware that they'd visited the Guild at any time over the last few weeks, but Master Aquinas didn't spend all his time here. Somehow my brothers had gotten to him.

Convinced him that I wasn't worthy. How *dare* they?

I sucked in a breath, the prentice chain at my neck—plain silver and iron—growing warmer as my anger increased. I could hardly convince Master Aquinas that my brothers were wrong about me if I lost control of my powers in his presence. I tried to let my mind go blank, to direct the power back down into the earth. The tiles beneath my feet began to feel too warm.

Hell's fucking fires indeed.

Where was a bucket of ice water when I needed one?

Just as I was wondering if I dared risk leaving the chamber, the Master's door finally swung open and Master Columbine stepped out. For a moment I thought I saw sympathy in her expression, but then it returned to its usual calm composure. "You may go in now."

I nodded, not daring to speak in case the curses still boiling in my head spilled out. My hands clenched in the folds of my skirts as I entered the Master's office.

Master Aquinas was slipping a book back into place in the ceiling-high rows of shelves that covered one wall. He no longer wore the Master's chain but that did little to alter the authority he wielded. The Guild Master's office was large and the metalwork that formed the decorations and furnishings was both beautiful and elaborate, designed to display the power of the Guild. Yet Master Aquinas was the thing that drew the gaze in this place.

His gray eyes were calm as he acknowledged me with a gesture toward the chairs by the fireplace.

"Prentice DuCaine, would you like to sit down?"

"Not particularly." I snapped my mouth shut before I could say anything worse.

"Then perhaps you would do so to indulge me?" Master Aquinas said. "There are things to discuss."

"Things called Simon and Guy?" I said, staying where I was.

Master Aquinas sighed. "Sit down, Saskia."

Despite the sigh, it was a command. I sat.

"You're upset," he said as he seated himself in the chair opposite mine.

"Why, Guild Master, whatever reason would I have to be upset? You just announced publicly that Sara Ledbetter is a better mage than I am. What could possibly upset me in that?"

His mouth quirked. "Would you like to swear at me a little?"

"No, sir," I said. "I believe I'll save that for my brothers."

Master Aquinas' face turned serious. "It wasn't your brothers, Saskia."

"Oh really?" I said, letting my disbelief color my words.

"No," he said firmly. "It was me."

For the second time that morning my mouth dropped open and the rage drained away, to be replaced by stark cold fear. Him? Master Aquinas had made the decision to exclude me himself? Sainted earth, did that mean I really wasn't good enough?

"What do you mean?" I stared at Master Aquinas, not sure I believed what I was hearing. "I've worked hard for this. You know I'm the best in my year."

He nodded. "Yes. I do. You're also the only one in your year with an affinity for iron. We need that skill, Saskia. It will be more important than ever if the negotiations don't go the way we want them to."

"You're saying I'm *too* good to go?" I was still struggling to take it in. I'd worked so hard and now that apparently was the reason they weren't going to let me reach my goal.

"I'm saying that we need to keep you safe."

"The negotiations are held under Haven laws. With the Veiled Queen present to enforce them. I'm hardly going to be at risk." I tried to keep the snap out of my voice and only partly succeeded. I bit my lip, twisted my fingers through my prentice chain before I made things worse.

Master Aquinas leaned forward, setting his chains chiming softly against each other. "That's not strictly true. This is not a normal treaty negotiation. Not with the way things lie in the City. Anything could happen. The negotiations may well be disrupted. I want you here safe at the Academy."

"You think someone is going to attack the Treaty Hall?" Really, I couldn't have been any more startled if Master Aquinas had announced he had decided he was now attracted to women and wanted to marry me.

"I'm saying that we don't know and I'm not taking any risks. Your skills are more valuable to me here."

I frowned. "You think the supply of iron is going to be reduced?"

"It could be. Which means we will need the best mages to work what we have. And to keep looking for substitutes." He nodded at me. "Your experiments have been promising."

"Mine and those of half the other mages in the Guild," I said. "Promising isn't the same thing as successful." None of us had hit the perfect combination of alloys that might mimic the strength and power of iron without causing pain to the Fae. Which was why, if Master Aquinas truly did think my efforts were promising, it made no sense that he would deny me the opportunity to gain an introduction to the Fae smiths and prove myself worthy of being taught by them.

"Yet."

I was torn. Part of me liked the compliment being paid to my skills, but mostly I felt the net of convention and obligation tightening around me from yet another angle. Yes, I wanted to help, but to do so by hiding away and denying my own desires didn't exactly sit easy. "You still need iron workers to be in the delegation."

"Yes, and that's why I chose Master DeLuca. The rest of you will stay here."

His tone made it clear that there would be no disputing the point. His argument was logical. Master DeLuca would work well on the delegation. He wasn't one of the more powerful iron workers but he was intelligent and diligent. So he'd do a good job whilst being expendable—not that any loss of a mage was acceptable. Despite the logic, I still wasn't entirely convinced that my brothers hadn't planted the hells damned notion in Master Aquinas' head. It seemed suspiciously convenient that this particular negotiation period was deemed unsafe for metalmages who worked iron when usually they had a strong role to play in negotiating the human iron ration. Not that I was officially a metalmage yet. No, I was still just a prentice and therefore bound by the will of the man before me.

I tried one last objection. "You picked Rebecca from the third-years," I said. "She's a silver worker. Won't the silver supply be affected too?"

"There are three times as many silver workers as iron workers. You know that. It's not the same thing."

He leaned a little closer, his expression softening. "I know this is disappointing, Saskia, but if you accept this, then your patience may be rewarded."

Oh yes? After everything had gone to hell in a handbasket, then I was going to get some special treatment? "How exactly?"

"Something good will come of it."

I narrowed my eyes at him. "Do I get to choose what that something might be?"

He smiled. "I take it you have something in mind?"

"I want to go to the Veiled Court," I said bluntly. "I want a chance to work with the Fae smiths."

Serious eyes studied me for a long moment, then nodded. "All right. I will see what can be done. In time," he added. "Your work has proved your skills." He stood, smoothing down his tunic absently. "Now, I have much to do and you must be missing classes."

Dismissed. Without a firm agreement that I would get what I had asked for. Anger rose within me again and I clamped down before it could strengthen. Master Aquinas would see the power sparking if I didn't. Then I would be in for a lecture about lack of control.

"Thank you, Guild Master," I forced myself to nod politely, stand, and dip a curtsy. I even managed to walk out of the room in a controlled manner and not slam the door. I maintained my sense of composure until I was through the building and halfway down the path that led to my workroom.

At which point I let myself break into a run, heading for the safe haven of my own space, where I could lock myself away—Master Aquinas having been mistaken about my class schedule today—and indulge my anger to my heart's content.

The workroom door—reinforced with heavy brass banding—slammed satisfyingly, shaking the various implements and piles of glassware around the room into a furious jangle of noise. I felt a moment's guilt, hoping that Silvio, who had the workroom that shared a wall with mine, hadn't been in the middle of a delicate process, then took the lack of shouted protest to be a sign that he hadn't.

I stomped across the room, yanked my heaviest leather apron off its peg, and dropped it over my head, heedless of the fact that I still wore my best tunic. It wasn't as though I was going to need it for the negotiations after all. What did I care if it got stained or burned?

I threw half a scuttle of coal onto the banked embers of my forge fire and stirred them viciously to life with a poker that threatened to bend in my hand as the power surged again in response to my mood. I channeled the fury into the fire, heating the coals far too quickly. The flames roared and blasted my face with heat that was a little too much for comfort.

Face nearly scorched, I scowled and pushed some of the excess heat down through the earth, into the deep aqueducts that ran under the Academy for exactly this purpose.

Once the fire was under control, the coals starting to glow red, I stepped back, dropped the poker, and looked around for something else to take my anger out on. Anything.

I spotted a sword that I had ruined with an incautious tempering several weeks ago hanging from the wall amongst some other failures waiting to be repurposed. *Perfect.* I snatched it down and plunged the blade into the fire to heat. While I waited for the forge fire to do its work, I paced the room, fighting the urge to throw things.

I had worked up a good sweat, pounding my frustration into the sword, when I noticed my wards flickering. Somebody at my door. Cursing, I plunged the sword into the quenching barrel—it was beyond ruined now—and stalked over to the door, still holding the hammer.

The man standing on my doorstep looked somewhat taken aback. "I wasn't that rude last night, was I?" Fen asked with a grin. He nodded at the hammer. "If I was, I assure you I apologize. If you put that away."

I blinked, my mind trying to catch up. Fen here, on my doorstep? Laughing at me. I was suddenly very conscious of my soot-stained, sweaty state. And that I was waving a hammer at him. I bent and leaned the hammer against the doorframe. "I was working. What are you doing here?"

He looked somewhat the worse for wear. He hadn't shaved and his clothes, though not the same elegant tailcoat he had worn to the ball, were rumpled as though he'd slept in them. He wore a navy tie knotted crookedly around the collar of a white linen shirt. The slightly lighter blue jacket fitted beautifully despite its wrinkles.

"May I come in?" he asked.

I hesitated. I wasn't in the mood for visitors, any visitors, let alone someone as unsettling as the man before me. Not when I had no idea why he'd sought me out. Regina and Holly had told me a little of his reputation—his wild ways and his legendary charm when it came to pursuing women— but surely he hadn't come here to woo me?

I sincerely doubted that I was the type of woman he wooed—if indeed he ever did have to do any wooing rather than just sitting back and letting women flock to him. And I had no inclination to become one of the panting throng. He was horribly attractive, even scruffy and unkempt—not the distant perfect beauty of a Fae but still enticingly hand-some. Particularly when his intense green eyes were focused on me like I was the gateway to heaven. "I'm busy," I said shortly, fighting the urge to step closer.

"Please?" He accompanied the plea with another flash of charming smile. It made me nervous, but I found myself stepping back and nodding before I could think better of it. Which only made me more nervous.

I had met attractive men before. I'd even dealt with Fae men whose beauty made Fen look plain. But none of them had made my sense of self-preservation itch the way Fen did. I hadn't let myself think about it last night when he had seemed so bored and eager to get away from the ball. Even those last few minutes on the portico, I had made myself dismiss whatever interest I had felt, knowing it could lead to nothing good. But apparently the events of this morning and my lack of sleep had rattled me sufficiently to make me vulnerable.

I held up a hand, warding him off. "This room has iron in it. Won't it hurt you?"

He shrugged. "No. I'm fine as long as I don't handle it directly."

I wondered if he was telling the truth, then decided I didn't care. If he wanted to be an idiot, it wasn't my place to stop him. I stepped farther back as he moved toward me. He might be an idiot but I wasn't going to be one.

Scooping up the hammer, I moved across the workroom, back to the forge to return the tool to its proper place, putting a good chunk of metal between me and the man who had me rattled in the process.

Fen, however, came to a halt a few feet inside the door, his head turning every which way, his expression fascinated.

"You had something you wanted?" I prompted. I didn't want to deal with this man while I was shaken and off balance. What I wanted was to be left alone to regain my composure. Because I was suddenly afraid that I might attempt to work off my anger by doing something foolish with him.

I wiped my hands on my apron, succeeding only in smearing more soot on skin and leather. Turning my back on Fen, I crossed to the sink at the rear of the room, untying the apron as I went. Scrubbing my hands gave me a minute to think. I would've dunked my head in the water if I'd thought it would help but I doubted it would. Besides, I didn't want Fen to see my nerves.

I dried my hands slowly. Behind me, Fen moved around the room, his footsteps light, then silent as he paused here and there. At least there was no crash of glass or clatter of metal. Or maybe that wasn't a good thing. Knocking something over would give me the excuse to toss him out again.

With one last nervous swipe of the linen towel over my hands, I forced myself to turn back to him.

"Are you going to tell me why you're here?" I came halfway back across the room, still keeping a reasonable distance between us. The Guild didn't apply the silly rules of chaperonage and etiquette that the human world imposed—it would make teaching students difficult if unmarried men and women couldn't be left alone together—but for once I missed the protection of the system I'd grown up with.

Fen moved—prowled, rather—around my room, looking somewhat like a wild thing hunting for . . . what exactly, I couldn't tell.

He paused near the forge, stared down at the flames. He still didn't speak.

I frowned, anger rekindling slowly now that I'd had a chance to steady my nerves. "I'm really quite busy this morning. If you're not going to tell me why you're here, I'm going to have to ask you to leave. Do you want something?"

His head lifted sharply, and those wild green eyes settled on me, narrowing slightly. "Such as?"

"I don't know. You came to me," I pointed out.

"And men never come to you just because?" His voice dropped a note or too, pitched just right to please the ear.

"Not very often." I pressed my lips together, swallowed against the sudden resurging flutter of nerves. "After all, they know who my brothers are." I angled a few steps toward the box under the window where I kept the weapons I made. I didn't truly believe I needed one, and I did have other tools of defense at my disposal, but it didn't hurt to be careful. Simon and Guy had drummed that much into me.

"Your brothers aren't that scary."

"Maybe not to you." Once again, I wondered if he was telling the truth. Usually I was very good at reading people. Fen, if he was lying, was a master at it. All the more reason to treat him with caution.

I'd seen him head out of the ballroom with Simon and Guy last night and seen him return, looking grim, before he'd pasted a polite look of indifference back on his face and stationed himself, back to the bar, watching the dancers while he drank. "But most men I meet have more sense"—*and less brandy,* I stopped myself from adding by clamping my mouth shut on the words and swallowing again—"than you."

"You don't know if I have any sense or not."

"I've heard stories," I said. Then cursed myself as the look in his eyes turned amused. "Besides, you look like you haven't been to bed at all. That's hardly sensible."

"I'm half Fae," he reminded me. "I need less sleep than a human. I work best at night."

His eyes gleamed with even more amusement. I ignored his innuendo. Fae blood or not, something told me that he was desperately tired. His shirt cuff obscured the chain around his wrist, but I could feel it, the purity of the iron singing to me cleanly through the myriad other notes of metal in the room. If nothing else, wearing iron had to drain him. He'd left the ball early, same as me. Who or what had occupied the rest of his night?

No. I wasn't going to think about how he might or might not spend his time. Find out what he'd come for and send him back on his way: that was the only sensible plan. "Less sleep isn't no sleep. But your sleeping habits are no concern of mine."

That made him look amused again. Sainted *earth*. I was turning simpleminded around this man. To his credit, he didn't say anything. He was being the perfect gentleman, mostly. I judged his flirtation to be mostly instinctive, something he used on any female—or male perhaps—to get what he wanted. *Nothing to do with me personally*, I told myself firmly.

But the not telling me why he was here was growing tiresome. My own lack of sleep was starting to take its toll now that the adrenaline of this morning had subsided. Fen's presence was still making me nervous enough to hold it at bay, but I could feel fatigue waiting to descend on me like an anvil dropped from the sky. I rested my hand on the copper trivet lying on the bench nearest me, drawing strength from the metal. Just a little. Not enough to damage it, just enough to keep my wits about me.

"What my concern is," I continued, "is why you're here. Are you going to tell me, or are you going to leave?"

He watched me for a long moment, then seemed to come to a decision. He straightened his shoulders, tugged his tie into a slightly more orderly position. "I came here to test a theory."

"A theory? You have some sort of metallurgical problem I can help with?"

He snorted. "Hardly. No, I have an entirely different sort of problem." He stepped forward. I moved back without thinking, but there was a high stool in my path. I couldn't go any farther without making it obvious that I was retreating. And really, what did I have to retreat from?

"Perhaps if you share it with me, it will make it easier to determine if I can help?" I sounded calm at least. That's one thing that years of being trained to be a properly behaved young lady does for you—teaches you to hide your feelings well. Though I was hoping for something closer to Lily's intimidating silent stillness than the studied politeness of a well-bred human girl. I got the impression that Fen would eat well-bred human girls for breakfast. Break their hearts and step over the pieces.

Sainted earth. There it was again. I didn't care what he did to women's hearts. Not in the slightest.

A few more steps and he paused, within arm's reach of me. I couldn't interpret the expression on his face; it was outwardly as calm as I was trying to pretend I was, but there was something strained in his eyes, making the dark circles and lines of fatigue suddenly more prominent.

"Forgive me," he said. "I haven't offered you a proper greeting this morning." He held out his right hand and automatically I took it.

Our skin met with a faint buzz and suddenly Fen looked ten years younger, his eyes unshadowed, the strain in his face vanquished.

Startled, I pulled back, but his fingers tightened around mine, warm and strong. His eyes looked past me—or through me. One breath. Two. Then he seemed to come back to himself and stepped away with a shallow bow.

When he straightened, he looked tired again, though not as tired as he had.

The room seemed distant around me as I closed my fingers to my palm, feeling the warmth he'd imparted. "What," I asked uncertainly, "was that?"

"That, Prentice DuCaine, was an answer." And before I had time to think of the next logical question—like "To what?"—he bowed again, turned abruptly, and walked out of the room, leaving me wondering what in the name of hell's fires had just happened.

It took a few minutes before I stopped gaping. By the time I regained my senses and ran to the door, Fen was nowhere to be seen.

I slammed the door savagely as the rage came flooding back. *Gods damn it!*

Yet another man thinking I would just acquiesce to whatever he wanted.

He thought he could just swan in here, smile at me, do whatever it was he had come to do, and then swan out again?

No.

Enough was enough.

I was going to get some answers. And no man was going to stop me.

The hall bell started to chime as I looked around me, wondering if I had any money in my workroom. I froze. Blighted earth. Classes. I was late for Master Tien. And she was not a woman to cross.

But then again, right now neither was I.

I had worked myself nearly to the bone for the last year, striving to be chosen as a student delegate. And the Guild had decided that my hard work meant nothing.

Which meant, right now, that I was more than willing to let their rules mean nothing as well.

I had far more important things to do.

Anger carried me back to my room to change and find a purse and money. It burned hot as I waited for the hour to end and the bells that tolled the change of class to sound, wanting the halls to be crowded so that I wouldn't be so noticeable. It had settled to a steady seethe by the time I went back downstairs and out onto the street to find a hackney. I had donned perfectly normal dark green day dress, but the gate guards knew me and looked at me strangely as I swept past them. They knew the Guild's schedule as well as anybody. Most students would have the last of the morning classes to attend at this time. Still, I was a fourth-year and we were allowed a certain amount of freedom. Neither of them made a move to stop me.

I got the feeling, however, that my leaving the grounds would be reported in short order. All the more reason to find a hackney fast.

I marched briskly down the street, in the direction of the nearest underground station. I would prefer a hackney or 'cab ride over taking the train into the border boroughs, but if it came to a choice between making my getaway and taking the safest mode of transport, I would choose speed.

Luckily I didn't have to make the choice. A hackney came trotting up behind me and stopped when I turned and signaled.

"The Swallow's Heart," I said to the driver, naming the tavern where Holly used to live and Fen still resided.

Bushy gray eyebrows shot skyward. "You sure that's the place, Miss?"

"Yes," I snapped, "I'm sure. And it's prentice, not miss."

He looked at me with uncertainty for a moment longer, then apparently decided that arguing with a metalmage might not be the smartest course of action. "If you insist," he said and tightened his reins.

I said nothing, just gathered my skirts and climbed into the carriage.

Chapter Four

SASKIA

⚡

Rage carried me all the way into Brightown—building again as the journey was held up several times by traffic snarls and other petty delays that normally wouldn't bother me. The journey, which should have taken thirty minutes at most, took nearly a full hour. I let irritation burn away any nerves as I climbed out of the hackney and walked down a narrow, disreputable-looking alley to the rear entrance of the Swallow's Heart. My temper only flared brighter when a tired-looking woman in a white apron opened the door in response to my loud knocking and gave me a knowing look when I asked for Fen.

"Bit early for him, dearie." She looked me up and down again. Doubtless I wasn't dressed the way that the kinds of women who visited men in these rooms were usually dressed. The Swallow was next door to the Dove's Rest, the biggest brothel in the City. Not exactly reputable. My gloved hand tightened around my purse. If necessary I would offer the woman an incentive to give over the information. I wished for a moment that I could pull out my prentice chain, but it was hidden under the high neckline of the dress.

"The room?" I prompted. "He's expecting me."

The woman grunted. "Takes all sorts, I guess. That one never turns down a bit of company. Third floor, room right at the end of the hallway." She paused for a moment as if expecting me to say something.

Instead I just nodded politely, bit back the stab of annoyance that her comment about Fen had evoked, and followed her directions.

The wooden staircase was nothing fancy but it was clean and polished. I'd never been in the back part of a tavern before. Actually, I had hardly ever been in the front part of a tavern on this side of town. The students at the Academy had a few favored taverns in Silvertown that sold cheap beer and didn't mind the odd explosion. I was too busy with my studies to venture farther afield, even I'd been interested in the sorts of entertainment that Brightown offered.

I climbed the stairs, breathing rapidly from exertion as well as from my temper by the time I reached the last landing and followed the corridor down to a door that was bare of anything but a slightly tarnished-looking brass six. No nameplate gave any clue as to the identity of the room's occupant, but the cook or whoever she had been had said the door at the end of the hall and this was as far as I was going. If she'd steered me wrong, then she would be the one to vent my temper on instead of Fen.

My knock was slightly less vigorous than it had been on the door downstairs, but it still sounded loud in the quiet of the hallway. If most of the people who lived here kept Fen's sort of hours, I might have just woken half the floor. I braced myself for an angry head or two to appear in doorways.

Nothing.

I knocked more forcefully.

From beyond the door came an irritated grunt, followed by the sorts of noises that someone half asleep makes when crossing a room while trying to get dressed and bumping into things. I'd made enough of that sort of progress myself after long nights studying to recognize the sounds.

There was a slightly louder muffled curse, a brief tingle as a ward was lowered, and then the door cracked open about a foot.

"What?" Fen demanded. His dark hair stuck up in several directions and he needed a shave even more than he had earlier. His white linen shirt was wrinkled and untucked

and for a moment I wasn't entirely certain whether the dark
trousers he wore were fastened, given he had one hand
clutched at his hip. Then I recognized the gesture. The instinctive grasp for a weapon of a man used to carrying one.

He must have been deeply asleep not to arm himself as
he woke, if that were the case.

He blinked bleary eyes, finally seeming to recognize me.
"What the hell are you doing here?" He peered past me
into the hallway. "Did Holly bring you? What time is it?"

"I brought myself," I snapped. "And it's nearly midday.
Let me in."

He frowned, his eyes squinting with the effort to wake
up. He shook his head as though to clear it. "No. Respectable girls like you don't come into my rooms."

"You came into mine," I retorted. "Let. Me. In."

His gaze sharpened, the blurriness of the newly wakened
disappearing. "Or what?"

"Or you'll find out how much fuss a metalmage can
make when she's thwarted."

"Veil save me from women," he muttered, rubbing his
stubbled chin. Then he shrugged. "Have it your way. But if
your brothers ask, this was your idea. Don't expect me to
save your hide."

"My hide is my own business," I said, making a shooing
gesture so that he finally opened the door wider and
stepped back to let me enter.

His room was in hardly better shape than its owner.
Clothes littered the floor, and books and other mysterious
objects covered all available flat surfaces. A long shelf running the length of one wall held still more books and several bottles of brandy in various stages of consumption.
Against the other wall, at the windowed end of the room,
was a massive four-poster, its disheveled covers confirming
that I'd woken Fen up.

It was the most decadent-looking bed I'd ever seen, a
four-poster with dark wooden columns carved with sinuous
figures and its surface covered in myriad layers of deep red
fabric and pillows.

I pulled my gaze away with difficulty.

"What are you doing here?" Fen asked again. He moved
past me, lifted a pile of clothing off a low chair, dumped the
clothes on another pile near a basket that was already full

of still more clothes, and gestured at the chair as if inviting me to sit. I remained where I was.

"I assure you, it's clean," he said. "It's just the day my laundry is collected."

I raised an eyebrow at this. An armoire that matched the bed stood against the wall opposite the foot of the bed. One of its doors was ajar, revealing a rack bulging with shirts and jackets. The man seemed to have more clothes than I did. Or more than I kept at my rooms at the Guild. Every time I returned to my room at my parents' house, more new dresses of the type my mother approved of—like the pale pink one I'd worn last night—appeared in my wardrobe.

"From the looks of things it's also the maid's week off," I said, a little more sharply than I'd intended.

Green eyes narrowed at me. "Not all of us have maids, sweetheart. Now, I was sleeping and I'd like to get back to that. So say what you came to say."

"You're mad at *me*?" I said incredulously. "You waltz into my rooms, act all mysterious, then disappear, and you think you get to be mad at me? Sorry, it's the other way around."

"Sorry if you wanted me to stick around a little longer, but I had other things to do."

"Like sleeping? What happened to 'I need less sleep than a human'?"

"Just because I need less doesn't mean I don't enjoy it when I can get it." He tilted his head speculatively. "Like many other things. Is that what this is about? You thought I came to see you for something else? To lay flowers at your well-bred feet perhaps? And now your pride is irked?"

"Don't be ridiculous," I said, fighting the urge to set something on fire. "I don't care about flowers. Or you," I added in rapid clarification. "I care about being treated like a convenience by men. A pretty thing who doesn't need to be given information or allowed to participate. I have a right to know what you were doing when you came to see me. I am a person, not a thing, and I don't care how you usually treat women, but it's not how you're going to treat me."

There was more than a hint of anger in his gaze now. "I generally treat women how they deserve to be treated. If they're nice to me, then I'm nice to them." ·

"I hate to think what you consider nice."

"Not waking me up to shriek at me is a good start."

"I am not *shrieking*. Besides, I wouldn't have had any cause to come anywhere near you at all if you hadn't started this." I stalked over to the chair and settled myself onto it, glaring up at him. "If you want to finish it, if you want me to go, then tell me why you came to see me. The truth. Don't bother trying to charm your way out of this, Fen. I'm not in the mood to be charmed."

I hoped I was telling the truth. True, I was in no mood to be sweet-talked out of my temper, but I had a horrible feeling that if any man could charm me, it might be this one. Despite his rumpled state he was still undeniably attractive. The room smelled like him too. Of male with a hint of brandy and something deep green and intriguing, which I assumed was his cologne.

He stared down at me. "I'm guessing you're just as stubborn as your brothers, aren't you?"

"Would it help if I told you that in our family I'm known as the stubborn one?" I said sweetly.

"I don't see how it possibly could." He scrubbed a hand over his stubbled chin, then grimaced. "Veil's eyes, I need coffee."

"Then talk fast and you can ring for some."

"You're not going to let this go, are you?"

"No. I'm staying right here until I get what I came for. The truth," I added. I had no doubt he might try lying if he thought it would get rid of me. But I wasn't going anywhere until I was convinced he had told me the whole story.

He said something under his breath that I didn't quite catch. Fae, perhaps. I knew some of that language, but mostly technical things about metalworking and magery and enough to get me by with basic niceties and conversation. I didn't think what Fen had just muttered fell into any of those categories.

"I can wait all day," I said.

"Maybe I'll leave, then," he said.

"I'll follow you."

"How?"

"Well, for one thing, unless you're planning to remove that chain—" I tried to keep the wince out of my voice as I looked at his wrist. The skin under the links looked both bruised and slightly swollen. Taking it off had to be a temptation. The fact that he kept it on meant he needed it. "I can probably track you anywhere you might run to."

He looked both surprised and appalled. "You can track a single object amidst all the metal in this city?"

"If I try hard enough." The effort would leave me drained and useless but he didn't know that. "So why don't you spare us both the trouble and just tell me?"

"You want the truth? So be it. You're probably not going to like it."

"Given a choice, I'd rather be informed and unhappy than ignorant and unhappy."

"How about ignorant and happy?"

"Not likely. I've had quite enough of that lately. Stop stalling, Fen. Think of the coffee."

"I'm trying not to." He settled himself on the bed, rubbed his face again. He looked so tired for a moment that I was tempted to allow sympathy to override my good sense and let him off the hook. Instead I pressed my lips together so I couldn't sabotage all the work I'd just put into getting him to this point and waited for him to start talking.

"All right," he said. "I came to see you because I wanted to test a theory."

Hardly enlightening. "What theory?"

"It doesn't make any sense," he said softly.

"Nor do you, right at this moment. What theory, Fen?"

He looked past me. "Last night. At the ball. Being around so many people in one room. That's hard for me sometimes."

"Because of your visions?"

"Yes. Sometimes I can keep things under control, but sometimes I can't. More people makes it harder."

That, at least, made sense to me. More people had to equal more potential futures for him to see. I didn't know a lot about how the powers of a seer worked, but I knew those who seemed to have true sight tended to be Fae or Beast Kind. I'd never heard of a human seer. Though Fen was only partly human.

"So you were having a bad night?" That explained the brandy. "What does that have to do with me?"

"I told you, it doesn't really make sense," he said.

"And it won't until you tell me."

"When I helped you into the cab you weren't wearing your gloves." His eyes dropped to my hands, folded neatly in my lap.

"No. They were uncomfortable. What does that matter?"

His eyes suddenly looked a far wilder shade of green. Like a window into a dangerous place. "When I touched you, the visions went away."

I couldn't help it. For the second time this morning my mouth dropped open and I stared at him. "Excuse me?"

"When I took your hand, I couldn't see anything—no visions at all. And it didn't hurt anymore." He added the last under his breath, his tone almost . . . wistful.

I ignored my pang of sympathy and focused on what he'd just told me. "But—"

"I told you it didn't make sense. I thought it must have been a coincidence, but then last night something else happened and I decided I needed to know. That's why I came to see you this morning. So I could touch you again."

I didn't know whether to ask him if it had worked first or ask him what had happened. My brain had half stuttered at the phrase "touch you again." *Gather your wits, Saskia. He's just a man.* My mother's voice in my head came to my rescue. "Did it work?"

He nodded. "Yes."

"If you touch me, your visions go away?"

"So far, yes."

I wanted to suggest we try again just to confirm things, but I was reluctant to touch him. My mind tried to come to grips with the implications. "Do you see anything now?"

He shrugged. "Nothing much. Faint glimpses. One on one I can usually keep them under control."

"Usually?"

He ignored that, studying me. I didn't like the speculative expression lurking in the depths of that gaze. What did he see around me? My stomach tightened as I realized that he might be seeing my future. I wouldn't ask. I didn't want to know. Or did I? "But surely stopping your visions isn't a good thing. You earn your living through them, don't you?"

"Yes. But that doesn't mean I like it." His left hand drifted toward his right wrist, then jerked back.

I looked again at the iron chain. "You told me that didn't hurt."

"I lied. I do that." The last held a hint of warning.

I resisted the urge to rub my temples. It seemed the combination of not enough sleep and the frustrations of the morning were combining to set me up with an aching head of my own.

"I don't understand—" I stopped for a moment. Tried to think. "It has to have something to do with my powers. I have an affinity for iron. Maybe that means my power is like iron to yours?" I stopped again, unsure of myself. "But surely if that worked, someone would have known about it before?"

Fen's expression was intrigued . . . if a little skeptical. I knew how he felt. My theory was just that, a theory. A wild-sounding one at that.

"Not necessarily." He spoke slowly. "The Fae and the Beasts don't really spend much time with metalmages, after all."

"The Fae sometimes do."

"Fae seers?"

I had to admit I didn't know the answer to that. "Where does your sight come from, anyway?"

Another fluid shrug. "Nobody knows the answer to that particular question. There aren't many Fae-Beast-human by-blows like me."

I could believe that. While Fae and Beasts both slept with humans, I couldn't imagine a Fae doing the same with a Beast. They would consider that far too undignified. Fen's heritage was, if not unique, then at least very rare. Much like his powers. That was unfortunate, but it also meant my theory was as good as any right now. No one knew exactly why metalmages had an affinity for one metal over another either. It was plausible that whatever made iron and me a good match could mean that I could be the human equivalent of iron for Fen.

Not that I had any idea what earthly use that might be. Did he? "Why did you want to know for sure?"

"Because, as Holly would say, information is power."

That didn't ring true to me. It wasn't as if this particular fact was any use to anybody but him.

I studied him. He met my gaze calmly, but I wasn't reassured. "Don't start lying now. What were you hoping to achieve?"

He made an exasperated noise, then stood and stalked over to the window.

Silence reigned as he stared out the window. He had good aural wards, that was for sure. The Swallow and the Dove were both large and constantly busy. They also faced one of the busier streets in Brightown. It was nearly midday now. The streets below us would be crowded with people and vehicles, yet all I could hear was the sound of Fen's breathing and the faint rustle of my dress as I eased my position on the chair.

Eventually Fen turned back to me. "I don't know."

"So it's just curiosity?" I paused. "Why don't I believe you?" I tried to remember everything he'd said here in this room and back at the Guild. "Wait—you said something else happened last night. What?"

"That doesn't concern you."

"It does if it sent you scurrying to my doorstep."

"I do not *scurry*."

"Fine. Sent you striding manfully to my doorstep," I retorted. "What happened?"

"I'm not going to tell you."

"This is going to be a long day then."

His mouth flattened. "You know, it's possible that you're even more annoying than your brothers."

I smiled. "I'll take that as a compliment."

"You like being annoying?"

"It's better than being invisible," I said.

"I hardly think many people would consider you to be invisible."

"You might be surprised."

"Humans are idiots," he said.

"Aren't you half-human?"

"Technically, it's three-eighths."

"Oh?"

"My father was Fae. My mother's mother was *immuable*. Do you know what that is?"

I nodded. "A Beast who doesn't change." I'd known he was part Beast but not the *immuable* part. No wonder he could charm the birds from the trees. I'd met only a few Beast Kind—those who sometimes came to the Guild to commission work—but they were invariably handsome men and women, radiating . . . something I didn't want to think too closely about. And the *immuable*—the Beast Kind who didn't change—were said to get all the other qualities of the Beasts in extra doses. Strength. Beauty. Charm. Temper. Along with a helping of Sight. Fen's grandmother must have been a very interesting woman.

And apparently her blood ran strong. Fen had those same qualities. He drew the eye. Amongst other things.

"Interesting," I murmured.

"That doesn't bother you?"

"I'm a mage. My brother's a mage. My future sisters-in-law are likely to be a wraith and a demi-Fae. If none of that bothers me, why do you think your parentage would?" I lifted my chin. He might have me in the category of "good human girl" in his head, but I'd rather he saw me for what I really was. A person in my own right. Someone who was capable of more than decorating drawing rooms and ballrooms, someone who valued more than just the strictures of the privileged human society I'd grown up in.

"Perhaps I underestimated you," he said.

I tamped down the immediate glow of pleasure. "Yes, you did. So now that we've cleared that up . . . are you going to tell me what happened last night? Maybe it's a problem that I could help with."

"I doubt it," he said. He looked for a moment over to the shelf that held the brandy. He probably wanted a drink. Holly said he drank too much. I was beginning to understand why.

"Tell me," I said again, trying to coax him.

Fen shook his head. He moved to the bed, sat, and dropped his head into his hands. Then he straightened. "I don't want to drag anybody else into my mess."

"Tell me or I'll tell Holly that you're in a mess and then you'll have more than me to worry about."

"You wouldn't."

"Care to put that to the test?"

His expression turned resigned. "No."

"Then tell me."

"Let's just say that last night I received several invitations to participate in the treaty negotiations."

I stared at him. "That's a bad thing?"

"Sweetheart, if you could see what I see, you wouldn't want to be anywhere near those negotiations. In fact, you'd be leaving the City."

"Then why are you still here?"

"Because apparently it's not only humans who can be idiots."

"You really don't want to be on a delegation?" Anger and disbelief sparked in my stomach. I had spent *months* trying to achieve what he was going to casually discard. Sweated and slaved and—

"No," he said shortly.

"Why not? Simon and Guy will both be on the Templar delegation," I said. "Holly too, I guess."

"I know," he said. "But just because Holly has lost her head doesn't mean that I want to lose mine."

My jaw tightened. "Did you ever consider that perhaps the way to prevent whatever it is you've seen happening is to work to stop it?"

His brows drew together, dark slashes that matched the dark worry in his eyes. "You think it's that easy?"

"I don't know. I don't know what you've seen."

"And you're not going to," he said.

"I'd do it," I said. "If someone gave me the chance to help, then I would." I bit down before I could say any more and all the disappointment of this morning came spilling out of me.

His mouth twisted. "Then that's the difference between you and me."

"I don't believe you," I said. "I know you helped Holly when Reggie was in trouble."

"Holly and Reggie are my family."

"Everybody's family might be at risk if what you've seen is true." It had to be bad, whatever it was that made him look so haunted.

"I can't help everybody."

"How do you know unless you try?"

"Spoken like a well-protected human girl. You don't know what it's like outside your safe little world. The Night World is dangerous."

I was all too aware of the costs that the Night World could impose. "I'm not—"

"Don't try and tell me . . . you didn't grow up in the border boroughs. You don't know what it is to fight for survival."

"Only because no one will bloody well let me!" My voice was louder than I intended, echoing around the room. "You think I just want to sit on the sidelines and embroider hankies? No. I want to make a difference. And I wouldn't throw away the chance if I was offered it." I rose from the chair, not sure exactly what I was intending to do. But I couldn't just sit there.

Fen rose as I did and took one step toward me before stopping. We stared at each other. I wanted to read something in his eyes, something to tell me he wasn't really so cynical. But all I saw was a flat resolve that I couldn't decipher any further.

"Are you really not going to help?" I didn't want to believe that he would turn his back on what was right.

"I don't think I'll have a choice," he said bitterly.

"What does that mean?"

"It means I either accept your brothers' offer to be on their delegation or I inevitably end up being forced into helping somebody else."

I wondered who else had made him an offer. Someone from the Night World, I presumed. The Fae had their own seers—I couldn't see that they would trouble themselves with a half-breed who seemed to be at war with his powers.

Night World then. Beasts or Blood.

"Would you really consider working for the Night World?"

"It wouldn't exactly be a choice."

"If you don't want to do that, then, it seems as though you should choose our side."

"I'd rather choose my own side and stay the hell out of things altogether."

"And I'd rather grow wings and fly to the moon, but that's not likely to happen, is it? You can help."

"That's part of the problem, I don't know if I can. I can put my bloody neck on the line and be completely useless. Or worse."

What was worse? "Because you can't control the visions?"

"Partly. But it's not just that. It's—" He stopped. "No. I'm not talking about this."

"Because it hurts," I said softly. "Doesn't it?"

I crossed to him. I couldn't help it. I wasn't a healer like my brother but I didn't have to be to feel the pain in Fen. I laid my hand—still safely gloved—on his cheek.

"Yes," he said simply. "And I can't make it stop."

Chapter Five

FEN

The touch of Saskia's gloved hand was warm against my cheek, the leather soft where it brushed my skin. But instead of leaning into the comfort she offered, as part of me wanted very much to do, I made myself stop, straighten, step away.

Admitting my pain had been an error in judgment. I wouldn't compound my mistake.

Saskia's hand fell slowly away, but she didn't protest my retreat. The weight of her gaze, the knowing look in those eyes, seemed to bore right through my skin, as though she could see into me. I didn't want her seeing that. The mess that I was.

"You can't stop it," she said hesitantly. "But maybe I can."

She started pulling off her gloves.

I held out a hand, palm out. "Don't."

"I can help you, Fen."

"No."

Hurt flared in her eyes, then turned to something hotter. Anger.

"Why not? Too proud to accept help from a female?"

"It's not that."

"Then what?"

I hadn't entirely understood my instinctive rejection, but her questions had made it clear. "Because," I said, trying not to snarl the frustration that knowledge brought, "knowing there is a way for it to stop will just make the rest of the time harder than it already is."

"Oh." Her expression softened again.

Which, perversely, made me angry. "Exactly. You can't just snap your fingers and fix everything. This is the real world."

Her hand twitched. Probably wanted to slap me. Wouldn't be the first woman to do so either. But her fingers curled into her palm instead, and her chin came up.

"I'm well aware of that," she said. "And maybe it won't work all the time, but surely some of the time is better than none?"

"You going to come down here every night and hold my hand? It's a tempting offer, sweetheart, but I'm not sure your family would approve."

Her eyes narrowed. "I'm not offering to go to bed with you, if that's what you're suggesting." Her chin tilted higher still, her eyes suddenly flinty. "You're not my type, anyway."

I let that one lie. I knew it wasn't true. Knew that she felt the same pull toward me that I felt toward her. But given that I thought the smart thing to do was ignore it, I was glad that she seemed to have reached the same conclusion. "Then what exactly are you proposing?"

"A mutually beneficial arrangement."

I lifted an eyebrow. I might be prepared not to act on the attraction between us, but I wasn't entirely above a little flirtation. Her cheeks went pink, but she just ignored that and kept going.

"I have something you need. You have something I want. We can help each other."

"And what is it of mine that you want?" I asked, curious despite my better judgment.

"I want you to join the Templar delegation." She paused, took a deep breath. "But I want you to tell my brothers you'll agree to join if they take me too."

"And in return for me sticking my head into the lion's den, I get what?"

"You get relief from your visions."

"How often?" How far was she actually willing to take this? She had determination, I had to give her that. Not to mention a certain degree of courage—or misplaced bravado—to come to see me in the first place.

"We can discuss that once you agree."

"Why should I agree before I know what I'm going to get out of it?"

She flapped her gloves at me. "Oh, stop being difficult. The choice is easy. You can suffer or you can help me and I'll help you."

Definitely Guy and Simon's sister. Ruthless in pursuit of what she wanted. Still as attractive as her offer—the thought of no pain, even temporarily—was, I wasn't going to drag her into a situation that I didn't want to be in myself.

"No," I said.

Saskia's mouth flattened. "I'm getting very tired of people telling me no."

"Be that as it may, no it is. Simon and Guy would have my head if anything happened to you."

"Simon and Guy don't get a say in what I do. Sainted earth, I'm twenty-three years old."

"They might not get a say but that won't stop them from coming after me."

She looked like she wanted to throw something. At me.

"Maybe you should be more worried about me than them."

"Excuse me?"

"I'm a metalmage, Fen. I'm not some delicate female flower who needs a big strong man to protect her. I don't see you telling Lily or Holly what to do."

"I have more sense than that," I muttered.

"Then I suggest you add me to whatever strange mental category you include them in."

"Lily is a wraith. *You* can't walk through walls to escape if something goes wrong at the negotiations."

"Nor can Holly."

"Holly can handle herself."

Her eyes had moved beyond flinty. Now they were a storm cloud shade. Lightning lurked in their depths. It matched her thunderous expression. "How do you know I can't?"

"You work metal, don't you? That's not going to help you if a Blood or a Beast comes after you."

"Oh, really?"

"Yes. Beside, you're not yet a metalmage. You're still a student."

"That's just semantics."

"Well, right now, in this city, your semantics might just get you killed."

"Is that so? Tell me, Fen, what special powers do you have that make you invincible?"

I shrugged. "I can see trouble coming." That was a lie, but nearly thirty years of life in the border boroughs had left me with a healthy instinct for trouble and the ability to fight my way out of it when I had to.

"I thought you wore that chain around your wrist to stop yourself from seeing. So I really don't see how your sight can be all that useful. It's hardly practical."

Before I could answer, she reached up and yanked a hairpin free from the neat coils of her hair.

"Whereas I can do this." She held the bronze-colored pin upright between her thumb and forefinger, then narrowed her eyes at it. The tip of the pin burst into flame.

Impressive. Not that I was going to tell her that. "I don't think any Blood or Beast is going to stand still while you stick a flaming pin in them." I did my best to sound bored.

She shot me a look that made me wonder why my head didn't ignite as the pin had. The flame on the pin died abruptly and she flicked it toward the empty grate, where it made a little sizzling noise as it hit the hearthstone. One quick glance around the room and she stalked over to my mantel and picked up a pewter candlestick. "Can I borrow this?"

It was obviously a rhetorical question. I sensibly stayed quiet, limiting myself to a nod. She shot me another flat glare, then moved her hands, one to each end of the candlestick.

I wondered if she was working up to braining me with it, but then she suddenly pulled her hands apart and the metal . . . stretched. That was the only word for it. As if it were rubber or clay or toffee. I stared as her right hand moved over one end of the candlestick, working it to a wicked point, more dagger than candlestick.

She made a satisfied sound, then moved her grip so that she held only the blunt end. Definitely more daggerlike. Perhaps I had underestimated her after all.

She aimed the sharp end toward me and snapped her fingers. The point lit up like a flare, burning with a clean white light. She smiled nastily at me and before I could say anything she threw the flaming dagger toward me with deadly force. It whistled past my head, close enough for me to feel the hot rush of air as it traveled past me and buried itself in the far wall with a solid *thunk*. At once the wallpaper began to smoke and char, the burning smell hot and acrid.

"That's going to cost me extra rent," I said. I didn't bother trying to put the fire out. Nothing I could do would extinguish a flame set by a mage.

Saskia made no move to douse the fire, just folded her arms, gaze locked on mine. The paper around the dagger caught with a soft whoosh of flame.

"You've made your point. Do you think you could put that out now?"

"Of course." She snapped her fingers and the flames died. I picked up the pitcher of water and crossed the room to toss it over the candle dagger and the wall. I was sure she could put the flame in the metal out, but I wasn't so sure about the wood. I didn't want to wake up in the small hours with my room on fire. Saskia said nothing.

I wrapped my hand around the end of the dagger, half expecting it to be hot. It was warm but not unpleasantly so. I pulled it free of the wall, carried it back to her.

"This is yours, I believe."

"Actually, it's yours." She laid it on the table. "Consider it a gift. Still think I'm helpless?"

"It was a good throw," I admitted. "But you're still not going to have time to fashion a weapon every time you need one."

Her mouth dropped open. "Do you think I'm an idiot? I carry weapons. And I can do that to any piece of metal around me."

My eyes traveled around the room, noting all the bits and pieces of metal. My chain around my wrist suddenly weighed a ton. But there was still no way I wanted to put myself in the position of having to explain to Simon and Guy exactly why I was going to demand that they put their sister in danger.

"How does that work, exactly?" I said, stalling while I tried to think of another way to dissuade her. "The fire?" I'd known that metalmages could manipulate metal, but the fire part was new.

She shrugged. "All metal was molten once. It remembers the heat."

"I'm not sure that makes any sense."

"It's magic. It's hard to explain. You try to explain how your visions work to me and, if you can, I'll try again."

"Touché."

"So?" Saskia lifted her chin.

"So what?" Playing dumb was my last bastion of defense.

"Do we have a deal? Throwing a dagger isn't the only thing I know how to do. I'm a pretty damn good shot and I can use a sword too."

"You can?"

"I grew up with two older brothers who wanted to be Templars. They got lessons, I paid attention. And as soon as I joined the Guild, I started up again. After all, if you're going to make weapons, it helps to know how to use them."

"What kind of weapons do you make?"

"Guns, daggers, swords. Lots of things. We have to learn all sorts of metalworking as part of our studies. I like the weapons."

The girl continued to surprise me. I shook my head. I should have guessed as much, given her brothers. "Was there a particularly bloodthirsty ancestor in your family?"

Her smile this time was almost scary. "We've had our moments, but really the DuCaines are just a normal human family."

"You and Simon are both mages."

"Guy and Hannah aren't, though."

"Two out of four is a high percentage, isn't it? For your sort of family."

"Two out of five," she corrected.

"Sorry?"

"There were five of us. I had another sister."

Had? Damn. There was a subject I wasn't about to delve into. Her face had turned shadowed.

"Five," I corrected. "It's still high."

"These things happen. My parents don't like it, but there's not much they can do about it."

Her parents would be worried about who would take over the family concerns once they were gone. Guy was a

Templar, and unlikely to give that up, from what I could tell. Simon was busy with his patients and St. Giles.

The senior DuCaines had to be hoping either Saskia or Hannah would marry the right sort of man and bring him into the family fold. I looked at Saskia, standing there ready to charge into battle to get what she wanted. She could run a family's estates. I didn't think she wanted to, though. I had trouble imagining her sitting sedately behind a desk, going through piles of ledgers and bills.

The faint images ghosting her didn't show such a fate. But right now they didn't show much of anything beyond the same sense of heat and flame I'd gotten the night before. Which was a good thing, and how I wanted it to remain. "You should listen to your parents. And your brothers. They'd all tell you not to do this."

"As I said, I'm very tired of being told what to do. Do we have a deal?"

"The situation is complicated . . ." If I couldn't convince her with logic, maybe I could intimidate her with something else. She was a good human girl, after all. Perhaps I'd taken the wrong tack.

"I can handle complications. I understand the politics of the negotiations—quite well." She looked me up and down. "Possibly better than you do."

"I wasn't talking about politics, sweetheart." I let my voice go softer, deeper. Holly called it my female catnip voice. She ribbed me relentlessly about it when she caught me using it, but even she couldn't deny it worked. I could talk most women into anything when I used that voice on them.

Saskia's cheeks deepened in color but she made no move. "What exactly did you mean?"

"You're volunteering to spend a lot of time in my company. And I know you feel something for me."

"Why, you—" She sputtered for a moment.

"Don't pretend you don't know what I'm talking about. Or if you truly don't know, then you really have no business trying to make this deal."

She continued to stare at me, seemingly struggling to come up with a suitable retort.

"If you're all grown up, as you insist, then you're old enough to recognize heat between a man and a woman.

And it's there between us. I'm not a saint, Saskia. I'm not one of your respectful human boys. If you ask me, I'm not going to be a gentleman."

"Sainted bloody earth." She'd finally found her tongue. Her cheeks still blushed pink, but her eyes were furious. "How is that no woman has killed you before now?"

"Women like me," I said. I let a grin spread across my face and watched her expression grow even more furious. Apparently Saskia wasn't most women. Which, in a perverse fashion, made her only more interesting. More fun to tease, definitely. "More than like me, actually."

"Maybe. Until you open your mouth," she shot back. "I assure you, Fen, I am perfectly capable of protecting myself. And pardon me for being blunt, but somehow I don't think resisting your . . . charms . . . will be all that difficult."

"You think that, do you?"

"Yes." Her hands were on her hips.

For a moment I was tempted to kiss her and prove her wrong, but that would be true insanity. Heat runs both ways after all and I had enough problems without availing myself of a temptation that I couldn't afford.

The silence stretched. Neither of us looked away. I frowned. I wasn't going to be the one to give in.

Saskia looked triumphant. "See. This should be easy. You find me annoying and the feeling may well be mutual. Now, do you want to come up with some more excuses or should we deal with this like adults?"

I muttered something not fit for her ears under my breath and stalked over to the window. But staring down at the mossy tiles of the Swallow's roof didn't offer any inspiration. There was, as Saskia knew, no choice for me to make other than to join with Simon and Guy.

Unless I was willing to leave the City. Which I couldn't think about.

The only question that remained was whether I was callous enough to drag Saskia into the mess with me. It didn't matter that she seemed to desire just that—she didn't know what she was asking for. She didn't know what I had seen.

The iron at my wrist burned for a moment as the memory of last night's vision returned. Should I continue to walk the narrow line I'd laid out for myself, skirting the edges, staying free, and risking even more pain?

Or should I actually make a choice and put myself—and Saskia, most likely—in harm's way?

Loathing soured the back of my mouth. It was a devil's bargain, no matter which way I cut it. Damned to the seven hells no matter which way I chose.

Shal e'tan, mei.

I wasn't ready to choose. Not yet.

Saskia stood there, watching me with the light of expectation in her eyes. The sour taste in my mouth grew sharper.

"I . . ." I paused, not sure how to tell her no. Then a knock sounded at my door. Perfect. An interruption was just what I needed.

Or so I thought until I opened the door and saw Holly, worry written large in her eyes.

"What's wrong?" I demanded.

"It's Reggie," she said. "She wanted to go back to the store this morning. She was meeting Viola there for a fitting."

"Viola?" I struggled for a moment to place the name.

"She works at St. Giles. She's Fae." Holly made that impatient gesture. "It doesn't matter. What matters is I was just at the salon and when I got there the door was open—half smashed—and neither of them was there."

Fear twisted itself into my stomach, pulling into a tight knot that clawed at me. "Maybe they'd already left." Holly's modiste salon was in Gillygate, safest of the border boroughs, but it was still a border borough. Burglaries and vandalism weren't unknown.

"Reggie's bag was in the office. She doesn't go anywhere without that bag."

True—the bag contained the notebook she used for working out her design ideas. She was always scribbling in that damned notebook.

"I think something's happened," Holly said. "Someone's taken them."

"But why?" It was Saskia's voice from behind me. Holly's eyes widened and she shot me an accusing glance. I ignored the look but opened the door wider so Holly could see into the room.

"Who would attack a modiste?" Saskia continued, coming up beside me.

"Someone who wanted to get to Holly," I said bluntly.

"Or at Guy through her. Or—Veil's eyes—who knows, it might have been Viola they were after. Or it was just a robbery and they were in the wrong place."

"We don't really have much worth stealing," Holly pointed out. "If someone wanted to clean out the stock, they'd do it at night. And the stock is all still there."

I didn't like the picture she was painting. My gut was increasingly certain that she was right. Someone had taken Reggie and Viola. But who? And why? Reggie had been kidnapped by Holly's father when he was trying to control Holly in the past. But he was dead.

Lady's eyes. It couldn't be happening again. Lightning didn't strike twice. Or did it?

One way to find out. I knew that much. "We need to go back to the salon."

"We should go to Simon and Guy," Saskia protested.

"We will," I said shortly, knowing that my choices were narrowing rapidly. The more I let myself get entangled with the DuCaines, the harder it would be to turn down their request. And in truth, the sense of honor I usually kept as tightly chained as my wrist was breaking free. This wasn't right. If someone as sweet and gentle as Reggie had been caught in the crossfire for the second time, the City needed to change. Even if somebody was going to have to force the issue.

Holly had a hackney waiting outside and it didn't take long for us to clatter our way through the streets back to Gillygate. Saskia rode with us. I'd tried to send her home, but she'd given one flat shake of her dark curls and set her jaw. Holly hadn't tried to argue the point, which told me she was even more worried than she was letting on, to put a DuCaine female in the path of potential harm.

The scene at the salon was much as Holly had described. The door was half smashed, though she'd hauled it back into position and bribed one of the street rats to watch the gap while she fetched me. What she thought a street rat might be able to do if whoever had done this returned escaped me. I tossed the kid a half crown and told him to bugger off. Holly reached for the door handle and I grabbed her wrist.

"No, let me." It wasn't politeness, it was necessity. To have any chance of seeing whoever might have done this, I needed something they'd touched. My power worked far better looking forward than back, but sometimes I could catch an echo of something that had gone before, particularly if what had happened involved strong emotions. Like fear.

I clamped down on the thought of Reggie struggling against an attacker. *Concentrate, Fen.* Time enough to get angry later. To see, I needed to be in control.

No spark of memory rose as I wrapped my fingers around the brass handle. *Buggering Veil's eyes.* I waited, took a breath, pressed my free hand against the wood.

Still nothing.

"Anything?" Holly said, an edge of pleading in her voice.

I shook my head, hating the flash of fear that rose in her eyes. I pushed the door inward, expecting more resistance from the shattered wood than I got and half stumbling forward. I stopped again when the three of us were inside, testing the air, trying for a clue. I couldn't smell Beasts, which was promising, but then again, if Martin was behind this, he'd probably be smart enough not to use his own men to snatch two women. A group of Beast *guerriers* would stand out in Gillygate, which was mostly human in population, and there were plenty of humans in the border boroughs or the Night World who would do a job like this for the right amount of cash. Particularly in the current environment, when steadier work was becoming increasingly scarce and dangerous.

I looked around, scanning for other signs of damage. The outer room of Holly's salon was a purely female place, decorated in pale greens and understated blues with lots of crystal and touches of silver. Long racks of dresses stood against two of the walls and there was a cluster of low chairs and couches at the far end. Those were where the clients sat while dresses were shown or while they were inspecting a fitted dress being paraded by their friends. The furniture was arrayed around a massive triple mirror. Off the sides of that space were curtained alcoves where the actual fittings and changing took place.

Beyond the alcoves a door led to the workroom, where Reggie made the dresses they sold.

All of it seemed untouched. Nothing looked out of place to me, but I didn't really spend that much time here and Holly and Reggie often rearranged things.

"Nothing is missing, you said?" I wished it were otherwise. A robbery involved touching things. This was starting to shape up more like a specific snatch and grab. The targets being Reggie and Viola. Or one of them with the other merely having had the misfortune to be in the wrong place at the wrong time.

Holly shook her head. "No." She looked as frustrated as I felt.

"What about the workroom? Is that where you found her bag?" If I couldn't get a read on the attackers from something they'd touched, I'd try another tack. Maybe I could see Reggie from her bag. She didn't like having her fortune told, but I'd snuck the odd peek on her behalf occasionally or caught glimpses without meaning to. It was hard not to. If there were two people in the world my powers should be attuned to, it was Regina Foss and Holly Evendale, given all the time we spent together. Of course, that hadn't helped me when Reggie had been taken by Holly's father, but for all I knew, Cormen—being the true prick he had been—may have done something to block me.

No time like the present to find out.

"The bag?" I prompted and Holly led the way back to the workroom. Saskia followed us, her expression curious as she looked around. The workroom was very different from the salon. Granted, the walls were painted in the same colors, but there was none of the froufrou femaleness, apart from an overabundance of gaslights wrought in the same delicately twisted shapes as those in the salon.

No, this was a working room, with several massive tables and shelves lined with row upon row of fabric bolts and bins that held more neat rolls of lace and ribbon and whatever else the hell you could sew onto a woman's dress than I cared to count.

Reggie's domain. Here, she bossed everyone else around and worked her magic in silks and satins.

Holly went to the desk, which was tucked into one of the corners, opened one of the two small cupboards that supported it, and pulled out Reggie's battered carpetbag.

"Here." She shoved it toward me. "Find her."

"It doesn't work like that," I said softly, but her expression was anguished enough to make me stop repeating things she already knew.

I closed my hands over the bag and closed my eyes, concentrating on the last memory I had of Reggie. At the ball, looking quietly happy as she danced with some nameless man, blue dress swaying like a bell as she turned in time with the music.

Reggie.

Nothing.

With a snarl I opened my eyes and yanked the chain free from my wrist with a few quick movements. Ignoring the sudden sharp throb of pain in my head, I closed my eyes again and dug my fingers hard into the worn fabric.

At first there was still nothing, but then suddenly, like a mist burned away by a lightning strike, I got something. Not an image but a sensation. Fear. Terror, in fact. My lungs contracted with my stomach as though it was my own emotion, and I fought to gain some distance.

Fear. Pounding through me. Hands gripping me. Then darkness.

I pushed harder again, trying to see more, and the pain in my head redoubled with a vicious stab. I staggered, nearly dropping the bag.

"Fen!" It was Holly's voice, but the hands that reached for me weren't hers. No. Instead Saskia's fingers grabbed for mine. The sensations suddenly vanished. Along with any sense of Reggie.

My eyes flew open. "What the fuck did you do that for?"

Saskia flinched but she didn't move her hand. "You're no use to anyone if you collapse," she said sharply.

"What did you see?" Holly interrupted. "Where is she?"

"I don't know," I said. Holly's face turned gray-white. "I think she's alive," I added quickly. "But I couldn't see her."

Holly's eyes squeezed shut briefly and then she shook her head. "All right. We're leaving. We need Guy and Simon."

Chapter Six

Fen sat silently beside me in the hackney as we drove across town. I knew Simon was home and that Guy was with him—I've always been able to tell where my family are since my powers first appeared—so we hadn't had to waste any time deciding where to look for them.

Across from us, Holly stared out the window, one hand toying with the chain of her pendant, her face pale and set. I'd never seen her look scared before. It made my own stomach twist queasily. I understood her fear, shared it, although I had only met Reggie a handful of times, through Holly, and then because my mother loved her dresses and bought me a whole new wardrobe. But the thought of anyone being taken . . . especially now . . . stirred up old memories I didn't want to contemplate.

I stole a glance at Fen. His right hand was braced against the carriage door, absorbing the jolts of the rough road. In the daylight, the livid bruising on his wrist beneath the tightly wrapped chain glowed a sullen purple, making me wish I had Simon's powers and could erase the damage. I didn't, of course. My brother was a sunmage, not a metal-mage, and our magic took different paths. I didn't like my chances of getting Fen to let Simon look at his wrist when we got to Simon's house, but I would try.

Fen's eyes were half shut, his head turned toward the window, and I let myself watch him for another moment. Despite everything else going on, he still caught my attention. Damn the man.

Women like me, he'd said with a smile that made it hard to refute his point.

He'd been trying to scare me off with his flirting, I knew that. But if he thought I was going to be put off so easily, he needed to reconsider. Still, I couldn't quite escape the images he'd put in my head. Of him and me.

And a bed.

Which was pathetic and wrongheaded. I'd only just met the man. And clearly he was not the type of man you should risk your heart with.

But he'd be fun, a part of me insisted stubbornly.

I pushed that part back into the deep dark recesses of my brain where it belonged. I didn't have time for fun. Besides, what that silly part of my brain was failing to recognize was that Fen's kind of charm was the sort it was hard to untangle yourself from. Too complicated. My mother would faint at the very idea of me spending time with somebody like Fen, but then, she probably still believed I was a virgin. Which I hadn't been for several years.

Mages thought differently about such things. In their view one should allow passion to burn and shine as the gods intended; otherwise it would interfere with the work and the power. I'd had a few partners during my time at the Guild and I'd enjoyed them, but I hadn't been broken-hearted at any of them moving on. I was at the Academy to learn. To master my powers. Metal consumed enough of my attention and time without trying to juggle a lover as well.

I wondered if Simon's years with the sunmages had been the same and what he told himself about what I might be doing at the Academy. He'd never raised the subject with me. Nor had my mother. I didn't know if that was due to rigid denial or rigid belief that I was her daughter and therefore would adhere to her standards regardless of circumstance.

I was happy to let her maintain her illusions.

I was trying desperately to maintain mine. I would not be distracted from my goals.

The fact that I was aware of the precise distance between Fen and me, not just because I could feel the iron circling his wrist but because I could feel the man himself, could feel his warmth like a banked fire inviting me closer, was irrelevant.

I knew better than to stick my hand into the fire.

At least I hoped I did.

The hackney turned onto the broad avenue that led past St. Giles, jolting and swaying. Like Fen, I braced myself with one hand, determined not to slide toward him on the smooth leather seat.

Keep my distance as far as possible.

If I got my way, if he joined the Templar delegation and if Simon and Guy let me join too, I was going to have to spend a portion of each day touching Fen skin to skin. I didn't want to increase the temptation any more than I had to.

I had to focus on the important things.

Find Reggie.

Help to secure peace in the City for the next five years. Stop whatever it was that was brewing in the Night World that might ruin everything.

The thing that I feared my brothers were at the very heart of. I had lost one sibling when I was too young to do anything about it, but I wasn't going to lose any more. Not if I could do something to prevent it. I knew that Simon and Guy felt the same way, but the difference was that I was still willing to let them take the risks they needed to take to bring about the goal we shared, whereas they thought that keeping me locked away would keep me safe.

The truth was none of us was safe as long as the City was at risk.

Reggie and Viola's disappearance proved that all too well.

FEN

"You didn't see anything?" Simon asked, his voice tight. His eyes studied me as though he doubted the truth of my words.

I tried to keep my own voice steady, tried not to let the

remembered sensation of Reggie's desperate fear wrap around me again. "I think she's alive. I couldn't see where she was."

"Which only leaves all of the City and the Veiled Court to search," Guy said. The big Templar stood by the unlit fire, fists clenching every so often. He wore mail and the red cross on his tunic seemed very bright. The color of fresh blood. Images of him bloodstained and muddy, rage twisting his face, floated around him as though the anger riding him was making one of his futures more possible.

I blinked and pressed the iron into my wrist, not wanting the distraction of visions right now.

Beside Guy, Holly shook her head. "I don't think it's the Veiled Court."

She sounded certain. I wished I shared that certainty. Holly's late unlamented father had been part of a plot against the Veiled Queen. His guilt had been revealed but he'd died without betraying his co-conspirators. There had to be Fae who had Holly high on their shit lists. The Fae, as a whole, didn't take well to anyone getting in their way. It was conceivable that one of them would come after Holly via her friend.

"It could be," I said.

"They'd go after me, not Reggie," Holly said.

"You're better protected," Guy said.

"Perhaps." Holly frowned. "But what good does taking Reggie or Viola do? They know the Veiled Queen would take action if she thought Reggie was being held somewhere in Summerdale again."

"It might not even be Regina they were after." It was Lily who spoke. She'd been silent thus far, staying perched on the edge of one of Simon's sofas, dressed in dark trousers and a simple green shirt, watching us all argue. Her low, cool voice cut through the room like a sword strike.

"Why take a Fae?" Holly countered. "If there was one thing guaranteed to stir up the queen against the Night World, that would be it."

"Truth is," I said, "we can keep arguing about this for hours, trying to work out the whys, or we can work out what we're going to do about it."

Across the room, Guy's pale eyebrows lifted a little, but he nodded approval. "Fen's right. The longer we wait—" He stopped himself before completing that sentence, with a sideways look at Holly.

It was Lily who broke the silence that spilled across the room as we all tried not to think about what could be happening to Reggie and Viola while we wasted time talking. "So we need options," she said. "And a plan."

I nodded. "I think we can safely assume that somebody from the Night World is behind this."

"Someone named Ignatius Grey," Holly muttered.

"Maybe. But there's another candidate," I said.

"Who?" Guy asked.

"Martin Krueger," I said.

"Martin? What the hell would he want with Reggie?" Guy demanded.

"It wouldn't be Reggie he wanted," I said carefully. I wasn't looking forward to this part of the conversation. "It would be me."

"What do you mean?" Saskia asked while her brothers both sputtered. She had stayed silent before this, sitting in a chair and following the threads of the conversation with stormy eyes.

"I mean that your brothers aren't the only ones who want to write their names on my dance card," I said with a shrug that was far more casual than I felt.

"Martin wants you for his delegation?" Guy demanded.

"Martin wants a seer," I said. "He thinks he can convince me I'm the one for the job."

"Why?" Guy asked.

I didn't know exactly how much Holly had told Guy of my history. It was easiest just to tell the whole story. "Because my *grand-mère* was a Krueger and he thinks, therefore, that he has a claim on me."

"And does he?"

The Templar's voice had turned cool. Too cool.

"I've obliged him from time to time," I said. "Before all"—I gestured around the room—"this began."

"And lately?"

"He sent for me the night of the ball."

I saw Saskia's and Holly's eyes narrow in unison.

"That's why you left?" Saskia said.

"You helped Martin Krueger?" Simon said. "For sun's sake, why?"

"He didn't exactly give me a choice. He sent one of his *guerriers* to fetch me. They don't take no for an answer." I said. "I'm part Beast, but I can hardly take down one of them on my own. And I'm kind of attached to walking around breathing, thank you very much."

"You went there after we'd just asked you to be on our delegation?" Simon's voice was as cold as Guy's. Lily rose to her feet beside him. I wasn't sure if she was on his side or ready to restrain him.

"To be clear," I said, "Martin issued his . . . request . . . for my attendance before I spoke to you."

"Did you give him a different answer from the one you gave us?" Simon asked.

"I gave him the same answer that I gave you. That I was staying out of things."

"Why should we believe you?" Guy said.

"Guy!" Holly protested.

"It's all right," I said to her. "It's a fair question."

Holly glared at me and then turned to Guy. "I believe him."

"I know you do, darlin'," Guy said, his voice warming for a moment. "But it might not be that simple." He turned his gaze on me. "Time's up, Fen. Sliding around the edges of things might have worked for you before, but now you need to make a choice."

"Or?"

"Or I'll have to ask you to leave," Guy said.

"You need me to find Reggie."

"I think maybe you need us more than we need you," Guy said, stony-faced. "We'll find her without your help."

"Guy—," Holly protested, her hand going to his arm.

"Is right," Lily said before Holly could say anything more. "We need to know if we can trust Fen."

"What's it to be, pretty boy?" Guy said. Saskia had a hand over her mouth, eyes round as she stared at me.

Guy looked casually confident, as though he knew which side I'd choose. Maybe he did. But he didn't know all of it. A certain petty surge of satisfaction slid through me. Maybe they were right—maybe I did need to finally make a choice. I knew they would try to find Reggie without me, but it would be faster if we worked together. Reggie was worth the pain that throwing in my lot with the DuCaines might bring. But if Guy was going to force my hand, then I'd repay the favor. Or make him back down.

"You want me to join your delegation?" I asked. "Very well. But there's one other condition."

I turned to Saskia, who had gone very still. Truth was, if I was going to partake in this particular insanity and be their seer, then I was going to need her help. I couldn't survive weeks of constant pain. Not and stay sane. I needed the relief she could bring. I told myself firmly that was all I needed from her. Besides, there was a chance that if I made this demand, Guy and Simon might change their minds about wanting me in the first place. "If you want me, you have to let Saskia be on the delegation too."

That caused another uproar.

Saskia cut through the noise with a piercing whistle. "Stop yelling," she said, directing her admonition to Guy and Simon with an exasperated look.

"You put him up to this," Guy said, returning her gaze with a look that was equally disgusted.

I stepped forward. "No." There was no reason for Saskia to be in as much disfavor as I was. Though given the anger on the faces of her brothers, maybe that was a mistake. "I'm the one who needs Saskia."

That didn't do anything to ease their minds. Beside Guy, Holly looked at me with a pointed "What stupid thing have you done now, Fen?" look that I knew all too well. But luckily she kept a firm grip on Guy's arm, having grabbed him as soon as I'd spoken.

"Needs her how, exactly?" Simon said in a dangerous tone.

"Not that way," Saskia said with an eye roll. "Give me some credit, Simon."

"I give you credit," Simon said, his tone not changing. "Him, I'm not so sure about."

"Well, he can't exactly have done anything to me without me letting him, can he now? Besides, I'm not sure exactly when you think we've had the time. I'm sure Fen is very flattered by your assessment of his ability to seduce a woman in three seconds flat, but that isn't what he meant."

"What. Did. He. Mean?" Guy asked through gritted teeth.

"It's his visions," Saskia said. "They're painful."

Simon's eyes flicked down toward my wrist. "You said you had them under control."

"I did. But lately, things have become more . . . difficult."

"What's that got to do with Saskia?"

"Saskia can stop my visions."

"What!" Holly exclaimed.

"How?" Lily said at the same time.

"I don't know how. But she touched me and the visions went away."

"What were you doing touching her?" Guy said. His voice was still ominous, but he had relaxed a little. Maybe. Or maybe that was wishful thinking on my part.

"He was helping me into my 'cab," Saskia said. "As either of you would have," she added. "I'd taken my gloves off because my hand was hurting." She broke off and held a hand up in Simon's direction. "Don't fuss, Simon. It was just a little burn. Anyway, Fen took my hand to help and apparently his visions went away."

"Coincidence," Simon said.

"No, it happens every time," I said, judging it safe to talk again. "Well, every time we've tried it."

Guy's pale blue eyes were the shade of frost on a window, the chill of his anger clear. "Oh really? How often is that, may I ask?"

This time Holly elbowed Guy in the ribs. "Calm down," she said. "Fen held her hand, not . . . anything improper." She hit me with another one of those looks. This one meaning "You'd better not prove me wrong about that." "If having Saskia around gives Fen some respite from his visions and the aftereffects, then surely that will make him more useful to the delegation?"

I hid my smile of relief. Holly was making the point for me far more effectively than if I'd tried to do it.

"We don't know that will work," Guy rumbled.

Simon sighed. "Maybe not. But if Saskia does help him—"

Guy looked outraged. "You're not going along with this."

"I can't in good conscience deny Fen this relief."

"So you just want to give him Saskia?"

"I'm standing right here, you know," Saskia said, exasperation equal to her brothers' rising in her voice. "Nobody is giving me to anyone. I've agreed to help Fen. Which means I need to be close to him when he needs me."

"The negotiations aren't safe, Sass," Guy said, obviously trying a different tack.

"Nowhere in the City is terribly safe right now," Saskia said.

"The Guild of Metalmages is protected," Guy countered.

"Hardly," Saskia said. "One of my fellow apprentices could screw things up and blow us all to the depths of hell at any moment. Or worse. You have to let me pick what chances I want to take, Guy. I want to help. And Fen needs me."

Guy's pale eyes narrowed again. He swung back to me. "You can't fix"—he stopped and pointed at my head with an accusing finger—"that any other way?"

"I've tried. But the iron isn't helping as much anymore," I said. "I don't know why exactly. There isn't much else I can do. The only other people likely to be able to help me are the Beasts or perhaps the Fae. I doubt they would help me out of the goodness of their hearts. They'd want something from me in return."

I paused, let that sink in. Guy knew all too well the dangers of the Veiled Court and the games they could play with their half-breed by-blows. Holly had almost fallen foul of her own father. With my power, I would be a valuable tool for an unscrupulous Fae. They had their own seers, but it was a relatively uncommon power. Plus Guy knew that not all the Fae were on the humans' side of things when it came to the treaty.

If he made me take that path, then he wouldn't get what he wanted from me either.

So the question was, just how badly did he want me? He was an interesting man, the Templar. Devoted to his duty and equally devoted to his family, including Holly. Sometimes I wondered how the strain of it hadn't split him in two before now, how he managed to balance on the knife's edge and not fail either side.

But now I was asking him to make a choice that squarely hinged on that dilemma. Who to put first? Saskia or the City? I hoped I'd made the right gamble as to which he was likely to choose.

"You'd sell yourself to the highest bidder?" Guy's voice was dark with distaste.

"I'm not selling myself," I snapped back. "I'm trying to make the best of a bad situation."

"Don't loyalty and honor matter?"

"Whom should I be loyal to? Nobody wants the mongrels like me." I refrained from looking at Holly and Lily and including them in my statement. Through those two, Simon and Guy knew very well what the demi-Fae went through.

"You'd choose to go to the Beasts for help?"

"I don't want to choose to go anywhere. I was quite content as I was."

"The world isn't going to stay as it was," Simon said.

"I *know* that." As much as I wanted to deny it, I couldn't.

"You've seen something, haven't you?"

I stayed silent. Guy started to swear, a long steady stream of curses half muttered under his breath.

"No point muttering," Saskia said to him. "You're not saying anything I haven't heard before."

Guy shot her a look but kept stalking around the room, his curses a little louder. Simon stayed where he was, eyes fixed on me as though he could read the truth in me. Maybe he might have been able to if he was touching me, reading a lie in my bodily reactions, but not even a Master Healer can read another's thoughts.

Saskia crossed to me. "You did see something, didn't you?" she asked, laying a hand on my arm. My skin warmed beneath her touch as the pain melted from my wrist and my skull. Involuntarily my head turned to her, our eyes meeting for a breath too long. She looked away first. Then looked back.

"Well?" she repeated.

I shook myself and stepped away. Saskia made no move to follow, though her cheeks flushed as she watched me go, something close to hurt flashing in her eyes. Damn. I didn't like the answering flare of guilt in my gut.

I couldn't care what she felt.

"If I did see something, I'm hardly likely to tell anyone until it's decided whose side I might be on," I said.

Across the room, Guy's cursing cut off midbreath. Simon's face grew even grimmer. "Is that a threat?"

I folded my arms across my chest. "Just good business."

Simon squared his shoulders. "What makes you think we'll just let you go?"

"What are you going to do, beat me up in front of your sister, then throw me in a Templar cell?" I stood my ground.

"If I—," Guy growled before Saskia stepped forward, shaking her head at us.

"There's an easy way to settle this," she said. "Without any of you having to act like petulant children."

Guy started to splutter. Simon nudged him. "Such as?"

Saskia nodded toward me. "Do as he asks. Let me be on the delegation. Then I'm sure he'll tell you whatever he knows."

I tensed as Guy and Simon turned their blue eyes on me. One pair frosted ice, one pair bright as summer, they held identical expressions of anger. Guy was glaring. Simon looked only resolute.

"Don't make me get a bucket of cold water," Saskia said. I wondered whose tone she was mimicking to get that snap of exasperated authority. Her mother perhaps? Or maybe one of the Masters from the Guild?

Saskia moved a few steps toward her brothers, putting herself between them and me. Foolish girl.

"Simon, you want Fen's help. Surely letting me be on the delegation isn't such a terrible thing?" she said.

Simon and Guy both stiffened. I knew what they feared, but I also understood Saskia's need to be allowed to make her own way in the world.

She looked just as determined as her brothers, hands planted on her hips as she scowled at them. "Guy, you always say you believe in the greater good. So do I. So you need to take your emotion out of this. If it were anyone else, you wouldn't blink."

"Maybe not. But it isn't anybody else—it's you. You're my sister," Guy said.

"And that's the mistake you keep making. I'm not just your little sister anymore. Not in the way you think. I don't need your protection. I can help. So stop cutting off your nose to spite your face and give in."

Another look passed between Simon and Guy. Then they turned to me.

"Will you tell us?" Simon asked. "The truth? If we agree to what you want?"

In other words, was I joining their side? *Veil's eyes*. How had I gotten to this point? I nodded, curtly.

"Say it out loud," Guy demanded. "I want your word."

One side of my mouth curled. "I'm not Fae, you know. I could lie."

"But you won't."

"How do you know?"

"I don't," Guy said shortly. "But Holly has faith in you. And you helped us when we needed it. I believe you're a good man. I hope you don't prove me wrong."

I paused for a moment, feeling the weight of the chain around my wrist, the aching bite of the skin beneath it. Thinking of Reggie, wherever she was. To be rid of one and to save the other, I would do this utterly stupid thing and help the DuCaines. "Yes. I'll tell you what I saw. I'll join your delegation. As long as Saskia is assigned to assist me. She has to be where I am."

Guy pressed his lips together but Simon nodded. "All right."

"Say it," I said. "Out loud. Your word for mine."

"You have a deal," Simon said. "If you join the delegation, Saskia will be assigned to you."

Guy nodded agreement. "Though if something happens to her—"

I nodded back. "You don't have to worry about that. I will look after her."

Saskia looked vaguely indignant at this exchange but she wisely didn't say anything.

Holly came forward to join Guy again. "Good. Now, if you boys are finished, can we get back to Reggie?" she said in a tight voice.

Guy and Simon had the grace to look vaguely sheepish. Guy reached out to put his arm around her.

"Ideas?" Holly asked, leaning into Guy.

"Either the Blood have her or the Beasts do," I said.

"I can search the warrens," Lily offered. "Once the sun sets."

Simon opened his mouth, then snapped it shut again. There was no point protesting. Lily was the only one of us who could get deep inside Blood territory without any risk of being discovered. She was a wraith and as long as there was no sun to snare her she could turn invisible and incorporeal, barred by no wall or door.

"I could go with her—," Holly said.

"No." Guy and I cut her off at the same time. Holly's charms were good but she wasn't a wraith. If she was discovered, we'd just end up with someone else in need of rescue. Holly looked mulish but she didn't argue any further.

"What happens if you find her?" I asked Lily.

Lily shrugged. "If she's somewhere that I might be able to get her out on my own, I'll try. If not, then I'll come back and we'll figure it out."

Meaning we'd lose more time, given that it was far more likely to be the latter option. If Reggie had been taken by the Blood, we didn't have time to spare. Every second she remained there was time she would be helpless. Unable to stop them from doing anything they wanted to her. The thought was terrifying. There was no time to waste.

"All right. And I'll go and see Martin Krueger," I said. I hoped like hell it was Martin who had her. He was definitely the lesser of two evils at this point.

"Why would he tell you if he has her?"

"He will if he thinks he's getting what he wants. That I will see for him."

"You'd lie to him?" Holly said.

"Why not?" After Martin learned the truth, that I'd picked a side that wasn't his, he would, most likely, seek revenge. Lying to him couldn't make things any worse.

"Or maybe you'd be telling the truth," Guy said.

"I gave you my word," I shot back. "You either need to accept that or not. This isn't going to work if you're going to jump down my throat every other minute."

"He's right," Simon said. "All right, Fen. Tonight, you go talk to Martin."

"What are we meant to do until then?" Holly said.

"Sleep," I said. "Go about our business. Whoever did this wants to get to us. We need to act like everything is normal."

"I agree," Guy said after a pause.

Thank the Veil for that. Gods, I wanted to sleep. Then I remembered Reggie once more and guilt sliced through me. Guilt didn't change how tired I was, though. Sleep would help me function. We all just had to pray to whoever might listen that Reggie would survive until we came for her.

I watched Holly lean into Guy, wrapping her arms around him, seeking comfort. My stomach tightened as I read the strain on her face. Once upon a time she would have turned to Reggie and me for comfort, but now Guy was the one she needed for strength. She'd gone through this before with her mother. I'd been worried then but not in the same way. That time I'd been fairly sure that Reggie would be okay, that Holly's bastard of a father wouldn't actually hurt them.

This time I didn't have that vague reassurance in the back of my mind. This time I felt as though there was a clock ticking. The worst of it was that I was too tired to tell if it was premonition or just worry. Veil's eyes, I needed a drink. There was no one waiting to wrap her arms around me and make me feel any better.

Guy whispered something to Holly, then straightened. "So now there's only one more thing to deal with." He hesitated a moment, looked over at Saskia. "Sass, why don't you go arrange some tea for everyone?"

Saskia shook her head. She had a slightly wild look about her, as though she wasn't quite sure she'd actually gotten what she wanted. Or that she wanted it now she had it. But the vague air of uncertainty was mixed with determination. "You're not getting rid of me that easily."

Chapter Seven

FEN

"Tea will have to wait," Saskia said. "We need to hear what Fen has to say." Lily nodded agreement.

I swallowed, mouth suddenly dry. These people . . . the DuCaines. Holly. Lily. They were all willing to fight to save the City. They believed they'd win. That their side was right and that right would triumph. How could I tell them that maybe that wasn't going to happen?

"Tell us what you saw," Guy repeated.

"You're not going to like it," I said, stalling.

"I don't like much of what's happening lately. One more thing isn't going to matter. Talk."

Five expectant faces focused on mine. There was no way I'd be allowed to leave this room before I told them. "I saw Ignatius Grey," I said bluntly. "Seated on what looked like a throne with Fae and humans kneeling before him."

Behind me there was a startled gasp. Saskia. *Damn*. Across from me, Holly's face had turned pale. Lily was pale to begin with, but her eyes had turned to silver ice.

"Anything else?" Guy asked.

"Isn't that enough?" I didn't want to remember anything more. Mostly I remembered the feel of the vision. The chill of hopelessness against the fierce, piercing heat of victory in

Ignatius' eyes. The dread that had opened up before me and swallowed the world.

"Did you recognize anybody else?" Simon asked.

"No." I made myself face the memory to make sure it was the truth. Ignatius on the throne was clear enough. I turned my attention to the faces of those in front of him. Not easy—they had their heads bent in homage or fear or both. I could see their hair and the clothes. The long robes of the Fae, which meant they were from the Veiled Court rather than those who lived outside of Summerdale. Which only made the vision worse.

Please be wrong, I thought, even as I turned the image in my head, looking for anything familiar.

Nothing.

Which might mean it was a false vision or just that there truly was no one I recognized who was present when this came to pass. I was hardly on intimate terms with the Fae who lived in Summerdale, nor did I know many of the humans from the DuCaines' level of human society. I'd attended exactly one ball. I wouldn't be able to identify any of the members of the human council if someone had offered me gold. I was more familiar with the humans and Fae who worked at St. Giles with Simon, but they, except for Lady Bryony—the Fae healer in charge of the hospital—and a few other senior healers, were hardly likely to be involved in the negotiations. And I couldn't imagine Lady Bryony kneeling for anybody.

"No," I repeated. "Nothing."

Not yet at least. I would be paying strict attention to the faces that crossed my path during the negotiations.

"Does that mean it's not a true vision?" Saskia asked.

"I rarely know if something's a true vision. Not at first."

"How, then?" Guy asked.

"If the same thing shows up over and over again, it's more likely to come true," I said. I didn't want to mention the flames and blood I'd been seeing for weeks now as an example. "Like you and Holly," I said. "When I see you together, I see gold bands on your fingers. Every single time."

Simon grinned at this, whereas Guy just grew still. Beside him, Holly looked somewhat astonished.

Saskia frowned. She'd pulled her prentice chain out from beneath the high neck of her dress, the bright silver and dark gray metal heavy against the dark green fabric. One hand strayed to it now, fingers twining around the wide links nervously.

"Perhaps. But it's not like I can re-create a particular vision at will. For a start, I usually have to be near the person. Or near someone who's spent a lot of time with them." I realized that the three DuCaines had identical expressions of concentration on their faces. I shifted my weight, uneasy to be the subject of their regard. Since Holly had first met Guy I'd learned that when you put Simon and Guy together, a plan to do something seriously foolhardy in the name of getting what they wanted was quite often the result.

Saskia, I had started to accept, was cut from the same cloth as her brothers.

"Someone like Martin Krueger, perhaps?" Simon said.

Fuck. I hadn't thought of that. "Maybe—" I shook my head. "No. That's not a good idea."

"Why not? You said Martin wanted you to see for him," Simon said. "That gives you the perfect opportunity."

I had the sudden nasty sensation of a net dropping neatly over my head and holding me fast. "If Reggie's there, I'll need my strength to get her out. The visions . . . they—" Hurt like hell. I didn't know how to say that to Simon and Guy. "They take power—energy. Simon, you're a sunmage. You know what I mean." Unlike Simon, I couldn't just step into the nearest sunbeam and refuel myself.

"If Reggie's there, then it will mean Martin's trying to force you to do what he wants," Guy countered. "And what he wants is your visions."

The net closed more tightly.

I could argue, but that wasn't going to change the reality of the situation. "I'm not promising anything," I said. "I can't control what I see."

"But you'll try?" Saskia said.

"Reggie is my first priority. But if I get a chance, then yes, I'll try."

"Good," Guy said. He sounded satisfied. Mostly. I doubted he was completely happy with a situation where he couldn't take direct action himself. But for now he was going to have to wait and see what Lily and I could find out.

I hoped like hell it was Martin who had Reggie. Getting

her free from the Beasts would be a lot easier than spiriting her away from the Blood warrens. Presuming she was alive . . . My throat tightened and I jerked my hand, wanting the sting of the iron to drive out the fear.

"I suggest everyone gets some rest until then," Guy continued. "Saskia, you should go back to the Guild."

She frowned. "Stop trying to get rid of me."

This time it was Simon whose face turned stern. "You may be part of our delegation, Sass, but you're still a student at the Academy. You need to go back and tell them that you will be absent for the length of the negotiations."

Saskia's expression turned . . . well, it was still somber, but there was a certain degree of satisfaction in it. "I do, don't I?" she said. "But you wanted tea—"

"We can manage," Simon said. "The Guild needs to know where you'll be. Come back afterward, if you must." He sounded resigned, as if he knew there was little chance that Saskia would choose not to get involved in the hunt for Reggie.

"I will." Saskia took a moment to hug Holly, smile at Lily, and then she dropped a kiss on Simon's cheek before walking to the door. She paused, looked back at me with something like reluctance in her expression. I looked away, not wanting to complicate things any further than I had already. But I still felt it when she slipped out of the room.

Saskia

The Guild hall was busy as usual as I walked toward Master Aquinas' office. I hoped he would be available. Better to get this over with quickly. I didn't think my announcement was likely to get a warm reception, but I wasn't going to change my mind. The negotiations were my chance to finally do something.

No one was going to dissuade me.

Besides which, I was eager to get back to Simon's house and rejoin the others. To do whatever I could to help them find Reggie. Even though I knew nothing could happen until the sun went down, worry gnawed at my stomach, making it hard to focus. Worry about what might happen to Lily and Fen. Worry about what might be happening right now to Reggie.

I'd gotten what I wanted today but there was no pleasure in the victory now. Though Reggie's disappearance made me even more determined to help set things right in the City.

The clerk outside the office informed me that the Master was busy but that if I cared to wait, he would be able to see me after his current appointment.

I settled into one of the chairs outside the office to do just that, spending my time studying the portraits of previous Masters of both the Guild and the various metals. The current Masters of Iron, Gold, Silver, and Copper stared down at me from their prize positions above the Guild Master's door.

I tried not to look up at the unsmiling face of the Master of Iron. Master Matthews had been nothing but supportive of me over the years I'd been at the Academy. An affinity for iron was rare in women, who tended to be more in sympathy with silver and gold for reasons nobody quite understood, but Master Matthews treated me as he did the male students. Hopefully that support would continue. Hopefully he would understand.

My stomach twisted again, nerves about what I was about to do mixing uneasily with the underlying stew of anxiety.

Eventually the clerk rose from his desk, a sheaf of papers in his hand, and tapped softly on the Master's door before slipping inside. I heard him say, "Prentice DuCaine would like to see you, Master Aquinas," before the door closed again.

I shifted in the chair. Although its upholstery was rich velvet and well padded, it was, like most of the furniture in the Masters' offices, made of metal. I preferred wood. It was both more comfortable and less distracting. Wood didn't sing to me like metal did.

I couldn't afford the distraction right now, even if part of me automatically listened to the songs, identifying the makeup of the bronzelike alloy that had been used by whoever had fashioned the chair. Percentages and alternatives started filling my head. A little more tin and a shift in the magics used to strengthen and the chair could have been—

The door opened abruptly and the clerk emerged. "The Master will see you now," he said, beckoning.

I rose, tried to smooth my somewhat rumpled skirt as my nerves bit harder. No turning back after this.

When I walked through the door, my heart sank a little. Seated across from Master Aquinas near the fireplace was the Master of Iron himself. Ellis Matthews looked exactly like one would expect a man who could bend iron to his will to look. Tall, broad-shouldered, and ruddy-faced. Dark hair tamed back from his face with a leather twist and eyes as dark a gray as the metal he controlled. Beside him, Master Aquinas looked almost small. But you couldn't mistake which of them was the Guild Master.

"Saskia," Master Aquinas said, "we were just speaking of you."

I wasn't sure I wanted to know why that might be. I forced my lips into a smile. "I don't mean to intrude, Masters."

Master Aquinas gestured to the chair beside Master Matthews. "You're here now, so why don't you tell us why?" He looked relaxed, slouching back in his chair as if he had not a care in the world, but his eyes were sharp. It had been only half a day ago that I had stood here and heard him tell me that I couldn't have what I wanted. How would he react when I told him that I'd found another way to get it?

I swallowed, my throat suddenly dry. "I need to request a leave of absence, Master."

Both men straightened. "Has something happened? Your family?" Master Aquinas asked urgently.

I shook my head. "No. Everyone is fine."

Expressions of concern turned to frowns. Master Matthews' forehead settled into deep lines of disapproval. "Then why would you want to leave your studies, girl? You've been making good progress."

I bit down my automatic "apparently not good enough" retort and lifted my chin. "I've received an invitation to be part of the Templar delegation. And I've accepted." I spoke the last in a rush before either of them could say anything.

"What?"

"You can't—"

I held out a hand. "I have," I said simply. "So I'm asking for leave from my studies for the period of the negotiations."

Master Aquinas rose from his chair, displeasure sharpening his face. The chain around his neck seemed to flare brighter for a second. "We discussed this yesterday. Your talents are valuable and we don't want you to be at risk."

"I'm aware of your views," I said, keeping my tone cool with an effort. "But I don't agree with them."

Master Matthews made a rumbling noise. "You're a student, here, *Prentice* DuCaine. It doesn't matter whether you agree with our views or not. You agreed to abide by the decisions of the Guild when you joined the Academy."

"I've done just that for four years. I've done everything you've asked," I said. "But now I'm asking for leave while I do something that's important to me."

"Does your family know about this?" Master Aquinas asked.

The metal in the room nearly quivered under the closely held disapproval in his voice, the song that lurked in the back of my head chiming an almost discordant note.

"Simon and Guy were the ones that invited me," I said. Not quite the entire truth. But explaining that a half-Fae seer from the border boroughs had coerced my brothers into extending their invitation wasn't going to help my case. I wasn't ready to share my newfound ability to quiet a seer's visions either. If the Masters heard about that, they wouldn't let me go anywhere until they'd figured out exactly how I was doing it and whether such a thing could be put to any other good use.

Neither man looked pleased about my announcement of my brothers' involvement. Master Aquinas' mouth was a flat, unhappy line.

"When it comes right down to it, your brothers' consent or otherwise doesn't really matter. You are under my authority," he said shortly.

"Are you saying no?" I said.

He tapped his chain with one long finger. "What would you do if I did? You can be asked to leave the Guild for disobeying the will of the Guild Master, Saskia."

My skin went clammy. I hadn't expected that level of displeasure.

Time to make a choice.

Fen had made a difficult decision when he'd agreed to help our side. He'd risked his entire life.

Was I willing to do the same?

I hesitated, thoughts whirling. I'd wanted nothing more than to be a Master since the first hints of my power had blossomed.

What good is having power if no one lets you use it? The voice in my head was savage.

"Are you saying that you'll expel me?"

"You're not qualified yet, Saskia," Master Matthews said warningly. "You can't throw everything you've worked for away."

Anger surged, the chain at my neck heating to a point just below uncomfortably warm. "If my skills are so valuable, then can you afford to let me go?" I said, trying my best to sound civil. "Maybe you need me more than I need you."

"Hold your tongue, girl," Master Matthews growled.

My hold on my temper slipped further. "No. I'm sick of being told what I can and can't do. You can throw me out, you can refuse to train me, but that's not going to change my mind. I know enough now that I can make a good living if I choose."

"Is that so?" Master Aquinas said.

I bit back my retort. Getting into a shouting match with the Masters of the Guild and my specialty wasn't going to help matters. I needed to appeal to their calmer sides. I took a deep breath, held out my hands, palms up. "These negotiations are important," I said. "If they don't go the way we all want, then nobody is going to care whether or not I'm qualified. Nobody is going to care if anybody's powers come with a Guild stamp of approval. We'll be at war."

Master Matthews made another rumble of displeasure.

"Which is exactly why we should be protecting anything that gives us an advantage. You can't help anyone if something happens to you," Master Aquinas said.

"I can't help anyone if I sit here doing nothing. I'm sorry, Guild Master. You're not going to change my mind. Will you grant my request or not?"

He stared at me, pondering earth knew what in his head. Then he made a noncommittal gesture, half shrug, half head shake. "The Masters will need to discuss this, Saskia."

I nodded. If that was how it was going to be, then that was how it was going to be. I felt sick to my stomach, but I had made my decision and whether the Guild approved of it or not couldn't make any difference to me.

"In that case," I said, "you can send word to me care of my mother to let me know your final decision." I curtsied respectfully. "Now, if you'll excuse me, Masters, I have to pack."

FEN

The Beast scent twined around me as I moved through the hallways of the pack house, following the *guerrier* who'd come to the gate to fetch me when I'd turned up demanding to speak to Martin.

I fought the urge to wrinkle my nose. There was something about the deep earthy smell that always set my nerves on edge. I didn't know if it was mere dislike or something deeper and more primal. A recognition of kinship I didn't want to acknowledge, or a lingering effect of the banishment my *grand-mere* had suffered. I wondered if it was even possible for a casting out to affect more than the person who'd been targeted—then I pulled my errant thoughts back as we drew closer to Martin's reception room.

I was here for one purpose and one purpose only.

To find out if Martin had Reggie and promise as little as possible to him in return for extracting that information. He was going to be angry enough with me when the delegations were announced and he discovered that I was working with the humans. It would be better not to give him even more ammunition for his fury by promising things I had no intention of delivering.

The halls of the pack house were busier than they had been the previous night. It was early evening still, but the Beasts were rousing to their nightly business. There were plenty of *guerriers* roaming the corridors, but we passed a number of women and a child or two making their way to wherever they were bound as well. Most Beasts lived close to the pack. The alpha's immediate family and closest *guerriers* and their mates and children lived within the walls of the pack house itself. I wondered if more than the usual residents were taking shelter here from the unsettled streets outside.

I had no love for the Beasts, it was true, and they were no angels, but it was hard to wish ill on women and children.

I gave myself another mental shake at the thought. The damned DuCaines were rubbing off on me. Well, Simon and Saskia at least—I couldn't see Guy sparing much concern for any Beasts. Luckily I didn't have time to be any further distracted. We reached the doors and I was ushered inside with a promptness that made me wary.

Martin's eyebrows rose slightly at the sight of me but his smile was blandly welcoming. "What brings you knocking on my gates, puppy?" he said. "Come to your senses, have you?"

No beating about the bush, then. I took a breath and reached deep for arrogance to match his tone. "That depends on whether you can give me what I want."

His head cocked, green eyes slanting a question at me in a manner that was all too reminiscent of the Beast that lurked beneath his skin. "And what might that be?"

His tone was mild, but around me the atmosphere changed as the *guerriers* came to a subtle alert. "I want Regina back," I said.

Martin looked genuinely taken aback and my heart sank. Either he was doing a very good job at pretending or he knew nothing about what had happened. "Regina? She's one of the humans you run with, isn't she? Works in that dress shop with the *hai'salai* you're so fond of?"

He knew that much. Which only confused me more. I knew he kept tabs on me but I didn't think he had much reason to be interested in Holly or Reggie. "She works with Holly Evendale, yes."

"And you say she's missing?"

"Yes."

The corner of his mouth turned up slightly. "Well, then. That is unfortunate. Dangerous times in the City right now."

The hairs on the back of my neck rose. I couldn't growl like a Beast but I wanted to. "Do you have her?"

Martin's mocking expression didn't falter. "What would I want with a human seamstress?"

"I rather assumed it was to get my attention," I said carefully. "That much worked. But rest assured, if Reggie is hurt you will regret it."

"And if I did have her, what then, puppy?"

"Then I would assume you want something and that we can come to a trade."

"A trade?"

"You want my services."

"You value the human girl that much?"

"I want her back."

Martin's face lost its smile. "Then perhaps it is a pity that I do not have her."

The words were both relief and terror. Because if Martin spoke the truth, it was likely that Reggie was either in the not-so-tender care of the Blood Court or dead.

Hard on the heels of that realization came another: Martin had admitted he didn't have Reggie too easily. Not his way to give up an advantage, so he must have another angle to play. Which meant that he knew more than he was telling.

"Do you know who does?"

On cue, his smile reappeared, more than a hint of cocky satisfaction playing in his eyes as his expression bared his too long canine teeth. "I believe that is information that is valuable."

And there it was. The bargaining. I'd known it was coming, as much as I'd hoped I might be able to avoid it. Even if I didn't intend to honor my end of the bargain, I didn't like letting Martin think he'd gotten his way. It grated against the habit of a lifetime. "What do you want?"

"Do you really have to ask?"

I didn't, but it was best to spell things out when making any deal in the Night World. "You want a seer."

Martin nodded, his grin just as self-satisfied as ever.

"I won't join your pack."

"Puppy, what makes you think I'd let a mutt like you in anyway? I need your visions, not your muscle. I don't care what you do with your spare time as long as you're around when I need you."

"What do I get in return?"

"Maybe I'll tell you where your little human is."

"How do I know that you even know?"

Martin folded his arms. "Take it or leave it."

Fuck. He had me. For now. There was always Lily, who was even now slipping invisibly through the Blood warrens, searching for Reggie. She could also search the pack house if she needed to. Beasts didn't tend to use sunlamps, so her powers would be free to work here. But Lily would be searching the warrens for hours yet and I couldn't afford to waste any time. I wasn't going to give Martin a total victory, though. "I have one condition."

"Oh?"

"I want your help to get her back. If she's somewhere I can't get to myself, then you'll lend me some of your *guerriers*." If Reggie was being held in Blood territory, as I feared, then I would need help to retrieve her. There was no way Simon or Guy could help me. There was too much tension in the City for either of them—known enemies of Ignatius—to appear anywhere in the Night World and not cause a riot. There were glamours, of course, but glamours could be broken. Too risky. No, if I was to have backup, it would have to be from those whose presence would not be remarked upon. The Beast and the Blood often mixed in the Night World. A squad of Krueger *guerriers* would do nicely. Muscle and camouflage all in one. They could pass me off as one of their own.

"And if I don't?"

"Then you will have to live without my services and I'll take my chances."

That sharpened his gaze and his smile dimmed. "Fuck, puppy, are you sleeping with the chit? In love with her?"

"That's none of your business. Do we have an agreement?" I met his eyes—glittering green with annoyance now, much as mine probably were—and waited.

Eventually he nodded. "All right. I'll give you four men. And whatever else you need once you find her. Is that sufficient?"

I returned the nod. "It will do."

Chapter Eight

SASKIA

⚡

The night stretched endlessly as we waited for Lily to return. Fen had been back from the Krueger Pack House for several hours and the five of us kept vigil in Simon's parlor, conversation growing thinner and thinner as we fell to watching the clock inch oh so slowly around the dial.

Simon started to pace around two a.m., fingers clenching and unclenching at his side as though he reached for a sword. I knew he would have given his right arm to accompany Lily, but there was no way for him to follow her into the shadow.

Guy, on the other hand, seemed calmer, but I didn't know if it was fatigue or willpower keeping him silent. He'd gone back to the Templar Brother House, ridden out on patrol, then rejoined us after midnight. He sat in one of Simon's chairs and stared into the empty fireplace, occasionally answering when Holly spoke to him. I didn't want to know what he was seeing wherever he was in his head.

Fen and Holly and I made some attempt to talk after Fen had laid out the story of his deal with Martin and reported that no, he hadn't had a chance to find out if he could see more of Ignatius. From time to time I saw Simon look at me and I knew he wished I could do for Lily what I could do for the others in my family. But Lily and I didn't share a blood tie, or whatever bond it was that let me track my family in my head, so I couldn't tell him where she was.

Which left me feeling useless.

Shortly after three, Lily came walking into the room as if she'd just stepped out. She wore black leather trousers and a black shirt and leather vest that made her look sleekly dangerous. Her red hair was braided and twisted around her head. She looked unhurt, her pace steady as she entered, but her expression didn't bode well. Simon started to go toward her but didn't get more than a few steps before Holly spoke up. "Did you find her?"

Lily wasn't one to draw out a conversation. "Yes," she said shortly. "She's at Lucius' mansion."

Holly, Fen, and Guy winced. From which I gathered the mansion was nothing good. I ran through the list of Blood Assemblies I knew of in my head. None of them had that particular name. But if it had been Lucius' mansion, then it was probably Ignatius Grey who held sway there now. Which meant wherever this mansion was, it was deep inside Night World territory and nowhere that anyone human would want to be taken against their will.

"Is she all right?" Fen asked, voice rasping slightly. He walked up beside Holly and took her hand.

My throat tightened. I knew what it felt like, to wait for news of a sister fallen to the Night World. Reggie, Fen, and Holly weren't related by blood, but they'd been raised together and they regarded one another as family.

I found myself muttering a prayer in my head to whatever gods might be listening that they weren't about to go through what Simon, Guy, and I had experienced when Edwina had died. I wouldn't wish that pain on an enemy, let alone on people I cared about.

Lily's face was grave, her voice soft as she answered. "She's alive," she said. "But they were giving her blood."

Oh, Reggie. My heart clutched. Vampire blood was horribly dangerous for humans. The pleasures it brought were highly addictive and that addiction couldn't be broken. Those who fell prey to the spell of it became blood-locked, mindlessly seeking more and more of what they craved and ignoring everything else—work, family, sleep, food—until they died. Or were killed by the Blood when they grew too weak and useless as entertainment. My sister, Edwina, had suffered that fate.

For a few long seconds we were all silent, equal expressions of horror marking our faces. Then everyone started talking at once.

It was Fen who shut us up with a whistle that almost made my eardrums bleed.

"I'm going after her," he said. "No arguments."

"How—," Guy began.

Fen cut him off with a gesture. "I have the best chance," Fen continued. "I can get in with Martin's help. I look like a Krueger, I'll blend in to a degree. Lily can come with me, to lead me to Reggie, but I'll get her out." He jerked his chin at Guy, who looked as though he wanted to argue, pale eyes sparking as he pressed his lips together. "Guy, you and Simon can't go into a Blood warren. Not one that's well within Night World borders. Not so close to the negotiations. It would play right into Ignatius' hands."

The muscles of Guy's jaw tightened but he didn't argue. The crosses inked into the backs of his hands rippled as he clenched and unclenched his fists.

Holly's fists were clenched too. "I want to come."

"No." Fen's voice was curt. Controlled. "You can help me—I'll need some charms—but you're staying right here where it's safe." He turned his head to me. "That goes for you too. Lily has the shadow and I'm . . . expendable."

"Fen!" Holly choked.

"It's true," he said, turning back to her as she stood leaning against Guy. "I'm an—" He looked at Guy. "What would you call it? 'An acceptable loss'?"

Guy nodded, still not talking.

"It's not acceptable to me," Holly snapped.

Fen's expression softened a little. "I know," he said. "But it has to be me. Believe me, I'm going to try like hell to come back in one piece."

Holly bit her lip, obviously wanting to say more. I knew how she felt. I wanted to tell him not to go, but I'd learned well enough from Guy and Simon that the words of a female were unlikely to sway a male intent on risking his fool life. Even when the female meant something to him.

I was useful to Fen, but I didn't want to fool myself and

believe there was anything more to it than that, despite whatever hints of heat there might be between us. He wasn't that sort of man. Not a good risk.

So why did I care so desperately that he was trying to get himself killed?

My nails curled into my palms, making the still-healing burn on the back of my hand throb a little in protest.

"How much time do you need?" Simon asked when it was clear no one else was going to protest.

"It's too late now to organize the Kruegers," Fen said. "I'll go back there and talk to them, but I doubt we can move before tomorrow night at the earliest."

Holly sucked in a breath at that. Tomorrow night. Meaning Reggie had another day in the hands of the Blood. Another day drinking vampire blood.

Another day closer to being blood-locked.

Those were the words that weren't being said.

The truth that all of us understood. But as my mother was fond of saying, it was better to deal with one thing at a time and not borrow trouble before it arrived on your doorstep. I took a deep breath, trying to get the images of the worst-case scenario out of my head.

"What can we do to help?" I asked.

FEN

My spine crawled as I stepped out of the carriage. *Not one of your brighter ideas, Fen*.

Not that I had any choice in the matter. Not really. The entrance to the massive building before me was lit by several hanging gas lamps, nothing about its appearance to spark any concerns other than the knowledge that we were far within Blood territory and about to go deeper still. My instincts suggested it would be best to climb right back into the hackney and leave.

Not an option. Not if Reggie was somewhere within.

Behind me Willem grunted, and I turned to watch him and Alec, another of the Krueger *guerriers*, follow me down

onto the cobbled forecourt. Both of them looked alert and
focused, not nervous. Willem scanned the surroundings ef-
ficiently, then nodded at Alec.

"All clear," Alec said in a low tone, and Martin's head
appeared in the carriage door. I still wasn't entirely certain
why Martin had chosen to come with us, but I hadn't had
time to try and decipher the deeper game he was playing.
What mattered here and now was that he'd agreed to get
me into the mansion and to help me take Reggie out. I
couldn't waste energy worrying about whether he was going
to double-cross me.

Hopefully Lily's invisible backup would be enough to
get me out of hot water if the worst happened and if not,
well, fuck it, at least I'd die trying.

Martin too paused a moment to assess the situation, then
apparently decided he was satisfied and descended from the
carriage. Willem came quickly to his side as Alec shut the
door and gave instructions to the driver.

Through it all, my nerves crawled. I'd never been here
before. Never ventured deep into the heart of Blood territory. In fact, I'd made it a rule in life to stay as far away from
the Blood Court's warrens—which lay beneath the grounds
of this mansion—as possible.

An Assembly was one thing—being somewhat the public face of the Blood, the Assemblies had the veneer of
civilization at least—but this, this was another thing entirely. Step inside the warrens and the Blood ruled.

"Fen," Willem snapped. "You take the rear."

I realized that Alec had taken his place on the other side
of Martin and all three Kruegers were staring at me impatiently. I moved into position, my hand clasped firmly over
the handle of the pistol at my hip.

Me and my bright ideas.

It had taken less fast talking than I had expected to get
Martin to agree to move so quickly. In the end, it was the
hint that me being near Ignatius might lead to some useful
visions that seemed to sway him. I didn't fool myself that he
actually cared whether Reggie lived or died.

Still, selling him on the idea without actually promising
anything more than I already had had been akin to walking
a high wire. One far more treacherous than any theater hall
acrobat ever ventured out on.

It was only going to get more precarious as soon as we entered the warrens.

We walked toward the entrance and I focused on looking like a *guerrier*. For once, I was glad of the Krueger resemblance that would hopefully let me pass unnoticed. I'd strengthened it with my rarely used and somewhat unreliable powers of glamour, enough that I didn't look exactly like myself, or so I hoped. Holly had given me a charm to help twist my scent too, so that I would pass as a Beast to the sensitive noses of the Blood and the other Beasts.

Still, the hairs on the back of my neck stood on end as we approached. I wondered where Lily was. Somewhere nearby, if everything was going to plan. But there was no way of knowing where. And no way of joining her in the safety of wherever it was she went when she shadowed. No changing form or substance for me.

I would have to do this as I had always done, with wit and bullshit in equal measure. Plus the old fallback of fighting dirty if it came to that.

Hopefully it would be enough.

Our little group came to a halt near the doors. Willem stepped forward to knock. The heavy brass ring rapped sharply and the door swung inward, revealing a white-clad man—one of the Trusted who served the Blood—who looked us up and down before bowing slightly to Martin and stepping back to let us enter..

No turning back now. I tightened my grip on the gun and followed the others into the warrens.

The scene inside didn't ease my nerves. In the Assemblies some semblance of restraint was maintained in the more public areas, but here that pose had been abandoned.

I wasn't more than twenty feet into the building before I spotted a Blood lord with his fangs buried in the neck of a scantily clad human girl through a half-open door. I steeled myself not to react, but my free hand drifted up to brush the lapel of my jacket, to check for the reassuring bump of the invisibility charm Holly had given me tucked beneath it.

The small weight of it was tangible, unlike Lily's unseen backup. Something to focus on other than my uneven pulse. I tried to breathe slowly, aware that the Blood and the Beasts could hear my heartbeat.

I wanted a drink. But that would have to wait.

The warrens were well named. The corridors seemed endless as we followed the Trusted who'd opened the door for us through the building. The man walked quickly, pausing only to bow to the Blood we passed—those he served in the hope of one day being turned. Our pace was too fast to truly take in any distinguishing features within the building or get the route we had followed straight in my head. Without windows to orient myself to the outer world, I was rapidly becoming confused as to what direction we were heading. Down into the earth—that much was clear.

Every few turns of the hallway, there was another short flight of stairs leading down. Exactly how far beneath the surface did the place go, anyway? Lily had told me a little about the warrens beneath the mansion—after all, she'd been raised here—but her words had not painted the full picture. The walls changed from brick to old stone as we went deeper. They pressed in on me, making me yearn for open air—even the somewhat murky night sky of the City.

An overwhelming sense of "This is a terrible idea, Fen" settled more heavily on my shoulders with each step. To distract myself, I set about studying the people we passed, searching the faces of the white-haired, black-clad Blood for anyone familiar.

It was too much to hope that we might actually come across Ignatius so that I could get the proximity I required for the visions that could help the humans. No, Martin hadn't been summoned to an audience; he was coming here on the pretense of joining the growing tide of the Night World who seemed to be throwing their fates in with Ignatius in the struggle to rule the Blood Courts and—presuming the eventual victor was as ruthless as Lucius had been—also gaining control of the Night World. Courting favor by dancing attendance on the Blood and their questionable pleasures.

In front of me, the three Beasts walked and I could tell from the subtle bristling in their postures that none of them was much happier about being here than I was.

Outside, above us somewhere, the moon was growing fatter. Most of the Beast packs spent the days before she gained her fullest stature in the relative comfort of the pack house, where their control would not be tested too strongly. Alec and Willem were the strongest and most experienced of the Krueger *guerriers*. Normally I would have had no doubt that they could maintain control, but as we went deeper into the warrens, even I could smell the dark salt hints of blood hanging on the air under the other smells. Granted, Beasts didn't usually eat humans these days, but any blood scent would be a distraction—and a temptation—right now.

Eventually our guide came to a halt outside a room with tall double doors. From Lily's descriptions, I didn't think this was the Blood Court's main audience hall, but if the height of the doors was anything to go by, the room beyond was still sizable.

"Stay here," the guide said curtly. He opened the door just wide enough for him to enter the room. From my position behind the other three Beasts, I couldn't really see into the depths beyond. Perhaps that was just as well.

We didn't wait long before the Trusted returned to usher us in. I kept my gaze on Willem's back. Now was not the time to gaze around at the room like an idiot. *Guerriers* focused on the job, not the decor. The room was big, the walls were dark, there were other Blood and Trusted here—though not many of them—and it was hot. Fine by me. I liked the heat. Plus it provided an explanation for the nervous sweat stealing down my back.

We advanced into the room, halted when Martin halted. Willem and Alec moved out a little, flanking him, leaving me with a small space between Martin and Willem where I could see the man we faced.

Ignatius Grey. Seated on a big black chair behind a massive wooden desk. Wiping his mouth with the back of his hand as a slight, dark-haired woman—a Trusted, judging by her attire—stumbled away from him, looking dazed. Blood ran down her neck, dripping onto the white tunic she wore.

The Blood do not have to hurt when they feed. Apparently Ignatius was one who liked to do so. One of the other Trusted came up and ushered the girl away. Ignatius ignored them, staring instead at us, his gaze direct.

Intended to be a challenge.

I clamped down on the instinct to grab him and beat him to a pulp until he told me where Reggie was. Instead I tried to let the part of me that responded to him with a wary prickle of the hairs on the back of my neck take over. The sensible, prudent part.

Martin bowed slightly to Ignatius. Willem and Alec did not, so I stayed still. Ignatius nodded his head, an even shallower motion than Martin's bow.

It wasn't the most effusive of greetings. I hoped Martin would remember his manners.

Ignatius was watching Martin closely. He pulled a white handkerchief from a pocket, scrubbed at the back of his hand where the blood had smeared. "So, Alpha, have you made your decision?"

I blinked, then reached for stillness. Decision? What decision? I felt as though a gaping hole had opened in front of my feet. Martin had been keeping secrets too, it seemed. I shifted my stance a little, bracing for action.

Martin's shoulders stiffened. "I thought I had another day."

Ignatius frowned. "You have had almost two weeks. It is not that difficult a choice."

My jaw tightened. Would one of them just come out and say what it was that they were talking about? The expressions of the other Blood around Ignatius were impassive. Either they weren't surprised by the conversation or they were good at hiding it. I had no way of seeing what Alec or Willem thought about the matter from where I stood at the rear of our foursome.

"The opening of the negotiations approaches rapidly," Ignatius said in his usual unpleasant rasp. "I need to know who I can trust before then."

"Are you saying you'll be certain of your position by then?" Martin responded.

"That is not your concern." There was a bite in the raspy voice.

"I beg to differ. You are asking me to throw the fate of my pack in with you."

"For which you will be amply rewarded."

"If you succeed."

Ignatius' frown turned ominous. "Now is not the time for any . . . decisive acts," he said. "You may be confident that my influence at the negotiations will be considerable."

What the hell did that mean? Did Ignatius think he would have control of the Blood by the negotiations? I hoped Lily was somewhere close, listening. Even if I didn't make it out of here tonight, someone needed to let the Templars know what was happening.

I should have listened to my better instincts. The ones that had recommended getting out of the City. But those baser instincts never factored in Holly and Reggie. And the honorable part of me—stunted as it might be—couldn't let them down. I couldn't leave Reggie here to rot. I'd die first.

The silence between Ignatius and Martin was stretching to the point where it was about to snap. Lady only knew what would happen if it did. If Martin knew what was good for him—and us—he would make some placating noises and let us get out of here intact.

"Well," he said after another second or two had dragged by, tightening the atmosphere in the room a few more notches, "if that is the case, then you can expect my support."

Veil's bloody eyes. Was Martin really going to ally with Ignatius? I suppressed the bite of outrage in my stomach. *Stupid*. Thank the Lady that I would be free of this mess soon.

Though if Martin was going to bond with Ignatius, then the repercussions of my defection were likely to be even more unpleasant.

But there would be time enough to worry about burning bridges and other disasters when Reggie was safe. I gritted my teeth and pretended to be a statue while Ignatius and Martin exchanged a few more rounds of coded banter. I committed it to memory, though I wasn't sure how useful it would be.

Eventually Ignatius dismissed us, inviting Martin to partake of the hospitality of the warrens. I didn't want to think too hard about what that might involve, but it was the chance we needed to look for Reggie.

The same white-clad Trusted guided us back to a higher level of the warrens. There he explained the available services—which, to my relief, boiled down to sex, alcohol, and gambling rather than blood or torture—and where they might be found, then left us to choose our poison.

Martin looked at me. "I don't want to stay here any longer than necessary," he said in a soft voice. "The boys and I will go play some cards for an hour or so. You poke around. If you find your girl, then get her out. Don't get caught."

I took that to mean that I couldn't expect much assistance from them. Fair enough. He'd agreed to get me in here and he'd done that much. I hadn't expected him to help me beyond that unless we actually stumbled across Reggie in the hallway.

"I'll try not to," I said and left them as they headed toward the rooms the Trusted had said were for gambling. I would look through the other public areas quickly, but first I wanted to find somewhere private.

There were more Beasts and Blood in the halls now, which made me think perhaps Ignatius wasn't making false promises. Maybe he was close to gaining control of the Blood Court. I moved carefully but some of the Blood I passed pressed uncomfortably close. Most Blood Assemblies are a crush but a certain amount of propriety is still observed. Random bumps and knocks are inevitable, but this felt different. Here, the bumps were deliberate and the "accidental" touches lingered too long to be anything but intentional. Their gazes lingered too, trying to snare mine and work their vampire allure. It made my skin crawl and I picked up my pace, muttering false apologies as I headed for one of the washrooms the Trusted had mentioned. I locked the door behind me with a shudder of relief.

"What are you doing?"

Lily's voice was soft in my ear. I jumped, then scowled. I turned on the tap in the basin, hoping the water would muffle our conversation if there were any hear-me charms in the room. And hide it from the all too acute ears of the Blood as well. I couldn't feel any magic, but who knew what the Blood could do? "Looking for you," I said in a voice just as quiet as hers. "Do you know where she is?"

Lily faded into sight. She wore stark black. Soft pants, boots, a shirt, hair drawn back in braids. Her dagger rode her right hip and a small black leather pouch hung from the other. She looked deadly, her mouth set and her eyes angry. "I need you to stay calm," she said.

"Why?"

"So you don't get yourself killed," Lily said. "Can you do that?"

I set my jaw against the greasy mix of fear and anger churning my stomach. "I'm calm. Tell me."

"She's here. Upstairs."

I reached for control. "Just her?" We'd promised we'd look for Viola as well.

Lily nodded. "No sign of Viola."

Fuck. Well, we would have to figure out where Viola might be and what it meant that she and Reggie weren't together later. Reggie was my first priority. "Show me where she is."

"No. Not right now."

"Why not? We came here to get her." I leaned against the edge of the basin, gripped the cool porcelain hard so that it pressed my chain into my wrist. The flare of pain helped me focus.

"I know, but she's busy right now."

"Doing what?" My voice was a little too loud. I clamped my jaw shut.

Lily tilted her head. "Calm, remember? She's with the Nightseekers they've brought out for the night. The ones being shared around."

I was halfway to the door before I realized what I was doing. Lily blocked me, pushing me back hard.

"Fen." She gripped my wrist, pressing the chain tighter against my skin.

I bit down against the pain, tried to shake her off. But she was strong and the pain seared up my arm, stopping my breath for a second. I stopped resisting. "I have to get to her."

"I know. But you can't charge in there and drag her out immediately. I've been watching. There's a system the Blood use with the Nightseekers. They choose one, take them off into private rooms."

Where they would feed. Some vampire had his fangs in Reggie's neck. And gods knew what else might be going on. Rage boiled through me. Lily's grip tightened.

"They go away for about half an hour. Then they come back to the main floor. They're meant to mingle and look pretty, but they're usually not used again straightaway. If you wait, she'll be brought back. It's crowded in the main rooms and there are Blood and Beasts and humans. We can get her away from there."

Lily's voice was cool. Reasonable. It made me even angrier. "You want me to just sit here and wait while they use her like that?"

"I want to get both of you out of here alive."

"You—" Nausea rolled through me. *Reggie*.

"I know this is hard, Fen. But they're giving her blood . . . It . . . it won't be hurting her." She grimaced with distaste even as she spoke the words.

She meant that if Reggie was under the influence of vampire blood, she'd be enjoying whatever was done to her. "Am I supposed to think that's better?" The words stung my throat. *Gods*. Reggie.

"No," Lily said flatly. "Trust me, Fen. I know."

Lily had grown up here. Been Lucius' slave. I had never asked Holly if she knew anything about what had happened to Lily here, but from her tone now, I knew it had been bad.

"I—"

"I know," Lily said. "There's nothing good about this. But no pain is better than pain. And alive is better than dead."

Her words seemed to come from a distance as I fought the rage, struggled for control. She was right. "How do we get her out?"

"If she's in the main salon, then none of the Blood have claimed her personally. So she can leave, if she wants to. We just have to get her to the front door and into a carriage. They won't be expecting anyone to come after her here."

If she wants to. That was the catch. Reggie had been here for two days already. Had drunk vampire blood. Would she want to leave? Would she even know who I was?

"And if she won't come?"

"Then we knock her out, slap an invisibility charm on her, and you carry her out."

"Like Simon did to you?" The story of how Simon and Guy had kidnapped Lily from one of the Blood Assemblies was one I had heard.

"Well, I'd prefer we didn't have to start a riot to cover our exit like they did," Lily said dryly. "Plus they didn't use a charm, but close enough. Now, are you going to be sensible and wait?"

I took a deep breath. It felt wrong but I knew I had to do as Lily had suggested. "Yes."

She let go of my wrist, stepped back. "Good. Because there's one other thing."

Chapter Nine

FEN

"Tell me," I said. I was sure I wasn't going to like what she had to say, but at this point there was little that would make the situation actively worse.

In response, Lily drew something out of the leather pouch at her hip. Dangled it in front of me. A heavy black chain about sixteen inches long.

I regarded it warily, much as if she'd hung a snake in front of my face. "Iron?"

She shook her head. "I think it's enameled. It belongs to Ignatius. I've seen him wear it."

Which made it even more dangerous. "What do you want me to do with it?"

"You said proximity to a person helps you see. And Holly told me that sometimes touching things works for you as well." She moved the chain closer. "So look."

"Right now?"

"When better? Ignatius is close by and you can touch something of his as well. You're unlikely to get a better chance to see."

I was beginning to think that Lily had ice water running in her veins. She had a ruthless practicality that I might admire if I was less angry. "I have other things on my mind right now."

"Worrying won't help Reggie," Lily said, her tone still unnaturally calm. "You need a distraction. We need the information. Take it."

I shook my head. "My visions . . . lately . . . there's a cost."

"They hurt, you mean? That's all right. Bryony gave me this." She pulled a small glass vial out of the pouch with her free hand. A dark green liquid sloshed within it.

"What's that?"

"It will stop the pain for a while." She waggled the vial. "She said it's very strong, so she wouldn't give it to you regularly but it would work this time."

Oh good, a Fae potion so strong even the Fae Master Healer was concerned about it. Just what I needed. But I couldn't come up with an argument. I'd agreed to try and use my visions to help the human delegation. And this was a prime opportunity. All I needed was to be able to forget about Reggie. Perhaps Lily could teach me how to master detachment in five minutes or less.

Maybe not. After all, she'd learned her lessons from thirty-odd years in Lucius' service. Her control was hard won.

Then again, I had, in the past—before the City started going to hell—prided myself on my own control over my visions. Perhaps that would stand me in good stead now.

"Not here," I said. "I've been in here too long already. We need somewhere more private."

The last thing I wanted was for someone to come rattling the bathroom doorknob in the middle of a vision. That would draw the sort of attention I needed to avoid.

"There's a sort of closet with cleaning supplies farther down the corridor," Lily said. "Let's go." She jerked her head toward the door.

The wraith was impatient. Wonderful. Easy for her—she wasn't the one who could be potentially discovered.

Nerves twisted my stomach, mixing uneasily with the coffee I'd downed earlier. Acid rose in my throat as I slipped out of the bathroom. I swallowed hard and kept moving. Sure enough, a little way down the corridor there was a plain wooden door with no markings.

"This one," Lily said, her voice coming from somewhere

close to my right side. Talking to thin air was hard to get used to.

I glanced over my shoulder. The corridor was still empty. I tried the door. Locked. I swore under my breath but I'd come prepared for this eventuality. Holly and I had been taught to pick locks by the same thief and while her talent surpassed mine, this one looked simple enough. There was no wardlight shimmering around it to indicate there might be protections other than the lock itself.

Luckily, my assessment was correct. The lock yielded easily to my picks and I stepped into the tiny room, pulling the door tight behind me.

"Lily?" I whispered.

She faded into sight. There were only a few feet between us; the walls to the right and left held cleaning supplies— buckets and rags and dark glass bottles of gods knew what. The wall behind me was bare except for a high row of metal hooks. Which left about four square feet of free space. In different circumstances, with a different girl, the proximity and semidarkness might have spawned some different urges, but I had no leaning toward dalliance with Lily. She was clearly taken and would probably stab me for trying.

For a moment Saskia's face appeared in my mind. I shook my head, willing it away. No time for foolish daydreams now.

"Ready?" Lily said.

I unwrapped the iron from around my wrist, gritting my teeth at the sting as it pulled away from my flesh. Too tight. But it needed to be lately. I slid the iron carefully into my pocket, averting my eyes from Lily so I wouldn't be distracted by anything I saw around her.

"Give me the chain." I held out my hand.

Lily dropped Ignatius' chain into my palm, the links cool against my skin. It didn't burn, so it definitely wasn't iron. I backed away, until my back was pressed against the wall. Then I wrapped my hand around the chain, closed my eyes, and thought of Ignatius, conjured up the casual viciousness of him. The arrogance. The low rasp of his voice. Then I opened my senses to the visions.

Pain arced through my head as they sprang to life, stronger than ever. Flames. The City skyline glowing red against a night sky. Templars fighting Beasts in the street. Dead bodies. Screaming women. All the things I'd been seeing for weeks.

Not enough, Fen.

Ignatius. I brought him to mind, fighting the spiking throb in my temples as I fought the visions. Saw the pale gleam of long white hair falling around pale skin. The bright red blood on his hand as he'd wiped it earlier.

Ignatius Grey.

The visions whirled again, flaring brighter and faster, at first the same images and then, after a minute or two, a change. Ignatius again. The same as in the pack house. Ignatius on a throne. Ignatius victorious.

Hells and fucking damn. The pain redoubled as I focused. But the visions of Ignatius didn't change, didn't offer anything new.

Fuck.

I pushed away from the wall, staggering slightly as I reached into my pocket for my chain. I needed to tether the visions again, push them back before my head exploded. My hand shook as I withdrew the chain and it slipped through my fingers and fell to the carpet. I bent to retrieve it and the pain suddenly worsened, making me retch. I fought the nausea, fought to stay silent as the room swam around me.

"Here." Lily's voice beside me hurt my ears, but there was a soft clink as she reached for the chain.

"Hurry," I managed to say before I clamped my mouth shut against another wave of nausea.

Her hand reached out, hit my arm, then slid down toward my wrist. But before she could wrap the iron into place, another vision exploded, arcing through me.

Not Ignatius.

Simon.

Simon standing with a vampire, a man with a horribly scarred face. Simon talking to him easily as they moved through what looked like a hospital ward.

What the fuck was Simon DuCaine doing with one of the Blood?

I couldn't form the words through the pain in my head, and then, as quickly as it had appeared, the vision slid away as Lily slipped my chain back into place and the iron bit into my skin like claws.

The pain receded under that touch, as did the dazzling spiral of visions, dulling to a manageable ache and the muted flames and blood I was used to.

I sucked in several heaving breaths, not quite willing to believe it was over.

"Fen?" Lily said softly. Her silver gray eyes were worried. "What did you see?"

Lily, I thought slowly. *Simon's fiancée.* If Simon was involved in anything, she would know about it.

Lily the *ex-assassin*, I thought, slightly less slowly. Who might well kill me where I stood if she thought I was a threat to Simon. Not the woman to demand an explanation of.

I forced myself to a crouch and then, when the room kindly stopped spinning, stood.

"Nothing new," I said roughly. "Give me the damned potion."

Bryony was right about her potion. It worked. And it was dangerous. It didn't just take away the pain; it replaced it with an almost reckless sense of well-being and power. I felt like I could tear down the walls of the warrens with my bare hands. Which, given that my mood was inclined in just that direction, was a delusion that could lead to disaster.

I leaned back against the wall of the tiny room, trying to convince myself that I wasn't invincible. But my anger rumbled and prowled beneath the surface of hard-won reason, demanding satisfaction.

Maybe this was what Beasts felt like when they changed form.

All the more reason to resist it.

"We should go soon," Lily said. "They'll be bringing her back to the salon."

Her words echoed, seeming to bounce softly around my head as I struggled to focus. I needed to get to Saskia. No. Reggie. I was here for Reggie.

I shook my head, trying to clear it.

"Are you all right?" Lily moved closer.

"Yes." I straightened, looked past Lily to the door. "Let's go."

I couldn't see Reggie when I first walked into the room. There were about twenty Blood, along with an equal number of Beasts. The space was lit by candles hanging in glass lanterns and the flickering light made it difficult to see exactly how many people were scattered around the room, lolling on the low black couches. Here and there the filmy white tunics the Trusted wore stood out like beacons in the intimate dimness.

No sign of Reggie's pale blond head. Anger surged again. Fine. If they wouldn't produce her, perhaps I'd make them.

As I took one step forward, a hand clamped around my arm.

"And where do you think you're going with that look on your face?" Willem said in a soft growl.

I tried to shake him off, but apparently Bryony's potion didn't confer superhuman strength despite how I felt. "I'm looking for Regina."

"Seems to me you're looking for trouble, puppy," Willem said softly. His grip didn't shift.

"I thought you were leaving."

"Martin's not done yet." He inclined his head a little and I saw Martin and Alec seated on the far side of the room, conversing with another Beast. Martin held a hand of cards and there were coins scattered on the table in front of him. I could see only the back of the third Beast's head. Brown hair. Which told me nothing.

I returned my gaze to Willem, baring my teeth a little. "Then why don't you go back to him and leave me to my business?"

"Because I don't want you going off half-cocked and causing a scene. Things are . . . delicate right now."

"Well, now, I wouldn't want to ruin your deal with Ignatius Grey," I snarled.

The grip bit harder. "No, you wouldn't. You've agreed to throw in your lot with us now, Fen. And in a pack, what the alpha says goes and we work to make it so."

I wanted to tell him what he might do with his pack and his goddamned alpha, but I might still need their help to get Reggie out of here. "We had an agreement," I said through gritted teeth.

"That we did. Just don't make trouble as you go about it." Willem let go of my arm and stepped back. My hands clenched as the weird certainty that I could do anything I wanted surged again. Bryony's potion could yet be the death of me. I eyed Willem speculatively, wondering if I could get away with just one punch when he looked past my shoulder and jerked his chin.

"Isn't that your girl?"

Reggie. It was hard to move slowly. Bolting across the room wouldn't be helpful. I counted to five before I turned and looked.

Sure enough, it was Reggie, standing a little apart from a group of Blood. Her expression was unfocused, eyes gazing off toward nothing in particular. An odd smile played around her lips. She wore a white shift like the Trusted wore and her hair hung in loose curls down her back. The hair hid her neck so that I couldn't see if she'd been bitten. I hadn't seen Reggie with her hair down in public since we'd been very young.

That, more than anything, pushed my anger to the boiling point.

"Don't mess this up."

The voice was the faintest hint of a whisper in my ear. Lily's voice. Good. At least she was here with me.

The jolt of hearing her was enough to ease the fog of rage a little. I managed to walk casually across the room, stopping a few feet away from the group of vampires and Reggie. They were ignoring her so far. Good. Maybe they were done with her.

Reggie was still just standing there, swaying slightly. Her gaze passed over my face without any sign of recognition.

Not good.

I took another step closer. The Blood didn't react, still intent on whatever they were talking about. I was too focused on Reggie to listen in.

Reggie's eyes drifted back in my direction.

"Hello," I said softly. She didn't respond. But her vacant smile faded.

I took another careful step. "Why don't you come over here with me?" I reached out a hand, laid it on Reggie's arm. I felt the tiny flinch of her skin as I touched her, but she didn't protest. I moved closer still, put an arm around her shoulders.

One of the Blood turned to me. His eyes were an odd dark blue in his white face. "That one's about done," he said. "But she's a pretty thing." He paused, looked me up and down. "You Beasts like your women compliant, don't you?"

I forced the laugh. "Why do you think we come to the Assemblies?"

The vampire shook his head, turned away.

I tightened my arm around Reggie's shoulder. "Come on, sweet," I said, loud enough for the vampires to hear. "You and I are going to have some fun."

My stomach twisted, bile rising in my throat as I felt Reggie shiver against me. But still, she made no protest. Gods. What had they done to her?

We made our way across the room and to the door. This was the difficult part. If what Lily had said was true, and none of the Blood here had claimed Reggie personally, then she was indeed free to leave. I just had to get her out the front door and make sure she said she wanted to go if we were questioned.

Lily and I had gone over it earlier. Initially she'd wanted to come in here alone and try to sneak Reggie out with an invisibility charm, but I'd pointed out that if Reggie resisted or they ran into trouble, Lily couldn't turn solid and physically take Reggie out. Every Blood in the City knew who Lily was. A great number of them would want to kill her on sight. She would never make it out of the warrens without shadowing and having to leave Reggie behind.

Lily had given in, with some protest. I'd added the fact that Reggie knew me and there was some chance that she would remember and trust me, regardless of what state we found her in. She was, however, less likely to trust a disembodied voice. Or even believe it was real.

Reggie's skin felt too hot under my hand, as though she was running a fever. *Gods*. What had they done to her? I tried to remember what the Trusted had said about the rooms available for sex. Maybe I should take Reggie there and use the time to see if she was hurt. Or should I just try for the front door? I hesitated for a moment, hating the feel of Reggie leaning so unprotestingly against me.

"Fen." It was Lily's voice again. "Martin and his boys are leaving. Use the charm. You can walk out with them."

Now or never. We were alone in the corridor. I could hear Martin's deep rumble behind me from the room I'd just left. I clamped my arm tighter around Reggie, pulled her closer to my side.

Willem came up on my other side, eyebrows arched. "Okay, puppy, you've got her. Now, walk with us."

My pulse was hammering hard enough that I was sure all the vampires in the building must be able to hear it. I could only hope they had enough playthings occupying their attention. The walk to the outer door seemed to take an eternity—my nerves braced for someone to challenge us, but nobody did, and we managed to walk out the front door in one piece. We all bundled into Martin's carriage and the driver urged the horses forward at a pace that seemed far too slow.

I kept one arm around Reggie and the other hand on the pistol I'd left in the carriage. There were no sounds of pursuit or outcry from the warrens as they receded from the narrow angle of view I had out the carriage window.

As agreed, the carriage came to a halt once we were back in Beast territory and I lifted Reggie inside the 'cab I'd hired and gave directions to St. Giles.

SASKIA

If the hands on the clock on Simon's desk didn't start moving faster soon, I was going to scream or fling the damn thing out the window. Each minute seemed to take an eternity, the hands moving slowly, so slowly, past midnight, then on to one in the morning with no sign of Fen or Lily.

Both my brothers had tried to convince me to go home but I'd refused, insisting on waiting with the rest of them. Simon sat behind his desk, pretending to read one of his medical books, though the pages weren't turning very often.

Holly and Guy had taken chairs near the window, trying not to look too much like they were staring down at the streets below. Every so often Holly said something to Guy, but his answers were short and to the point. I'd tried to read as well, but made a worse job of pretending than Simon.

After a while I gave up and alternated drinking tea with staring at the clock. The combination was fraying my nerves.

Which was stupid. I barely knew Fen, after all. So why was I so worried?

"How much longer can this possibly take?" I said to the room in general, after the hands had counted off another interminable ten minutes. "Something must have gone wrong." I stood to return my empty cup to the tea trolley. My hands trembled and the china rattled as I placed it back on the brass tray.

"Don't jump to conclusions," Simon said. "They would have triggered their alarms if they needed help."

"Or they both got into trouble too quickly to do so," I countered.

Simon closed his book with a thump that belied his pretense of calm. "Unless Ignatius has somehow employed a sunmage, that's not very likely. Even if Fen was in trouble, Lily would let us know."

I glared at him. It was easier for him to be casual about this. As he said, Lily wasn't the one at risk on tonight's little adventure. Frustrated, I turned my attention to Holly. "What do you think?"

She was pale but composed. "I think Simon's right. There's no point panicking before we need to." Her hands tightened around the arms of her chair for a moment. She wasn't quite as calm as she pretended to be either.

"I think we should—"

"What?" Guy said, in his don't-be-an-idiot rumble. "Go in and rescue them? How exactly would that work, Sass? Simon's right. We just have to wait."

I stayed standing. "I don't want to just sit here and do nothing."

"If you can't keep better control of yourself than this," Simon said, "then you're never going to survive the negotiations."

"The negotiations are hardly the same as going to the Blood warrens!"

Simon shook his head. "There's less difference than you might think. Don't fool yourself, Sass, the negotiations— these negotiations in particular—are life and death."

"All the more reason we need Fen's help," I pointed out. "And why we should be worried about him."

"We are worried," Simon replied. "But that doesn't mean

we go charging off into the night. What exactly do you think we could do at the warrens, anyway?"

"But—" I broke off, chewed my lip. He was right, of course, but I didn't want to admit it. There was nothing we could do. That just made the waiting even harder somehow.

I forced my hands into my lap, gripped them tightly together, and shut my eyes. I stretched out my senses, trying to identify all the different metals in the room—an old focus exercise that the Masters used to drive first-year students mad—to calm my mind.

At first there was just a blur of sensation, overlaid by the peculiar pulses I recognized as Simon and Guy—pulses I could sense anywhere in the City—but gradually I started to focus in on the individual strands of metalsong that made up the whole. A pen nib on Simon's desk, that was silver. As was the cross around Guy's neck. Brass nails in the furnishings—the alloy given a little bit of help from a mage—more brass in the tea trolley and the tray and then the myriad tin lids on the jars of gods knew what lining some of Simon's shelves. Plus the bones of the building itself. St. Giles was largely made of stone and wood and marble, as were most buildings in the city, but there was iron here too. The founders of the hospital hadn't spared any expense when they'd built this place.

I sent my senses deeper, following the iron, feeling it grow stronger as I went further into the depths of the hospital. The call of the iron started to drown out the other metals . . . which made no sense . . . Iron was rare and expensive; it couldn't be the most used metal in this building. Unless—

"There's a 'cab," Holly said suddenly. She leaned closer to the window, staring down into the darkness.

"Is it—" Simon started to ask.

"It's Lily. And Fen. And, oh gods. Reggie." She whirled and headed for the door at a run. Simon almost beat her to it and Guy was hot on their heels. I hesitated, looked back to the window, wanting to know what Holly had seen. But then I realized I was being silly. The fastest way to find out what had happened would be to follow the others. So I picked up my skirts and ran.

*   *   *

My heart was pounding by the time we reached the main reception hall of the hospital, and not just from the exertion. No, with each step, worry about what might be waiting for us had grown in my stomach, until my pulse pounded with nerves and I wished I wasn't wearing a corset. Then at least I might have been able to feel as though I could catch my breath.

At some point during our mad dash through the halls of St. Giles, Simon and Guy had overtaken Holly. But even so, by the time we reached the main entrance of the hospital, Lady Bryony had appeared and was already ushering Fen and Lily toward one of the treatment rooms, her face grave as she looked down at the burden Fen clasped in his arms. His knuckles pressed whitely against the olive skin of his hand as though he was determined that nothing would make him let go of the woman he carried.

Reggie. Her eyes were closed, and she was too still as she rested against Fen's shoulders. Her long hair fell in a tangle of ratty curls covering half her face. She wore a nearly see-through white shift that bared her arms and her legs below the knees. She'd been gone for only a few days, but she looked thin. Smaller than I remembered.

Had Edwina looked like that before the end? Too thin? Too small? I bit back the sharp tug of grief. I couldn't afford to break down here. Reggie was the one who needed taking care of.

Fen held her as though she was spun glass. Like he was both afraid she might break and determined that no one would take her again. It was only Holly's coaxing that persuaded him to lay Reggie down on the bed and let Simon and Bryony examine her. He and Holly, their eyes fixed on Reggie, both hovered as close to the bed as they could be without getting in the way of the healers. Guy, Lily, and I hung back, me closest to the door. I was half tempted to slip out of the room—I felt helpless and useless—but I wanted to know what happened.

Reggie moaned softly in response to something Bryony did and Fen jolted forward with a noise that was half growl.

"Stay where you are." Bryony fixed him with a glare. Then her gaze sharpened and she turned from Reggie and stepped closer to Fen, examining his face. "How much?" she asked, looking past Fen to Lily.

"He took the whole thing," Lily said.

I had no idea what they were talking about.

Bryony tilted her head, studied Fen. "How do you feel?"

"I'm fine," he snapped. "Reggie is the one who needs your help." His tone was sharp, edged with something that made me want to step back a little.

"We're taking care of Reggie," Bryony said carefully. She turned back to Lily. "And what of Viola?"

Lily shook her head. "I couldn't find her. I didn't have a lot of time, but she's either very well hidden or not in the warrens."

Or dead—that was the other alternative.

Bryony's lips compressed, a quick glint of red sliding across the rainbow-metaled chain she wore at her neck. Fae work, some exotic alloy I'd never been able to fully deconstruct, it shifted color with her moods, giving fair warning to those who crossed her. Just as well. Lady Bryony was the most powerful Fae healer at St. Giles. She might just be the most powerful of the Fae who chose to live outside Summerdale's walls. No one with good sense crossed her. She could probably raze the building if she chose.

But as much as her temper and low tolerance for fools was legendary, so was her skill. She held Lily's gaze a little longer, an unspoken question in her indigo eyes. Then she took a quick breath and bent to Reggie, laying a hand on the blond curls, brushing them gently back from her face.

"Is she going to be all right?" Holly asked.

Simon looked up at that. I didn't like the bleak expression in his eyes. "How was she when you found her?"

Fen's face twisted. "They were feeding on her. I don't think she knew me, but she came with me willingly enough."

"Did you see her drink any blood?"

A shake of his dark head. "No. But . . ."

"But what?"

"She was so . . . compliant . . . There's no way Reggie wouldn't have fought them if she'd been herself. So she must have drunk."

"There are other drugs," Guy offered.

"Not in the warrens," Lily said softly. "She has the look about her." She looked toward Simon. "There's a way to find out."

Simon shook his head.

"What's she talking about?" Fen demanded. "If there's a way to find out, then do it."

"If she's blood-locked we'll know soon enough," Simon said. Beside Fen, I saw Holly bite her lip.

"Isn't there anything you can do? Or is it already too late?"

"I—"

"This is cruel, Simon," Guy said suddenly. He'd stayed silent until now, a looming presence next to Lily, his eyes fixed on Holly as though he wanted to do something to help her but didn't know what or how. But now he was looking at Simon with an undecipherable expression. "Tell them."

Simon straightened, eyebrows lifting with surprise. "Guy—"

"I think he's right," Bryony said.

"So do I," Lily said firmly. She lifted her chin, one hand toying with the hilt of the dagger at her hip.

She and Simon exchanged a long, level look. For once, he looked unhappy with her. What in the name of earth's fires was going on? The five of them—Bryony, my brothers, Holly, and Lily—knew something. That much was clear. But what?

"It's too risky," Simon said.

"If they're on the delegation, it's likely they're going to find out sooner or later," Guy said.

"Find out what?" Fen and I said together.

Simon glared at Guy. "Saskia should leave."

I folded my arms, prepared to do something drastic if they tried to make me go. "Not a chance. Tell us what, Simon?"

"Bryony?" Simon said, with a note of last-ditch appeal in his voice.

"It's ultimately your decision," Bryony said. "But I think you should tell. It might even help the process."

"What process?" Fen growled.

"It's not a process, exactly," Simon said.

If he prevaricated any longer I was going to scream. "Sainted earth, Simon. Just tell us what the hell is going on."

He looked down at Reggie, seemingly considering something. Then he straightened. "Fine. But if I tell you this, it's dangerous. So one last chance to change your mind."

"I think we're clear on the situation being dangerous," Fen said. "Tell us."

Simon's eyes suddenly looked very blue as he looked at me, and I wondered what he was thinking about. But I was more interested in what he was about to say.

"I think it's easiest if I just show you."

Chapter Ten

SASKIA

"Let me guess," Fen said. "This has something to do with you and a vampire."

"What?" The exclamation left my mouth before I could stop it. "Simon?" I took a step toward him. Guy put a hand on my shoulder.

"Well?" Fen asked.

Behind him, Holly was watching carefully, as though she was not exactly sure what he might do. Bryony had an equally concerned expression, though one hand still rested gently on Reggie's shoulder.

"What's going on?" I mouthed at Holly. She shook her head and pushed past Fen, coming to stand between him and my brother.

Fen stayed silent, his gaze fixed on Simon over Holly's head. His eyes glittered—too green, too sharp. He looked almost feral.

"Simon? What's he talking about?" I asked.

Simon shrugged. "I said, I'd show you. Guy, can you bring Reggie?"

"I'll carry her," Fen said sharply.

Holly stepped closer to him, her hand lifted as though to touch him. Fen flinched away. "I said I'll do it."

"It's safer if Guy does," Bryony said. "That potion you took can be unpredictable."

That news didn't seem to improve Fen's mood any. "How?" he gritted out.

"Sometimes it keeps people going for a few hours and then it knocks them out cold. Where they stand. It's probably better if you aren't carrying Regina if that happens."

Fen's lip curled, but he stepped aside. Guy picked Reggie up as though she weighed no more than a kitten. He held her as gently as Fen had, worry frosting his eyes as he looked down at her still face. He turned from the bed, adjusted his grip. Then he paused. "Don't we need charms?"

Charms? For what? And for that matter, why the hell did everybody else in this room seem to know what was going on except for Fen and me? "Why would we need charms?"

"The only people who know about this are in this room," Simon said.

For the first time, I realized that no one else had come to help Simon and Bryony. Normally there would be others—prentices, orderlies, other healers—watching and learning and assisting as needed. But nobody had come into the room since we'd entered. Now that I thought about it, I could feel a ward humming gently behind me, sealing the room to prying eyes and ears.

Simon's or Bryony's work? If they were worried about being overheard here in St. Giles—which was not only a hospital but a Haven, a place of supposedly inviolate safety—then whatever it was they were hiding was serious indeed.

But I had no idea what it could be. Fen had said something about vampires. But that couldn't be right.

Holly pressed a charm into my hand, a twisting dangle of glass beads and leather that looked small and simple. But the thread of magic that pulsed from it was complicated.

From the taste of the power, it was Holly's work. Which meant we couldn't be going far. Holly's charms worked spectacularly well when she used them on herself but usually lasted only a short time for others.

"All right," Simon said when everyone—apart from Lily, Simon, and Bryony—had been handed charms. Holly had tied one of them around Reggie's wrist as well. Fen had looked at his as though he recognized it and his brows drew down, the anger in his eyes sparking hotter. Obviously he knew what the charm was for.

I couldn't tell.

"Lily will go first, then Holly will activate the charms for the rest of you."

Lily faded from sight, which was something I still wasn't used to, even though I'd seen her do it a number of times. When the last smokelike image of her disappeared completely, Holly did something and everyone else in the room disappeared from view as well. Invisibility charms. Well, that solved that mystery, though it didn't provide any answers as to why we needed such things within the walls of St. Giles.

After a minute or so, Simon gave the order for us to follow him. How exactly we were going to achieve that when all of us were invisible remained to be seen, but the more immediate problem was how we were all going to be able to leave the room without crashing into one another.

Holly took care of that, making me jump as she brushed past me to take up a position somewhere near the door and issuing instructions for how we were to proceed in a low voice. Bryony left the room first and as she passed me I noticed a tiny, faint glow of light floating in the air roughly at the height her shoulders would be. Follow the invisible Fae.

Holly's system worked and we set off on a strange, mostly silent journey through hospital corridors that seemed too empty. I wondered if Bryony had given orders for no one to be wandering around for a certain period of time or whether she was using a spell to contain people where they were, but as I had to focus on walking—being invisible was an odd and unsettling sensation that made me prone to tripping over my skirts—I didn't try and feel for any magic.

Bryony's light led the way to the back corridors of the hospital, then down into its bowels via a series of staircases I'd never used before. Down and down and down. What exactly had the founders of the hospital been expecting when they built the buildings with several levels belowground?

As we traveled deeper, the notes from the metals in the building grew muffled by the earth that surrounded us . . .

except, that is, for the familiar song of iron. That grew
steadily stronger as we filed along, until the walls almost
pulsed with the sensation. I wondered how Bryony bore it
as well as she did. Or *if* she did. As the sensation from the
iron grew even stronger, the little flickering orb of light
dimmed, until it was only the faintest of sparks.

We turned at a final junction in the seemingly unending
tunnels and suddenly the source of the ironsong was appar-
ent. A massive door—warded so heavily it fairly glowed—
blocked our path. I stopped in my tracks, heedless of Fen
walking behind me, trying to calculate how much the door
must have cost.

It was a horribly expensive barrier to whatever lay beyond.

A chill shivered through me. What was worth spending
so much on to protect?

I was about to find out. Simon blinked into sight and
started working the wards. The door swung open silently to
his touch, making me itch to inspect it more closely, to see
how it was wrought. To balance such a weight of iron so that
it moved so easily was a skill indeed.

Simon beckoned and beside him Lily also faded into
view. She stepped through the door and then Bryony and
Holly also appeared. Bryony waited by the door, drawing
on a pair of slim leather gloves while Holly held out a hand.

"Saskia, then Fen. Come up to me and put the charm in
my hand."

"I can kill a charm." Fen's voice was sharp.

"I'd prefer you didn't waste all my work," Holly said. She
sounded like she was holding on to her temper with both
hands as well. "Saskia, you first."

I did as requested, moving carefully, hoping that I
wouldn't crash into Guy. I'd lost track of where he might be.
Fen, I knew, was behind me. I reached Holly, dropped the
charm into her hand, and then had to suppress a sigh of
relief when I could see myself again. I rubbed my arms, one
after the other, both to relieve the chill I felt and to prove
to myself that I was indeed all here.

I didn't envy Holly, who used such charms regularly in
her work as a spy. Not being able to see my body was unnerving. I preferred seeing that both my feet were firmly on
the floor.

Holly jerked her head toward the door and I walked through. Behind me, Holly said, "Fen?" He didn't reply. I didn't look behind me, focusing instead on my surroundings. We stood in another stretch of St. Giles' seemingly endless tunnels. About fifty feet or so beyond us was another massive door.

More iron. More wards. My chill increased.

Soft footsteps came up behind me. Holly walked past me to stand by Lily and Guy joined her, Reggie still safely in his arms. Fen stopped beside me. I snuck a glance up at him. His eyes still looked too bright as he stared at Reggie. The air around him almost vibrated with his anger. I wanted to touch him, to help with the pain he had to be in, but I didn't think he'd welcome it right now.

Bryony closed the iron door behind us and the resonance between the iron of each of the doors made the air sing softly around me. I found myself caught by the song, listened to the metals with wonder. I didn't think I'd ever been in such close proximity to so much iron. My prentice chain warmed around my neck as my power flared in response.

"How can you stand to be down here?" I said to Bryony. Down here, the sense of power that usually surrounded her was muted and she looked pale.

She made a fluid Fae gesture, smoothed the leather gloves. "I can bear it for a little while. As long as I don't touch the iron directly."

I wondered how much she was underplaying. Being so close to so much iron had to hurt her. All of the Fae who chose to live in the City had to get used to some degree of discomfort from the iron in the buildings and machines, but that was different from being this close to what must be at least half a ton of iron.

Simon cleared his throat. "Before we go on, there's something I want to tell you."

Fen made a sound that was almost a growl. He had to be close to his limits of tolerance as well. Which couldn't be helping his anger. He was frowning at Simon, his mouth set in a tense line.

I was suddenly reminded that he had grown up in the border boroughs, running half wild in those streets. Part Beast. Part Fae. Surviving. And thriving. He wasn't the simple pleasure seeker he affected to be, this man. No. He was strong. Powerful in his own right. Not a man to cross.

And probably full of secrets that I didn't necessarily want to know about.

Much like my brother, it seemed.

When had things gotten so complicated? My head ached, fatigue and apprehension tightening the muscles in my neck and back. I wasn't sure I wanted to know any more, despite my curiosity. Didn't want to risk having my relationship with Simon altered by what he was about to reveal. He was my brother and I loved him and I wanted things to be easy between us.

But in these times of rising dark, perhaps things could no longer be so black and white. In the half-light, it was never easy to see the truth, after all. But it was important to try.

"Tell us," I said to Simon.

He nodded and took a few steps closer to Lily, seeking the comfort of her closeness, perhaps. "A few years ago," he said in his quiet, calm voice, "I was coming here, to St. Giles, very late—or early, perhaps. I found somebody in one of the laneways near the hospital. Injured, horribly burned."

"One of the Blood?" Fen said.

"Yes."

I stifled the pained laugh that rose in my throat. Only my brother would do such a thing. He hated the Blood for what they had done to our sister, yes, but his healer oaths would bind him to help anyone who needed it. "You took them into the hospital? Gave them Haven?" Anyone who wanted it had to be granted refuge in any of the Havens in the City.

"He was too far gone to ask for it," Simon said. "But he managed to say something about being hunted, so I took him down to one of the old disused quarantine wards here in the tunnels. It was too close to dawn to take him anywhere else."

"Why try to save him? Easier to let him fry," Fen muttered. I got the impression he would have chosen the latter option.

"I'm a healer," Simon said. "I had to try. So I worked on him. It was too late to do much. Someone had used silver and holy water on him. The Blood heal fast and the scars were already forming. I did what I could. But he'd been blinded."

"How do you—" I cut my words off. On second thought, I didn't know what kinds of torture it would take to blind a vampire. They, like the Fae and the Beasts, heal inhumanly fast. They can survive and heal wounds that would kill a human many times over. To lose his sight, well, the only thing I could think of was that someone had actually gouged out his eyeballs and then burned him with molten silver to seal the wounds. My mouth tasted a sour rush of bile, and I swallowed. Hard.

"So you saved him," Fen said. "Then what?"

Simon looked toward the door at the end of the corridor. "I couldn't just send him back out into the world. A blind vampire wouldn't last long without help, and he said that Lord Lucius was the one who'd hurt him, so there was truly no hope for him if the Blood Court found him."

"So you kept him? A vampire?" It seemed crazy, even for Simon.

"He asked for Haven. I couldn't have turned him away."

"The Blood would not scruple to turn humans away," Fen said. Guy made what I thought was the start of a nod of agreement before he caught himself and stopped the movement.

"Not if someone had claimed Haven."

"You believe that?" Fen said incredulously. "Do the Blood even operate a Haven?"

"There are Havens in the Night World."

"I'd imagine they're pretty dusty and disused," Fen retorted. "Anyone fleeing the Night World isn't going to stick around in that part of the City. If they don't leave the City entirely."

"Be that as it may," Simon said. "How the Night Worlders deal with their supplicants isn't my concern. How *I* treat anyone who comes to this hospital seeking help is."

I stared at my brother, fascinated. I'd never quite understood until just now how deep his healer instincts ran. Hells, it was still hard to reconcile either of the naughty, hell-raising big brothers I'd grown up with with the Master Healer and the Templar knight who stood here, both looking tired and resolute. It didn't seem that long ago that it had been the five of us playing croquet in the gardens of our house, happy and carefree.

Now we were only four and I didn't know if even Hannah could be called completely carefree.

Perhaps, that is why Simon and Guy have difficulty seeing you as a metalmage, a guilty little voice in my head said. I chased it away. I was allowed nostalgia if I didn't let it color my actions now. My brothers were just being stubborn and pigheaded in their desire to keep me hidden away.

"So what happened next?" Fen asked. "Healing him is one thing"—he stopped, gestured at the doors—"but you wouldn't need all this if you had just healed him."

Simon nodded agreement. "I thought it safest to keep him hidden until I knew his story. I told Bryony and she agreed we should keep his presence a secret. For his safety and for the safety of everyone else at St. Giles. Over time, I slowly got to know him. He had to trust me—I supplied his food and everything else and he told me a little of his life in the Court. It took time for me to see that perhaps not all the Blood were the same. Atherton—that's his name, Atherton Carstairs—told me that he'd been in the retinue of a Blood lord who had opposed Lucius' ways. He's quite young, as the Blood count such things. Anyway, Lucius killed his mentor and tortured all those who followed him, to set an example. Atherton's Trusted somehow got to him and set him free. She didn't survive to escape with him, though."

Simon rubbed his hands along his thighs, fingers stretching. "As I was saying. We talked. Became friends of a sort, and one day I happened to say something about a cure for blood-locking."

"A cure?" Fen took a step toward Guy and Reggie, hope flaring on his face. "There isn't a cure."

"No," Simon said. "Not quite. Not even the hint of one back then. I hadn't expected Atherton to help me. But he said that perhaps we should look for one. He thought that the one way to loosen Lucius' grip on power would be to break the Blood's hold over the blood-locked. Stem the tide of humans falling to the Night World."

"Damn fool idea," Guy said.

"You don't approve?" I was surprised. I would have thought that anything that spiked the Night World's guns would be manna from heaven to Guy.

"Let's just say that Simon and I disagree on the consequences of his cure, should he find it," Guy said.

"You're looking for a cure?" Fen asked. His face twisted as he looked down at Reggie. "That's madness."

"Why?" I said, puzzled.

"A cure just gives those who choose the Night World less reason to be afraid of the Blood, doesn't it?" Fen said, with a flick of one long-fingered hand. Across from him, Guy made an approving noise. "If they don't have to fear being blood-locked, why should they stay away?"

"I disagree," Simon said. "A cure will help so many people. It's vital if we're going to survive."

A cure. My head throbbed. All I could think was that it was too late for Edwina. My throat was tight with sorrow. Too late for my sister. But maybe not too late for Regina. "This is all academic unless you've actually found a cure," I said. "Have you?"

"We can talk about that inside. I just wanted to prepare you first." Simon looked from Fen to me.

Prepare us to meet a vampire, he meant. Not that it would be Fen's first time. I'd seen Blood before, of course. They attended the opera at the Gilt and other amusements in the border boroughs, but I'd largely avoided contact with them. Vampires only reminded me of Edwina.

Who'd died blood-locked and estranged from us. And now Simon thought he could find a cure?

I tried not to think of Edwina but it was impossible. The hurt was always there. And, part of me whispered, maybe it was that same hurt that drove Simon now. Could he really find a cure or was he just trying to right a very old wrong? One that could never be mended.

Our family would never be whole again. All of this ran through my head like a litany as Simon opened the next door.

"Give me a moment." He slipped through the door.

Preparing the vampire, no doubt.

Sainted earth.

Guy stood closest to the door, shifting his stance slightly as he waited for Simon's return.

"I can take her," Fen said to him.

Guy shook his head. "She isn't heavy." He glanced down at Reggie and then back at Fen, his jaw tightening, lips settling into a grim line, and for a moment I saw a glimpse of the warrior Guy usually hid around us. Saw that his rage went deep as well.

Just what we needed.

I hoped Simon's vampire—no, Atherton—I could at least extend the courtesy of using his name, was good at being circumspect. I didn't think it would take much to set either Fen or Guy off tonight and a vampire would make a tempting target for their anger.

Simon's reappearance was a welcome break to the tension brewing in our little group. We followed him through the door into a moderately sized room. It was dimly lit, only a few of the gaslights on the wall burning. It was also mostly empty. A few tables set against the wall to our left held a clutter of notebooks and various medical-looking devices, and a somewhat neater desk and chair stood closest to the very ordinary-looking wooden door in the wall opposite us.

As Holly pulled the iron door shut behind us, the wooden door opened and a vampire stepped through, his posture wary, tensed, head swiveling slowly from side to side as though he was scanning the room.

Which he couldn't do. Where his eyes should have been was a mass of scarred flesh and ruin. Burns. I knew the look of burns—they were somewhat of an occupational hazard for metalmages—and these were definitely burn scars. Horrifying, scorching burns.

The room swam around me for a moment. Blighted earth. I swallowed and took a deep breath.

"This is Atherton Carstairs," Simon said, moving to the vampire's side. "Atherton, do you know who is here?"

"Hello, Lily," Atherton said. "Lady Bryony. Guy. Miss Holly. I do not know the other three. But I gather we have a new patient?" He turned to face Guy, the surety of the movement uncanny. The Blood have senses far beyond those of humans—their hearing and smell and sight are all honed to the acuteness of the predator—but seeing Atherton's casual display of just how good they were was alarming.

"The patient is Holly's friend, Regina," Simon said.

"The one who was missing?" Atherton's mouth turned down. "I am sorry, Holly." The vampire turned back to Simon. "How did you retrieve her?"

"Lily and Fen—you've heard Holly talk about Fen—went after her. They were able to get her out of the warrens."

"Can we do the niceties later?" Guy asked, shifting his stance carefully. "Where do you want Reggie?"

"Bring her inside. There's a bed readied." Atherton turned and opened the door he'd come through, then walked into the room beyond. Guy carried Reggie through and the rest of us followed.

I was first through the door after Simon and almost stopped short again when I found myself in a much larger room that resembled a hospital ward.

That's because it is *a hospital ward, idiot*, I chided myself. Simon had said that he'd taken Atherton to an old disused ward. What he'd neglected to mention was that it was no longer disused.

No, now it was full. There were at least eight rows of beds, each occupied by a sleeping person. Guy put Reggie down on the empty bed Atherton indicated, settling her gently. Atherton bent and pulled the covers around her. I saw Guy stiffen as the vampire reached to move one of Reggie's arms, but he didn't interfere.

"Are they all blood-locked?" Fen's voice came sharply from behind me.

"Yes," Bryony said calmly. "More or less."

"What does that mean?" Fen asked. His voice rang loud in the hushed room. None of the patients stirred, though, which meant either that their sleep was charmed or that they weren't capable of responding.

"We're getting closer to a cure," Simon said. "But—" He stopped, turned to Lily with a raised eyebrow.

Lily shrugged. "I said you should tell them. That means telling all of it."

"All right." Simon rubbed his thigh again, then gestured at the various chairs that stood beside some of the beds. "Sit. Let me go back to the beginning. Bryony, will you see to Reggie?"

Bryony nodded and went to help Atherton. The rest of us carried chairs closer to Simon and then settled ourselves.

Simon looked tired as he began to speak. "All right. The beginning. Fen, you know a little of this, I think, from Holly."

Fen, on his chair, was tense, his brows drawn together in

a thick black slash over his eyes. "Perhaps. Do you mean Saskia doesn't?"

"No."

Oh good, more secrets. I held my tongue.

Simon drew in a breath, let it out heavily. "A few months ago, Lucius sent Lily to try and kill me."

"What?" I'd never known exactly how Simon and Lily had crossed paths, what had driven her defection from the Night World, apart from falling madly in love with my brother. I turned to face Lily. "You did what?" Around my neck, I felt my chain begin to heat.

"Easy, Sass," Simon said. "You don't understand."

"She tried to kill you!" I said indignantly.

Lily's eyes lit with amusement for a moment before her expression returned to its neutral gaze.

"Well, she failed," Simon pointed out. "Besides, she didn't want to do it. Lucius—" He stopped, looked again at Lily. She nodded. "Lucius had a secret. Lily's secret. He'd addicted her to his blood."

"*You* were locked?" Fen said, looking shocked.

Lily shook her head. "Not exactly. I'm a wraith. Vampire blood doesn't work in the same way for my kind, apparently. I had the need, but it didn't damage me like it does a human. I kept my senses and I could control my hunger, to a degree."

"That may be debatable," Guy said with a snort. "After all, you fell for Simon."

"True." She looked at Simon affectionately. "It's that DuCaine charm, I guess."

"Simon cured your addiction?" I asked.

"No. Lucius' death cured my addiction."

"And they killed Lucius," Fen added.

I gaped at him. "I don't understand."

Fen shrugged, his chain clinking softly. "Your brother and Lily. They're the ones who killed Lucius."

Sainted earth. I dug my fingers into the back of my neck, the pounding in my head stronger than ever. My chain warmed again. Too many secrets. All this time and they'd never told me. "You killed him so you'd be cured?" I asked Lily.

"Because he needed killing," Lily said. "He was a danger to everyone."

"But it cured you. Killing the vampire who addicted you cured you?"

"It did. In my case."

"What about others?" I turned to Simon. "Have you tried this on others?"

Simon rolled his shoulders. "We can't just go around slaughtering vampires to test out the theory."

"More's the pity," Guy said with a grumble.

"The problem is that by the time we get our hands on anyone who's blood-locked, they're too far gone to tell us who locked them anyway."

"But you have tried?" I prompted.

"Yes," Simon admitted.

"On who?" Fen said suddenly.

"Patients brought to St. Giles," Simon said.

Fen's brows lifted. "Then how has this been kept a secret? If people's families bring them here for treatment . . ."

Simon looked away. My stomach curled uneasily, the pain in my temples intensifying. "Simon?"

He took a deep breath, sighed it out. "The families don't know."

"What?" Fen and I spoke in unison.

"They don't know," Simon repeated.

"So what do they think has happened to these people?"

"They think they're dead," Lily said.

Fen made a half-choked sound of outrage. "That's horrible!"

Lily shrugged. "The locked were already lost to their families. Offering false hope would be crueler. So Simon chose not to."

"Is it false, though?" I asked.

Fen ignored me, still focused on Lily and Simon, his green eyes very dark, body tensed. "What gives you the right to make that decision? Those people brought their daughters and sons and parents to you and you . . . what, lied to them? Told them they died? How can you do that?"

"I admit, I struggled with it," Simon said. "But Lily is right. It didn't seem fair to offer false hope, to prolong their pain. Bryony and I agreed this was kinder."

"Either that or you just didn't want anyone to find out about what you were doing. Because you knew people would try to stop you," Fen said, his voice dangerously close to a growl again.

"That was obviously a factor."

"Is it even legal?" Fen asked. "If the Blood have a right to the locked under treaty law, is it even legal to try and take that away from them?"

"Everything under the treaty is negotiable, Fen," Holly said.

"Which is part of why it's a flawed system," he replied.

"You don't believe in the treaty?" Guy asked.

"I don't . . ." Fen stopped, shrugged. "I think it leaves a lot of people to fall between the cracks." He looked at Simon again.

"Then why join our delegation?"

"Sometimes you have to pick from several bad choices," Fen said.

I winced as Guy's expression darkened. "I'm sure Fen means—"

"Let him speak for himself," Guy said. Beside him, Holly put a hand on his arm and he shook her off. Definitely not good.

"Do you really care?" Fen said. "You got what you wanted."

Guy leaned forward. "Did we?"

"What are you implying?"

"That we don't need someone whose loyalty is questionable."

"I gave you my word." Fen's jaw clenched. I held my breath, not daring to speak as Guy and Fen locked gazes.

"But you don't believe in the treaty."

"I said it was flawed."

"Isn't that the same thing?"

"Not necessarily. Not the way I see it."

"You and I have different ways of looking at things, then," Guy said.

"Yes, I suppose we do," Fen said. "You grew up in safety and comfort. Your family are the kind who build places like this hospital." He waved his arm at the room. "I grew up in an attic above a whorehouse. You can afford to be black and white about the world, Templar. I can't."

"Is that so?" Guy's voice was starting to stretch to a drawl. Never a good sign.

Simon held up a hand. "Calm down. It's late and we're all tired. Why don't we—"

"No, Simon. I want to hear what he has to say," Guy said.

"And I want to hear Simon answer my question," Fen said. "Is it even legal, what he's doing?"

"That's a gray area," Simon said carefully.

"Gray as in 'nobody knows' or gray as in 'we're all in it up to our necks'?" Fen said.

"We don't know," Lily said.

"Is this why Lucius tried to kill Simon?" Fen said.

"He never gave me a reason," Lily said. "But I would assume so."

"Which means we can also assume that maybe some of the Blood know about what you're doing. And that they really don't want this to happen."

"I don't think any of us particularly care if Ignatius Grey and his cronies are unhappy," Lily said.

"Only those of us who have to live with the consequences of that unhappiness. What if they use this at the negotiations? Surely Lucius didn't keep it to himself."

"I had heard no whispers of it in the court," Lily said. "But we think it's wise to plan for that."

"And if they do, what if the Fae side with them? It could be a disaster," Fen said.

"Or our salvation," Lily countered.

"If there is a cure, maybe. Is there? You said there were others. Were they cured when Lucius died?"

"It's complicated," Simon said slowly.

"Why? Seems like a yes or no answer to me."

"That sounds very black and white," Guy said to Fen.

"You don't like this either," Fen shot back.

"True, but that hasn't convinced Simon to stop, as yet." My brothers exchanged a scorching look. My stomach churned. No. I couldn't handle this if my brothers were fighting as well. I didn't want our family to splinter.

"And now you want to experiment on Reggie?" Fen said. "Make her part of this—"

"Fen." Holly's voice cracked across the room. "This is Reggie's best chance."

"How is it even a chance? Better that she died than stay like this."

"Simon will find a cure," Holly said stubbornly. "He will."

Fen scowled. "I like Guy's idea better. I vote for going back to the warrens and chopping off heads until we find the bastard responsible for this. Better yet, we can set fire to the whole fucking place. Let them burn."

"Killing all the Trusted and the Nightseekers and the Blood who do not feel as Lucius and Ignatius do in the process?" Lily snapped. "Oh yes, excellent plan. Of course, you'd probably die before you got too close. Do you want to do that to Holly?"

"Not to mention that an attack on the warrens would blow the treaty negotiations all to hell," Guy said. "But maybe you don't care about that."

Fen's eyes flared brilliant green, then darkened again. His mouth twisted. "I — "

"If you won't help, then you can leave," Holly said coolly. Her eyes were very large in her face as she looked at Fen and I got the feeling she was only stopping her voice from trembling with a fierce effort of will. "Simon's right. It's late and it's been a difficult night. You should go home, Fen. Go home and think about what you want to do. Think about whose side you're on exactly. Think about what Reggie and I mean to you."

Fen flinched. Ever so slightly, but I saw it. I was watching him far too intently to miss even the smallest move he made.

Then he spun around and stalked to the door, pulling it shut behind him with a thump that reverberated through the room like the final toll of a funeral bell.

Chapter Eleven

SASKIA

⚡

The echo of the door's slamming seemed to take a long time to fade away. I stayed where I was, looking at the beds around me — and the people in them — trying to understand what Simon had just revealed. That he had secretly been working on a cure for blood-locking, working with one of the Blood. For *years*.

"Well?" Simon said. "Anybody else have anything to say on the subject?"

"You already know what I think," Guy said. His voice was grim. I glanced at him, took in the set of his jaw and the way his scarred eyebrow was drawn down. Guy disapproved. Though obviously he had decided to side with Simon at the moment. Would he continue to do so?

"Saskia?" Simon said.

I looked back to where Reggie lay. Holly had taken a seat beside her and Bryony and Atherton stood on the other side of the bed. The vampire's ruined face was tilted down toward Reggie, his hand on her wrist, his manner so like Simon's when he was with a patient that it stole my breath for a moment.

"I don't know," I said honestly. A cure . . . it was something straight out of the pages of the cheap novels Hannah devoured. The stuff of legends, not reality. Even if it could be true, it had come too late to save the one person our family had needed to save. And it might yet have a terrible cost. "I need . . . time."

"You have until the negotiations start," Simon said. "You need to make up your mind."

"Are you going to announce this during the negotiations? Does it even work?"

Simon and Lily exchanged a long look. "It's hopeful," Simon said eventually. "We're moving in the right direction. We know it has something to do with bloodlines amongst the Blood."

"When Lucius died, did it help any of the others? Or just Lily?"

"Some of the others responded. They awoke. We're helping them, but they are mostly . . . damaged. We've been trying to determine when the best time is to tell their families."

That was a conversation I was glad that I wouldn't have to be involved in. I could see Simon's reasoning for keeping what he was doing down here a secret, but the families who thought they'd lost someone . . . what would I feel if I found out that Edwina had been hidden away from me for years and years whilst someone tried to cure her?

Happy if they'd been successful. But also deeply angry about all the time stolen from me. And all the needless grief.

"There must be magic involved as well," I said. "When the Blood turn, they change physically. There's magic involved in that process, yes?"

Simon nodded. "As far as we understand it."

Thinking about it made me dizzy. I understood a little about blood—metalmages can sense the iron in it, after all, and those of us attuned to iron more keenly than others—but I knew very little about how a human is turned to a vampire. I doubted anyone outside the Blood themselves knew much about that.

"Vampire blood must be different somehow, or else it wouldn't be addictive in the first place."

"Exactly. We're trying to understand how it's different and how it changes the locked. And if it can be reversed."

I rubbed my forehead. "And until you do, the only sure way you know is to kill the vampire who locked them." Blighted earth. It was a mess. Like reaching for something precious only to have it continually dangled out of reach.

"Not just the vampire who locked them," Lily said. "You have to kill the oldest vampire in that bloodline. At least, we think so. That why killing Lucius worked. He was the oldest left in his bloodline."

"His death changed the magic? Or ended it?"

Lily looked thoughtful. "Changed, maybe. It can't have ended it or the vampires he'd sired would have died too, surely?"

I just wanted to go home, go to bed, forget for a few hours. Maybe Master Aquinas and my brothers were right. I should stay safely tucked up behind the Guild walls and let the troubles of the world be someone else's problem.

Of course, if I could have chosen that path, I wouldn't be standing here in the first place.

"The Blood will go crazy. If you tell them you can cure blood-locking by killing vampires . . . it will be war."

Simon looked almost as tired as I felt, his blue eyes shadowed. "Hopefully we won't have to tell them. Hopefully we can find the true cure. Something that won't require bloodshed. Anyway, if things go smoothly, if the Blood don't overreach during the negotiations, then maybe we can keep this to ourselves a while longer."

I doubted that he believed the negotiations were going to go smoothly any more than I did. I was tired of being lied to. "Who else knows?"

"Just the people in this room."

"And probably some Blood," I said. "Fen was right. If Lucius tried to kill you, he couldn't have kept his reasons entirely secret. Someone amongst the Blood knows."

"Maybe."

"Yes." Guy and Lily spoke at the same time as Simon. Apparently they too thought Simon was being overly optimistic. Which made me feel somewhat relieved. At least I wasn't the only one struggling with the news.

"But if the Blood know, won't they try and use this against us in the negotiations? A cure is . . ." I had no idea of the legal implications of seeking to release those who were blood-locked. I knew that the locked were considered different from normal humans under treaty law. Once they were addicted, they forfeited their rights to protection. That meant the Blood had some claim on them, didn't it?

"We don't know," Simon said. "It somewhat depends on who is in charge during the negotiations. They could be one united bloc or they could still have factions. Atherton says there are still those amongst the Blood who don't agree with what Lucius was doing. Those who want to try and live alongside the humans and not rule over us."

"It's likely to be Ignatius Grey, isn't it? That's what Fen said. He saw Ignatius." And Ignatius Grey didn't want peace with the humans. I had been paying attention to the news and rumors afoot in the City in the lead-up to the negotiations. Ignatius Grey would be a new Lord Lucius if he gained control over the Blood Court. He was power-hungry and ruthless. There were other, more moderate, factions within the Blood, but until one of their leaders played the game as ruthlessly as Ignatius to get what they wanted, it seemed unlikely that they would defeat him. If they didn't . . .

"It's starting to seem that way, yes," Simon said.

"Which is why we wanted to keep you out of this," Guy said. "This isn't going to be a picnic. It's dangerous. We don't know what's going to happen during the negotiations."

"You think Ignatius will try something?"

"I'm not making any guesses as to what anyone will do," Guy said.

That was a lie. It was his job—his duty—as a Templar to try and outflank the enemy, to be a few steps ahead of them. Which meant that, as usual, they were still trying to keep things from me. My fingers curled and I relaxed them with an effort, feeling heat run through my prentice chain. "Surely no one will try actual . . . violence with the Fae there. The Veiled Queen would crush anyone who did."

"We have to hope that you're correct in that assessment," Lily said, "but we don't know."

"Which is why you need to think about whether you still want to be part of this," Simon said.

"The alternative being to sit in my room while I wait to find out what's happening or for war to break out?"

"You'd be safe at the Academy," Simon said. "I want you to consider this carefully, Sass. If not for your own sake, then think of Mother and Hannah."

A low blow. "I can't be wrapped in cotton wool because Edwina died. That's not fair."

"Life isn't. So please, think hard. You know too much now," Simon said. "If something happened . . ."

"I won't tell."

"Not willingly," Guy muttered.

Lily shot him an exasperated look. "Stop trying to scare her."

I shivered suddenly. Did Guy really think it might come to that? Being coerced to tell what I'd learned here? Did that mean Fen was in danger too?

"I—"

"It's late," Guy said. "There's nothing more we can do here. We should leave Simon and Bryony to do what they can for Reggie. The rest of us need sleep. We can talk more in the morning. Saskia, you should go back to Mother's. Lily will go with you."

I felt my jaw clench. Dismissed again, like a schoolgirl. I was starting to understand Fen's anger all too clearly. But I wasn't going to convince Guy or Simon that they should let me stay. There wasn't anything I could do to help. I looked to Lily, who was watching me with an odd expression. "All right," I said. "Lily, are you ready to go?"

She nodded, and after kissing Simon and stopping to squeeze Holly's shoulder briefly, she led me out of the ward. I was quiet as we made our way back to the main tunnels. Lily moved soundlessly, as she usually did, looking formidable in her black leather, her hair still braided tightly. I hadn't seen her wear it like that since the first few weeks after Lucius died. She'd seemed to be growing more relaxed amongst our world, but tonight she was on alert, her body telegraphing the same readiness for action that Guy's usually did.

As we turned out of the tunnel that held the first door, she glanced back the way we'd come.

"Did you leave something?" I asked.

"No." She tilted her head at me, as if considering something.

"Did Simon send you with me to see if you could convince me to do what he wants?"

"No. To keep you safe." Her smile flashed briefly, lightening her expression like a flame leaping to life. "But safety is not the only thing that's important. I think you should do what you think is right. Your brothers do too, deep down. That's why they're so busy trying to convince you to stay out of things. They know you're too much like them."

"That's hypocritical."

"They're men. They don't always make sense. They just want to keep you safe." She hesitated.

"Is there something else?" Lily didn't usually prevaricate. She either stayed quiet or said exactly what she was thinking.

"It's about Fen."

I hadn't expected that. "What about him?"

"The vision he had at the warrens. It was . . . painful."

My skin chilled. "How painful?"

"From where I stood, very. Enough for him to take Bryony's potion without arguing. And I'm not sure that stopped the pain entirely."

"Why are you telling me this?"

"Your touch helps. Perhaps you should go to him."

I stared. "Simon and Guy would throw a fit if they found out."

"I thought you didn't care what your brothers thought." Lily's eyes held a challenge. "Fen was brave tonight. It's not easy to be the outsider stepping into this fight."

I looked at the clock. "It's almost four a.m."

"You're always telling me you don't want to be just a well-behaved human girl. So why do you care?"

Definitely a challenge. I wondered why she was encouraging me to do something that Simon would disapprove of. They were most often a united front. But apparently Fen had won her respect. Or else she had a different agenda in making sure that he was all right.

"You think I should go to him?"

"Yes."

"He seemed very angry."

"All the better that someone try to talk to him before he has a chance to do something stupid because of that anger."

"He might not want to listen to me. I am Simon's sister, after all."

Lily smiled at that. "Oh, I think of all of us, you probably have the best chance of persuading him. Except maybe for Holly, and she's too busy with worrying about Regina right now to worry about Fen too much. Not to mention calming Guy down."

"Guy . . . he doesn't like what Simon is doing?"

"No, he doesn't. But that's something that Guy and Simon have to deal with. They've dealt with philosophical differences before."

"Whose side are you on?"

She cocked her head, studied me in her unnerving way. "I'm not for Ignatius Grey, or for the Blood destroying the treaties. The rest is semantics. Whose side are you on?"

Mine. But then I saw Fen's face again. Not just mine perhaps. It seemed my night was not yet over.

The night felt very dark, pressing in around the 'cab despite the fact that we were still in the relatively well-lit streets of Greenglass, deep in the human boroughs. We hadn't even reached the border boroughs yet.

What was I doing?

Well past the middle of the night and I was going to seek out a man and offer him . . . what exactly?

I didn't know him terribly well.

Didn't know why I wanted to help him.

Didn't even know if my help would be welcome.

Crazy. I should just tell the driver to turn the 'cab around and go home. Tomorrow would be soon enough to seek out Fen.

Tomorrow would be soon enough to face all this craziness.

But if I went home—back to my mother's house, or back to my room at the Guild—then I would be doing exactly what everyone wanted me to do. Playing it safe. Staying out of trouble. Following the rules set down by my brothers. One of whom had been breaking the rules all along.

And Fen would be left alone and hurting.

I tightened my grip on my purse and set my teeth. Simon had been lying to me. Would probably keep lying to me if he thought it would keep me out of trouble.

Fen, on the other hand, seemed willing to tell me the truth.

The 'cab hissed when the driver slowed as we hit a rut in the road. A quick glance out the window revealed that we were passing into Brightown.

Even at this hour, there were taverns and theater halls

doing business, their lights spilling out across the darkened streets, mingling with the sounds of laughter, music, and frivolity—though the crowds were thinner than usual, thinner even than the lateness of the hour would explain. I had been in this part of the City before in the early hours, out with fellow students or attending one of the performances at the Gilt, the largest of the theater halls.

There had always been more people than this. I shivered and clutched my wrap around me. Despite the warmth of late summer, there seemed to be a chill in the air. I told myself that the weather must be the reason for the lack of people, but I knew it wasn't true. No, the real reason that was keeping people off these streets was plain and simple.

Fear.

I knew how they felt. Fear was riding with me in the 'cab right now. Fear for my brothers, for Reggie, for the whole damned city. And, more pressingly, fear of how Fen might react to me turning up on his doorstep. Nerves jittered through me like angry wasps. Only when the 'cab came to a halt outside the Swallow did I look across to Lily, who had insisted on accompanying me this far. She nodded encouragement and I managed a smile before I opened the door and stepped out into the night.

The 'cab driver took off in a hurry after I'd alighted, leaving me facing the wide double doors of the Swallow's Heart. Where hopefully I would find Fen.

I hesitated, studying the windows of the tavern's upper levels, trying to remember if Fen's faced the street. But the windows were uniformly dark, curtains tightly drawn and letting out no light. In contrast, lights shone on the first and second floors of the Dove.

I tried not to think too hard about what the occupants of those rooms might be doing. I had come here to see Fen, to make sure he was all right. That was all. Wasn't it?

Two large men leaned on either side of the door, seemingly relaxed. But they came alert as I walked closer, studying me carefully. One of them smiled at me.

"Not smart to be out so late alone, miss," he said. "Ain't safe."

"I won't be alone for long," I said, then regretted my choice of words as his grin widened and a knowing look came over his face.

"If you're looking for customers, love, then you're in the wrong place too. The Figgs don't take kindly to poaching."

I gave him my best imitation of one of my mother's withering looks. "I am not a prostitute. I'm looking for somebody."

"Oh? And who would that be?"

"Fen—" I realized with a start that I didn't know his last name. If he even had one.

The grin changed again, and this time his friend joined in with a laugh. "Him, huh? Guess you told the truth, then. That one doesn't pay for it."

"Is he here?" I wanted to cut them off before I heard more about Fen's preferences than I wanted to hear.

"He came in a while ago," the first man said thoughtfully. He stroked the waxed tips of his moustache. "Whether he's still about is anyone's guess. Tricky, our Fen is." He made a half bow. "Why don't you go in and find out? Tell you what—if he's not, you come back here and we'll see you get home safe."

I didn't know exactly how to take that. I decided to pretend I didn't know there was more than one interpretation. "Thank you," I said. "That would be very kind. I'll be sure and tell Holly that you were so helpful."

Their demeanor changed somewhat. "You know Miss Holly?"

"She's a friend of my brother's."

One of them went pale. "Your brother wouldn't be Guy DuCaine, would he?"

"Yes."

They exchanged a look. "Right. Well. Like I said, miss, if that Fen ain't in there, you come out here and we'll get you another 'cab or a hackney quick enough. We take care of Miss Holly's friends here."

Or took care of women whose brothers had swords almost as tall as they were, I thought cynically, but I summoned a pleasant smile. "I will."

They stepped back to let me pass and I walked into the Swallow. Here at least there was a crowd. The room was awash with light and sparkle and noise and the almost overwhelming stink of too much perfume, cigars, and spilled beer and whiskey.

Not all that different from the last hours of a ball, actually.

I let my eyes adjust to the bright lights and started to look for Fen.

It was difficult in the crush to see more than a few feet past where I stood. So I took a punt that he might be at the bar and headed toward the lines of people who I assumed were trying to get their drinks made up.

I drew a few odd looks and one leering proposition that I dealt with by applying the heel of my boot to the instep of the offender. I could have set his ugly brass tiepin on fire, of course, but I was trying not to draw too much more attention to myself.

I wormed my way through the crush to get to a point where I could at least see the bar.

No Fen. Damn. Or words even less polite than that. I hesitated, wondering whether I should go up to his room or just take the more sensible route and go home.

I was halfway back across the room toward the exit when I paused, a vision of the pain on Fen's face floating before my eyes for a moment.

Was I a coward to leave when I could help him?

No, just sensible.

Well. It might be sensible, but I also knew that Lily had been right. It was the right thing to do to come here. I could help him. And if I helped him, he might actually decide to stay in the delegation, which I needed him to do. If he backed out, I had little doubt that my brothers would try to sideline me again.

So being a coward would just hurt him and me.

I braced myself to fight my way back through the crowd to the staircase that I thought led to the rooms over the Swallow rather than to the entrance of the Dove and its services. That would be a mistake I didn't want to have to explain.

On a normal night, in a normal time, I might have admitted to some degree of curiosity as to what the inside of a brothel looked like, but tonight I couldn't afford the distraction.

I chose correctly and soon enough found myself at Fen's unassuming door. Unassuming except for the wardlight turning it to glimmering silver. I couldn't remember if the wards had been active when I was here before—I'd been too angry to really pay much attention at the time. Still, surely he was unlikely to have anything too harmful. I raised my hand to knock, then paused again. Or was he? He'd seemed so angry when he stormed out.

I still wasn't sure why. I didn't like the fact that Simon had kept me in the dark, but I could see that there was some merit to finding a cure—if they could find a true cure rather than one that required killing vampires. But something had obviously touched a nerve with Fen. Touched it to the quick.

Before I could make up my mind, the door swung inward to reveal Fen glaring at me. "Do you always stand around in hallways in the middle of the night making people's wards buzz?"

"I—" I'd woken him. Again. He wore a pair of trousers—loose black cotton, not quite buttoned properly—that I couldn't imagine him wearing in public. No shirt.

Which left a lot of bare Fen available for my perusal.

For a moment, I couldn't quite remember why I'd come. Rake and border boroughs half-breed hedonist he might be, but he obviously did something to keep his body well honed. He was lean and muscled and there was an intriguing trail of dark hair leading down his abdomen and disappearing under the waistband of his trousers.

"Why are you here, Saskia?" he asked, not sounding pleased.

I dragged my wits back together. As attractive as I might find him, right now it seemed the sentiment wasn't returned.

"I thought you might need me."

"Oh?" His voice deepened and his look of sleepy irritation turned altogether more speculative.

I decided to ignore both the look and the little answering jump of my pulse. "I thought you might be in pain," I said. "Lily said your vision at the warrens hurt you."

"I'm fine," he said bluntly. "I took Bryony's potion."

I studied him. His pupils were large in the dark green of his irises, their darkness echoed by the circles under his eyes. He didn't look like a man feeling no pain. Rather more like one fighting his demons. "I think you're lying." I dropped my gaze to his wrist. The chain wrapped around it. "And that tells me I'm right."

He blew out a breath, rested his head briefly against the doorjamb, then lifted it again. "Saskia, I'm tired. I'm not in the mood to deal with any DuCaines right now."

"Isn't that cutting off your nose to spite your face?"

"It's my nose." He tilted his head. "Do your brothers know you're here?"

"Why do you care?"

"I think there's enough tension in this situation right now without adding fuel to the fire. Don't you?"

"I think that I can help you and that what Simon and Guy don't know won't hurt them."

"Is that the family motto?" There was an edge of bitterness to his tone.

"Let me in and we can talk about it."

"I don't think that's such a good idea."

"Why not?"

"Because if I let you in, I might do something stupid."

"Are you forgetting the fact I can set you on fire?"

"No. But I have a feeling that you might be the type who does stupid things too."

"Let me in, Fen. Let me help you."

He looked at me for a long moment, then stepped back. "So be it. But this was your choice—don't forget that."

He let me past him, then shut the door. The room was nearly dark, the only light coming from a couple of almost spent candles set in brass holders on the mantel.

There were gaslights on the walls. I walked over and turned one on. Somehow illumination seemed a safer option than intimate darkness. When I turned back, Fen still stood by the door, watching me.

"Afraid of the dark?" he said softly. He leaned against the door, seemingly casual, but there was something too careful in his stance. Something trying to mask pain or . . . I couldn't quite decide. Something both tightly wound and carefully held at bay.

"Anyone who lives in this City and isn't, is an idiot," I said, deliberately ignoring the challenge in his tone. I looked around the room, then moved to one of the low armchairs. I removed my boots with quick movements and sat, tucking my legs up in the chair, finding my favorite position. "Why don't you come sit down and I'll see if I can make you feel better."

Fen cocked his head at me. "If you go around talking like that to all the boys you meet, Prentice DuCaine, then you have reason to be afraid of the dark."

Apparently he thought flirting was going to scare me away. He needed to think again. I wasn't going to play his games. "Right now I'm worried about you."

"About the delegation, you mean?"

I shook my head at him. "That's not why I came. But I won't lie to you—"

"Well, that puts you in the minority," he interrupted.

"Oh, be quiet. I have just as much reason to be upset with Simon and the rest of them as you do. If not more. Come and sit down." I patted the velvet chair next to mine, trying to coax him like I did Hannah when she was in one of her moods.

He waited a long moment, then obeyed. But not before he picked up a shirt from another chair as he passed and dropped it over his head, hiding all that expanse of muscle and chest from my view. I tried to ignore the part of me that wanted to protest. I was here to help him. Nothing more. This was about ease and comfort. Nothing different from the touches we'd already shared.

But once he'd lowered his long, lean form into the chair, I hesitated, not entirely sure where to put my hands. Should I take one of his? Or lay my hands on his head? Simon would do the latter, I thought, but whatever it was that let me do this for Fen, it wasn't healer power.

And Fen had been right—I wasn't entirely sure I wouldn't do something less than sensible.

"What's wrong?" he asked, tilting his head back to look up at me, eyes half closed against the light. He looked like a big black cat, half languid ease and half coiled power.

He looked . . . tempting.

I was determined not to be tempted. "Nothing." Setting my jaw so I wouldn't ask him to put some more clothes on, I looked at his right arm, where the chain snaked around his wrist. "Have you been wearing that all the time?"

He made a noncommittal noise.

Even in the yellowish light I could see that the skin beneath the chain was bruised and angry-looking. But, if I judged his mood correctly, this was hardly the time to ask more about his visions. I should talk to Holly when I got a chance. Perhaps I could come up with an alloy that might work to block the visions without hurting him. After all, the main reason that metalmages with an affinity for iron were valued was because they did best at creating alloys with the same properties. Not that any one of us had actually cracked the code yet and come up with something that did everything iron did.

We had alternatives, but none of them were true substitutes. They didn't last as long as iron, or if they did, they lacked the same strength when you tried to work them.

"If you're going to do something, do it," Fen said from beside me. His voice sounded slightly strained . . . as though he was fighting with himself.

I took a deep breath, then laid my hand on his forearm. That seemed safe enough. His muscles were tense beneath my palm, but as I closed my fingers gently, he let out a breath and I could almost see some of the strain releasing. His eyes drifted shut and he leaned his head back against the chair.

"You were hurting, weren't you?" I said.

Another untranslatable noise.

"Men," I muttered. Then, slightly louder, "We had a deal, you and I. I said I would help you with this. You should have asked me."

"I had other things on my mind," he said.

Simon, he meant. Ignatius. Atherton. Reggie. Things I didn't want to talk about now. Not when I was so bone-tired and couldn't really remember why I couldn't just lie down on Fen's bed and go to sleep. But still, there was no sleep to be had if I didn't know whether Fen was coming back tomorrow to reaffirm his decision to join the human delegation.

First, though, a few minutes surcease for him. If nothing else, it might improve his temper.

I stayed quiet, watching him breathe. Feeling the rhythm of my own breath synchronize with his. His eyes stayed shut and I wondered for a moment if he had fallen asleep, but then decided not. He was more relaxed, but there was still an underlying awareness in his body, and traces of fatigue and pain still tightened his face.

And this was before he was expected to use his powers for us, to deliberately open himself to more pain. I believed in the necessity of the treaty, that the City would fall if we didn't have it to limit the excesses of the Blood and Beast Kind. Fall for humans, at least.

But I was starting to realize that there was also a cost to keeping the peace. I'd known what Guy risked in the Templars, but he'd been a knight for so much of my life, I was almost inured to that danger. I'd learned how to shut off the worry and anxiety and wall it away in a part of my brain that I could ignore most of the time.

Simon had seemed safe enough once he'd left the Templars for the healers. Yes, his work carried risks, risks that had been amplified with the appearance of Lily in our lives. I hadn't truly known how much risk until tonight.

And here was another man at risk. One who didn't even seem to care, like Simon and Guy did. Which made me wonder exactly why I cared about him. Because the truth was, I did. Maybe that was why Holly and Lily had warned me off Fen. Because he could charm and snare an unwary woman. Well, charm me he may have, but I would do my best to avoid the trap. That would just be putting myself at risk of an altogether different kind. Right now I needed to focus on the negotiations.

If I got to be part of them.

If I could convince this man to stay with us. I knew one way to try, of course. That was simple enough. I could give in to temptation and try and snare him first.

I didn't think he'd fight too hard, even though he might offer a token protest.

As if he could hear my thoughts, Fen stirred, his arm flexing beneath my hand. I fought the temptation to stroke him, to soothe, to run my own hands along the warm skin and see what happened. At his throat, I saw his pulse beating a little too fast.

And that made me wonder what *he* was thinking about. Made my own pulse bump up a notch or two.

Don't be stupid, I thought fiercely. I needed to do something to break the air of intimacy that seemed to have stolen into the room and surrounded us, weaving a web that was drawing me closer to him.

I took a breath. "Are you feeling better?"

"Define better." One eye cracked half open. "My head hurts less."

"What about your temper?" It was a risky course of conversation, but I had to ask.

The other eye opened and his head lifted. "My temper?"

"You were . . . angry when you left."

"Don't you think I had a right to be?"

"I didn't say you didn't. I asked how you were feeling." I pulled my hand away.

Fen winced. I reached to put my hand back and he moved his arm out of reach.

I leaned back in my own chair. If that was how he wanted it, so be it. "Well?"

"What you really want to know is if I'm still going to be part of the delegation."

Well, so much for skirting the subject. I had to remember that he was quick, this man. "Yes." I nodded, folding my arms across my chest. "Yes, I would like to know the answer to that question."

"So that you get to go."

"No. Well, not entirely," I amended. "I want to know that you'll do it because I think that we need you, Fen. You might be able to see something coming that no one else has a chance to. Something that might make all the difference."

"Or I might see nothing. Or kill myself trying. Or get killed."

Kill himself? Was the pain that bad? He'd added the "or get killed" as an afterthought. Trying to cover up the bit of truth he'd blurted unknowingly.

"If you don't try, then you'll definitely see nothing. As for the rest, well, the future is uncertain. You know that better than anyone." I tried to coax a smile from him. "But I will help you with the pain and I'm sure Simon will too if you ask. There are Fae healers at St. Giles. Lady Bryony or—"

"Bryony sa'Eleniel would want nothing to do with my kind."

"Bryony? Why would she have any issue with you? She was perfectly civil tonight."

He looked away. "Tonight was different. You don't know—"

"I do. And I also know that she has helped both Holly and Lily. And Lily's a *wraith*." The Fae hated wraiths. But Bryony had made her peace with Lily. Which meant she should have no issue with Fen's heritage. "Bryony's a healer, Fen. She'll help you if she can."

"I don't want any help from the Fae."

I bit down my retort. Exasperating man. "Have it your way. You're the one who has to bear the pain."

"Nice to hear that acknowledged."

I sighed. I didn't think that this conversation was going to get any easier. Or any more useful. Lily had been wrong. I should have waited until morning. Let him sleep it off and give him time to think. If Fen was anything like Simon and Guy, he would prefer time on his own to let his temper cool.

Pity that we're almost out of time, the waspish voice in my head said.

I stood abruptly. "I should let you sleep." I looked around for my boots, spotted them a little ways from the chair.

"Going so soon?" His tone was almost nasty and I felt myself flinch a little.

"I don't think there's anything else for me to do here."

"Gods, Saskia . . ."

"What?"

He hesitated, then shook his head. "No. You're right. You should go."

"And you should learn some manners," I snapped, my own temper suddenly biting under the strain of fatigue and confusion and tangled attraction.

"Oh?"

"You could at least thank me for helping you," I said. "And perhaps see that I got to a 'cab safely."

"You want thanks?" He seemed to flow out of the chair, his eyes suddenly sparking green. "Really?"

"Yes."

"Fine. Then let me say thank you, Miss DuCaine." His voice was almost a growl and I was too distracted by the glare on his face to react when he closed the gap between us with one sudden step and pulled me close.

"Wha—"

The protest died on my lips as his mouth closed over mine.

Chapter Twelve

SASKIA

⚡

He tasted dark and dangerous. Hot and sweet. His kiss was fierce, almost desperate, and an answering wave of desperate heat flowed up through me, making me wonder if my chain was burning. But no, it wasn't the metal that was hot—it was my skin. As though all my nerves had sparked to life with wanting.

The chain against my throat was chill in comparison.

Fen pulled me closer, flush against him, so there was no escaping the evidence that he wanted me too. His erection pressed against me, sending another wave of pleasure shivering over me.

Desire. Gods. I wanted to lose myself in it, to chase away what had happened tonight, but I fought to keep my head above the rising tide of lust. To think rather than feel.

Because desire wasn't the reason—or at least not the only reason—that he was kissing me, and with that realization came an equal one that if desire wasn't the reason, then I didn't *want* him to kiss me.

I pulled away, making the movement even more definite as he tried to pull me back toward him, until I was free from his grasp and several steps separated us.

"What did you do that for?" I said.

He looked both annoyed and half amused. "You wanted me to thank you."

"You think that's a thank-you?"

"I don't usually get complaints." His pupils were large, darkening his irises to a green like midnight.

"Then you are kissing the wrong sort of women."

"Oh? What sort would that be?"

"Idiots," I spat.

"You didn't seem to mind."

"Of course I mind!"

"Why? Didn't you enjoy it?" His eyes narrowed. "You're not a virgin, are you?"

"I mind," I said slowly, ignoring his question. I wasn't going to give him the satisfaction of answering. It was none of his business. "Because you were kissing me to make a point."

"You're wrong."

Wrong? Did he think I was stupid? The chain around my neck suddenly felt very warm as my temper flared and I directed the power into the fire behind me, which suddenly whooshed to furious life. "Is that so? So why did you kiss me exactly?"

His eyes glittered dangerously, his mouth twisting, then relaxing before he spoke. "Because this has been a pretty horrible day, and right now I don't want someone to hold my hand. What I want is another sort of touch altogether."

My skin was catching on fire, I was sure of it. His voice seemed to slide over it like warm velvet, stoking the flames higher. "I—"

"Which is why you should leave. Because right now, I figure the only thing that might make me feel better would be tossing up your skirts and fucking you."

My mind went blank as the breath left my lungs. And then with a rush, filled again with images of him doing exactly that.

My gaze slid to the bed, to the rumpled sheets, the dark velvet counterpane that was a deep and dangerous red. Deep enough to sink into. I could feel the cotton and velvet against my skin as truly as though I lay upon them, pressed into them with the weight of the man before me. The sensation, true or not, ignited another wave of desire, a pulse that started between my legs and exploded out from there so swiftly, I felt my knees tremble.

Control. I bit my lip, forced my gaze back to Fen. He couldn't have meant it. He was trying to get me to leave.

I didn't want to go.

I didn't want to do the sensible thing, the right thing, the well-behaved-human-girl thing. I wanted what he wanted. Wanted to lose myself in whatever madness caused this heat between us and forget the world beyond the walls for a time.

But the fact remained that he was saying the things he was saying to scare me away.

Or was he?

There was color in his face too and his pupils were dark pools, shading out the green. His breath came, I fancied, a little faster than it should as he watched me.

What would happen were I to call his bluff? And how exactly could I do that?

"You should go," Fen said, his voice a low hum that seemed to only increase the tension vibrating in the room.

My mouth was dry. I swallowed before replying. "What if I don't want to?"

"Saskia . . . ," he said warningly. "Don't push me. I'm not one of your nice safe human boys."

"Maybe not. Maybe I'm not who you think I am either."

"Is that so?" He tilted his head, his expression suddenly intent. "I'm not playing a game here. If you stay, then I'm going to take you to bed. Is that what you want?"

I managed a single nod, unable to look away. Unable to deny what I was feeling.

"Very well. Take off your dress."

I had the feeling he was still testing, still seeing if I would stay or flee. But even as I tried to work out how I felt about that, my fingers reached for the buttons that held the front of my dress together. One small mercy of wearing one of my student dresses, I could get in and out of it by myself. Only now I wasn't by myself, was I?

I almost missed the next button at the thought. Glanced down at it to find my place again, glanced back up, hit the wall of Fen's searing gaze and almost lost my nerve. My fingers trembled but I continued on, freeing the buttons one by one until I was able to shrug my shoulders and have the dress fall to my feet.

Fen sucked in a breath. I stayed very still, very aware of the thinness of the cotton of my chemise and my drawers, of the tightness of my corset against my skin. Of how that skin tingled as Fen watched me, motionless. The silence in the room seemed to sharpen, making the air crystal, likely to shatter with one false move. The only tiny sounds were the breaths we each tried to control.

Through that silence my pulse roared in my ears, a beat that grew stronger and stronger each second I stood there, submitting to his gaze.

Feeling the hunger for him fire within me as if his hands were stroking my body, finding all the places I most liked to be touched. Yet he hadn't even touched me yet.

How could I stand it when he did?

How could I bear it if he didn't?

Fen moved then, one step, two. Bringing him close enough that I could feel the heat of his skin, could smell the faint echoes of the cologne he wore and the scent of excited male and a trace of smoke and alcohol. Not close enough to touch, though.

I stayed still, not daring to move. Not wanting to move. Somehow, waiting for him to tell me what to do next was everything I wanted right in this moment, some relief from fighting so hard to be seen. Giving in to someone who saw me perhaps too clearly.

Fen leaned closer, his lips almost touching mine. I wanted his kiss, wanted the taste of him again, but instead he moved to my ear.

"I want you kneeling on the bed. Hands and knees."

I didn't know if my legs were even capable of holding me up, but I did as he asked, part of my mind still wondering why. The rest of me knew all too well. I would do whatever it took to get him to touch me, to take me. To ease this hunger he'd ignited and chase away everything else that was tumbling through my head.

The mattress gave beneath me as I climbed onto the bed, the velvet soft against my skin, the combination both welcoming and intimidating. There was no hiding from the truth of what I wanted and what I was going to do here. My arms trembled as I arranged myself as he wanted, tiny tremors that echoed the shivers of sensation that traveled across my skin.

It was tempting to bend my arms, drop my head to the mattress. But that would be hiding. And not what he'd asked of me. Instead I bowed my body sideways so I could look back at Fen.

He hadn't moved from where he stood. But as I watched he pulled the shirt over his head and dropped it.

Then he moved. Stalked across the room so fluidly that it was clear that he wasn't entirely human. Something about the way his bones and muscles moved was too swift. Too sleek.

Too wild.

It made me want him even more.

I could feel the pulse of it, beating between my legs, could feel my nipples hard and tight against the confines of my corset. Wanted to rip every scrap of clothing from my body so that there was nothing to stop him from touching me.

I'd never felt this before. The sheer wanting of it.

Madness.

I was happy to lose my sanity if that was the case.

Fen stopped at the foot of the bed, his eyes locked with mine.

"Look away," he said.

I moved my head, gazed straight ahead, feeling the loss of eye contact like a wound. I held myself there, feeling as though I might just come apart entirely if he didn't touch me soon.

One heartbeat. Two. Three. *Four*. My nerves tightened, stretched, quivered. I fought to stay still, not to turn around or roll over and scream, "Take me."

And then it came. The flat of his hand stroked the length of my spine, caressing me from nape to hip. Then both hands seized my chemise, clenched, ripped, let the ruined cotton and lace fall off me. Then they returned, stroking my skin, circling restlessly, yet carefully. Coming near all the places I wanted to be touched, dipping toward the slide of my buttocks and drifting down my sides a little but never quite touching me.

I bit my lip, trying not to moan. I managed to stay silent, but I couldn't quite still the impatient arches and dips of my body as it responded to his touch.

"Like that, do you?" His voice sounded rough, hungry. "Good."

His hands slid up my back again, slowly this time, so I could feel the small pauses as his palms slid over the small obstacles of the lacing of my corset. I held my breath, sure that he would free them. I wanted him to. My breasts ached, nipples screaming to be released, to feel his fingers and his mouth. But he didn't. Instead he tracked the curves of my corset, the places where it drew my waist in, contouring the lines of my body. His hands slid down, then around, and then, finally, finally up to my breasts, cupping them through the satin and cotton, the pressure of his hands only deepening the longing to be able to really feel him.

His hands pulled the fabric tighter against my skin, so it scraped the too sensitive buds of my nipples and I moaned and pushed into him.

"Gods." The word was soft but urgent. His hands moved again, sweeping around to my back, sliding down, down, until he was gripping my thighs, pulling me back against him, so I finally—finally—felt the hard length of him against me. I moaned again and he moved away, his hands repeating their tearing act with my drawers this time.

I went still as he pulled them free. Gods indeed. I was bare to him now, nowhere to hide or go or pretend. He could, no doubt, see the evidence that I wanted him.

"A little farther up the bed," he said, and I could hear the fierceness of him in his voice. Knew suddenly that he was struggling for control just as I was.

Gloried in the knowledge.

I made my movements slow, deliberate, as I eased myself a little farther up the mattress. Took the stance he wanted again. Held myself there against every instinct I had to beg him to come close again. I closed my eyes, not willing to look.

I heard the rustle of cotton, then felt the mattress dip as he climbed up behind me.

Felt him slide against me, his cock slipping between my legs, rubbing against me as he put his thighs either side of mine. "Gods," he muttered again as for a few seconds I couldn't help arching against him, easing the ache between my legs against him, feeling pinwheels and starbursts of pleasure with each slippery contact.

I didn't have long to tease him. His control was slipping as fast as mine. His hands tightened on my hips and he pulled himself back and then took me with one hard thrust that felt so good I almost came.

But that would be too easy.

"Not yet," he said roughly, and he eased back, then thrust again. Long and slow and fierce, setting a rhythm that wiped every thought from my head. I didn't know if he was taking me or I was taking him as he drove me higher and higher.

Slow became faster, then faster again. His breath was fast and rough and mingled with my gasps. I felt myself begin to quiver around him and one of his hands slid around and pressed once, hard and sharp, and I came with a shuddering moan, sliding forward in a boneless heap of pleasure.

"Oh no," he said. "We're not done yet."

He freed himself, rolled me over and settled himself against me once more, not yet sliding home. The feel of him made all the nerves that were still pulsing with delight shiver and tremble all over again. I lifted my arms above my head, lazy with satisfaction. Fen's eyes were dark, wild almost. He reached up to grip my wrists and his chain brushed my skin, the iron a sudden shock.

"Take it off," I said.

He froze. His pupils flared wider as he studied me. I didn't know why I was asking what I was. Only knew that I wanted him as naked as he had me.

"Just us," I said.

He nodded once then, slowly eased back a little so he could undo the chain. He unwound it carefully, hissing at one point as though it hurt, then dropped it over the side of the bed.

"You can't stop touching me now," he said. "I want you against me."

A smile stretched my lips. "I can do that." I settled myself, draped my legs around him, arching to invite him back in.

Then it began again. Not so fast or wild this time. Instead, we moved together, a sliding, twisting dance that moved us across each other and the bed, bodies straining, skin touching.

His mouth came down on mine and the kiss was dark and deep, almost desperate. We followed each other over the bed, at no point breaking contact altogether, always lips or hands or bodies joined, drowning in the pool of pleasure we created, our own moment of escape.

I lost count during the night of just how many times I came or he came or which of us started each new round. It was only Fen and I and, at the end, all I knew was his body curled around mine as I finally surrendered to sleep.

I woke when the mattress dipped beside me, the warmth of Fen's body suddenly gone. I rolled over, intending to coax him back to my side once more.

He sat on the edge of the bed, twining the iron around his wrist.

My stomach chilled. "What are you doing?"

He didn't meet my gaze. "It's past seven. You need to go home."

The chill in my stomach stole outward, making my arms and legs feel strangely numb. I reached for the velvet counterpane, dragged it around my body. "You want me to leave?"

That brought his eyes to mine. "I think it's best. Don't you?"

I blinked. "I thought—"

"Don't." He cut me off as he stood and started dressing. "This was just one night, Saskia. Don't start weaving any stories of happy endings around me."

My jaw clenched even as my stomach twisted. "You enjoyed it."

He nodded. "Yes. I did. So did you. But that's all there is. Now, you need to get home before your brothers find out you're not there already."

"My brothers? Is that what this is about? You're worried about what Simon and Guy will think?"

"No. I'm just trying to be clear. I'm not—" He broke off, ran his hands through his hair. "There's no future in this."

"What if I'm not looking for a future?"

"Girls like you always want a future."

That finally tipped me over. The curl of anger I felt was stronger than the humiliation of being tossed out of his bed. "I told you last night. I'm not the girl you think I am."

"Oh really? You just want someone to fuck when the urge takes you?" One dark eyebrow arched, skeptical as the tone that turned his voice to a knife's edge.

"What if I do?"

"The answer's still no."

"I see." I spoke the words carefully, feeling as though they might shatter in my mouth. The anger was still there, but beyond it was a lurking pool of hurt that wanted to rise up and wash over me. Obviously I had been wrong about him. I thought we had connected last night. Thought there had been something more to it than just satisfying the roar of want we shared.

I pulled the counterpane tighter, climbed out of bed and found my dress and my corset. I didn't bother with the shreds of my drawers or my chemise. After a moment's hesitation I dropped the corset as well. My dress would fit well enough without it, thanks to its practical cut. And I'd be damned if I was going to ask Fen to help me.

I pulled the dress on over my head, did up the buttons with jerky motions. My boots—where were my boots?

Then I remembered. By the armchair. I straightened my spine and crossed the room to fetch them. I avoided looking at Fen until I had the shoes on and had found my purse.

Then I turned to face him. "It seems I was right about one thing," I said with a snap in my tone that would hopefully hide anything else that might be lurking beneath the surface.

"Oh?" His voice was as edged as mine.

"Yes. The women who kiss you *are* idiots."

There were far less polite things I could think of to say, but I was trying to keep the last shreds of my dignity. Hard to do when a large part of me was desperately hoping he would reach out to me. Say "Stop. Don't go." Apparently I was as much an idiot as any woman when it came to Fen. Still, I didn't have to be a complete fool and let him know that. "Good-bye, Fen."

I wasn't going to ask him if I'd see him again. If he was going to still be part of our delegation. He could make up his mind himself and the lords of the seven hells could damn him if he turned his back on our bargain.

We could do just fine without him, I was sure.

I turned to leave. I could feel his gaze boring into my back, feel the temper and other things sparking between us, but he didn't speak.

And if he didn't, then I wasn't going to either.

I made it all the way back to my mother's house and into the safety and seclusion of my bedroom before I let the tears come.

Much later the same morning I woke in a foul temper and far too early given how late—or early, rather—it had been when I'd finally slept. I crept down to the garden, carrying my tea, so that I could stand on bare earth for a while and let the power fill me and chase away some of my fatigue. Pity that it could do nothing about my mood.

The day was clear and warm, the powdery blue sky promising heat later. The late-summer sunshine was preposterously cheerful, making everything in the garden shiny and bright. Birds sang and bees buzzed around the flowers, which were blooming riotously, filling the air with scent.

It seemed ridiculous to think that the City outside our garden walls had any troubles at all, let alone that it might stand on the brink of disaster. Surely disasters didn't happen in perfect weather? Surely there should be clouds and storms and a slinking darkness, like the end of the twilight, the half-light the City got her ancient name from?

But no. It seemed not. Reality didn't work that way. Bad things happened regardless of weather or place or rank or if the person they happened to deserved any pain or suffering. The world wasn't a safe, sunny fairy tale.

I needed to remember that. The next few weeks were going to be dangerous. Outward appearances weren't to be believed. Everything needed to be watched and weighed and balanced, and any actions taken carefully. Time to be the adult I was always telling my brothers to believe I was.

I sighed and swallowed the last of the tea, before shaking the few stray leaves at the bottom of the cup onto one of the flower beds. *Fen could probably tell my fortune from the tea leaves*, I thought, and then cursed myself for bringing him to mind. I gritted my teeth, determined not to cry again. So, I'd been an idiot. I'd slept with a man and had my feelings bruised.

It had happened before.

But never quite like last night.

I heard his voice again then and felt his touch, felt my body pulse in remembrance of the things we'd done.

The things we would not be doing again.

Any more than I would be remembering the sweetness

of his kisses and the way he looked at me as he touched me for all those hours we'd shared.

It had been more than just sex.

For me, at least.

Which meant nothing, if Fen was of a different opinion. My fingers curled around the teacup, wanting to fling it at the brick wall just for the satisfaction of hearing it shatter.

No.

Giving in to a tantrum wouldn't make me feel any better. I walked back toward the house, my steps dragging even though I did feel the tiniest bit better for the time I'd spent outside. Part of me wanted nothing more than to climb back into bed and pretend there was nothing to worry about.

This was what I had wanted, I reminded myself. To be let in on the inner secret. To know the truth about what was happening. And I'd wanted Fen too.

It seemed the old saying about being careful what you wished for was true indeed.

As I passed through the back door, Ian, one of the footmen, handed me a letter. "Message for you, Miss Saskia," he said.

I took it cautiously, wondering who was writing to me. Master Aquinas, to tell me I was expelled from the Guild?

Don't be melodramatic. I thanked Ian and headed for the stairs, turning the envelope over to see if the seal might give any clue. But no—it was an unmarked blob of red wax, unrevealing as a mummer's mask.

I was half tempted to leave it unread, but it could well be something important. I tore it open and pulled out a single sheet of paper.

Prentice DuCaine, it read in a carefully elegant hand.

You were wrong. I am the idiot.

If you would come to see me, I'll let you say I told you so.

Please come.

The signature was nothing more than an *F* slashed in three bold strokes.

I stared at the note, not knowing whether to be happy or even more outraged.

So he thought I would come if he called, did he? Well, that was just . . . perfectly correct, I realized with a sigh as I reached my room.

I would go.

I couldn't help myself.

Which, as far as I could tell, made me an idiot beyond any reasonable meaning of the word.

It was well past one o'clock before I got to the Swallow. I had taken time to bathe and dress, carefully choosing something that was flattering but simple. I didn't want Fen thinking I'd made any particular effort, after all. Even if it had taken me twenty minutes to decide on a pair of earrings and longer still to determine how I wanted to wear my hair.

Idiot, indeed.

I hadn't actually expected the Swallow to be open this early, but there were two men at the door as usual, though not the same men as had been there when I'd left the night before.

But like those two, the new bouncers looked somewhat surprised at my appearance. I didn't blame them. I would imagine that men brought the majority of any business that the Swallow did so early.

Still, they let me pass without too much comment. *I should have sent a reply*, I thought as I scanned the tavern. *Should have made him come to me.*

But that would have meant having this meeting with the entirety of Mother's household plus Simon, Guy, Lily, and Holly present.

No thank you to that particular scenario.

It took a moment or two for my eyes to adjust to the dimness, so different from the blaze of the chandeliers that had illuminated the place previously.

Then I saw Fen. At the bar, a place he looked far too comfortable in. I hesitated. This was stupidity. Nothing more or less. But I couldn't make myself turn around and walk away.

Instead, I just watched. The room was nearly empty, maybe twenty people in total, a number that would only fill half the stools along the massive wooden bar, let alone make any sort of impact on the small tables scattered around the place. They were all men—I'd been right about that. Half of them wore evening clothes, so presumably they had been out all night. The others, more plainly dressed, were mostly eating or reading newspapers. Perhaps they were staff rather than patrons. I didn't know or care. They weren't the ones I had come to see, after all.

Fen was alone at the bar, talking amiably to the barman. The green stone dangling from his ear glinted in the low light thrown by the flickering gaslights. There was a glass in front of him—brandy, judging by its color—but it was still mostly full and he didn't reach for it in the long moments while I watched.

Then he turned, saw me. The smile he shot me had me stepping forward before I could think any more. Nerves bloomed with each step.

Silly little girl.

Silly, foolish, stupid little girl.

No matter what I called myself, there was someone deep inside who tossed her head and insisted she didn't care. That what she wanted was sitting before her on that barstool, grinning at her. I still hadn't decided whether I felt sick or happy by the time I reached Fen and hoisted myself onto the stool next to his.

"You came," he said.

"Did you think I wouldn't?"

"Saskia, there's not a oddsman in the City that would've accepted a bet that you would show."

I wasn't entirely sure what that meant. What was he doing here if he was so sure that I wouldn't come? Trolling for a replacement?

I squelched the thought. It was unworthy. "I'll have a brandy," I said to the barman. Fen cocked his head at me but didn't comment. Good. Maybe he was learning.

But still the considering gleam in those green, green eyes made my nerves flare higher.

"How are you feeling?" The question came more out of automatic politeness and my need for something to say than anything else. I dropped my eyes to his wrist, but he wore a long-sleeved white shirt whose cuffs hid his chain from view.

He shook his head. "Nothing to concern yourself about."

That could mean anything from "better" to "hurting like

hell." How long did a person have to know this man before he relaxed enough to actually let her in? A long time, it seemed.

More time than I had in hand and perhaps more time than I wanted to give. The doubts were starting to win. I twisted on the stool. Fen's hand shot out, circled my wrist. "Don't go."

"This was a bad idea."

"I know."

"Then why am I here? I don't understand this, Fen. Why ask me here? You made your feelings perfectly clear earlier."

His head tilted again. "I'm not all that sure myself."

My heart sank again and I looked away. "Then I should go. And you can bother somebody else. I'm sure you don't lack for choice."

"No, I don't."

This time I did slide off the stool. "In that case, I think it's better that I go now, before we both make any more *mistakes*."

Fen moved to block me, coming to his feet and stepping around me in that fluid movement that reminded me of his very mixed heritage. Grace and speed and strength. Power. From the Fae and the Beasts. He radiated heat as well as charm, hard not to step closer, to bask in him.

"Don't go," he repeated.

To my horror, tears rose in my eyes. "Why not?"

"Well," he said, "for one thing, there's this." Then he laid his hands either side of my face and bent down to kiss me.

It was just as good as I remembered. And this time it wasn't backed by anger. No, this time there was a dangerous sweetness to his touch, a warmth that stole through me and melted the walls I'd constructed to defend myself.

I had a horrible feeling that the taste of it could be addictive, potent as any pleasure the Night World, or anywhere else, could offer. And I had even less chance of fighting it than a Nightseeker snared in the grasp of a Blood lord.

Still, I had to try. I broke away from him. "You said this isn't a good idea."

"I also said I'm an idiot," Fen said. He stepped forward. "Is that supposed to be an apology?"

"Yes."

"Try again."

His expression turned serious. "I'm sorry."

"An explanation would also be helpful."

"I'm not sure I can explain." He leaned in again.

I stepped back. "Not here."

His eyebrow lifted. "Are you inviting yourself upstairs?"

"It was a kiss, Fen. Don't get cocky."

"It was a bloody good kiss."

"As I said, don't get cocky." But I had to look away when I said it so I wouldn't move nearer.

He pressed his lips together, lifted his hands, shifted on the barstool slightly as though he were uncomfortable. "All right. I bow to your decision."

"Don't sulk," I said.

"I don't sulk," he shot back. "I'm being gentlemanly."

He said the last with a wicked look, letting me know that he might be behaving himself but what he was thinking was not the sort of thing a gentleman would contemplate. Which didn't help me. I was thinking exactly that sort of thing myself. It was all I could do not to step toward him and ask for another taste.

Which only proved my theory about my level of idiocy. He had tossed me out of his bed this morning, told me there was nothing between us. Yet here he was calling me back. Kissing me.

I wasn't going to be at his beck and call.

"We have things to discuss," I said, settling back on my own stool. I smoothed my hair, then my skirts, then clasped my hands together to stop myself fidgeting like a nervous schoolgirl.

"Discussions aren't much fun," he said.

"This is not the time for fun."

"No?" His tone was lazy. "I think it's the perfect time. Make merry while we still can."

I didn't think I liked the sound of that. It hardly sounded like a man who thought he was about to take part in the treaty negotiations.

"I, for one, would rather make a little less merry now, and make sure there's still time for it later."

"That's because you're a DuCaine," he said.

I found myself suddenly wondering if he'd been drinking. He hadn't tasted of alcohol, but maybe . . . "What's that supposed to mean?"

"Very serious, you DuCaines."

"Because we care about things other than ourselves?"

"Maybe. Maybe you've just forgotten how to have fun."

I felt my eyes narrow at him. "If you're trying to bait me, don't bother. You're the one who asked me here, or have you forgotten?"

"No. I'm hardly likely to forget that."

"Then shall we stop beating around the bush?"

Fen straightened slightly, then looked around the bar. "Not here."

"I think we've already established that I'm not coming up to your room."

"There's a room in the back. It's more . . . private."

Warded, I assumed that meant. Sensible. In his position I might not want the news that I was joining the human's delegation broadcast any sooner than it had to be. My mood lifted slightly. Surely this meant he was going to help us. After all, if he was going to say no, why did he need privacy to say it?

Chapter Thirteen

FEN

I led the way to the back room, hearing Saskia's heels tapping out a staccato rhythm that spoke of irritation—if not outright anger—on the floorboards as she followed me. No doubt she was wondering what the hell I was up to after my less than reasonable behavior this morning.

Which made two of us.

Only I wasn't so much wondering why I had tried to cut her off this morning as why I'd found myself writing a note to ask her to come back so I could apologize.

It had all seemed so clear this morning. Clear that tangling any further with Saskia DuCaine could only bring ruin upon both of us. I couldn't afford to care about someone else. Not when my heart was already torn by the memory of Reggie lying so still and pale down in the bowels of St. Giles.

Surrounded by others suffering her fate. The ones that not even the combined powers of a vampire, Simon DuCaine and Bryony sa'Eleniel had managed to heal.

Sweet Reggie, who had never hurt anyone if she could help it, now perhaps fated to live out her years in a sleep that was only half a step above death.

My little sister, for all intents and purposes. Lost.

Lost to me, as so many others had been lost.

I didn't want to care again. Caring only hurt.

But still, as soon as Saskia had closed the door of my room behind her, I had wanted to go after her.

I had argued with myself all morning. I still wasn't entirely sure if I'd changed my mind because I couldn't afford to fall out with the DuCaines right now—though I wanted to believe I wasn't quite that much of a bastard—or because I wanted the relief Saskia's touch could bring me—again, bastardry—or whether, when it came right down to it, I just wanted her.

The memory of her standing before me, letting the dark gray dress she wore fall to the floor, was seared in my memory. But stronger still was the feeling of her curled against me, skin to skin, her warmth and the sound of her sleeping breath chasing my demons away as easily as her touch held the visions at bay.

For a time I'd been able to forget. To relax.

To be me.

Pity that her brothers would likely make mincemeat of me when they found out I was sleeping with their little sister. Saskia wasn't for the likes of me—even Holly had told me that much.

I knew they were all right.

But I also knew that I couldn't let her go. Not just yet.

Of course, I had to convince her of that. Right now it wasn't the DuCaine males I had to worry about.

No, as I watched Saskia take a seat at the table, tidying her skirts primly around her before she settled to stillness—except for the hand that toyed with the prentice chain around her neck—I was well aware that I was dealing with an angry DuCaine female.

One who could set things on fire with her will. One who didn't need her brothers' help at all to express her displeasure, should she so choose.

I truly had an excellent skill for landing myself in trouble far, far over my head.

I took a seat opposite her. Perhaps I should have brought the brandy with me. A few more shots might have calmed her temper.

Though the stormy shades of gray and green riding her

eyes suggested that the Figgs didn't stock enough brandy to achieve such an outcome.

"Well?" Saskia said after she had studied me for an uncomfortable length of time.

"You said we had things to discuss," I said politely.

Her eyes narrowed. "You wrote a note asking me to come here. You first."

"I apologized already," I said. "I'll do it again"—I added hastily—"but that was why I wanted to see you to apologize."

"Why?"

"Why what?"

"Why are you apologizing? What exactly are you sorry for, Fen? Taking me to bed, or throwing me out of it this morning? Or maybe the way you stormed off last night?"

"Definitely not the first one." I wasn't that stupid. "Unless you want me to be sorry about that . . ."

Her mouth twitched slightly, but her severe expression didn't alter. "No. Not about that."

"I'm definitely sorry about this morning. I don't know exactly what happened."

"That's hardly an explanation."

"Bryony's potion made me temporarily insane?" I offered with a half smile, seeing if I could coax one out of her as well.

"Given the time frame, wouldn't that mean that you took me to bed under the influence of the potion and thought better of it in the clear light of day? I'm not sure that's—"

"That's not what I meant. Definitely not. How about we chalk it up to general male idiocy?"

"I'll take it under consideration," Saskia said with another twitch. "Very well, so you don't regret sleeping with me and you do regret the way we parted this morning. That just leaves the rest of last night. Care to enlighten me as to your thoughts on that?" Her tone had grown very careful with that last sentence. As though she was worried about toppling something fragile over with the wrong choice of words.

"I'll be honest with you. I don't like that your brother didn't tell me what he was doing sooner."

She nodded. "I can understand that. I'm not overly happy with him myself right now, but I can also understand why he is keeping secrets. Can you?"

"Yes. But they're asking me to take a big risk and they don't trust me."

"They don't know you that well—"

I made a noise of protest and Saskia held up a hand to stop me.

"It's true. They know that Holly trusts you, and that helps a lot, but they don't know you, Fen. And you insist on telling everybody that you're not one of the good guys." She tilted her head, something odd riding her expression for the briefest of flashes. "You can't be hurt when some people believe it. But they will trust you if you prove yourself."

"Is that what you're trying to do? Prove yourself?"

"I'm just trying to help. I want the City safe."

"Is that all?"

"I have other goals in life." She reached up, stroked her prentice chain briefly. "But those are not important for the next few weeks."

A few weeks. Not much time. There were a few more days of preparation left to us and then the negotiations would commence. Two weeks to secure the future of the City for another five years.

It seemed ridiculous.

I knew that the treaty was a good thing, that peace—or what passed for peace—amongst the races saved lives and allowed the City to function and prosper, but sometimes it also seemed to cause more problems than it fixed. Perhaps it would be better to let it go, let us all battle it out, let the victor take the spoils and the losers slink off elsewhere.

But that didn't seem very likely, plus it would be a violent and bloody mess of a struggle. One the humans would likely lose.

A few months ago that thought wouldn't have concerned me overly much. But now one of my best friends was in love with a human and the other was lying in a hospital bed with little hope of salvation other than at the hands of another human.

And then there was the very human girl sitting across from me.

Did I want to let her world be swept away?

No.

Which meant that, reluctant as I might be, I was going to take part in these negotiations. Which also meant playing nice and biting my tongue about what I thought of Simon's search for a cure for blood-locking. It also, I imagined, meant Saskia and I were going to have to be circumspect about the fact that we were anything more than friends.

Turned out I didn't need to be concerned. I didn't get a chance to be alone with Saskia over the next two days. No, we were too busy being drilled on delegation protocol and the seemingly endless rules of the negotiations. Who could sit where, who could talk to who, what could or could not be brought into the Treaty Hall.

The lists went on and on and on.

Because we were late to join the delegation, we were sequestered separately with our assigned tutors and had the details drummed into us for hours on end.

I was glad for the excuse to be away from other people, but midway through the second day I would have sold my soul to whoever asked for it in exchange for brandy and the chance to get away from Brother Anthony, the very serious Templar who'd been assigned to instruct me. Saskia's tutor was another Templar, a younger man with dark hair and skin, eyes greener than mine, and a left arm that ended at the elbow. Brother Liam, he'd been introduced as when we'd met.

Saskia had smiled at Liam in welcome, making me think that she knew him already before they had gone off together to wherever their lessons were being held. Brother Anthony had told me to sit, then proceeded to open an ominously large brown leather book at page one and started drilling me as though I was one of his novices, and a particularly recalcitrant one at that.

I'd always been a relatively quick study—it helps in my business to have a good memory for faces, places, and facts—but at times I felt as though my brain would likely burst if I had to parse one more of Anthony's horribly complicated protocol scenarios.

When a knock at the door was revealed to be one of the novices sent to call us to lunch on the second day, I almost ran from the room.

I made my way toward the dining hall without thinking. I knew the way well by now. Over the last few days the only places I'd been within the Brother House were the dining hall, the small chamber where Anthony and I were studying, and the even smaller cell where I was sleeping. Saskia, as far as I could tell, was sleeping somewhere in St. Giles. Guy and Simon had decided it was safer for both of us to stay within the walls that surrounded both St. Giles and the Brother House, where Haven laws were enforced. My cynical side thought the fact that I'd been found a room in the Brother House and Saskia had accommodations in St. Giles was somewhat deliberate on the part of her brothers.

Still, I did see her a few times a day, when we gathered for delegation discussions or when Lily came to take me to the hidden ward to visit Reggie. Saskia was diligent in making sure she got to touch me to relieve my visions, but the small amount of contact was hardly enough to satisfy my need to do more than just hold her hand.

I wondered what Brother Anthony would do if he knew exactly what I was thinking about some of the times I lost my place in our endless lessons.

But there was no time to try and steal away. Between the endless study and the strategizing and spending time with Reggie, I barely had time to eat and snatch a few hours' sleep each night. The few times I'd thought I might have a spare hour to myself, Guy had appeared and dragged me down to the Templar weapons hall, putting me through my paces with sword and pistol until he was satisfied that I knew what I was doing with a weapon. I liked to think he'd even been a little impressed with a few of the sneaky moves I knew.

I wasn't a trained warrior like his brother knights, but I knew how to keep myself alive. Still, I was sporting a number of bruises from our sessions that didn't make sitting down and studying for long stretches any more comfortable.

But even the exertion of sparring with a Templar hadn't really done much to ease my need for Saskia.

I planned to snatch some time to see Reggie after I'd eaten. I wouldn't be able to stay for long. There was meant to be another meeting tonight of the Templar delegates and I was expected to attend. Though attendance consisted largely of listening to the discussions and making notes and trying to ignore the images conjured by my powers. Images of bloodshed and death that followed some of the Templars around like ghastly smoke.

I was starting to dread the visits to Reggie. She was still and silent in that damned hospital bed. She was awake, at least, and sometimes she even responded when asked simple questions. And she still ate and drank. But she showed no signs of improvement beyond that.

My head pounded as I took my place in the queue for food. I could smell coffee, which might help, but what I really wanted was brandy. It was harder to be here in the dining hall; more Templars meant more visions swarming around me.

At least spending time with Brother Anthony meant that I had only one person to deal with, and so I'd largely kept the visions at bay. But even then, spending so much time with a single person meant it was inevitable that I would start to see things surrounding him. So far it hadn't been anything too terrible, but there was a darkness around the man that made me want not to see much more. Or maybe that was just my bad mood.

I filled my plate with food, not really paying any attention to what it was, and then my luck improved and I spotted Saskia and Brother Liam.

As usual, the visions swirled brightly around both of them. Liam—someday I would have to find out more about him—was shadowed by a large black wolf and I also saw him on a horse looking desperately tired and determined, riding toward a burning city through terrain that wasn't familiar to me. The city was walled, which meant it wasn't our City. And everywhere images of the sun followed him. I'd managed to discover that he was a sunmage, so that much made sense, but I hadn't figured out the rest.

I tried not to look too closely at Saskia's fates. It felt like spying on her, and the images around her were far less clear anyway. Sparks of metal and swords and a group of three Fae men wearing mail. Her family. An impossible wall of iron spikes. And Saskia herself weeping, kneeling and looking at something I could never quite make out. It caught at me, that image, every time it swirled past. Even worse was the one where she was wearing a beautiful silver gown, smiling with delight and holding out her hands to some-body.

It looked far too much like a wedding gown to me. If it was, I was glad I couldn't see the man who was going to win her eventually.

I shook off the thought. Saskia was laughing at something Liam had said, which only soured my temper further, but I made myself smile when they noticed me.

The delighted expression on her face faltered a little before she got it back under control.

I didn't know how to interpret that. Did she not want to see me? Or had she taken something amiss from my expression? I could hardly ask with Brother Liam within earshot. He would no doubt be quick to pass on anything he learned to Simon and Guy. I wasn't ready to have that particular conversation.

Biting back my need for more information, I nodded at the two of them and walked closer to where they stood. "Saskia. Brother Liam. Are you eating?"

"Saskia is," Liam said, with a return of my nod. He suddenly looked pleased. "I actually have something else I need to do. Perhaps you could see that she is escorted back to St. Giles after the meal?"

"That would be my pleasure." I tried to keep my tone neutral, hiding the grin that threatened to break my composure. I closed the gap between us and extended my arm to Saskia. "I'll take good care of her."

Liam nodded and took his leave of us, moving briskly through the crowd of men, stopping only once, to speak to someone. I noticed that some of the Templars grimaced as he passed them, their eyes resting on his mangled arm.

Liam didn't notice, or didn't react if he did. He was very controlled, but I wouldn't have liked to be the person who finally made him lose his temper.

"I'm perfectly capable of walking back through the tunnels myself," Saskia grumbled, but she smiled as she said it. "Go find us a seat while I get some food. I'm starving." She shooed me away with a little flap of her hands.

She wasn't wearing gloves and I wished I could take her hand so she could chase the visions away for a little while. But that would have to wait.

I found a seat and Saskia joined me. We ate quickly, talking of our lessons and inconsequential things. I tried not to let my gaze linger on her face too long or dip to where the sensible blue dress she wore hugged her curves.

When she pushed her plate away and swallowed the last of the tea she'd chosen, I rose, impatient to be away from the crowded room. If we were lucky we might actually get a little time alone on the walk back to St. Giles.

"Shall we?" I looked down at her, trying to decipher the expression in her eyes.

She nodded, and rose. We carried our plates and cups back to the counters where they would be collected—the Templars were fond of neatness and order. Saskia snatched up an apple and put it into the purse she carried.

"Is your head hurting as badly as mine?" I asked.

She turned toward me. "Your head? Are you having visions?" Her hand slid down my arm toward my hands. "Do you need—"

Was she worried about me or reluctant to touch me? Her hand hovered where it was, midway down my forearm, the warmth of her skin penetrating the fabric of my jacket. Should I lie? Tell her I needed her so that she would touch me?

No. Not until I knew how she felt. If I had scared her or upset her, then I would at least give her the courtesy of not forcing her to touch me more than she had to. "No," I said. "It's just all this damned protocol. I don't know about you, but if I hear one more thing about the degrees of separation in the nuances of Fae Court bows, I'm going to tell Simon and Guy I've changed my mind."

To my relief, that drew a smile from her. A somewhat smug smile, I thought.

"You don't know Fae protocol?" she asked.

"You do?" That surprised me.

"Well, some," she said. "We learn some treaty protocol at the Guild and how to deal with the Fae." She frowned for a moment, then shook her head as if dismissing an unpleasant thought.

Of course she had. She was a metalmage. And a DuCaine. And of course she would have been tutored in human etiquette and mingled with the higher echelons of

human society since she was tiny. There was no way she felt
as out of her depth as I was starting to.

"I see," I said, trying not to sound irritated. I wondered
if anyone had ever made a charm to accelerate learning.
Probably not. The Fae wouldn't need such things.

"If your head hurts, Simon or one of the healers can help
you," Saskia said.

"I'm fine," I said. "At least it can't go on too much longer."

"No," she said, her face turning serious for a moment.
"No, tomorrow we have to start using what we've learned."

That wasn't a thought to improve my mood. Anything
could happen at the negotiations. I tried to see what the possibilities were, tried to make some sense out of all the images
I saw around the Templars and St. Giles, but the truth was
that until I was at the Treaty Hall with all the players in one
place, I wouldn't see the whole picture.

That chance would come soon enough.

"We should go," I said, nodding in the direction of the
door.

Saskia's expression turned . . . speculative. A dimple
winked into view in her cheek and she twined her fingers
through her prentice chain, just at the point where it
skimmed the modest neckline of her dress. The sudden
change in mood made my heart speed up a notch or two. I
made myself look down at the floor. The last place I wanted
to be caught staring at Saskia's arresting curves was in the
midst of a group of Templars who were brothers-in-arms to
Guy.

"Still hungry?" she asked softly. I lifted my head. Mis-
chief and something hotter danced in her eyes.

"I have an . . . appetite," I said cautiously.

She smiled. "Let's take the long way. We can walk across
the grounds. Get some fresh air."

"The tunnels are safer," I said, then smacked myself
mentally. That was definitely not the argument to use with
Saskia. Too much like her brothers.

"It's the Brother House and St. Giles," she said, with
more than a hint of wheedle in her tone. "Probably the two
most protected places in the City right now."

I could hardly argue that point. It was the reason we
were both sequestered here, after all. I glanced at the near-

est window. It was still light; the sun wouldn't be setting for a few more hours. "I—"

"Please, Fen," Saskia said. "I've been cooped up for almost two days. I really need to be outside."

Was she telling the truth? Did she really need to recharge her powers or whatever it was that mages did?

Or was she just being rebellious?

She moved a little closer, smiled a little sweeter. "Besides," she said, glancing up at me from under her eyelashes in a demonstration of flirting prowess that Holly would have been proud of, "there are some interesting little spots in the hospital's garden." She reached out, let her hand drift over the back of mine.

Sweet Lady, I was an idiot. But I couldn't say no. Not with my cock leaping to life at the touch of her hand and my blood suddenly pounding. After all, I had a pistol and a sword, and no doubt Saskia was carrying some sort of weapon in her purse as well.

It was still daylight. Everything would be fine. "All right," I said, hoping I didn't sound too addled with lust. "But just for a little while."

Everything was fine. At first. We made it across the grounds of the Brother House and passed through the gates between the Templars' land and the hospital under the watchful eyes of the knights guarding it. They looked slightly suspicious as we went, but apparently none of them were going to argue with a metalmage. Or, perhaps, with a DuCaine.

Either way, I was grateful to them for letting us pass. As soon as we rounded the corner of the first of the St. Giles buildings and found ourselves in one of the many little alleys that crisscrossed the hospital complex—a delightfully deserted little alley—Saskia came to an abrupt halt, turned, and pulled my head down to hers.

Sweet Lady. As her mouth pressed to mine fiercely and opened to me, I thought my head might just explode. Not only from the sudden relief from the unending visions and the pain that accompanied them, but also from the sudden surge of lust that set my belly alight. I backed her up against the wall, lifting her, pushing up her skirts so she could wrap her legs around me, getting as close as I dared.

It was pleasure and pain. I wished I could throw caution

to the wind and take her here and now, burying myself in her until we were both lost. But there were some far reaches of my brain that knew that to be an impossibility. And, thank whoever might be looking out for me, that part managed to keep control of the rest of me.

It didn't stop me from slipping a hand between her legs and driving her to the orgasm I so fiercely desired, though.

I blocked her cries with more kisses, feeling her pulse against me with satisfaction. When she stilled, I pulled my head back.

Her eyes were half-closed and languorous, a smile turning up her swollen lips. "Well, now you've done it," she said.

"What do you mean?" I eased her down, let her smooth her skirts before I was tempted to do something really stupid—like try for another round. Her dress seemed none the worse for wear, the material seemingly not prone to crushing.

I wished the same could be said for my shirt, which was sadly rumpled. But at least my coat was long enough to hide the erection that was demanding satisfaction with a strident voice. I gritted my teeth, tried to think of something distracting. Buckets of ice water. Rotten fish.

None of it worked with Saskia so close and flushed before me.

"We'll have to take longer now," she said when she'd arranged her dress to her satisfaction. "Atherton would be able to smell exactly what we've been up to. Lily too, if she's there. Though she might approve."

"She would?" That was enough to take my mind off my cock for a minute. *Lily* would be happy I was shagging her future sister-in-law?

"Yes, she—" Saskia broke off, her brows drawing down in a sudden frown. "Someone's coming."

My hand clutched my pistol. "Which way?"

Saskia had stooped to a crouch, reaching for the purse she had dropped. She yanked it open and withdrew a pistol of her own. She jerked her chin toward the nearer end of the alley. "That way. Whoever it is, they're carrying iron. Weapons, I think."

"Templars?"

She straightened. "I can't tell."

I grabbed her free hand in mine. "All right. Where's the nearest way in?"

"We need to go left at the end of this alley. There's a door in the next building over."

"Then we head that way. Quickly."

"I'm sure it's just one of the hospital staff."

I wished I shared her certainty, but there was a nasty prickle at the back of my neck that told me a hasty retreat would be a sensible option right about now. I started backing down the alley, as fast as I dared, keeping my eyes focused on the other end, the direction Saskia said our unexpected visitor was coming from.

We got only about twenty feet down the alley before a man rounded the corner and the prickling on my neck turned into a sinking stomach.

This was no human healer or Templar. Not a Fae either. No, the man coming toward us was Beast Kind. And he drew a sword as he spotted us, launching himself into a leaping run that closed the distance between us with frightening speed.

"Run!" I roared at Saskia. I stood my ground, took aim, and fired. My pistol wasn't loaded with silver bullets; silver wasn't allowed anywhere near the Treaty Hall and even though our weapons would be confiscated before we entered, the presence of silver bullets would be taken as a treaty violation. Guy had made sure my weapons wouldn't cause any issues the first day I'd spent in the Brother House.

Silver or no, my bullet hit the Beast in his right shoulder, making him falter and fumble his sword. I fired again, aiming for the same spot, hoping the damage would slow him down enough that Saskia could at least make it to safety.

I didn't dare risk a glance to see where she was. The beast stumbled again as my second bullet hit home and this time he did drop his sword.

Cursing loudly, I launched myself forward, desperate to get to him before he could rearm himself. But he was fast— Beast fast—and he twisted and scooped up the sword. I got off another desperate shot, which went wide, and then I flipped the gun into my left hand and grabbed for my sword just in time to meet the slashing blow of his.

Our blades clashed with a force that sent me rocking back on my knees. I'd thought Guy's blows savage enough, but I'd forgotten the force a full-grown Beast could wield, even in human form.

I rocked backward, trying to deflect some of the shock. The Beast grinned at me, flashing fangs. Fuck. That was all I needed. If he managed to transition to hybrid form I was well and truly screwed.

My left hand was sweaty and the gun was an awkward grip, but I fired again, aiming for his torso.

I couldn't miss at such a short distance, but though the Beast's grin changed to a snarl and a howl of rage as the bullet tore through him, he still lifted his sword for another blow.

My pistol wasn't doing enough damage. And I had only two more bullets.

But any time I could hold him off would be time for Saskia to get to safety, to get help, perhaps—though that was too much to hope for.

I blocked another blow, managed to twist and parry before darting away. The Beast was fast, but I had speed too. Beast and Fae blood flowed through my veins. I moved backward, trying to entice him back in the direction he'd come from, away from Saskia. The Beast crouched, readying himself for a leap, and I spotted Saskia standing in the mouth of the alley.

Fear rushed through me with a whooshing roar. What the fuck was she doing?

But then she shouted something and there was yet another whooshing roar as a fireball ignited around the Beast's sword. He let it go with a yelp, but not fast enough. The fire sprang up around him, blazing with heat that made me fall back under the force of it.

His clothes ignited and then his hair, and he screamed as his flesh began to blacken. The stench of burning meat roiled toward me and I retched. And then did the only thing I could think of—raised my gun again and shot him in the head.

Chapter Fourteen

FEN

The Treaty Hall was an imposing marble building located in almost the exact center of the City. I studied it cautiously, suddenly feeling unprepared for what was to come despite all the hours of lessons Saskia and I had undergone in the last few days.

The building rested on vast granite tiles that marked out a square several hundred feet long on each side. To its left and right, across the borders of the square and further separated by cobbled avenues, were the human council chambers and the elegant wooden building that housed the offices of the Speaker for the Veil.

I'd passed the hall many times, but I'd never been inside. Few had. Between negotiation seasons, the hall was generally sealed, protected by wards set by all four races, so that, in theory, none could get inside. Occasionally it had been used to receive dignitaries from outside the City, but otherwise, it sat empty and inviolate, each of its four corners flying a flag of one of the four races, supposedly to demonstrate harmony and equality.

But now, thanks to Brother Anthony's hours of tutelage, I knew quite a bit about the hall and what happened in it during the negotiations.

The first task of any treaty season was the undoing of the wards and the inspection of the building itself, followed by the setting of lesser wards and the establishment of patrols to protect the perimeter, both aboveground and below, where tunnels provided daylight access for the Blood. Most of the negotiations were actually held in the evenings in deference to the preferences of the Blood and the Beasts, but some ceremonies were held during daylight hours. Those took place in one of the windowless rooms at the heart of the hall.

After the hall was opened and inspected, heavily supervised teams of cleaners and workmen were allowed in to make the place fit for the negotiations. They polished and swept and repaired any cracks in the wood and stone of the building. As it didn't contain a single scrap of iron in its construction, it was somewhat susceptible to the ravages of wind and weather. No ward can completely gainsay the weather, after all. Or the rats and mice and other creatures that manage to exploit any small pieces of damage and get inside to take up residence.

That work had been going on for several weeks now and today, or this evening rather, it was finally time for the actual business of the negotiations to commence.

The building rose several stories above the square, the marble gleaming pink and gold and white in the light from the setting sun. It should have been welcoming. Instead, I couldn't help feeling dread as I waited with the rest of the delegation in the area designated for the humans to gather.

All four races entered the building at the same time, watched by guards from all the races and, of course, by the extra forces of the Fae.

In theory we were all equal, but all of us were aware that the Fae could change the game with a blink of an eye. The Veiled Court's delegation had gathered in the area to the right of ours and I found myself watching them, unable to look away.

I generally avoided contact with the Fae. I've never been to Summerdale, let alone the Veiled World. Too much risk for a half-breed like me. All it would take would be for one of my father's family to decide to stake a claim on me for my abilities and I could find myself bound there for good. Safer to stay here in the City, free under the sun.

Still, despite the threat they represented, they drew the eye, those of the Veiled Court. Tall, slender, and fair in the twilight, more beautiful than anybody should be. All of them acting calm and collected and yet you couldn't mistake the fact that every last one of them had half an eye and ear on the palanquin that rested atop the elaborately carved wooden platform they were gathered around. Hung with walls of silks of all possible shades that hid the interior from sight, and topped by the standard of the Veiled Court, it held a single occupant. The Veiled Queen.

Holly had met her, not all that long ago. Met her and found both loss and freedom at her hands. The queen was not a woman to be trifled with. The Fae queen had the power to flatten the whole City if she chose. It was her power that had bound the races to the treaty all those centuries ago and that same power had enforced the treaty all these years. But now she was fighting a rebellion in her own courts, if what Holly and Guy believed was true.

I couldn't see a future swirling over the palanquin, hard as I might try. I didn't know if the queen was protected against seers or if it meant that everything was going to go horribly wrong. I hoped it was the former. After all, I tried to tell myself, the queen had been holding the City together with her will for a long time. A petty squabble amongst her people wasn't enough to make her abandon us now. Or was it?

As we waited, the tension in the air wound higher and higher, until you could practically smell the nerves—like acid and ashes—floating around us. Mail jingled and horses blew nervous snorts, and all around were the sounds of men and women making the kinds of small movements that soothe anxious nerves.

If one more person cleared his throat, I was going to have to punch him. Beside me, Saskia was not entirely immune from the general mood. Her hand dallied with the prentice chain around her neck, fingering the loops with twirls and taps that were no less damning for their air of long habit.

I resisted the urge to adjust my chain—wrapped as tightly as I could bear it, to ease the endless whirl of visions smoking the air—or my coat or my cravat. I would stand still if it killed me. The last thing I wanted was for the

Kruegers or the Fae or anybody, hells take them, to see how sick I felt.

The DuCaine brothers stood on Saskia's other side. They too avoided looking anywhere other than at the Treaty Hall. Which was fine with me. They had been furious with Saskia and me last night, though I hadn't entirely worked out if that was because we hadn't used the tunnels or because we'd killed the Beast and therefore ruined any chance of questioning him.

No one had come looking for him. Yet. Simon and Guy both seemed to think that the death might be thrown at the humans in the course of the negotiations.

But given that he had attacked us within a Haven—which we could prove, given the nice little preservation charm Bryony had worked over the charred patch of stone where his body had fallen—and that we could also demonstrate that his body had several bullet holes in nonlethal places—further demonstration that we'd tried to warn him off before killing him—I didn't see what we could actually be blamed for.

Still, it hadn't exactly put me in Simon's and Guy's good graces. They were grateful that I'd defended their sister, but they had taken both of us to task for nearly an hour over our general idiocy.

My announcement that I was going to remain part of the delegation after that had been something of an anticlimax.

As the clock struck eight and the last of the sun slipped below the horizon, the gaslights around the square whooshed into life. Then, as all of us turned to look, the final delegation came to meet us.

The Blood.

Descending from the long rows of black, windowless coaches that had been making a slow queue across the city from Sorrow's Hill and LeSangre for the last hour like silent ghosts. I'd never liked groups of Blood together. There was something beyond inhuman in having so many of them in one place. White skin, white hair, black clothes, and the wink of too bright eyes against all that noncolor made the hairs on the back of my neck rise. Made my brain sound a song of "predator, predator, run" in the way the Beast Kind never really managed.

The coach closest to the square was the last to open its

door and I caught myself holding my breath, waiting to see who stepped down from it. I knew, of course. Knew without a doubt who it would be. Had known it since I had first seen the vision of him at the Krueger Pack House.

Ignatius Grey.

Stepping from the carriage with a slow precision that told me everything I needed to know. He believed he'd won already. Believed he would rule the Blood and, though the gods only knew what he might be planning, rule the City as well.

All the small noises in the square died as he descended. Everybody watched as he adjusted his long velvet coat and gazed around the square to survey those of us who waited. And I wasn't the only one who shivered when a far-too-satisfied smile spread across his features.

Part of me wondered whether, if he'd raised his voice and commanded us to kneel, we would have obeyed. Hypnotized en masse, like rabbits under the gaze of a raptor? Could he have won with a word?

Luckily we weren't going to find out just yet. Because just as the silence deepened beyond bearing, there was a ringing peal of trumpets and all eyes turned to the Fae.

I kept watching Ignatius. His smile didn't falter but it did grow tighter as he too turned to look at the Fae delegation. Lights bloomed, pale glowing orbs floating above the heads of those closest to the palanquin, a myriad of miniature moons casting silvery light that made the silk banners shine. Slowly the curtain at the end of the palanquin drew back. Stairs unfolded and then the Veiled Queen stepped out and descended.

The veils that covered her face were, for now, a pure white that glowed in the light of the floating orbs. That was either diplomacy or a promising start. The veils of the Veiled Queen reflected her moods, thickening and shifting color with her will. If they turned black, someone was going to die. White was safely neutral, neither good nor bad. Or so the protocol lessons had informed me, reinforcing what I'd already heard elsewhere. The square grew even more hushed as the queen moved slowly down the stairs, then extended one hand to the Speaker of the Veil, who waited for her.

Like his queen, the Speaker was robed in white, his dark

hair—black in this light—bound back with a silvery band that echoed the silver of his eyes. I assumed the band wasn't actually silver—which could be an insult to the Beasts and the Blood—but some Fae alloy. The Speaker's face was carefully blank. He bowed deferentially to the queen as he released her hand but his expression didn't give away any other hint of how he might be feeling.

I wondered how it felt to be him right now. Usually the Speaker was the Veiled Court's liaison with the outer worlds. Grievances were taken to him and he spoke the queen's will. But at the negotiations the queen herself took the reins and he was just another of the Fae courtiers of the delegation, albeit one of the most powerful amongst them.

Looking at his face, you wouldn't know that he was probably older than the City itself. There had only been one Speaker in all the time the Veiled Queen had ruled. The two of them held centuries of knowledge and power and secrets.

The hairs on the back of my neck prickled, a feeling of supreme insignificance swamping me as the queen stood and surveyed the assembled delegates. Finally she nodded and the horns sounded again and the doors of treaty hall swung inward. The air buzzed suddenly as even more layers of magic sprang to life around us.

Wards. Many of them.

It eased my nerves temporarily. Of all the places in the City, the Treaty Hall had to be one of the safest. Granted, taking part in the delegations, being a known delegate for one side or the other, exposed you to risks outside the walls of the hall, but inside, nobody would dare to commit an act of aggression. Not unless they wanted their delegation to lose a large portion of its rights, if not all of them.

The queen turned toward the doors and walked slowly to them, still grasping the arm of the Speaker. The rest of the Fae delegation followed her, and its allotted quota of guards.

After the queen had passed through the doors, the rest of the delegates moved in their predetermined order of entry to take their places.

Which had taken almost as much protocol and wrangling to decide upon as the treaty itself.

It was an accounting of the balance of power in each of

the races, if you knew how to decipher it. How each race set precedence and how it assigned its delegates provided insight into its power bases and alliances.

The Blood votes had previously been held by Lord Lucius and he spoke for them all, but this year, since his death and the lack of a clear victor in the race to be the new Blood Lord, they had split their voting rights into blocs, as the Beasts and humans did. Still, we all watched with interest as the first group of Blood moved to follow the queen.

Unsurprisingly, it was Ignatius who led the way and after he had left, the numbers of Blood still assembled were substantially reduced. I wasn't the only one swearing under my breath at this development.

It was official: Ignatius was winning. Something needed to be done about the man. Unfortunately, given it was treaty season, that something couldn't be anything along the lines of someone making him disappear the way Lucius had, thanks to Simon and Lily.

After the Blood, the first of the human blocs, the council's delegation, entered the hall. They were followed by the first Beast pack. Again I watched with interest to see who had won that honor.

The Roussellines, as it turned out, which did manage to surprise me.

I would have bet on the Favreaus being most in favor with Ignatius, but apparently the Beasts hadn't yet made up their minds completely.

As the Roussellines moved toward the hall, I suddenly spotted Martin standing amidst the other Kruegers. He saw me too, and his lips drew back in a silent snarl.

Damn. My secret was out. Not that I could've kept it any longer than the next hour or so of the naming ceremony, but still, ice formed in my stomach as I read the rage in Martin's eyes burning into me from across the square.

I'd known my choice would bring a reckoning with my erstwhile relatives, so I would just have to deal with it when it came. Hopefully *after* the treaty, after I had earned the right to rope Guy and maybe some of his other Templar brethren into helping me deal with whatever that reckoning turned out to be.

It seemed to take a long time for the rest of the delegates to process into the hall. The Templar delegation wasn't the last of the humans to go in, so I didn't have to wait until the very end.

But as I crossed the threshold and felt the tingle of wards brushing across my skin, I was forced to wonder again what exactly I thought I was doing. Then Saskia came up beside me, her hand moving subtly to brush against mine, easing the pressure building in my head, and I remembered.

I could just picture my mother laughing at me. "All that for a girl," she'd say. "Only fools let love lead them around by the nose, Fen lad."

She'd tried her best to teach me that lesson, but apparently I was a poor student of common sense as well as protocol.

I followed the rest of the delegates into the entryway, keeping pace with Saskia and, like many others, craning my neck to look around me, now that I was actually inside the mysterious Treaty Hall. I hadn't really known what to expect. All four races had contributed to the construction of the hall, in money or labor or materials, and it was a testament to leashed power.

The floor we walked was a polished gray stone—granite, I thought—the color of the dark heart of a frozen river. From it, the walls rose to curve to a vaulted ceiling far, far above our heads. Or, I thought, suddenly confused, as I considered the outward appearance of the hall, perhaps that was an illusion. The chamber we stood in seemed taller than the walls outside. The walls were covered in an intricate mosaic depicting each of the four races and parts of the City—some of which I didn't recognize. Perhaps the buildings in them had fallen into obscurity and ruin long ago. The hall was old, like the treaty itself.

But as astonishing as that room was, it couldn't really distract me from the room we were walking toward: the Treaty Hall itself. Tall brass doors stood ajar at the end of the entrance hall and the delegates were filing through, one by one, past the Fae guards who were checking names against the pages of a thick leather-bound book. From beyond, I heard the hushed humming of many muffled voices, but I couldn't yet see the room itself.

I reached the door and got my first glimpse of the hall—it was even more imposing than the entrance hall. The walls here weren't tiled; instead they were paneled in carved woods. Arches and columns twined with vines and flowers and tiny animal faces, seeming to grow up toward the ceiling like a forest run riot. The four sides of the hall were lined with tiered rows of seats, each divided into subsections by carved wooden screens, some waist high, some higher, so that the space seemed to be almost like a series of small rooms. Each wall had two narrow aisles running up the tiers to allow access to the seats. Behind the top tier was another series of screens that I had been told hid the corridors used by the servants of the hall and the guards who accompanied the most important members of each race.

The tiers were filling with the delegates, those who had entered first taking the prime seats nearest the front, closest to the floor.

A floor of white marble veined with the palest of green, the expanse of it broken by a sparkling golden circle inset in the stone. This was the speakers' circle, where those addressing the delegates stood while they held the floor. It marked the dead center of the room, and around it, several feet back from the circle itself, the four points of the compass were marked by smaller circles of black stone set in the marble. On the circles stood pedestals of the same dark stone—each of them about four feet high. The pedestals were topped by polished ebony chests, bound with locks and chains of gold.

The circles served only to draw the eye to the circle. I was glad I wasn't going to have to stand there under the gaze of so many hostile eyes and speak my piece to try and convince the races to agree to one concession or another. No, it was bad enough being part of the delegation without bringing myself to further attention than was necessary.

Saskia and I followed Liam, filing up the stairs to take our place in the fourth row of seats, behind the councils' delegates and the official representatives of our own delegation. I managed to ensure that I sat next to Saskia. I might as well have some small pleasures in the days to come. Though as I settled myself beside her and breathed in the scent of her skin, I began to think that that might be a mistake. I needed to focus on what was about to happen here, and she was a definite distraction.

But it was too late to move. Protocol demanded that once you had taken your seat, you moved only at the allot-

ted times for breaks or discussions or to leave the chamber
for the official sessions of negotiation and bargaining that
each delegation undertook in the myriad rooms that filled
the rest of the building. We would be locked in the Treaty
Hall from dusk until dawn neared and the Blood had to
retire for the day. Then everyone would leave and the hall
would be sealed again until the next day.

I watched the seats around me fill. The humans had the
east side of the hall and the Blood the west. The Fae were
north and the Beasts south. The volume of conversation in
the room grew louder and louder as the delegates continued to take their places. The buzz of voices had a nervous
edge to it.

The process of getting everyone situated took a long
while, during which time I had nothing to do but sit and
watch. The seats were padded, but only thinly, and my legs
already felt cramped. Perhaps humans had been shorter in
the time when the hall had been built. I was a little taller
than most human men, thanks to my ancestry, but it didn't
usually disadvantage me. Now I was beginning to think that
the next two weeks might cripple me.

After the seemingly endless parade of delegates making
their way into the hall, they had all finally taken their places.
The keepers of the hall—one representative from each race
who had been tasked with opening the building and ensuring the security of the wards—then appeared and took their
places at the four pedestals around the speaker's circle.

The whispered conversations died away instantly, the
tension in the room rising. All eyes turned toward the keepers. One by one, they stepped forward and produced the
keys that were the symbols of their position. Then, each of
them in turn used the keys to open the boxes on the pedestals and draw out the treaty stones, raising them to display
to the delegates before placing them on the pedestals.

One by one, the stones glowed to life, turning a warm
gold. The power of the stones added another tingling layer
of magic to the room. They were supposed to enforce peace
and truth for those who stood under the lights and spoke
from the circle. I had a feeling that it would take more than
four ancient glowing stones to make that happen for this
particular round of negotiations.

Looking across at the carefully controlled smirk on Ignatius' face as he watched the keeper only confirmed my fears.

Duties done, the keepers withdrew and the Speaker for the Veil rose to his feet from his position at the queen's right hand and moved across the floor to step into the circle.

When he reached it, he paused for a long moment before circling to face each of the races in turn. I fought the urge to roll my eyes. The endless protocol lessons had been dull enough, but actually seeing the rituals in person was somehow worse. With so much at stake, this posturing and pointless ceremony seemed like the games of children vying to secure the possession of a favorite toy.

I couldn't see that it mattered that the Speaker stood a certain way or that the stones glowed or that the ceiling was the right shade of whatever. What mattered was that the races would manage to come to an agreement and prevent the City from falling into chaos and anarchy.

I moved on my seat, my head already starting to ache in the presence of so many people in one place. The visions were an added layer of strangeness, swirling so quickly I could barely make anything out.

Saskia shifted beside me and once again, as though she could sense my mood, her hand brushed mine in a movement so subtle that I doubted anyone but me would have noticed.

All too soon she moved her hand away again, but even the brief respite had let me catch my breath and clear my head.

I schooled myself to patience, letting my mind drift a little into the haze of the visions, trying to slow their crazed circling and see if there was anything useful to be gained from the jumble. But nothing came clear.

The Speaker began to recite the text of the treaty law that governed the negotiations. The rules of order and the bindings that all the delegates were agreeing to submit themselves to. His recitation took a long time and because I'd only so recently had the words drummed into my head, hearing them yet again made it even more difficult to concentrate.

The visions surged forward, making my head throb sharply as my focus slipped. I made myself snap back, settling my free hand over my wrist to press the iron more firmly against my skin. Beside me, Saskia turned her head, eyebrow lifting slightly. I shook my head at her and turned my attention back to the Speaker.

He continued to speak, the lines of convoluted legalistic language flowing effortlessly. I wondered exactly how many times he had spoken them before. I could probably figure it out if I wanted to, but math had never been my favorite endeavor. Not unless I was counting money.

The Speaker eventually fell silent, looking around the hall gravely. The last words he'd spoken were a challenge for anyone who did not intend to work toward the renewal of the treaty to speak first. The silence in the chamber settled deeper, but no one spoke.

The Speaker nodded once, then called the first of the delegation leaders to announce his delegates. In this case the first was Ignatius.

Ignatius stood and walked—no, "strutted" might be a better word—onto the floor. He too paused before he started to speak, taking his time to look over those assembled. I wasn't the only one unwilling to meet his gaze, I noted. Still, the silence held as he spoke in his rasping voice, reeling off the names of his delegates with decisive force. I only recognized one or two of them.

Yet another cause for concern. I had a passing familiarity with those of the Blood who frequented the safer Assemblies and occasionally showed up at the Gilt or others of the theater halls. The more civilized of them. One couldn't really function for long in the border boroughs without knowing some of the players.

The fact that I didn't know many of Ignatius' supporters meant either that they were newly risen to power—which I didn't completely discount—or that they were of the Blood, who kept to their own world where they could play by their own rules. Older Blood who had perhaps been biding their time under Lucius' rule, or indeed may have supported Lucius in whatever it was that he had been planning. But I'd never been able to judge the age of a Blood lord because of their ageless faces, so I had no way to tell which of the two theories was correct.

After Ignatius finished his remarks and returned to his seat, a slow whisper gusted across the hall, as though half the people present had let out a breath of relief. It seemed that more than just our delegation had been concerned that Ignatius might try something early in the process. Apparently for now he was playing by the rules.

Thank the Lady for small mercies.

After Ignatius, the leaders of the other delegations took their turns, announcing the names of their delegates and the other members of their delegations.

Eventually it was the Templars' turn. Their Abbott General took his place. Only middling tall, his graying hair cropped short, and dressed simply in Templar gray and white, Father Cho had none of Ignatius' strutting pride, but his quiet air of command meant that he caught and held the attention of the assembly effortlessly.

I schooled my face to stillness as I listened to the list of names he announced in his steady voice. Until eventually mine was spoken. I risked a sideways glance at where Martin sat with the Kruegers. His expression was grim, but he was pointedly not looking in my direction. From behind him, Willem's lips had drawn back in a snarl. I got the feeling that when Martin decided to take his revenge on me for this betrayal, Willem would be the one volunteering to carry out the sentence.

Pity. I liked Willem, after a fashion. Still, I would fight him if I had to and do everything in my power to win if it came to that. Of course I would first do everything in my power to avoid having to fight him. Just what that might be escaped me right now, but I was sure I would think of something eventually.

After Father Cho, the parade continued. By the time we'd made it through another two or three delegations—the human council and the Guilds and one of the Beast pack alliances—the mood in the hall was starting to relax, the silence disturbed by people shifting in their seats and, here and there, by the unmistakable sounds of discreetly smothered yawns. Of all the things I'd imagined the negotiations to be, I'd never really considered that they might be boring.

I was close to smothering a yawn myself as we neared the last delegation. The Veiled Court. The queen stayed where she was, seated on a carved chair that looked more comfortable than the rest of our seats. Her veils moved slowly, though there was no breeze to stir them. The effect was both hypnotic and vaguely unsettling.

I wondered if she took advantage of the cover of her veils to hide boredom when she needed to. Or if she was even paying attention. The Speaker rose again from his place beside her and walked to the circle. He raised a hand, like all the others before him, ready to swear the oath of amity, when a groaning rumble suddenly sounded from beneath us and then, without warning, the room seemed to catch fire as the walls around the doorway exploded inward.

Chapter Fifteen

SASKIA

⚡

The sounds of explosions—screams and rumbles and a overwhelming smothering, roaring noise that punched into my ears—crashed around me as Fen pulled me out of my chair and down to the floor, throwing himself on top of me as debris rained from the ceiling.

My back hit the marble, which shook below me. With no metal in the building, I had no way to tell what was happening. A steady rain of small pieces of debris struck the parts of me not covered by Fen, but I didn't feel any larger blows. I twisted my head, tried to push Fen away a little so that I could move, but he only pressed me more firmly into the floor.

"Stay *down*."

Idiot man. I could probably do more to protect myself than he could in this situation. But he was too heavy to dislodge.

"Tell me what's happening," I demanded.

His face was close to mine, smudged with a dark streak of something across one cheek. A trickle of blood oozed from a slice above his eyebrow, the flow thickening as his brows drew down. "Something blew up." His voice seemed to come from far away, distorted by the ringing in my ears.

"I know that," I said sharply. "Are you hurt? You're bleeding."

He shook his head, as though he was more trying to clear his ears than to answer my question.

"What about you?" I shook my head in turn. I couldn't feel anything immediately painful, so presumably there was nothing worth worrying about.

Fen lifted his head sharply as Guy's voice cut through the roar in my ears, calling my name. "Stay down," he repeated. His weight vanished from me as he lifted himself to a crouching position. "We're here," he called.

His movement cleared my line of sight and I stared up at the gaping hole in the ceiling. The air was full of ashes and bits of falling—well, I wasn't entirely sure what they were other than the fact that they were on fire. I pushed myself up to a seated position carefully, checking for any protesting muscles or bones. I took a deep breath—a mistake— then coughed as the smoke hit my lungs. Fen's head twisted back toward me. He glared.

"I'm still down," I said. Though I didn't intend to stay that way for very much longer. My back hurt where I'd hit the floor and the sleeve of my dress was torn, but I seemed otherwise unharmed. Which meant I should start helping those who were hurt.

Guy's face suddenly loomed above me, peering over the remains of the row of chairs in front of us. "Are you two all right?" His voice was faint but clear.

I nodded while Fen said, "Yes."

Guy's answering nod was brisk. "Good. Let's move."

Fen reached down and grabbed my hand, pulling me carefully upward as he stood. "Where?"

"Out of here," Guy said shortly. "The building is on fire."

"But—" I started to protest.

Guy slashed a hand through the air, cutting me off. "No arguments. You're leaving."

"Where's Simon?"

"He's fine. He's helping people."

"I can help."

"No." Guy reached across Fen to take my arm. "Let's go."

I looked around the room. Chaos reigned. There were bodies sprawled across the floor and some of the rows of seats. Those who were moving were either doing so dazedly or pushing and shoving toward the doors. In the Beast Kind area nearest the door, a whole section of chairs about fifteen feet across had seemingly vanished. Where were the delegates?

I peered harder through the smoky air and started to pick out bloody shapes. Too small to be whole bodies. I swallowed hard, then coughed again, fighting the urge to spit ash and bile. *Sainted earth.* Who had done this?

Guy tugged on my arm and we moved as quickly as we could along the row of broken seats toward the aisle. The human section seemed to have been spared too much damage. I didn't see any bodies, at least. But when I reached the aisle and turned to look back down at the speaking floor I saw something that made my stomach heave.

"Sweet Lady," I said. "Guy, is that . . ." I turned away, not wanting to look at the crumpled figure of the Speaker for the Veil lying across the golden ring of the speaker's circle. A massive spike of darkened wood speared his side. The uncanny stillness of his pose and the huge pool of blood spreading across the marble floor made it clear there was no hope he had survived.

Where was the queen?

I searched the room and found her. No longer robed in white, her twisting veils turned pitch black, she stood stock-still in front of the chair that was hers, staring down at the Speaker, heedless of the rest of the chaos around her.

Sainted bloody earth. The Speaker was dead. And the queen's veils were black. Guy was right—we needed to get out of here. *Fast.*

People were going to die.

I hastened my steps, but before I'd moved even a few feet down the aisle there was a second thunderclap of sound. All around me, people flung themselves down, arms wrapped around their heads protectively. But this sound wasn't followed by a blast and flying debris.

No, instead, in its wake it left a ringing silence, as the flames died and the air cleared. I felt the sizzling sting of wild, powerful magic scrape across my skin and rose to my feet cautiously, unsure what had just happened. Everyone else was doing the same thing. One by one, we turned toward the queen, who stood in the middle of the room, with her hands raised.

"Who," she demanded, "has done this thing?"

The silence was absolute. The feeling of power rolled across the room again, making the air close around me like the pressure before a storm. The jewels on the queen's hands sparked color like fireworks.

"Who?" she repeated, her voice full of a rage so deep it seemed as though it might drown us all.

Nobody answered. Which, given the tug and roil of the magic she was pouring into us, I had to imagine meant that whoever it was either wasn't in the room or lay amongst the dead. No one could have resisted the urge to speak in the face of that terrible voice.

Not unless they were protected by magics I couldn't even begin to imagine. The hall's wards were meant to prevent such a thing.

The queen's veils whipped and coiled around her, edged with dark light, as though lightning bolts might spring from them at any second. She was the Fae queen. The gods-damned Fae *queen*. She could raze the City if she chose.

"Who?" she said again, and this time I heard not just rage but grief in her voice. Grief like ice and darkness. I shivered and reached blindly behind me for someone, anyone, to shelter me against the weight of it. I felt a hand grip mine and knew it was Fen, but I couldn't look away from the queen to turn to the comfort of his touch.

"Justice will be done," she said. "Until then, these negotiations are ended."

"Somebody has to stop her," I said to Guy. Around us, everybody seemed to be standing frozen in place. The only figures moving in the entire room were those working on the wounded and the Fae who had started to swirl protectively around the queen.

"I don't think that's a good idea," Guy said, staring at the queen.

"Seconded," Fen agreed.

"The negotiations have to go ahead. If they don't, then whoever did this will try and take advantage. They could end the treaty. She knows you," I said to Guy. "She might listen to you."

Several of the Fae had knelt beside the Speaker's body and were covering it with a cloth produced from gods knew where. "You have to try."

Guy's face was grim, but he nodded, once. "I'll try. If she kills me, then I'm telling Holly it was your fault."

I wasn't sure how that would work, but I wasn't going to argue. If Guy could make any kind of a joke right now, no matter how feeble, then he must not be too worried that the queen actually would kill him. He sheathed his sword as he descended to the floor. Before he got within fifteen feet of the speaker's circle, he was surrounded by Fae guards, bristling with weapons. He held up his hands, stopped where he was.

"My name," he said carefully, "is Sir Guy DuCaine. I wish to speak to the queen."

The queen's head turned slightly, but then she focused back on those tending to the Speaker.

"Her Majesty will be leaving," one of the guards said, his voice no less icy than the queen's had been. "Stay where you are, human."

Guy, wisely, didn't move. He did, however, raise his voice. He was a Templar knight, used to working in noisy situations. He knew how to make himself heard.

"Your Majesty," he called. "Please. Listen to me."

This time her head turned fully, the veils writhing like serpents. "Do you know who did this, Templar?" she asked.

"No, Your Majesty."

I held my breath, watching. For a moment I thought she was going to be reasonable, but, "Then you are no use to me. Be silent." Her hand snapped out and Guy's mouth snapped shut.

Holy mother of . . . Had the queen just cast a spell on a Templar knight?

If that was true, then we were indeed in deep, deep trouble.

Guy's face turned thunderous, but he didn't say anything more. I didn't know if it was because he couldn't or because he had decided that discretion was the better part of valor if he was to avoid being turned into a frog or incinerated by a fireball, but no one else tried to approach the queen in the few minutes before the Speaker's body was fully wrapped and then carried—floated—out of the hall.

The minute the last of the Fae passed through the charred and shattered doorway, the noise in the hall erupted again with a vengeance. Everyone, it seemed, started talking at once. I ran down to Guy. "Can you speak?"

He shook his head. I turned to Fen, who was right on my heels. "Find Simon. Or Bryony."

He nodded. I patted Guy's arm, trying not to notice the fury in his eyes and the too white knuckles tightened around his sword hilt. He was furious. He jerked his head toward the door.

"Nobody is going anywhere just yet," I said. It wasn't strictly true. The Blood and Beast Kin delegates were streaming out of the hall, some escorting the injured or carrying bodies. Their expressions were a mixture—shaken, terrified, oddly calm, intent. The humans were hanging back, probably thinking it was wise not to get caught up amongst a crowd of Night Worlders just yet.

Fen returned, with Bryony right behind him.

The Fae healer looked at Guy with a careful expression, then laid a hand on his arm. The strain on her face eased a little. "It's all right," she said. "It's just a glamour. It will wear off in a little while."

"Can't you remove it?" I asked.

Bryony shook her head. "Saskia, if I could undo enchantments wrought by the queen, I would *be* the queen. It will wear off. It's not hurting, is it, Guy?"

He shook his head, but I wasn't sure I entirely believed him.

"Good," Bryony said. "Then we should leave. This building can't be safe, particularly not now that the queen has gone. And we need to make plans."

Plans for what exactly? Hunting down whoever had done this? How on earth were we supposed to do that? Someone had subverted the wards of the Treaty Hall and managed to kill the Speaker for the Veil. Anyone with that sort of power wasn't going to be easy to find.

Still, I couldn't argue with the proposal to leave. There wasn't much metal in the building—only the small traces in the stones it was constructed from and some of the furniture—but I could feel the strain in what little there was, the tiny faltering song of it speaking of stresses almost beyond bearing. Whatever magics had held the hall together for all this time had been torn, if not snuffed out altogether, and I would be surprised if it didn't collapse. Soon.

So I did as I was told, helping to gather the wounded and

the still standing and herding them through our retreat
back out into the night.

FEN

The Beasts and the Blood had vanished into the darkness
by the time we got the last of the human delegation out of
the hall. There was no sign of the Fae either, not that I had
expected there would be. No, they would be headed back to
Summerdale, speeding their queen to safety.

Fuck the Veil.

This was a disaster beyond anything we could have expected. The queen had shut down the negotiations. My days
of being tutored hadn't made me into an expert in treaty
law, but even I knew that with no negotiations, the treaty
stood to fail.

The square had attracted quite a crowd, people who had
come running when the explosion had occurred, at a guess.
Fortunately, amongst them were healers from both St. Giles
and Merciful James who'd arrived with wagons and started
loading up the wounded to transport them back to the hospital.

"What now?" Saskia said as we watched the swirl of
people milling around.

"We wait," I said. It went against my instincts, which
were currently strongly suggesting that getting the hell out
of the City would be the best plan at this point. I couldn't.
Not yet. I couldn't leave Holly and Reggie. And I'd given
my word to the DuCaines, including Saskia.

But I hoped that we would, at least, be leaving the square
soon. The magics in the hall had kept my visions at bay a
little, but now, out here amongst the panicking crowd, they
were starting to press in on me, making my temples throb
as I tried not to see. I dug my fingers into the back of my
neck, trying to ease the pressure and tension.

"Are you all right?"

I nodded curtly, but Saskia reached for my hand anyway.
My fingers curled around hers, grateful for the assistance.

And if I were to be strictly honest about it, grateful for the familiar feel of her skin against mine. A sensation I was becoming accustomed to, starting to anticipate with more enthusiasm than was sensible. Even here and now, amidst chaos and destruction, I was keenly aware of the fact of her, standing close and warm and female.

My mother had always said that men were the stupider sex, led around by their baser instincts. Right now I had to agree with her. What was I doing thinking about anything other than how we were going to get out of this mess?

Simon, Guy, and Bryony eventually came over to us. Lily was with them.

"What's going to happen?" Saskia asked even as I squeezed her hand in warning. Simon looked pale and drawn, but his face, like his brother's, was set and tight, radiating a deep fury. The chain around Bryony's neck was a deep and sullen purplish red, echoing those emotions.

"Bryony and I are going back to the hospital," Simon said. "Guy will go back to the Brother House. Lily"—he stopped for a moment to think, rubbing his forehead with a grimy hand—"will go with the two of you back to Mother's house. Then we'll come fetch you."

"Fetch us where?"

"Wherever it's decided it's safe," Simon said curtly. "Don't argue, Saskia. Not now. Just go. Get everyone packed and wait for us."

For once, she closed her mouth and nodded agreement.

Saskia

The trip back to Mother's was less eventful than I'd feared it might be. Lily had brought Simon's horse, Red, and one of the carriages and we made it back through the streets without incident. Fen sat silent and tense beside me the entire time, his expression fiercely alert as he kept watch out the carriage window.

I wondered what he was seeing floating in front of those dark green eyes. More than just the City streets we were passing through—he'd let go of my hand once we'd entered the carriage—and most likely nothing good. He'd been pessimistic enough about the City's fortunes before tonight's turn for the worse.

Right now he must feel like one of those soothsayers in the stories, doomed to speak the truth and never be believed. Doomed to watch the things they feared come to pass as they had seen them.

I shivered at the thought. His was a power I had no desire for. Give me the clean singing strength of metal bent to my will beneath my hands. That I could understand. That I could do something with.

The sight was another thing entirely.

A curse rather than a blessing.

It could very well be the death of Fen if he didn't learn to control it or didn't survive that which he'd seen if he couldn't stop it coming to pass. I left Fen and Lily to see to the horse and carriage and went inside to find Mother. I didn't have to go very far.

She was pacing the hall beneath the watchful eyes of my father and our house steward, Edwards.

"Saskia!" She bustled toward me as I appeared, her face turning pale as she took in my smoke-stained and rumpled appearance. "What in the name of all that—" She broke off, made a visible effort to restrain herself. After all, proper ladies didn't swear. "What happened? We heard an awful noise and there have been people in the streets saying all sorts of terrible things. We thought it would be better to stay here. Is everyone—where are your brothers?" Her voice sharpened with anxiety.

"They're fine," I said quickly, knowing she would be thinking of Edwina. "Simon is at St. Giles and Guy has gone back to the Brother House."

Though for all I knew Guy might well be patrolling by now. I couldn't see the Templars doing anything but heading out to try and keep some semblance of peace. Of course, Father Cho might want Guy to stay behind to help form a strategy to deal with all of this.

"But what happened?" Mother repeated. Edwards' face echoed her curiosity and behind him, peering down from over the railing of the stairs, I could see most of the other staff listening. Hannah was there—her bright blond curls standing out amongst the white-capped maids—though she should have been in bed.

"There was an attack—no, an explosion," Lily said.

I agreed with her correction. It had been an attack, but without knowing who was behind it there was no point in further fanning the flames of confusion. But neither was there any point in trying to conceal the truth. There was no way to keep what had happened at the hall secret—it would be all over the City in a few more hours—so we told the rest of the story as quickly as we could, though by unspoken agreement we left out the part where the queen had glamoured Guy, trying to cast her retreat from the negotiations as temporary.

Who knew, maybe it would be. Maybe the queen would see reason and reconvene the negotiations tomorrow. I didn't think one of Fen's oddsmen would think that a very good bet. Still, even with my glossing over some of the more distressing details, there were gasps as I told of the Speaker's death.

My mother, though, did what she always did in a crisis. With her immediate fears laid to rest and with the facts at hand, she went into organizing mode, sending everyone around the house to pack things as Simon had commanded. I didn't have the heart to tell her I thought he'd probably meant just her and Father and Hannah.

If nothing else, I agreed with Mother that the servants would be safer away from our house too. If Ignatius was one of the people behind the attack, then the DuCaines were a likely target. The servants could go back to their families or perhaps seek shelter at one of the Havens.

With nothing more to do and feeling fatigue start to crash down on me like an anvil, I climbed the stairs, determined to go to my room and wash and change if I could. A bath would be heaven, but I didn't know if there would be enough time for that.

Hannah was waiting for me near my room, having retreated when Mother had told her firmly to go back to her room. The back of her hair was caught into a rapidly disintegrating braid and she looked far younger than her fifteen years, face pinched with worry.

"Is it true?" she said suddenly. "Is it really true? There

was an attack at the negotiations?" I went to put an arm around her, then hesitated, not wanting to smear soot and gods knew what else all over her gown. She seemed not to care; she ducked under my arm anyway and hugged me.

"It's true," I said, dropping a kiss on her hair. "But it will be all right. It will be fixed. Simon and Guy and Lily and Fen will make sure of that." I blushed a little as his name came so easily to my lips as someone I depended on.

Foolish. He had stuck by me so far, but he wasn't bound to me or my family. I couldn't say whether he would stay, or even if I expected him to.

Wanting him to—that was another thing. I was getting to know the man he kept carefully hidden beneath his devil-may-care exterior. The man who chose to stand with those he counted as family rather than save himself. The man who'd thrown himself across my body to protect me, risking his life for me. I wanted more time with that man. In and out of bed.

"You go back to your room and help Sylvie pack some things. Then try and rest." I smoothed a hand over her head. Sylvie, who had looked after me before I'd left for the Guild and now was maid and confidante to Hannah, was both sensible and comforting. She would be able to keep Hannah calm. "I need to change. If you can't sleep, then read. I'll come to you once I've dressed."

I gave her another squeeze. Hannah so far had shown no sign of the powers that Simon and I had. She hated being the baby and the ordinary one. She must feel even more frustrated and helpless than I did. Well, I would make sure that she got to find her own place once things had settled again and she was old enough to make her way.

If she didn't turn out to be any kind of mage, then Guy and Simon would be even more protective of her than they were of me, so I would have to make sure she had a chance to live life as she chose. "Go, now."

I lifted my arm from her shoulders and gave her a gentle push toward her room, watching for a few seconds until she slipped inside her bedroom, then went to my own rooms, heading directly into the bathroom. I ran hot water in the basin and splashed my face before scrubbing it and my hands as best I could, making a mess of the towels.

The feel of soap and hot water made my longing for a

bath even stronger, but I made myself start to think about what I might need.

Sylvie had wasted her time unpacking what I'd brought with me from the Academy when I'd taken my leave of absence. Packing would've gone faster if those clothes—my most sturdy and sensible—were all still in my trunk. The things I kept at Mother's were pretty and frivolous, suited to the human world, but I didn't think they were going to be what was required for the next few days.

What I really needed were pants and tunics like Lily usually wore, something that provided ease of movement. I hadn't packed the tough canvas trousers I sometimes wore in my workroom—I hadn't expected to need them. Perhaps I could steal some of Simon's old clothes. Lily was shorter and slimmer than me, so hers wouldn't fit.

I had dragged most of the clothes I wanted out of the armoire when there was a soft knock at the door.

Hannah, I thought. Wanting company.

But when I opened the door, it was Fen, not Hannah, who confronted me. Fen looking as weary and worried as I felt. He held a decanter in one hand and two glasses in the other.

"Fen?" It was one thing to be alone together in his rooms at the Swallow, but inviting him in here in my mother's house suddenly felt far more intimate.

"Your mother," he said softly as he reached out and pushed the door farther open, "sent me to tell you that there was a note."

I stepped back without thinking as he moved forward. He came into the room, put the glasses and the decanter next to the pile of clothes on my bed, and lowered himself into the chaise longue I kept by the window to read in. He moved as if his very bones hurt, none of the usual languid, graceful prowl of him evident in his movements.

"A note?" I stayed where I was by the open door.

"Simon." He closed his eyes for a moment. "Simon sent word. We're to stay here tonight. The City is quiet for now, so we're all"—he grimaced suddenly—"to get some rest and he'll come in the morning."

I understood the grimace. Frustration.

Simon and Guy wouldn't be sleeping tonight; they'd be doing what they did best. Healing. Defending. Fighting back. Whereas I was trapped, as usual, into being able to do exactly nothing. I couldn't leave. Lily and I were, if it came right down to it, the strongest two in the house. "Is Lily still here?" I asked. If I knew Lily, she'd be off to help Simon as soon as she could. Unless he'd asked her to stay put and help protect the house.

Fen nodded. "Yes. Simon asked her to stay."

I expected she was about as pleased with being asked to remain here as I was. Not with having to protect us—she wouldn't hesitate in that—but being separated from Simon was not something she liked at any time, let alone on a night like this when he was in danger.

But knowing she was here made me rest a little easier. The house had strong wards . . . Simon and Holly had worked on them, strengthening them even more, over the last few days. Fen would know if there was anything wrong with them, as would I.

"I guess we should sleep, then," I said tentatively. Sleep sounded wonderful. Or even better, a bath before sleeping. But as tempting as both those things were, I made no move to usher Fen out of my room.

"Personally, I'm going to drink first." Fen laid his head against the back of the chaise, staring up at the ceiling. His face was streaked with soot like mine had been, his dark hair rumpled. His left hand was rubbing his right arm. He squinted up at the light coming from the gaslights in the walls, a wince splitting the dirt on his face. The bloodstain from the cut on his head was rusty brown now, blending with the rest of the dirt.

"Does your head hurt?" I asked. "The visions . . ." I hesitated. Should I ask? Or had there been enough catastrophe and disaster for one night? But if I didn't ask, I would just lie here for what was left of the night and wonder about it. "Have you seen anything?"

Fen let out a long breath. His hand moved from his wrist to his temples, long fingers pressing into the flesh there as if part of him wanted to reach right inside his head and pull out what it was that pained him. "Nothing good," he said.

"I hardly expected rainbows and flowers," I said. "Tell me the truth."

Fen didn't move. "Pour me a drink first," he said.

I looked at him, then at the decanter. It would be better

for him if I eased the pain with my powers rather than him dulling it with brandy, but I had the feeling that tonight he would drink regardless. I didn't really blame him. The notion of oblivion was awfully appealing right now.

Almost as appealing as the man himself, rumpled and stained and smoke-scented as he was. I bit my lip, then shut the door, turning the latch quietly. After all, it wouldn't do for Hannah or one of the servants to find Fen here.

I walked across to the bed, stared down at the glasses. "Tell me," I said. "If you drink, you'll forget."

"Good," he muttered.

"No, not good. I'm not asking anything that plenty of people aren't going to be asking in the morning. If you tell me now, you won't have to repeat it for them."

"Much good my visions are," he said, the words so bitter I could almost taste the sting on my tongue.

"If I were any sort of a seer, surely I would have seen what happened tonight."

"Who would have believed you if you had?" I said, wanting to ease his anger. I knew the perils of that particular emotion. Had seen it drive my brothers into danger. Had felt it myself. In Fen, I sensed that he would drink anger and guilt like raw alcohol and the mixture might bring him to a breaking point. "Besides, the Treaty Hall is so full of wards and magics and bindings, it's surprising that any of us could stand up straight, let alone use our powers. Tell me. Please?"

"I saw the Fae in Summerdale," he said. "The queen in black. I saw the hall in ruins and the Fae's chambers in the City empty. Fire. Blood ashes. More of the same."

"Did you see Ignatius?"

Fen rubbed his head again. "Ignatius laughing. Ignatius on that gods-damned throne. And this time there were more people around him. Whoever did this tonight, it's made things worse."

"You think it was him?"

A grimace. "He couldn't do it alone. Enough power to break all those wards . . . it's not something the Blood have. He would've needed Fae help."

That was a thought to chill the bones. My urge to join Fen in drinking ourselves into a stupor grew stronger. Not

that I'd ever actually managed to achieve that goal before.
Mages have to work very hard to get drunk.

According to Simon it has something to do with our bodies burning the food we eat more quickly to fuel our power—
the reason he said I could eat almost as much as he and Guy
could and still fit into my corsets. Personally I think it has
more to do with lugging iron bars around and sweating over
my forge half the day, but I'm not a healer. So I choose not to
argue with my brother over that. Still, I usually lose my stomach for alcohol well before it has the appropriate effect on
me. But maybe I'd just never had quite the right incentive.

I eyed the brandy decanter speculatively. "Surely the
queen will see that. Then she'll have to reconvene the negotiations if she wants to bring him to justice."

"I don't think the queen is thinking quite that rationally
just now. The Speaker—"

"Were they . . ." I let my voice trail off. Lovers? Friends?
Did the Fae queen take lovers? Presumably she was supposed to produce an heir eventually—though I realized I
didn't know anything about the Fae's rules of succession, it
having been centuries since there had been a change of
power in the Veiled World—but I didn't think she had.

Fen shrugged. "I don't know, but he's been Speaker as
long as she's been queen. Her most trusted courtier. Her
advocate and her voice. That's got to be like losing a limb
even if they weren't sharing a bed. Plus our queen has never
taken harm to what is hers lightly. She was already on edge
about the court after Holly's—" He stopped suddenly.

"I know about that," I said. Knew that Holly's father had
been involved in some kind of plot against the queen.

"Ah. Yes. Well, anyway, she has good reason to be para-
noid."

"But what does that mean?"

"Well, if my visions are right, it means we should all be
leaving the City about now."

He looked perfectly serious. And for some inexplicable
reason, even though I knew he could well be right, his tone
made me want to laugh. It was all too much to take in. Pre-
posterous that somebody had blown up the Treaty Hall, had
brought the negotiations to the teetering edge of ruin before they had even begun.

It couldn't be real. I bit back the giggle that rose in my throat. I felt suddenly as though I had drunk several glasses of his brandy in rapid succession. Light-headed and reckless. I didn't want to think about any of it anymore.

And I knew what I did want to do instead.

Chapter Sixteen

SASKIA

⚡

"So everything is pointless, there's nothing we can do, and we're all going to die?" I said.

Fen looked grim. Grim yet delicious. I didn't doubt that he believed what he saw, but I wasn't quite ready to give up the fight just yet. But we had both had just about enough of everything tonight. I could think of one thing that would make me feel better. It would also take Fen's mind off the visions plaguing him.

"Yes," he said shortly. "So can I have my damned brandy, please?"

I grasped the decanter round its throat and held it out to him. "This brandy?" I tilted the bottle, walking toward him.

His eyes flicked to the liquor, then back to me. "Yes."

"No," I said as I came within arm's reach.

"No?"

"No," I repeated. To emphasize my point, I tossed the decanter toward the wall. It hit with a dull thud, then dropped to the floor, where it shattered with a pleasing crash.

"What the hell?" Fen said, half rising.

I stepped closer, put my hand on his chest, and shoved him back into the chair.

"I have something better than brandy, Fen," I said, watching his furious expression turn wary even as his pupils widened.

"What's that?"

"Me."

"Excuse me?" He sounded startled, but his pupils flared wider, his eyes deepening to the darkly delicious shade I was coming to know all too well.

"You heard me," I said. Beneath my hand his heart sped faster. He wanted me. I knew that much. Well and good. I wanted him too. All I had to do was convince him that it was all right to take me.

"Saskia . . ." he said warningly.

"Shut up, Fen." I lifted my hand so I could straighten. "You think too much like my brothers."

His mouth dropped open. "This is your *parents'* house."

"I know," I said cheerfully. "But they have other things to worry about. And this room is well warded. I've told you before. I'm not a good human girl. Well-bred, I have to admit, but that hasn't stopped either of my brothers from doing what they want. I'm a mage, Fen. I can call fire. I can make metal dance. I can hear the song of the iron. I can hear the chain around your wrist and I can hear the blood in your veins. I hear it rushing, Fen. Rushing because your heart is pounding. You want me."

"I—"

"I said, shut up." I smiled down at him. "Stop making things complicated. I'm not asking you to marry me. Hellfire, Fen, if you're right, there's really not much time left, and I, for one, intend to at least have one last piece of fun before I die. I'd like to have it with you." I stared down at him, arching an eyebrow as I let my hands rise to the button at the collar of my blouse. "But if you're determined to sit there and sulk, then I can go find—"

His hand shot out, circled my wrist. Drew me toward him.

"I. Am. Not. Sulking."

"Well, then," I said, "prove it." I stepped back, turned around and headed across the room to the bathroom door.

"Where are you going?"

"I need a bath," I said. "So do you. Perhaps you'd like to scrub my back?"

He tilted his head. "Are you sure about this?"

"Yes, I'm sure. So perhaps you'd like to make up your mind now?" I walked into the bathroom without waiting to hear his reply and bent to turn the water on in the tub before I could change my mind. The rushing sound of steaming water pouring into the bath matched the whoosh and pound of my pulse in my ears as I stood there waiting to see if he would join me. I picked up a flask of my favorite bath oil. Undid the stopper. Poured it in. One heartbeat. Two. Three. Four.

Then I heard his footsteps on the floor behind me. Felt his eyes on my back.

"What took you so long?"

"I had to take my boots off," he said.

I turned to face him. Sure enough, he was barefoot, leaning against the doorway in his shirt and trousers. His jacket, apparently, had been abandoned along with his boots.

"Couldn't you have taken them off in here?"

"Water's bad for the leather," he said.

I smiled at his perfectly serious tone. "Scared I was going to pull you in fully clothed?"

He came closer still, and now there was a smile on his face to match my own. "No. Scared you wouldn't. Scared that I might be hallucinating all of this at the end of a very long day." He reached out and ran a finger along my face. "You feel real. Are you real, Saskia?"

"I think so." My voice shook slightly. I echoed his gesture. "And you?"

"I don't know anymore." He shook his head, then smiled again. "But if this is a vision, it's the best one I've had in a very long time and I'm more than happy to keep having it."

"Good." I stepped into him, reached up and kissed him lightly. "Let's see what we can see together then."

He pushed the door shut and turned the key in the lock. I felt a tingle of magic that meant he'd added another shield to the lock. Thoughtful of him.

I risked a quick glance at the tub, nearly half full already. Steam rose from the surface of the water, curling invitingly. But I was more interested in the man than the bath right now.

Fen came back to me and pulled me close. This time our kiss was anything but light. It was as heady and heated as the steam rising around us. Warming me from my head to my toes. Both of us exhausted and dirty and disheveled, yet he still smelled and tasted better than any other man I'd taken to my bed.

I pressed myself closer, eager for the feel of him against me. I tugged his shirt free of his trousers and ran my hands up and under, skimming the muscles of his back. He made a pleased noise against my mouth and his hands started working at the buttons that fastened my back. Too many buttons, I thought resentfully. Reggie did beautiful work on her gowns, but once she was well again, I would need to speak to her about making them quicker to get out of.

Not that Fen seemed to have that much difficulty. In no time at all my gown slid from my shoulders, as though buttons and fastenings had simply evaporated under the touch of his clever fingers, leaving me in my petticoats and corset.

The corset seemed suddenly too tight. I couldn't draw a deep enough breath as Fen stepped back and just looked at me.

I let him look as long as I could bear, then, when I couldn't stand it anymore, I turned and shut off the taps before the bath could overflow. The steam no longer felt quite so warm. I figured that was because my skin now felt hot enough on its own.

Fen came up behind me and ran his hand down my back, stopping where my spine ended. Then those keen fingers ran up and started working on my laces with as much proficiency as he'd shown with my buttons. Once those were free, he slipped the corset aside and tossed it into one corner of the room before spinning me and taking my mouth.

When we drew apart, both breathless, I noticed the smear of ash across his face where I'd touched him and started to laugh without meaning to.

"What?"

I just shook my head, bent down and dipped one of the washcloths into the bathwater. I used it to wipe his face gently and giggled harder when the water ran down onto his shirt, turning the fabric somewhat transparent.

His eyes went wide. "Two can play that game."

He picked up a washcloth of his own. He didn't even pretend to wipe my face though . . . just laid it across my chest, then squeezed the water out so it ran down the curves of my breast, the rapidly cooling water making my nipples spike harder against the thin silk of my chemise.

"Gods," he muttered and flung the cloth back into the water, where it landed with a splash. His hand splayed across my breast, thumb teasing the nipple with a pressure that made me shiver despite the heat in the room. "I know you wanted a bath," he said, voice gone husky, "but I'd like to propose an alternative."

It took a moment to find my voice, so distracted was I by the dual sensations of his touch and watching his dark olive skin against my own paler flesh. "Such as?"

"Bed first, then bath. Later. Much later," he added as he bent and replaced his thumb with his mouth, sucking gently, then fiercer. At that point I no longer cared where we were or what we used as long as we got to some suitable horizontal surface quickly.

"Bed," I agreed and pushed him away. I pointed toward the door he'd warded. "That way."

He laughed, then took my hand and pulled me toward the door. We half stumbled back into the bedroom, coming together again to kiss and shed the rest of our clothes in a frenzy as we moved toward the bed.

Fen's shirt and trousers vanished somehow and he dispensed with my chemise with one rapid upward tug, throwing it over his shoulder.

He dispensed with the neat piles of clothes laid on my bed in much the same fashion, tumbling them onto the floor with an impatient sweep of his arms. I laughed again at his eagerness until he turned back to me and the heat burning in those dark green eyes stole the laughter from my lips, replacing it with an urgent hunger that made me gasp.

I walked closer, pushing him backward until he toppled onto the bed and I could straddle him, feeling the long length of his cock underneath me with a sigh of satisfaction.

He looked up with an expression that was both surprised and pleased.

"I have to remember this," he said.

"Remember what?" I paused, half leaning toward him.

His grin was wicked. "You're really not a good girl."

"Oh, I'm very good," I promised him with a wriggle of my hips that made him catch his breath.

He reached up and his hand closed over the back of my

neck, tugging my face down so we could kiss again. "So am I," he breathed, and then he proceeded to show me that he hadn't been boasting.

The next morning, breakfast was subdued. I woke far too early, alone in my bed. While I appreciated Fen's discretion in disappearing, I missed the warm weight of him beside me. He didn't appear at breakfast. That made matters somewhat simpler. My mother had enough on her plate without having her illusions about the life I led shattered as well.

Lily and I sipped coffee and attempted to distract Hannah from her unending stream of questions. Mother hardly ate anything before vanishing off to organize yet another detail in her planning of the exodus.

After a few more minutes I convinced Hannah to go and see if she could help.

"How much longer, do you think?" I asked Lily. The sun was well into the sky now and the ornate clock on the end of the breakfast buffet said it was nearly eight. Surely Simon had to come soon.

Lily shrugged. "They'll come when they come." She took a sip of her third cup of coffee, the toast on her plate growing stone-cold as she ignored it.

Not so calm as she pretended. I forced myself to take a forkful of the bacon I'd put on my plate. I had no more appetite than Lily, but unlike her with her wraith's endurance, I needed to eat to function. "What do you think will happen?"

Lily regarded me for a moment. "I think the Blood will make a move," she said bluntly. "If the human council and the Templars don't step in to keep the peace and get the negotiations back on track, then Ignatius will almost certainly take action."

It seemed that Fen wasn't the only pessimist I had to deal with.

Or maybe he and Lily were merely pragmatic enough to face what the rest of us weren't yet ready to deal with. The possibility of war. Of death and violence. Of *losing*.

No. I wasn't going to think about that. Just like I wasn't going to think about the fact that my urge to go and find Fen was growing stronger with each minute I sat here. If I concentrated, I could probably work out where he was. Our house was large, but his chain would still be easy enough for me to sense. But no. We had to keep things between us simple and, for now at least, discreet. Anything more was too difficult to contemplate.

I'd had enough coffee to make my stomach feel like I'd been drinking acid by the time Simon finally arrived. He didn't have Guy with him, which only intensified the ache in my gut.

Simon kissed Lily, then gulped down the coffee she offered while I watched silently. He looked worn out. Guilt about the few hours of sleep I'd gotten tugged at me. As did the fact that I could have gotten quite a few more if I hadn't been occupying myself with Fen.

"We should go out into the garden," I said. "Simon needs sunlight." And outside, I too could touch the earth and draw power and strength from the metal beneath her skin.

Simon drank more coffee. "The garden is too exposed. The drawing room will do."

I didn't see that sitting in a room with huge glass windows was necessarily any safer than sitting in a garden that was also heavily warded. But Simon knew the house's defenses even better than I did and he was the one who'd spent time training as a Templar before he'd decided to become a healer.

"I should find Fen," I said. "He'll want to hear this too."

"No need." Fen appeared in the doorway. I wondered if he'd been waiting in his room all this time, avoiding me. He could have seen Simon arriving out his window and known when to come down.

"Good morning." Fen nodded politely at Lily and me and came to sit at the table, his gaze focused on Simon, his whole body carrying an air of only barely leashed need for action.

I felt a pang at his casual greeting. Which was foolish. He was being discreet. At least I hoped he was. I dug my fingernails into my palm under the cover of the tablecloth. Time to focus, not pout after a man.

"Are Holly and Reggie safe?" Fen said next, only increasing my pique.

"Yes." Simon nodded. "We've increased the wards at St. Giles, but there have been no incidents. Holly's there now with Reggie."

Fen's posture eased a little, but his mouth turned down

at the mention of St. Giles. He was thinking about Reggie and Holly down in the hidden ward, no doubt, not about all the other patients wounded in the explosion.

"We were going to go into the drawing room," I said. Lily nodded, tugged at Simon and set him in the direction of the door. Then she started piling food on a plate, obviously intending to take it with her and make sure he ate.

"You should eat something too," I said to Fen.

Lily shot me a sidewise glance. I ignored her.

"I'm not hungry," Fen said. But he had to be starving.

I didn't press the point. I poured myself another cup of coffee and raised it to my lips before my stomach twinged in protest at the thought. I put the cup down.

Lily looked pointedly at Fen, then gestured toward the food. "Eat while you can. We don't know what's going to happen today."

Simon was sitting on one of the deep window ledges when we all trooped into the drawing room, his expression distracted as he stared down at the street below us. Mother had joined him. She was seated in her usual place, her hands busy winding up tapestry wools from the jumble in the basket that lived beside her chair and stowing them in a sewing case.

She was watching Simon. His gaze didn't shift as we entered, his focus absolute. Watching for Guy?

I wanted my brother home too. Of all of us, Guy was the one who put himself most at risk day in and day out and even though I was accustomed to the sensation of being worried about him, it never went away entirely. There was a part of me—sometimes pushed deep below consciousness and sometimes front and center in my brain—that was always braced for bad news.

I joined Simon and extended my own power, seeking the faint spark of Guy's blood. As long as he was within the City walls I would be able to sense him. Much past that and my power reached its limits. I hadn't been able to feel him during those few years he'd spent in the Voodoo Territories— which had driven me crazy at first— nor when he'd gone into Summerdale with Holly, though I suspected in Summerdale at least, that was more to do with the Veiled Court's protections than a lack of power on my part.

"Can you feel him?" Simon said.

It took a moment more, but then I caught it.

Guy. Moving. Alive. A smile broke over my face. "He's somewhere near the Brother House."

Who knew if that was good or bad, but for now knowing he was alive was enough to ease the tension in the room. Mother breathed a sigh of relief and then, to cover her lapse, reached for another hank of thread.

"Here." Lily gave Simon the food she'd brought in. "Eat."

Simon nodded and took the plate. He started to eat while the rest of us found places to sit. I took a chair opposite the window after Fen sat on one of the small sofas. I wasn't going to sit beside him. That would be inviting unwelcome scrutiny.

Lily stayed by Simon at the window.

"Can you tell us what happened?" I asked Simon.

He swallowed, then shrugged. "Guy will know more than me. I spent most of the night tending the wounded."

"Did anyone die?" It seemed unlikely that all of them would have survived. Not with the extent of the some of the injuries.

"Franklin Jones from the human council and a few others who were supporting that delegation."

The council delegation had had the front rows of the human quadrant of the hall, so they would have borne the brunt of the blast. A councillor dead. That just added another layer of complication to the situation.

"What about the Beasts and the Blood?"

"I assume they're taking care of their own. None of them presented themselves for treatment at St. Giles."

I'd expected as much. Each race would be sticking close to home and trusting its own at this point. No point risking further fanning the flames by causing an incident at a Haven.

Unless further fanning the flames was what you wanted to do, of course. Ignatius seemed to be the most likely candidate to want to do that, but for now, it seemed, he hadn't made a move. Not one that had reached the hospital, at least.

Guy would know more. If he ever got here. "What does Bryony think?"

"She's not . . ." He stopped, looked at Mother, then at

me. "It was hard to talk last night. Some of the Fae healers went back to Summerdale when they heard what had happened. Bryony spent half the night trying to convince the rest of them to stay."

I winced. The sunmages like Simon were powerful healers, but the Fae had skills that went beyond human magics. Beside which, sunmages were not that commonplace, and Fae healers who were willing to risk a potential schism with their Family to come and work amongst the human healers were scarcer still. Any depletion of our healer ranks was a bad thing.

"She seems to have succeeded for now." Simon's face was grim.

I wondered how long "for now" was. "Did she know the Speaker?"

All night I'd tried to avoid thinking about the Speaker. Seeing a dead Fae had been . . . shocking. Worse than a human body somehow—not that I'd seen many of those. The Fae lived so long, and looked so young, it had seemed like a violation to see one so still and broken. Even now, the memory made me feel ill.

"All the Fae know the Speaker," Lily said when Simon didn't reply. "He's been part of the court forever."

It wasn't exactly what I'd meant, but I didn't want to push the topic. Things were bad. Maybe worse than we knew, but we'd have to wait for Guy to find out exactly how bad.

FEN

The waiting stretched into an hour and then slid toward two. When the cathedral bell rang the half hour, I drew Simon away.

"How much longer are we going to wait?" I asked softly.

Across the room Saskia made no pretense of not watching us, even if Lily and Hilary DuCaine hid their interest better.

"Guy will be here soon," Simon said. His voice was calm, but there was a thread of strain in the tone.

"What if he isn't?" I asked. "There are a lot of people in this house to move. Isn't it better to do it now? While the sun is up." And while it was early enough that most of the Beasts would be sleeping. Unlike the Blood, they were free to walk under the sunlight, but they still led largely nocturnal lives. If they'd stayed up strategizing, then the alphas and *guerriers* would need to sleep for at least a few hours before they took any action.

Like Martin coming for me.

I was keen to be somewhere more protected than this house if and when that happened.

Simon frowned. "I told Guy we'd wait."

"That was when Guy was expecting to be here early in the day. It's midmorning now. You have to give your servants time to get home to their families too, after they help you. You have to make sure they go." I'd overheard the house steward, Edwards, arguing with Hilary DuCaine about leaving earlier that morning. He wanted to stay and ensure that the house was safe. Hilary had flatly forbidden such a thing, but I wouldn't have been surprised if Edwards, who from what I'd been able to gather had served the family since before Guy was born, defied his mistress and tried to sneak back.

"Plus we need to strengthen the wards once everyone has gone." So that there would be a house for them to return to. If all went well. "That takes time." I was half surprised by my calm tone. Just as I was surprised by the fact that I was apparently staying with the DuCaines through whatever happened.

I still didn't know quite when I'd made that decision. But at some point last night, with Saskia curled in my arms, I'd known I couldn't leave. But I didn't know what my decision meant, by any stretch of the imagination.

Other than that I was well and truly screwed.

And didn't that just make me as big an idiot as any man who'd ever set his cap for a woman who belonged to an entirely different world? It was one thing for Simon and Guy to choose partners who didn't exactly fit the human standards of normal, but it would be lot harder for Saskia. Unfair, but there it was. Humans had different rules for men and women.

So I needed to keep a cool head. I wasn't going to say no

to her if and when we found a chance to be together again.
But I was going to keep a firm grip on my reason. Not let
myself be fooled into believing that there could be more
between us than the desire we shared. I still wasn't sure that
that desire wasn't fueled, in large part, by Saskia wanting an
escape from the reality that faced us.

I couldn't ignore that reality, not when a dozen variations
of it, each more disturbing than the last, danced in front of
my eyes every time my control over my power slipped.

Which was happening more and more, no matter how
tightly I wrapped my wrist in iron. Maybe I needed a thicker
chain.

I knew in my heart that wouldn't help. I could climb into
one of Guy's mail shirts and it still wouldn't be enough iron.
In fact, I could probably lie across Saskia's forge and let her
beat me with a hammer and that pain still wouldn't drive
away the visions.

Holly was right. I needed more help than I currently was
getting or the visions would kill me eventually.

But there was still time before I reached the point of
desperation. There was only one avenue left to me now. I
had cut myself off from the Beasts last night when I'd let my
name be read out as part of the human delegation. There
was a very slim chance that Martin might take me back if I
crawled to him on bloody hands and knees, but it was far
more likely that he would kill me for denying him.

Which meant I was left with the Fae for the solution to
how to control my powers. I doubted that they were any
more likely to be setting out a welcome mat for half-breeds
than any of the other races. Especially not after the explosion last night.

So until I grew desperate enough to bargain away whatever they might demand of me in return for their help,
Saskia was my salvation, the way to hang on a bit longer
before necessity forced me to go to Summerdale.

Hell, maybe we'd all be dead before that happened anyway. But I needed Saskia's touch until then, in more ways
than one.

I glanced up and realized that all three DuCaines were
watching me expectantly. I'd obviously missed a question
somewhere in my musings. "I'm sorry. I was thinking. What
was the question?"

"I asked if there was anything you needed from the Swallow," Saskia said.

I shook my head. I had clothes at the Brother House and whilst there were things in my rooms that I valued, my money and other valuables were either banked or stashed in various hidey-holes around the City. There was nothing that I needed badly enough to risk going to the border boroughs and potentially running into a Krueger or three.

"Good," Simon said. "Then the plan is to take Mother, Father, and Hannah to St. Giles. They need me there anyway and it will be safe for now. We can move Mother and the girls to the Brother House once Guy's free."

I wondered if he really thought he'd be able to convince Saskia to do that. The elder DuCaines would probably comply, to protect Hannah if for no other reason, but Saskia wasn't going to sit quietly by and let herself be locked away.

Besides, she was a named member of the Templar delegation. If my recall of treaty law was clear, that meant she had to be present during each day the negotiations took place. The system was designed so that no decisions could be made without each race's full complement of delegates. Though what the hell happened now that some of those delegates were dead and injured, I had no idea.

I imagined that both the human council and the Templars had probably spent large parts of the night reading the fine print of the treaty law, trying to decipher just that. Hopefully at some other point in the City's history somebody had died or been taken ill during the negotiations and had had to be replaced. Because if the law didn't cover substitutions, either there would be endless wrangling about what would be acceptable or the delegations would have to go on with their reduced numbers, which might have some interesting impacts on the voting blocs.

"All right," I said. "Then let's move."

Chapter Seventeen

SASKIA

St. Giles was orderly rather than frantic. I'd expected crowds of worried relatives and harried healers. Instead there was a sense of things being under control, even though the foyer under the great dome was busier than any other time I'd been there. Granted, some of the healers looked tired as they greeted Simon, but that was not entirely unusual. Healers tended to run their powers low in saving their patients.

Simon herded us up to his office—a tight squeeze once Mother, Father, Hannah, Lily, Fen, and I were all in the room. Then he left again to direct the servants, find out where we were to be lodging, and check on his patients.

Being this much closer to the action made the waiting even more difficult. My skin crawled with the need to know what was happening, my eyes felt like I'd rolled them in sand after my shortened night's sleep, and my stomach ached. Surely someone could provide us with an update.

It seemed from the lack of chaos downstairs, that the immediate problems presented by the wounded from the explosion had been dealt with. Maybe Bryony could give us an update. I knew where to find her office; it was another

floor up and across in the metal-free part of the hospital. I
could go fetch her and—

"Sit down, Saskia," Fen said, and I realized I'd half risen
from my seat without knowing it.

I sat. No one was going to let me go anywhere. Not yet.

Luckily for our collective sanity and patience, the next
person to open Simon's door was Guy.

Mother rose as he stepped through and Hannah flew
across the room and hugged him hard.

"Whoa there, halfbit," he said, squeezing her in return.
"Let me breathe."

Hannah let him go reluctantly. Guy pushed her gently
back toward the chair she'd been sitting in.

"Good morning." He nodded a general sort of greeting, then came over and sat down in a spare chair, a weary
noise of relief escaping from him as he leaned back and
stretched.

I studied him carefully. His face was grubby and he
seemed just as tired as the rest of us, but there were no signs
of injury or any lasting harm from the queen's binding. He
could speak again—that much was plain.

I let out a breath of relief and rose from my chair. "Shall
I go and fetch Simon?"

Guy waved me back down. "I ran into Holly downstairs."
His expression lightened briefly as he spoke her name.
"She'll bring him."

"What can you tell us?" Mother said, her hands twisting
in her lap.

"Let's wait for Simon," Guy said gently. He craned his
head backward, twisting his neck until I heard it crunch. His
pale hair stood up in messy, sweaty spikes, as it always did
when he'd been wearing his helmet.

My stomach tightened painfully. How had he spent the
night? Not doing what I had been doing, that much was
certain.

Simon and Holly appeared soon enough and with them
came Bryony, carrying a steaming silver teapot. Holly had
the matching tray laden with cups. Fae tea. I kept my expression polite. I had never really warmed to the Fae's
herbal brews, which tended toward green and astringent-
tasting rather than sweet. I drank my coffee black but with

enough sugar that Guy used to tease me about wasting time actually adding water and suggested that I just mix ground coffee and sugar grains straight and have done with it.

Everyone said hello again, and chairs were shuffled and rearranged so everyone had somewhere to sit or stand. I wound up close to Fen, with Hannah on my other side. Fen was watching Bryony with an expression I couldn't quite interpret. I looked at her, then down at myself with a sigh. Bryony had no doubt been up all night, yet she looked as beautiful as the sunlight streaming through the window. Her deep blue dress was immaculate and unwrinkled and her long black hair was piled in neat coils at the back of her head. The rainbow silver of the chain she always wore around her neck glittered faintly, throwing little hints of the blue and purple of the Family ring adorning one of her long fingers into the air.

She moved gracefully amongst us, pouring the tea. In contrast, I felt stumpy and shabby and slept in. I frowned as I watched Fen watching Bryony. Was she the sort of woman Fen liked?

Probably.

Still, I forced a smile as Bryony extended a cup toward me, taking the tea politely, though I didn't drink. It would probably make me feel better if I did, being brewed by a Master Healer after all, but I couldn't bring myself to do it. Childish. Certainly. But it somehow made me feel better.

I noticed that Fen didn't drink either and my small spark of satisfaction increased to a glow.

"All right," Father said after Bryony had completed the ritual of giving everyone tea and speaking a Fae blessing over us all. "Is someone finally going to tell us what is happening?"

Mother scowled at him, but Guy half smiled as he drained his tea. Some of the strained look left his face and he held out his cup for more. "Actually there isn't that much to tell."

Was he lying? If he was, I'd brain him with the teapot, precious silver or no. But I couldn't see any sign of deception in his face. His pale eyes were clear as he looked around the room.

"The Blood didn't make a move?" Simon sounded surprised.

"There were a few skirmishes last night, but nothing out of the ordinary. If you ask me, the Blood were holed up doing exactly what the rest of us were doing."

"Which was?" I said impatiently.

"Reading the bloody treaty to try and work out what sort of mess we're in."

"Did you come to a conclusion?" This time it was Bryony who asked.

Of all of us, I would have thought she was the one most likely to have the answer. The Fae hold the balance of power in the treaty and they are all schooled carefully in its minutiae. Then again, Bryony was somewhat disconnected from the Veiled Court, spending the majority of her time here in the City and at St. Giles. Maybe she hadn't brushed up lately.

Guy gave another shrug, though this one was more a frustrated hitch of his shoulders. "The best the Templar advocates can come up with, the treaty holds until the negotiation period is over. But that's their interpretation. Others might take a different view."

All of us fell silent for a moment. The negotiations happened every five years. The treaty was re-signed on the last day of the negotiation period, or sooner if all the relevant grievances and reallocations had been agreed. But it was always signed before midnight of the last day of that fifth year. Thirteen days from now.

"What happens if it isn't signed?" Fen asked eventually.

"Nothing good," Guy said

"War," Lily added.

Guy nodded and beside me Hannah bit her lip. I reached over and took her hand, wishing that I could reach out my other hand to Fen and feel him too.

"Is there someone who can take Hannah to wherever it is we'll be sleeping?" I suggested, not liking the pallor in her face.

"I'm not a baby," Hannah objected.

"No, you're not," I agreed, feeling somewhat hypocritical. "But there are things we have to talk about that you can't know."

My mother rose. "I'll come with you, Hannah. Simon will tell us what we need to know later, won't you, Simon?"

Simon nodded. He reached out and pulled the bell on his

wall. A few minutes later one of the hospital staff appeared and ushered Mother and Hannah out. Hannah's last-ditch objections floated back from the corridor.

Fen stood and closed the door. "We were talking about war," he said as he returned to his chair.

"There won't be war if we can help it," Guy said.

There was another long silence. We all knew the history. The treaty had come about the first time because the Fae had decided to side with the humans against the increasing depravations of the Blood. Without the help of the Fae, could the humans beat the Beasts and the Blood?

"It seems to me that the question is what we do to ensure that that doesn't happen," Bryony said.

"That means getting the Fae back to the negotiations," Simon said.

Another brief silence as we all contemplated that.

"Has anyone been looking into what happened at the hall?" I asked.

"Yes," Guy said. "Mages from each of the Guilds are looking over the wreckage. There were some Beasts there too."

"No Blood?"

Guy shook his head. "They waited until sunrise. It seemed safer that way. But they can only look outside. The Fae sealed the hall."

Bryony twisted toward Guy. "The Fae sealed the hall? I thought I felt something odd a few hours before dawn."

"Yes. No one can get inside right now. There are wards that, to quote Liam, would take your f—" Guy caught himself, suddenly remembering that Father was still in the room. "That would prove fatal to anyone who tries to cross them."

Well, that wasn't good. Not least because the longer the humans were denied access to the hall, the more time there was for the traces of whatever had caused the explosion to fade. "Were there any Fae there?"

"Not that they could see. Of course, anything could have been going on inside and we'd be none the wiser." Guy shifted in his seat, stretching his shoulders with another crack of muscles.

"Do you need healing?" Bryony asked.

"No. I'm not hurt. Just stiff."

"So what do we do now?" I asked.

"Father Cho is speaking with the council now, along with the Guild Masters. I'd imagine they're trying to figure out how to send a request to the Veiled Court that the negotiations recommence. I wouldn't be surprised if they decide to give the queen another few days to calm down."

"The rites for the Speaker will have to be held before sunset today," Bryony said.

I wondered if a funeral would help the queen or just make her angrier. My memories of Edwina's funeral were of vast grief and the abiding rage that simmered beneath the depths of all-encompassing sadness. If I could have torn the Blood who'd addicted her limb from limb, I would have done so. Watching her coffin being lowered into the earth, knowing it held only her ashes—burning was the law for the bodies of the blood-locked—hadn't eased my hurt and fury any. If anything, it had made it worse.

But perhaps the Fae were wiser than me.

The memory of the queen's voice demanding to know who had caused the Speaker's death suggested otherwise.

"Well, then," Fen said, "I'd imagine the council will wait until tomorrow. Unless they're idiots. The Speaker wasn't the only one killed, after all."

"Did anyone figure out the issue with replacing delegates?" Simon asked.

Guy nodded. "In case of death or sickness, yes, it's allowable. That was the other thing that the advocates managed to get to the bottom of last night. But they have to move fast. There has to be a full complement of delegates for the opening rituals to be completed."

I looked across at Fen, wondering what he was thinking. I hadn't asked if he was sticking around last night, but I'd wondered.

"Can the rituals even be completed? With the hall so damaged? The stones . . . what if the stones were destroyed?"

"There's nothing unique about the stones," Bryony said. "The spells could be re-wrought. The magics of the hall go deep. It's likely the rituals can still be performed. If not, well, the first negotiations were held in the open air outside the City. Maybe we'll just have to re-create history."

Out in the open at night? That would give the Beasts and

the Blood a degree of advantage I didn't like to contemplate. But it would be up to the Fae to police the negotiations, and it seemed unlikely that the Veiled Queen would be in the mood to brook any attempts to subvert the proceedings. If she was in the mood to attend the negotiations at all.

"There's no point just sitting here and speculating," Guy said. "We can't do any more until the Fae make their move. I need to get back to the Brother House and Simon and Bryony have work to do."

"Is there something I can do to help?" I asked.

Simon nodded. "I'm sure you can help somewhere. I'll ask. But I want you to see that everyone is settled first."

"I will." Hopefully I could think of something to say to Hannah, to make her feel better about being kept out of things. I had no idea what, though. "Maybe you can think of something for Hannah to do as well. That will keep her mind off everything that's happening. Make her feel useful."

Stop her from doing something foolish, hopefully.

None of us had truly had a childhood after Edwina's death, but Hannah, as the youngest of us, had lost the most. The rest of us had had to grow up fast, but she'd had the same life-changing loss and not so many years of happiness before it to buffer her. Guy was already sworn to the Templars when Edwina died and Simon had changed his path to the healers shortly after the funeral. My powers coming in had been another blow to her. She was older than she should be for her age, but at the same time still somehow innocent. I wanted to keep her that way a little longer, even though I knew she had to stretch her wings sometime.

Bryony rose and gathered the teacups from those of us still holding them. "I'll find one of the orderlies to take you to your family."

Fen moved restlessly in his chair, stretching his arms. The iron at his wrist was a bright blip in the song of the room. It was pressed tight against his skin. I wanted to take it off, soothe the pain he must be feeling.

And what did it say about me that I still thought of him in the midst of all this chaos? I needed to concentrate on what was important. There would hardly be any opportunity for us to be together, anyway.

Though as I thought about the size of St. Giles and the

miles of tunnels and abandoned wards belowground, there were still some possibilities available to us. Lily and Simon regularly spent nights here, and those two, as much as they tried to hide it, could hardly keep their hands off each other at the best of times. Guy and Holly were little better, but Guy at least had an apartment outside the Brother House, one that Mother had procured for him after he'd taken his final vows.

Simon had his house too, of course, but he worked so many nights that St. Giles was like a second home to him.

I hoped it wasn't about to become mine as well.

An orderly, a slim young man with bright red hair, appeared rapidly in answer to Bryony's summons.

"So," Fen said, as I rose, "what happens now?"

Guy stood and stretched. "Personally, I'm going to see if I can sleep for a bit before Father Cho wants me again." He looked around the room. "The rest of you should get some rest too."

The last thing I wanted was sleep. I was tired, yes, but I couldn't imagine actually being able to sleep if I did lie down. I needed to *do* something. Anything. "I'm not tired," I said. "I'll look in on Mother and Hannah, but then I can do whatever you need, Simon."

We dispersed rapidly. I helped Mother get the rooms we'd been assigned organized to her satisfaction. When Bryony came looking for me an hour or so later, I was glad to escape. Hannah seemed eager to come with me, so I brought her along, hoping to give Mother a chance to rest.

Bryony put us to work helping serve lunch to the patients and making sure that the relatives who were filling the halls and waiting rooms were given tea and other refreshments. It wasn't difficult work but it was unrelenting. The hours flew by.

The trolley the kitchen had given me to wheel the tea things around on had a slightly crooked wheel that made it apt to steer itself into walls and doorframes. I probably could've fixed it, given the right tools, but there wasn't any time.

I had just barely avoided spilling another pot of tea by bumping the trolley into the doorframe of one of the last wards we'd been asked to take care of when I stopped short. Hannah, bearing a basket of scones, almost ran into me.

"Careful," she said.

I ignored her, staring at the bed nearest the door. In it, half her head swathed in bandages as well as her arms and whatever else of her I could see, lay Sara Ledbetter. The prentice who'd been given my place in the Guild's delegation.

That could have been me.

Bile rose in my throat. It *would* have been me. If I'd been sitting with the metalmages.

"Excuse me," I muttered to Hannah and then bolted from the room. Fortunately there was a bathroom just a few feet down the corridor.

I hung over the washbasin, retching as the images of the explosion and death and body parts welled up before my eyes again. The air seemed to fill with the stink of the smoke and burning flesh. Like the Beast I'd killed yesterday.

I retched again.

Then jumped as someone pressed a cool towel to the back of my neck.

"It's just me," Lily said quietly.

The towel, and the faint green scent Lily always brought with her, seemed to help. Still, I hung over the basin for a minute more until I was sure my stomach was under control.

Lily didn't say anything as I ran the taps to rinse the basin clean and wiped my face with another towel.

"Better?" she asked as I stood, still breathing carefully.

"Mostly," I said. "Sorry."

"I've seen worse things than you throwing up. What brought it on?"

I shook my head. "I'm not sure. One of the patients—Sara—I know her from the Academy. She's burned." I pressed my hands into my eyes as though I could block out the image of Sara and all those bandages. It didn't work. I opened my eyes again and faced Lily.

"Is she a friend?"

A friend? No. More like a rival. Truth was, I didn't particularly know her other than where she stood in our classes. "No. But somehow it brought it all back."

"The explosion at the hall?"

"That, and the Beast we killed."

"Yes, I thought you were taking that a little too well. I

threw up for days the first time I killed somebody." She smiled an odd smile. "If that makes you feel any better."

"A little."

"The memories get a little easier. Over time."

I shivered. If anyone would know about that, Lily would. I didn't know exactly how many deaths she'd caused when she was Lucius' assassin, but the number wasn't trivial.

"I'll be all right," I said.

"I know," Lily said. "You're strong. Like your brothers."

I threw the towels into the tall, narrow basket that stood at the side of the basin. "I'm starting to think they were right. It would be better to stay out of it."

"No, it wouldn't. But that doesn't mean it's easy to do."

That was the truth. "How did you know where I was?"

"I was coming to find you." Her clear gray eyes looked sad for a moment.

A chill ran up my spine and my stomach moved uneasily again. "Has something happened?"

"Yes. The Fae have summoned the delegates back. They will be at the hall at sunset."

FEN

The missive from the Fae turned out to be something of an overstatement. When we arrived at the Treaty Hall a few minutes before sunset, having hastily made our way there with the rest of the delegation, everyone rumpled and not looking half as impressive as we had yesterday but still garbed correctly, we weren't greeted by the sight of the full Fae delegation.

No, instead a lone Fae man waited for us, clothed in black and holding the reins of a black horse whose ornate black tack glittered darkly in the twilight. Standing before the soot-stained white marble of the hall, they made an ominous picture. The golden light from the setting sun glowed behind them, somehow making them even more unsettling.

Hardly a promising sight. The Fae wore black gloves, which hid any Family ring that might give a hint to his identity, but I'd have bet good money he was either from the queen's Family or the Speaker's. Someone high up in the court.

I looked at Simon. "Any idea who that is?"

He shook his head.

The Beasts were also arriving in their packs. Once the sun slipped below the horizon, no doubt the Blood would arrive too.

Or would they? Maybe they would be split—some, like Ignatius, wanting to twist this to their own advantage and others, who might want to maintain the treaty, seeking their own path. One thing was certain. The Blood war for power that had been bubbling and simmering since Lord Lucius had died was about to erupt in deadly seriousness. Those who wanted to try for absolute power had to act now or miss their chance.

If my visions were correct, it would be Ignatius who rose. Lady help the rest of them.

Lady help the rest of us as well. Lady grant that my sight wasn't true in the first place.

We all stayed frozen in place while the light faded, seeming to take an age to finally slink away. True to my hunch, as soon as the sunlight winked out, the Blood began to arrive, not in coaches but coalescing out of the darkness in a way that raised the hairs on the back of the neck and made something very like a Beast Kind growl rumble in the back of my throat.

The Blood are very fast when they want to be. And they could stay hidden in the shadows . . . not truly incorporeal like a wraith but hard to see if they did not want to be seen. I scanned our surrounding quickly. How many of them might be hidden on rooftops or in the alleys and buildings surrounding the square? Ignatius might be planning a massacre.

I forced the thought away. I hadn't seen such a thing and I had to hope that Ignatius wasn't bold enough to act just yet, not until the Fae had given some indication that the negotiations might fail. If he acted before that, he would be the one to have broken the treaty, not the Blood. Which would open him up to retribution.

He was too smart for that. He wouldn't move until he was certain of his advantage. He'd worked hard to manufacture this situation—it had to be him. I knew it in my bones, but of course there was no proof. And never would be unless someone got the opportunity to force the truth from him or the Fae let the human mages into the Treaty Hall to examine the evidence left behind by the explosion.

But the arrival of the Blood seemed to satisfy the waiting Fae representative. He summoned a ball of pale light that hovered over his shoulder, providing more illumination than the gaslights that had survived the explosion.

"Are the delegates all present?" The Fae asked. His voice didn't sound loud but at the same time managed to seem as though he was speaking right beside my ear. The effect did nothing to ease my disquiet.

This wasn't going to be a good announcement. My instincts shrieked at me, but I had to follow the lead of the delegation around me. No one was speaking.

"Are the delegates present?" he repeated.

Ignatius stepped forward then. "All the Blood still living are here."

One by one the delegation leaders from the humans and the Beasts stepped forward to speak as well. Several of the alphas reported deaths but said that their delegates had been replaced, awaiting a renewed naming ceremony. The Templars had a couple of delegates who bore bandages and bruises, but we were all here. The mages also reported replacing delegates where needed. I noticed that Saskia flinched slightly when the Master of the Metalmages spoke several names. Was she regretting her choice now?

Was she wondering if they would take her back when all this was done?

Then Barnabas Stoke, head of the human council, stepped forward. I was expecting him to announce that they were missing a member but instead he too reported a replacement delegate to step into the dead councilor's shoes.

It didn't really matter. What mattered was what our Fae friend was about to say.

He began to speak. "I bear a message from my queen, Ruler of the Veiled World, protector of Summerdale, and Keeper of the Peace between the races."

The atmosphere thickened as he paused and looked around the square. Bloody Fae. Always putting on a show. I'm sure I wasn't the only one longing to shout "Just get on with it" as his silence stretched longer still.

"Her Majesty has declared that she will not return to these negotiations until the killer of her most honored and beloved Speaker is brought to justice."

Another long pause, this one broken by the soft hum of whispered comments. Was he about to announce that the Fae knew who that killer was? Was someone about to be dragged from out of our midst and carried off to Summerdale for retribution?

Lady, let it be Ignatius if that is so. I could think of nothing better. But common sense told me that if the queen knew who the killer was, he would likely already be dead and we would be seeing some Fae-conjured images of exactly how painfully he had died. And the queen would be meting out punishments on the killer's race that would probably mostly obliterate their privileges under the treaties. If they had any sense they wouldn't argue with her. The Fae queen would hardly have to lift a finger to annihilate them. She had the whole power of the Veiled Court to draw on, after all.

For not the first time, I was very glad that I'd stayed clear of the Veiled World. As uncertain as things were in the City right now, being in Summerdale had to be like trying to walk on a spiderweb suspended over a deep abyss lined with poisoned razor blades. Anyone with any sense would be laying very low.

The whole square was silent as everyone stared at the man in black. Unsurprisingly, no one stepped forward to claim responsibility for the destruction at the hall.

"Very well," the Fae said after an almost unbearable length of time. "If no one will confess to this crime, then it is up to all of you to bring the guilty party to light. You have one week."

Chapter Eighteen

SASKIA

The uproar as the Fae stopped talking was nearly deafening.

Finally Guy stepped forward and bellowed for silence. It didn't work. But Liam's moving up beside him, raising his sword, and setting it alight did. Uneasy silence rippled over the square like a fog.

Liam nodded once, then let the flames go out.

The leader of the human council, Barnabas Stoke, stepped forward. "This is not acceptable."

The Fae didn't blink. "There will be no debate. The queen has spoken."

"The humans have done nothing to act against the queen or the Fae."

There was no more expression on the Fae's face than there would have been on a statue. He was as shuttered and remote as a glacier. "My queen has yet to determine the guilty party."

"Has she found anything?" Bryony's voice cut across the square.

The Fae man cocked his head at her, as if surprised by her presence. "My queen did not ask me to impart any information about her investigations."

"Well, that's convenient," Fen muttered under his breath.

Bryony looked equally unimpressed as she stepped forward. "If the other races are to clear their names, they will need access to the hall."

He shook his head. "No. Access will not be granted. Until the queen knows who is guilty there is too great a risk that the evidence would be tampered with or destroyed."

"Guilty until proven guilty?" Bryony said. "That is not our way."

"The queen makes the rules, not you, Bryony sa'Eleniel." He seized the reins dangling from his horse's bridle. "I have spoken. That is all."

Before he could mount, Ignatius moved into the patch of light.

"I'm afraid I have to agree with my human colleagues," he said. "This is not acceptable."

The Fae stared down his nose like he was looking at an insect. "You're in my way."

Ignatius stiffened. "You tell your queen that if the negotiations are not resumed and completed by the appointed time, the Blood will judge the treaty to be dissolved."

A babble of outrage and horror rippled through the crowd.

Ignatius nodded up at the Fae. "She should think on that."

I saw Guy's hand close over his sword. Beside him, Liam nudged his side, frowning.

Sainted earth. Was this the beginning of what Fen had seen? The visions he had been tormented by had shown Ignatius victorious. Was this how it was going to come about? My stomach heaved, but this time I managed not to throw up. Barely. I gritted my teeth, willed the shaky chill to leave my body, trying to draw warmth from the metal around me.

It helped a little. As I watched the Fae man ride slowly out of the square, I could think of only one thing. We had to stop Ignatius.

"So what now?" Fen was the one who first spoke the words when we were safely back at the Brother House. Guy looked like he wanted to answer, but he deferred to Father Cho. Around us the other members of the human council and the representatives of the metalmages and the sunmages were seated around the Brothers' long council table. I avoided meeting Master Aquinas' eyes as I settled into my chair.

Father Cho paused a moment, as if considering his words. "Without access to the hall, we have no hope of determining who committed this atrocity. I believe our only real option is to convince the queen to reconsider."

"How do you propose that we do that?" Barnabas Stoke asked. He was an older man, balding and well fed, his weathered skin pink around the nose and cheeks, speaking of a fondness for good wine. A gray velvet jacket strained over the swell of his stomach.

"That's what we're here to discuss," Father Cho said.

"I think we need to act to make sure the Blood have no chance to plan anything," Guy said.

"What do you suggest?" Father Cho said. His tones sounded as frustrated as Guy's. "We can't attack them. Not while there's still a chance the Fae will return to the negotiations."

"We can find out what they're planning." Guy gestured at Lily. "We have the perfect spy at our disposal."

Simon's face turned thunderous, but Lily laid her hand over his. "No, he's right, Simon. I have to act now. No one else can do this."

"And if you're caught—captured?"

"The Blood aren't overly fond of sunlight," Lily said with a smile. "They can't stop me any other way."

"What if they—" Simon caught himself, cutting off whatever it was he'd been about to say with a snap of his teeth. Lily's eyes widened slightly and she pressed her lips together before looking away. I wondered what the hell he'd almost given away. Something to do with the secret of the blood-locked?

"Even that might stretch the terms of the treaty," another of the human councilors said thoughtfully.

"Everybody has spies," another countered. "The Blood, the Beasts. Us. Even the Fae do. No one is going to be able to point an accusing finger at us over this."

"We should pull in Henri Favreau and his cronies. They know who amongst the Fae is disgruntled with the queen," Guy said.

I blinked. Henri Favreau? I knew he'd been mixed up in

what had happened with Holly's father—along with a number of other younger male Beasts who were estranged from their packs—but I didn't know exactly how. From Guy's words, mixed up was perhaps too gentle a term.

"Which would also be a treaty violation," Liam said. "We don't have enough proof."

"Who knows what anyone is going to use as an excuse in this situation," Father Cho said. "We need to make the queen see reason. Send a delegation to speak to her."

"She'll just turn us away at the border."

"Not necessarily," Bryony said. "Lukar didn't say we were forbidden the Veiled Court. The queen presumably won't deny any Fae who want to return. She has to let them rejoin their families. I could go."

Lukar? Was that the Fae man's name? I wished Bryony had used his full name. His family name would give me more of an idea where he fit into the Fae courts.

"We need you here at St. Giles," Simon said.

"We have enough healers for now and you can keep St. Giles running."

"You can't go alone," Barnabas interjected. "How do we know what you'll say?"

Bryony gave him a long, cool look and he had the grace to look a little ashamed. But he didn't back down.

"I daresay I can take a few people with me," Bryony said. "They'll have a better chance of getting in if they accompany me than if they go alone."

"Who then?"

"I'll go," said Guy.

"No," Father Cho said emphatically. "You're needed here, Guy. We're going to need all our able-bodied men. If we need to send a Templar representative then we'll send Brother Liam. He's a mage and he's well versed in treaty law."

Guy scowled, but Father Cho made a curt gesture at him and he stayed silent.

Fen rose then. "I'll go." He looked across at me, eyes questioning.

"If he goes, I need to go too."

Most of the delegates looked confused, Master Aquinas amongst them.

Damn, I'd forgotten that my peculiar ability in relation

to Fen's talent wasn't common knowledge. "I mean . . ." I tried to think of a plausible cover story. "I volunteer to go. I'm a mage too and I can be useful." For one thing I could help with weapons suitable for the Veiled Court where iron and steel weren't tolerated.

Barnabas made a humphing sound of dissatisfaction. "She's a prentice. Someone from the council should go. And a Guild representative."

"I can't take a cast of thousands," Bryony objected. "Fen is all right. He's *hai'salai*, and he can claim he wants to find his Family anyway. I can take Saskia and Liam as my retainers. I'm High Family. If I make enough of a fuss, I should be able to take them through. They can represent the Guild and Templar interests too. Three should be sufficient."

This started a round of arguments that went in circles for an age as I bit my lip and tried not to wonder what I'd gotten myself into.

The argument was still going on when there was a knock at the door and one of the gray-clad Templar novices walked in and handed Father Cho a note.

He opened it, eyebrows shooting up. "Truly?" he asked.

The novice, who looked somewhat wild around the eyes, nodded.

Father Cho held up a hand and the room fell silent. "We will have to continue this discussion a little later," he said. "Lady Bryony and I are required at the gates."

Bryony lifted her head. "Why?"

"It seems there is a group of the Blood waiting to talk to us. It also seems they wish to claim Haven."

The only way Father Cho and Bryony could have stopped the rest of us following them would have been to set his knights on us. But they were the first two who approached the gates of the Brother House.

Through the metal bars, the white skin and hair of the group of Blood waiting for them seemed very bright in the moonlight. Tempting targets. They were heavily armed. As were the white-dressed humans who surrounded them. There were almost as many of them as there were Blood. Trusted, I presumed.

The only one who wasn't glowing like phosphorous was

the woman standing at the very front of the group. She wore
a dark cloak with a hood drawn up over her hair. The fabric
shadowed her face, hiding her identity.

Guy and several of the other Templars weren't far behind the Abbott General, swords and guns at the ready.

"What is your business here?" Father Cho asked.

"We seek Haven," the woman said.

"It's a ploy," someone in the crowd behind me muttered.
I didn't recognize the voice.

"Why?" The Abbott General's tone was blunt. I managed to bite back my murmur of surprise. Technically, if you
asked for Haven, it had to be granted.

"Because if we stay in the Night World, I doubt we will
live to see the end of the negotiations or even this night,"
the woman replied. "Ignatius Grey is making a play for
power. He has already killed about twenty of our number
tonight."

"Why should we believe you?" Bryony asked.

"Can you not tell if I am lying, Lady?" The woman's
voice sounded amused, if steely with it. "Are you gainsaying
the laws of Haven?"

"You can understand our position," Father Cho said.
"This is not an easy time."

"It will not get any easier if you allow Ignatius to kill all
of us who oppose him," came the reply. "We are willing to
give up our weapons and provide surety for our behavior."

Giving up their weapons was small comfort. A vampire
didn't really need weapons to wreak a lot of havoc amongst
a community of humans.

"If that is not enough, perhaps there are those amongst
you who can vouch for me." She drew back her hood, revealing a starkly beautiful face. It would have been more beautiful without the jagged gash that bit through her cheek.

"That's Adeline," Holly said softly.

As she spoke I saw Guy move up to Father Cho, bend
down, and whisper something in his ear.

Father Cho turned. "Holly, would you come here, please?
Lily, you too, if you would be so kind."

Fen growled softly as Holly joined the group near the
gates, Lily a few steps behind her. I moved a little closer to
him. "Can you see anything?" I asked softly.

"Violence," he said, his voice rough. "Death. But I think she's telling the truth."

"Holly, do you know this woman?" Father Cho asked.

"Yes, Father. Her name is Adeline Louis."

"And?"

"And my belief is that she is no friend to Ignatius Grey. She has never played me false, sir."

Father Cho nodded and turned to Lily. "And you?"

"She was not one of Lucius' inner circle. From what I know of her, she is . . . moderate." Lily's voice was cool in the darkness.

Father Cho met this with another short nod. He looked at Bryony, head tilted, as though inviting her views.

"They cannot come to St. Giles," Bryony said. "There is too much temptation. And it would cause too much fear amongst my patients. That will hinder their healing."

"There are tunnels below your hospital, are there not?" Adeline said. "Disused wards. Closed-up rooms. Those will suit us. We have resources to compensate you."

Bryony stiffened. "It is not a question of money."

Father Cho pressed his hands together. "But it is a question of finding somewhere safe for them to be. They need to be protected from the sun. Though . . ." He turned and looked back at Guy. "What of the storage cellars? Some of those are empty, are they not?"

"Yes." Guy's voice was grudging.

"Very well." Father Cho sounded resigned. "I will grant you temporary Haven in the Brother House. You will surrender your weapons, you will submit to guards, and you will abide by all the conditions we set. If there are any infractions, you will be ejected."

"Thank you, Father," Adeline said. "We accept."

As Guy began to unlock the gates, Simon moved up behind me. "You should go back to Mother and Hannah," he said.

I stiffened. "Why?"

He made an exasperated noise. "We're about to let thirty-odd vampires through those gates. It's dangerous."

"Then you should leave too."

"I'm a sunmage, I'm safe enough."

I swiveled around, tried not to raise my voice too high.

"And, as you so frequently seem to forget, Simon, I am a metalmage. I'm not unprotected. I can call fire just as you can call sunlight. Besides, I'd imagine the delegation will want to discuss this."

He closed his eyes for a moment. "Sass—"

I touched his face. "Simon, I know you want to protect me, but that's not your job here. I'm staying."

He opened his eyes, looked at Fen. "I don't suppose you want to try and convince her."

"I have more sense," Fen said. "Besides, if she won't listen to you, why should she listen to me?"

Simon sighed. "Very well. We'll be reconvening in the conference room after we get them settled. Wait for us there."

FEN

When Father Cho finally returned to the conference room, he wasn't alone. Adeline and another of the Blood, a man I didn't recognize, accompanied him. Adeline had removed her cloak. The black satin of the dress she wore was stark against the snow white skin.

Her cheek was cut, an ugly tear that had to hurt, though to be honest, I wasn't entirely sure how much the Blood experienced pain. She gave no indication of it if she did, merely regarding the assembled group of us calmly.

The man who accompanied her had his long white hair pulled back in a tail. Eyes as green as mine blazed in his face as he scoped the room, anger lurking in their depths. Not reconciled to the change in his fortunes, that one. Though, of the two of them, Adeline's contained stillness seemed more unsettling and dangerous. I'd met her a time or two at Assemblies when I'd been escorting Holly on business but had never exchanged more than a few words with her, all of those cautious.

I knew that Holly preferred dealing with her to others amongst the Blood, but that had been back before Holly had chosen the humans' side. Back then she'd appreciated clients who paid on time and didn't harass her. Adeline fitting those particular criteria didn't mean that she was trustworthy.

Father Cho gestured to two of the vacant chairs and the male Blood pulled out one of them and helped Adeline to her seat.

"Well," said Father Cho as he took his seat after everyone had settled. "It seems we have things to discuss." He sounded not entirely certain how to proceed. Which was unusual. I'd known him only a short time, but he was a born general, making decisions rapidly and giving orders with a quietly confident air that made it difficult not to automatically start to do whatever he was asking.

Father Cho steepled his fingers, regarding Adeline steadily over his blunt fingertips. "Lady Adeline, you have requested Haven to protect you from Ignatius Grey. As you can imagine, those of us in the human delegation have no wish to see him rise to power either. Perhaps we can join in a mutual cause."

There was a murmuring buzz at that.

Adeline inclined her head. "We thank you, Abbot General, for the gift of Haven. We are open to exploring options. Ignatius Grey ruling our court . . . would not be a welcome development. He needs to be curbed."

My stomach twisted Was Ignatius even further along in his quest for power than we had feared? I reached down to loosen the chain at my wrist a little, preparing to see what my powers might reveal about Adeline.

But as the chain moved from my skin, the vicious bite of pain from the visions was so intense that I flinched and locked it back into place, choking back the curse that rose in my throat. Struggling for control, I dropped my other hand below the table and groped for Saskia's free hand, curling my fingers around hers with a spasming grip that had to hurt. To her credit, she didn't so much as blink.

By the time the pain had retreated, the conversation had moved on. Adeline and her companion—whose name was apparently Digby Goodall—were being grilled to determine what they knew about Ignatius and his plans.

Unfortunately it was less than we might have liked to know. Still, they were able to name his main supporters and give rough estimates of the numbers of Blood who were likely to follow him as well as the locations of some of his favorite haunts outside the warrens.

Some of this was information the Templars already knew, judging by the nods that met some of Adeline's disclosures. Other revelations caused murmurs of disquiet amongst the group as a whole. After an hour or so, Father Cho called a halt to the proceedings for a meal break.

I wasn't hungry, though I would have killed someone for a brandy. I hadn't had a drink for several days and sometimes the need to blur reality pressed in on me, making my hands itch for a bottle.

As the assembled delegates began to disperse, Simon approached Adeline. He gestured at her cheek and I drifted toward them a little, interested to hear the conversation.

"I can do something about that," Simon was saying.

Adeline started to smile, then winced at little. "Thank you," she said. "But perhaps Lady Bryony could assist me?"

Simon frowned. "Why her, in particular? If you are worried about my powers, then I can assure you that I have treated Blood before and none of them came to any harm."

Adeline's brows lifted at that. "Do you often get my kind at St. Giles?"

"Not often," Simon said. Then he fell silent. Which was probably just as well. He risked giving away the fact of Atherton's existence if he spoke too much on the subject of how exactly a human sunmage had come to heal vampires.

"I see," Adeline said. "In any case, it wasn't your powers that I was concerned with. Rather, I have a matter that I wish to raise with Lady Bryony. It is somewhat . . . delicate."

Simon cocked his head. "Keeping secrets?"

"No. Not entirely. If Lady Bryony wishes to share the information after I have told her, then I will not try to stop her."

My curiosity was definitely piqued. I wondered whether Bryony would agree. The Fae and the Blood have an uneasy relationship at the best of times, and this was hardly the best of times. The Fae do not go so far as to call the Blood abominations, as they do wraiths, but nor are they easy with the existence of vampires. Drawing their power from the earth and the energy of all living things, they do not like the living dead.

Simon looked unconvinced. "I will pass your request on. But I cannot allow you to be alone with Lady Bryony. Security, you understand?"

A nod. "Certainly." Adeline's head turned slowly, surveying the room. "What about the metalmage?" She gestured toward Saskia. "She can call fire, I presume? Surely that is security enough for Lady Bryony?"

I felt myself bristle at the suggestion. *Careful, Fen.* This was not the time to give myself away and reveal to Simon and Guy the exact nature of my relationship with their sister. Still, I didn't want Saskia anywhere near Adeline. Not that I had any say in the matter.

I watched Simon, as he obviously debated the matter with himself. Would he be more curious about what Adeline might have to reveal or would he put his need to protect his little sister first?

Finally he nodded his head, bowed slightly to Adeline, and crossed the room to Bryony. After a minute or so in conversation with the Fae healer, he sighed and walked over to Saskia.

SASKIA

I wasn't about to give Simon a chance to change his mind, so I stuck close to Bryony as we were escorted by two Templars to a small office not far from the conference room. The Templars took up station outside the door, the suspicious looks they aimed at Adeline as she passed them speaking volumes.

Bryony shut the door behind us, but she didn't lock it. Nor did she make any move to set wards. Not taking any chances. I couldn't argue with that. Adeline was unnerving, so still and pale, her skin, even in the well-lit room, seeming to glow a little, like a moonlight on a pearl.

Or maybe that was my imagination.

I shook myself. *Pay attention, Saskia.*

I was here to guard Bryony, not be distracted by just how beautiful the Blood were up close.

Remember Edwina.

Bryony indicated that Adeline should sit, set the small bag of supplies she carried on the desk, and then began to inspect the vampire's cheek.

"Silver blade?" she asked in a cool professional tone.

Adeline nodded. "Yes. Ignatius used Trusted. He armed them well. Though not well enough." There was a certain ring of vicious satisfaction in the last statement. I guessed that whoever had attacked Adeline had not survived to tell the tale.

That made me shiver. I didn't understand why anyone would become a Trusted—a servant of the Blood, one who hoped to be turned one day—but I still didn't like the thought of Ignatius casually throwing away the lives of those who presumably believed in him.

All in the quest for power. I understood wanting power—the magical kind—but dominion over others was a different goal altogether. What type of mind gained satisfaction from such a thing?

Bryony's fingers touched Adeline's skin lightly. The chain around the Fae's neck was a curious mix of pale silvery green and tiny sparks of red.

"I will clean this before I heal it. There shouldn't be a scar."

She turned back to her bag, withdrew some cotton cloths and a small glass bottle. She tipped the bottle over one of the cloths, filling the air with a pungent herbal scent.

"This may sting."

"I'm sure I can bear it," Adeline said dryly. She didn't flinch as Bryony started gently dabbing at the edges of the wound, removing the traces of dried blood with precise motions. "Aren't you going to ask me why I wanted to speak to you?"

"First things first," Bryony said. She reached for another cloth, dampened it, and continued her cleanup. When she was finally satisfied, she gathered the cloths into a small pile, returned the bottle to the bag, and then laid her hand against Adeline's cheek. I felt the cool flow of power, like stepping into a mountain stream. It felt so different from the warmth of my own power or Simon's sunmagery, but not bad. Like chilled bubbles flowing over my skin.

The sensation didn't last long enough for me to analyze it in any depth. Bryony took a final deep breath, then lifted her hand. The gash was gone, leaving only a fine white line across Adeline's face.

"That will heal further," she said. "Now, what do you want to tell me?"

Adeline's hand drifted up to her cheek, but she allowed herself only a brief touch before she returned her hands to her lap. "I have good reason to believe that Ignatius has been abducting Fae women," she said.

"What?"

The two of them locked gazes, Bryony's chain sparking true red now.

Adeline nodded. "I see you take my meaning."

"How long has this been going on?" Bryony's voice was ice.

"It came to my attention not long after Lucius . . . vanished. Though there were occasionally rumors before Lucius died."

"And you think he's trying to . . ." Bryony trailed off with a glance over at me.

I held my breath. I was desperately curious as to what they were discussing but feared if I interrupted to ask, the topic might be closed. What would a vampire want with Fae women? Perhaps Holly might know . . .

"Yes." Adeline lifted her chin. "There are not many things worth risking the wrath of the court for. But this, this may be enough of a temptation. It would strengthen his position considerably."

"Surely the rest of your court would not want him to gain such an advantage?"

"True. But no one has yet been able to discover where he may be keeping them. Whoever is assisting him must be well protected. And well compensated to keep this secret."

"How then do you know it to be true?"

"I have made inquiries of my own." Adeline smoothed down the long ruffle of satin at her wrist. "I have confirmed some of the disappearances. And then Holly's friend was taken, in company with a Fae woman, I understand?"

Sainted earth. My stomach twisted. Was that why Reggie had been taken? Had she simply been in the wrong place at the wrong time? Gods. She deserved far better luck.

Bryony's lips thinned as she nodded. "Yes. I see. Thank you. I will consider what to do with this information."

"Good. You understand my concern that this information not become widespread? It is not an experiment we wish to encourage others to attempt."

"I understand," Bryony said shortly. "The Fae have no desire for such an outcome either."

I watched the two of them exchange another inscrutable gaze, the air between them boiling with tension. Whatever Ignatius was doing with Fae women, it wasn't good—though I had no idea what it might be.

But it seemed they weren't going to discuss things any further. Bryony gathered up her bag and the cloths and then opened the door. "Please escort Lady Adeline back to her quarters," she said to the Templars outside the door. "Saskia, you will come with me, please." She swept out of the room without a backward glance and I had to half-run to catch up with her.

"Why does Ignatius want Fae women?" I asked. I didn't think she would tell me but it was worth a try.

As I expected, she didn't answer my question. "I have to find Simon," she said. "Do you know where he is?"

I bit back my protest at her change of subject. There was no point trying to wring information out of a Fae who didn't want to tell me. Fae couldn't lie, but they could avoid answering just like anyone else. And I had no desire to be zapped into oblivion because I'd angered Lady Bryony.

It didn't take long to home in on the little spark of sensation that told me Simon's direction. It was bright and strong, a blue-edged yellow feeling that pulsed calmly in a way I associated with him being at ease. "He's in his office. I think Lily may be with him," I added.

Bryony halted abruptly. "You can sense Lily?"

I shook my head. "Not exactly. But he feels more content when she's nearby. I don't know how to explain it better than that."

Bryony tapped a finger on her chain. "One day you and I need to have a conversation about this ability of yours."

"I'm not the only metalmage who can do it." Some of the other ironmages shared my ability.

"No, but you are the one I see most often. Still, it saves me going looking for Lily as well. You should go back to your family. You need sleep."

It was a dismissal, but I was hardly sleepy. Not when my brain was suddenly putting together a whole new and disturbing possibility. Adeline had told us that Ignatius was taking Fae women, and the first people that Bryony wanted to see were Lily and Simon. Not any of her fellow Fae, not sending a message to the Veiled Court, but my brother and Lily. Lily the wraith.

A wraith, who like all her kind, had a parentage that was shrouded in mystery. Born of Fae and . . . Sainted bloody earth. What if Ignatius was trying to breed more wraiths?

Chapter Nineteen

SASKIA

⚡

I wasn't ready to return neatly to bed as Bryony had ordered. I was too alarmed by the possibilities that my suspicions had aroused. And, though I was ashamed to admit it when there was so much going on around me that was far more important, I wanted to see Fen. To breathe in the scent of him for a while. I missed him, I realized. Missed those moments we'd shared when we'd been skin to skin but sated. Of course, I missed what came before as well, but that wasn't what I longed for just now—I just wanted time alone with him.

Perhaps we could find a private nook somewhere. We hadn't shared anything more than the sedate touches that Simon and Guy expected of us since the night after the explosion, let alone a conversation that didn't involve the negotiations.

I sent my powers roaming again. I couldn't sense Fen in the same way I could my family, but the iron around his wrist should be detectable. Though here in the Brother House, there was probably more iron and steel than almost anywhere else in the City, except for the railways and the Guild of Mechanizers. The Templar armory was worth a fortune. They used other metals—the best that the metal-mages could come up with—but nothing was as true as cold iron and steel for swords and armor. As well as the silver they had for weapons used to subdue Beasts and Blood.

If one had a suicidal desire for wealth, stealing Templar arms would be a quick source.

Not that anyone in the history of the City had ever been quite that stupid.

I sorted through the various metalsongs, searching for the thread of Fen's chain. Finally I found it . . . after I widened my search toward St. Giles. I should have thought of that sooner. He was in the hidden ward. With Reggie.

"All I'm saying is that you should ask him," Fen was saying as I opened the door to the outer room of the hidden ward. I paused, door still in my hand. Fen was standing with Holly, both of them looking tense and tired.

"You don't even know if they'll help," Holly replied.

"They won't if he doesn't ask," Fen snapped.

Holly flinched and I stepped forward, not wanting to see any more arguments tonight. "Ask what?"

"Simon should ask Adeline about blood-locking," Fen said. "It might help him find a cure."

"It's not exactly a subject that you can bring up in casual conversation," Holly said. "You don't talk to the Blood about the locked. It isn't done."

Fen dismissed this with a flick of his fingers. "When is there going to be a better time? She needs us right now, so she'll have to cooperate."

"He has a point," I said, thinking of Adeline's conversation with Bryony. "Without us, Adeline and her friends will wind up dead."

Fen nodded. "It's important, Holly."

Holly threw up her hands. "So is not having our own version of a blood war here at the hospital if the Blood decide to take offense. Or have you seen something?"

"Can you even see down here?" I asked curiously. I would have thought that the doors were enough to give a boost to the chain around his wrist. Maybe that was part of the reason he spent as much time here as possible.

"No and no," Fen admitted. "It's just a feeling. Don't you want to see Reggie cured?" He aimed the last at Holly.

"Of course I do," she said with a scowl. "But that's not the point."

"It's the only point," Fen said. "Reggie is our sister. If there's a chance of finding the cure, you need to ask Simon. And you need to make sure he tries whatever he comes up with on her."

Holly bit her lip. "What if it makes things worse?"

"She's stuck down here, hidden from the world, barely conscious. It can hardly be worse," Fen said with a shake of his head that made the gem in his ear spark green.

His voice was strained—edged with guilt? Anger? I couldn't quite tell. I moved closer still, wanting to reach out and touch him. But I didn't. I didn't know if he'd told Holly about us, but if he hadn't, I didn't want to be the one who gave us away. "Fen," I said, "give Holly a chance to think about it. You're both tired and worried about Reggie. And it won't make any difference tonight. Everyone's going to bed."

He took a deep breath and his face eased. Holly looked relieved. "Why are you here?"

I thought fast. "I was on my way back to the hospital. I thought Simon might be here. Bryony is looking for him." I hoped neither of them would remember that I could tell where Simon was without any need to come and look for him.

"You came here alone?" That brought the frown back to Fen's face. "You shouldn't have. Not with the Blood here."

"The Blood are all safely in the Brother House."

"So we hope," Holly muttered. "I'd imagine they could get past a bunch of Templars easily enough if they wanted to. Atherton almost threw a fit earlier when Simon told him what had happened. He made us promise not to tell them he was here unless it was absolutely necessary."

"Is he scared of Adeline?" That was not a good sign, if it was true. Atherton had been amongst the moderates of the Blood Court before Lucius had tried to kill him. If he didn't think Adeline was trustworthy, then perhaps we should pay attention.

"I think it's more a case of him not particularly trusting any of the Blood," Holly said, pushing back her hair. "I don't blame him."

I didn't either. And I had to admit I hadn't given much thought to exactly how the Templars intended to keep the Blood contained, other than relying on the vampires' goodwill. The Blood can wrap themselves in shadow—not as a wraith does, stepping into another world—but they are very good at illusion and concealment.

Which gave me the perfect excuse to ask Fen to escort me back to St. Giles. Surely we could find an empty room somewhere along the way and spend just a little time alone.

"Perhaps Fen could walk me back," I said, trying to sound nervous. Hardly difficult. "Holly, are you staying here?"

"I'll sit with Reggie a while longer," she said. "Guy is patrolling tonight. I probably wouldn't sleep well anyway."

I knew that worry all too well. Guy had been a Templar for a good portion of my life and I'd never gotten entirely used to the anxiety. I squeezed Holly's hand, then tilted my head at Fen. "Well?" I asked. "Care to play escort?"

His face was shuttered, eyes dark and unreadable. He glanced at the door that led to the inner door as though torn.

"You should go," Holly said. "You have long days ahead of you. I promise I'll think about what you said. You take Saskia to her room, then get some sleep yourself." Her voice was soft but somehow big sisterly. I realized I didn't know exactly how old Fen was. He looked about the same age as Holly and Simon, but with Fae and Beast blood he could easily be older. I would have to ask him. But not right now.

I faked a yawn. "Come on, Fen," I coaxed. "I'm going to fall over if I don't sleep soon. And then you'll have to carry me."

We didn't speak until we were back in the corridors, safely past the junction that led to the hidden ward and able to shed the invisibility charms that I still hadn't quite gotten used to.

I moved closer to Fen, slipped my fingers through his. "Holly will come around," I said. "You're right. Simon should talk to the Blood. My guess is he will. He's determined to . . ." I looked around, conscious that we could be overheard. "Well, you know."

Fen's hand was warm around mine. "I know. I just don't like feeling helpless. Reggie—"

"I know," I said soothingly. "Let's just walk." I leaned my head against his arm for a moment, wishing I could curl up somewhere with him and fall asleep. Perhaps that would make my dreams easier. They were full of nameless unpleasantness that had me bolting awake at least once a night. I didn't have clear memories of them, but I was grateful that most nights I was too tired to worry too much about them before I fell asleep again. I was thinking about where there might be an empty room, sighing a little as Fen dropped a kiss on the top of my head when we turned a corner—and almost ran into Guy.

I dropped Fen's hand and straightened, but it was too late. Guy's expression turned thunderous.

"I thought you were patrolling," I blurted, hoping to stave him off.

"I thought you were in bed," he said. His icy blue gaze turned to Fen. "Care to explain?"

"Fen was just walking me back to St. Giles," I said.

"I didn't ask you," Guy said. "Fen?"

"I don't owe you an explanation," Fen said.

"Really? Because it looked to me like you were taking advantage of my sister."

I rolled my eyes. "Good grief, Guy. I'm not sixteen."

Guy ignored me, his eyes still on Fen. Fen's face was equally stony.

"Saskia and I are—"

Guy held up a hand. "Do not say what I think you're about to say." His free hand curled around the hilt of his sword. "Is this the thanks we get? For including you in our—"

"Oh, am I meant to be grateful that I've been dragged into this debacle?" Fen snarled. "I thought I was helping you."

"And I thought you were trustworthy. But now I see I need to reconsider that opinion."

"Guy!" I snapped, appalled. "Shut up."

"This is between me and Fen."

"I'm standing right here," I pointed out.

"You don't know any better. He should. He knows the rules when it comes to—"

"What, human girls? *Hai'salai* scum like me shouldn't soil them with our touch? Is that what you think, Guy?"

The fury in Fen's face had me rocking back a step. Oh, my *idiot* brothers. The links of my prentice chain suddenly warmed against my neck as my temper climbed to match Guy's.

"I think you shouldn't be taking advantage of girls half your age," Guy said. "Especially not my sister."

"I'm hardly half his age," I snapped.

"Be quiet, Saskia. Let your brother say his piece." Fen's voice was a rumble of ice. "I'm interested in knowing the truth about what he thinks of me."

"Don't tempt me," Guy snarled. "I should have seen this coming, I guess. Well, I know better now. This changes things."

"Fine with me," Fen snarled in response. "I know when I'm not wanted." He turned on his heel and strode off down the corridor, leaving me gaping after him with a rapidly growing ache in my heart. I turned back to Guy.

"You *moron*!" I yelled. "How dare you speak to him like that? Do you want him to leave the delegation?"

"We'd be better off without him," Guy snapped. "He can't be trusted."

"I trust him," I ground out.

"You're not thinking straight, he's seduced you and—"

"Maybe I seduced him! Gods, Guy, you are such a hypocrite. You're with Holly, Simon's going to marry a wraith, and I'm not allowed to see Fen?"

"It's different."

"Don't make me set your helmet on fire," I warned. "Because I'm starting to think that would be the only thing that might make you see sense. It's not different. I am a girl but I am a mage. And a person in my own right. I'm not going to follow all those neat little paths that you and the rest of human society seem to think I should."

"You don't know what you're saying," he said. "He's turned your head."

I smacked his shoulder then. Hard. Then winced as my hand throbbed after connecting with the mail beneath his tunic. "I am not an idiot. Unlike my male relatives. Nor am I a simpering virgin who's been taken by a pretty face. For your information, I've never simpered and I lost the other qualification for that particular title quite a few years ago."

Guy's mouth dropped open. I wanted to hit him again. "Honestly, Guy. What world do you live in? Even you Templars have sex. Simon wasn't exactly celibate before he met Lily and I don't think you were either, before Holly."

"I love Holly," he said stiffly.

"Really? And you were in love with her the first time you slept with her?"

"That's not up for discussion."

"Then pay attention. Neither is my relationship with Fen. It is my choice and my business. And I swear on the earth that binds us, Guy, if you've chased him off, I will never forgive you. And I'd imagine that Father Cho isn't going to be very impressed with you either. You need Fen. You need his visions."

Guy squared his shoulders. "Not that much."

"You want to risk it? Besides, I need him and you're just going to have to get used to the idea."

"Sass, listen to me. I know his history. Fen is not the type who settles down. He's a . . . He's fickle."

"That's my problem, not yours. For now, I'm choosing him. If I get my heart broken, then that's also my problem and you can say I told you so as many times as you like. But you can't blame Fen. And you can't treat him like you just did, no matter what happens. What do you think Holly would have to say about it?"

That made him grimace. "Holly would understand."

"No, she wouldn't. Fen's her family. Have you thought about that? Holly would never cut him out of her life. You're going to have to put up with him no matter what."

Guy stayed silent for a long stretch, his lips pressed together. "I don't want to see you hurt," he said finally.

"I know," I said. "But as I keep telling you, that's not your job. You can worry about me—the same as the rest of us worry about you every fucking time you go out on patrol—but you don't get to tell me how to live my life. You just get to be on my side when I need you."

"I—"

I held up a hand. "No. I'm not going to argue about this anymore. You owe Fen an apology and you will not bring this up again. Or I will melt every sword and piece of armor you own. I swear it." I glared up at him, willing him to see that I was serious. It scared me a little just how serious I was. I hadn't realized exactly how I felt about Fen until just now, when I'd seen the pain in his face before he'd left.

I needed Guy to understand, once and for all, that he didn't run my life.

Guy met my gaze, giving me his best "I am a Templar warrior and I always win" expression. Fortunately I was relatively immune to that particular gaze, though I'd seen him make Templar novices quake with it. He wasn't going to get his way this time. "The only words I want to hear are 'Yes, Saskia,'" I warned. "Or it's puddles of steel for you and you can explain to Holly why you're charbroiled."

The side of his mouth quirked. "You wouldn't."

"Try me," I said sweetly. "I'm just as stubborn as you or Simon. After all, I had both of you as role models. Well?"

Guy sighed. "I don't like this."

"You don't have to like it. You just have to accept it."

"Isn't that the same thing?"

"No. I accept that you are a Templar and that you risk your life daily. I grant you the courtesy of respecting your choice and doing my best to live with it. So you can try and do the same for me. Doesn't your God preach acceptance, amongst other things?"

Guy pressed his fingers to the space between his eyebrows, as though his head hurt. "Yes."

"Well, then. What do you have to say to me?"

"Yes, Saskia."

"Good." I smiled at him, then stood on tiptoe to kiss his cheek. "Now, I'll bid you good night. I have to go find Fen."

I was worried that Fen might have left the hospital altogether, but as I moved farther away from the hidden ward and its iron, I could sense his chain again. Outside.

Perfect. He was aboveground in the middle of the night with Blood all over the place and Ignatius throwing his weight around. Still, I wasn't going to leave him to think that Guy's stupidity had made any impression on me. I had to find him.

I followed the small song of his chain to one of the sheltered garden areas in the midst of the hospital buildings, where he sat with his back to the trunk of a massive oak. The moon was full, or near enough, shedding a silvery light over the expanse of grass and plants, turning them deep and mysterious green. Like the eyes of the man I was seeking.

"My brother is an idiot," I said softly as I settled down beside him.

Fen stayed silent.

"I told him as much. And that he needed to mind his own damned business. I'm sorry he spoke that way to you."

"Maybe he was right."

I sighed. "Please don't make me lecture you too. I've had enough for one night."

"I'm not good for you," Fen said. "I'm not good for anyone." He sounded miserable. I shifted to my knees, leaning back on them so he could see my face.

"Don't say that."

"It's true. I've never been good for anyone. I make a living spinning pretty tales and half-truths to part people from their money. I have no family. No loyalty."

"You're loyal to Holly and Reggie."

"And look where that got Reggie."

"You're as bad as Guy," I said. "There was no way you could have guessed that Reggie would be in danger. Besides," I added, "Adeline thinks Ignatius is taking Fae women. So it was Viola they were after. Reggie was just in the wrong place."

For a moment Fen looked interested but then he shook his head. "I'm meant to be a fucking seer, Saskia. What use am I if I can't see?" His chain clinked softly, the iron very dark against his skin in the moonlight. "All this pain and I couldn't even see that my best friend was in danger."

"But you saved her," I said. "You got her back. Simon can cure her."

"What if he doesn't?"

"Bad things happen, Fen. Even if you can see them, maybe sometimes you aren't meant to stop them. Maybe sometimes they need to happen."

"Do you think your sister needed to die?" he asked softly.

"No. But she did. Simon tried to save her and she died anyway. The world doesn't always work the way we want it to."

"All the more reason you should stay away from me. You think you can change the world to suit you. All you Du-Caines do. But you can't, Saskia. Guy's right. You're human. Your family is important. You shouldn't be with someone like me."

"Guy and Simon have hardly made conventional choices."

"All the more reason you should."

I shook my head. "No. All the more reason I shouldn't. Our society isn't perfect. Maybe it needs shaking up a little."

"I don't want to be your rebellion."

The breath rushed out of me. "Is that what you think this is? Rebellion?"

"Isn't it?"

I shook my head. "No."

"Then what is it?"

Love, maybe. The word quivered on the tip of my tongue. But I didn't think he was ready to hear it. Not so soon after Guy's little performance. "I don't know, exactly," I said. I rocked to my knees, straddled him, suddenly not giving a damn about Blood or Beasts or danger. The only important thing was Fen and finding a way to take the ache out of his voice. So that it stopped hurting me. "But I know that I like being with you."

He looked away, hands flat on the earth beside him.

"I like talking to you." I traced my hand over his cheek, then laid it on his shoulder. "I like who you are." I repeated the gesture with my other hand.

He lifted his head, his eyes searching mine.

"I like touching you," I breathed and I dropped my mouth to his.

Soft. So soft, this kiss. Soft as the moonlight and as heady as the scent of green and earth and damp surrounding us. I felt as though I were melting into him as his mouth moved against mine, as though skin was trying to say what words couldn't.

He tasted sweet and hot and dark. Of Fen. I wasn't sure I'd ever get enough of the taste of him. I made a noise deep in my throat and his hands came around my waist, tight and strong. He pulled me tighter against him and the kiss turned fierce. Wilder than the moon and the earth beneath us, heat sparking between us quick and true.

I tugged at my skirts, trying to free them where I knelt on the fabric. My bare knees hit the earth and a surge of power mingled with the roar of desire in my blood.

The world dissolved to a dizzying whirl of Fen and heat

and the sensation of skin on skin. Hands found buckles and buttons and removed obstacles, though I doubted either of us could have said who did what. All that mattered was the drowning kisses that built the fire between us, sparking the flames as sure as the bellows' breath over a banked forge fire.

Fen's hands slid beneath my skirts, found me, moved against slick skin, driving me higher. I writhed against him, but fingers weren't enough. I wanted him inside me, as close as he could get. I pulled him toward me and toppled backward, almost screaming when his weight settled against me.

His eyes were so green in the moonlight, nearly glowing. For a fleeting moment I wondered if his Beast Kind heritage meant that he felt the moonlight like I felt the earth. But then the thought passed as he angled himself against me, teasing me. I wrapped my legs around him and arched my hips, drawing him into me, feeling the slide of him through every inch of my body, relief and desire and a sense of rightness like the turn of a key in a lock I hadn't known I possessed.

"Fen," I whispered and he smiled down at me.

"I'm right here," he said and then he began to move, his rhythm exactly what I needed. Strong and sure.

I tugged his head down to mine again, wanted the taste of him as he filled me, completing the circuit between us, mouth meeting mouth and skin meeting skin.

Not soft any longer. Hard now, and hungry. Frantic. I heard him groan and then his hand found me again, those clever fingers pushing me over the edge in time to fall with him.

FEN

All of the human delegates were bleary-eyed and disheveled when we reconvened far too early the next morning. My own eyes burned as though I'd dipped them in raw alcohol. I hadn't snatched more than an hour or so of sleep by the time I had finally returned Saskia to her family's rooms within St. Giles and then taken myself back to the Brother

House. I'd half expected that the brothers guarding the gate would turn me away on Guy's orders.

But they let me through with no more than a slightly raised eyebrow from one of them. Fortunately he was too well trained to inquire as to where exactly I had been.

Guy hadn't said anything when I'd taken my seat beside Saskia this morning. He hadn't really looked pleased to see me, but that was better than trying to take my head off with that bloody big sword he carried, so I would take it for now.

Simon's gaze was also somewhat disapproving, from which I deduced that Guy had shared his discovery with his brother, but he too held his peace. Saskia greeted me with a pleased smile, though perhaps in deference to her brothers' sensibilities, she didn't do anything more than that.

Not surprisingly, none of the Blood were present. Adeline and, I assumed, quite a few of the others she'd brought with her were old enough not to need to sleep the day away, but the Brother House wasn't designed for vampires, and the room we had gathered in had stained-glass windows that let in multicolored sunlight, tinting the faces of the delegates. The orange patch floating on Guy's forehead made him just a little less intimidating.

I swallowed coffee and waited for Father Cho to open the proceedings. He did so soon enough, dismissing the problem—or opportunity—of the Blood refugees for the moment and returning to the equally thorny issue of the Veiled Queen.

The conversation quickly revealed that the majority of the delegates were still in favor of an envoy being sent to Summerdale. Lady Bryony reasserted her case that she was the logical one to go.

The discussion circled for some time as the last lingering objections were raised, but it didn't have the heat of the night before. It seemed that Adeline's news of Ignatius' bid for power had focused everyone's minds on the urgency of returning the queen to the negotiations.

Finally Father Cho called a vote. I wasn't surprised when it passed with very little objection.

"Very well," Father Cho said gravely. "Lady Bryony will be the one. Have you changed your mind on those you would have to accompany you, Lady?"

Bryony shook her head. She wore a dress of a deep, deep

red today, a color I hadn't seen her wear before. The chain around her neck sparked with flashes of the same color, and the red also glinted off the purple and blue jewels in her Family ring and the matching dark jewels in her hair. She looked beautiful.

Beautiful and deadly. If I'd been Father Cho and the other delegation leaders, I would have just murmured, "Whatever you wish, Lady" and fled before I was turned into a frog.

"No," Bryony said. "I will take Fen and Saskia and Brother Liam."

Liam, who was sitting a few chairs farther down the table, bowed his head at this news. I wondered if he was trying to hide fear or satisfaction. It couldn't be easy being a maimed Templar, kept away from the action. I just hoped this chance wouldn't drive him to do anything stupid if we should stumble into trouble.

"How long do you need to prepare?" Father Cho asked.

Bryony considered the matter. My stomach began to churn and I regretted the coffee.

"There are some matters I need to organize at St. Giles," she said and I sucked in a breath, hoping I might at least get a day to prepare myself for what was to come. A fate I'd worked to avoid since I was old enough to understand what could happen to me in the Veiled World.

"But those won't take more than a few hours," Bryony continued. "I suggest we leave by midday. That will get us to Summerdale with plenty of daylight left."

Father Cho nodded agreement and I slumped back in my chair, feeling suddenly sick.

Fuck.

I was going to Summerdale.

Chapter Twenty

Saskia

⚡

Summerdale.

I was going to Summerdale. I gripped the seat of the carriage, trying not to bounce with excitement. I knew that our
mission was serious but I couldn't help the joy bubbling up
inside me.

Summerdale.

I'd wanted to come here since I'd been a child and my
nanny had told us tales full of the wonders of the Fae. And
once my power had come in I'd wanted nothing more than
to study with the Fae smiths and learn their secrets. Learn
how to make metal do some of the things I had heard they
could do.

I curled my fingers tighter into the leather, determined
not to smile. No one else seemed to feel as I did. Bryony
and Fen were both grim-faced, though if I'd had to guess, I
would have said that Bryony was worried and Fen was
alarmed. Liam was, perhaps out of respect for the mood in
the carriage, silent, his good hand holding a leather book of
treaty law. He flipped it open occasionally and read something before returning to staring out at the countryside we
were passing through.

I looked too. I'd been to the villages around the borders

of Summerdale once or twice, but I'd never come to the actual Gate that guarded the Veiled World before. I'd seen pictures, of course, but pictures rarely did justice to Fae-wrought things.

The closer we got to the border, the more the earth hummed around me with a slightly unfamiliar sensation, as though the presence of the Fae was changing the earth itself. It was both unsettling and enticing and I reached out my power a time or two to lightly touch the earth and reassure myself that my connection was still there.

Finally the carriage drew to a standstill, the driver clucking to the horses in a tone that was meant to be reassuring but sounded somewhat nervous.

I was the first out of the carriage, eager to get my feet onto the ground and study the difference in what I was sensing more closely.

But my attention was turned from the changes in the earth's song by the massive marble tower that confronted me. It blazed white in the sunshine, a vast structure that stretched toward the sky, its smooth curved walls unbroken by anything except a single massive door at its base. It looked like it had been carved from one vast piece of marble, no sign of mortar or seam. Surely that wasn't possible? It had to be a facade of marble over a normally constructed tower. I couldn't even begin to imagine how the tower might have been built if that wasn't the case.

Some of my jubilation receded. The tower was taller than any of the buildings in the City, taller than either the Cathedral or St. Giles' huge dome by a good measure. And this was just the entrance point to the Veiled World.

Perhaps Fen had the right attitude after all.

But no, I wasn't going to be scared until I had to be. I turned back to the carriage, watched Bryony climb down, followed by Liam.

Fen came last, his face settling into even grimmer lines as he took in the tower. He turned on his heel almost immediately and moved to help the driver unload the small amount of baggage we'd brought with us.

Delaying the time when he had to face that tower, I thought.

But with so few bags, there was a limit to how long even

Fen could procrastinate. After only a few minutes, our small party was assembled, baggage in hand, all four of us gazing at the tower.

Behind us, the carriage was retreating at a speedy pace.

The driver only wanted to get back to the City before nightfall, I told myself. He wasn't nervous about lingering here on the borders of the Veiled World with the Veiled Queen presumably somewhere within, her fury over what had happened at the Treaty Hall still to be dealt with.

Summerdale.

I held my breath as Bryony stepped up to the door and pressed her hand against the dark wood.

The urge to grin and bounce up and down where I stood flared again. Luckily my mother had trained me well and I managed to tamp down all the emotion and merely toy with the buckle of the belt at my waist.

Beside me, Fen was still and silent. For him this was a completely different sort of homecoming.

One that could be far more dangerous for him than for the rest of us, despite Bryony's promises that she could keep any stray members of his father's Family from trying to lay claim to him.

I didn't think he truly believed her.

I wasn't sure I did either.

Some of my ebullience melted away. Fen could be trapped here. We all could.

Or worse.

But worse was nebulous. The risk of being separated from Fen had a more immediate impact and I wasn't sure I liked the fact that it upset me so. He had settled himself under my skin, sliding in without me noticing, like the smooth-tongued charmer he purported to be. I felt as though he'd marked me somehow, leaving a trace of himself, something I could no more get rid of than Guy could erase the Templar sigils on his hands.

My hand moved to my prentice chain, warming under my fingers. The Fae would be able to feel the magic it carried. Would they also be able to decipher the emotions that charged it when my control slipped?

I could just imagine the expression on Master Aquinas' face if I gave myself away like a raw first-year student.

I'd told everyone that I could handle this, that I could represent the Guild and face down the Veiled Queen. Now I had to prove it.

I took a deep breath as the door finally swung inward and Bryony turned to beckon us forward.

Summerdale.

Where everything was at stake.

I wanted to reach for Fen's hand, but we'd agreed to try and be circumspect here. No one could say what the queen might choose to take offense over, so it was important to be on our best behavior.

The room we entered was large and echoing. More white marble lined the walls. Here, though, it was intricately carved, flowers and trees and all sorts of fantastical creatures from tiny to life-sized cavorting over the walls and ceiling. Tiny stone tiles covered the floor, their colors forming patterns as well.

I took in the details, letting the beauty of it distract me from everything else, but eventually my attention was drawn back to the far side of the room. Three doors of bare, gleaming wood stood out starkly against the carved walls. One of them was the true entrance to the Veiled World and the Fae lands that lay beneath the ground. I didn't know which one. But once we passed through that door, the Fae would have control over us.

The leftmost door opened and a tall Fae woman, robed in white and silver—the same silver as her coiled hair— moved toward us at a stately, gliding pace. We came to a halt behind Bryony. When she bowed to the stranger, we copied her.

The woman returned our courtesy with a much shallower bow. "Bryony sa'Eleniel," she said. "It is long since you were in this place." She looked past Bryony to the three of us. "Now is not the time to bring in those who don't belong to the Veil."

Bryony inclined her head. "I understand, *al'car*. But I am here on a matter of great importance."

Al'car. I knew that one. This woman was the queen's Seneschal, keeper of the Gate, in a sense that went beyond just answering the door. As I understood the court hierarchy, she wasn't quite as high in status as the Speaker but she was powerful nonetheless. She could deny us entry—stop our mission with a word—unless any of us attempted the riskier route into Summerdale by facing the trial of the Door. Holly had told me a little about her experiences with the Door and I'd never managed to persuade Guy to tell me anything about his. Which made me hope that it wouldn't come to that.

"You wish to speak to the queen." The Seneschal's voice was flat. "She is not in a receptive mood."

It wasn't an out-and-out denial, at least. I made myself stand very still, not wanting to do something that might sway the Seneschal's opinion against us.

"She has closed the Court?" Bryony asked.

The Seneschal's lips pressed together. "No."

"Then she has to hear my petition, does she not?" Bryony said. Bryony was formidable at the best of times and she ruled St. Giles with a grip of gentle iron, but I'd never seen her quite so icy and regal as she was here. I knew that she was from a high Family, but I didn't exactly know how high. By the careful politeness with which the Seneschal was trying to persuade her, I gathered it was high enough.

"She will hear, perhaps. But I do not think you will garner an answer that you like."

"That is my choice," Bryony said. "So will you let us pass, or do I need to summon my father?"

Her father? Who exactly was her father? The Seneschal's expression had turned even more careful.

Interesting.

"That won't be necessary. You may enter."

"And my companions? They are necessary to me here."

"Really? A *hai'salai*, a mage barely out of childhood, and a crippled knight are necessary to your well-being? Life in the outer worlds must be very . . . educational." The Seneschal managed to make the words somehow sound far more insulting than they actually were. I could only see Bryony's necklace where it ran across the back of her neck, bared by her piled-up hair, but I saw the brief flare of dark purple that shimmered across it all the same.

"My well-being is my own concern. If the queen has not closed the court or the borders, then it is my right to bring whomever I wish. So again, will you admit us or shall we discuss the matter with my father?"

The Seneschal looked like she'd like to argue but

apparently thought better of it. She bowed. "I will admit you." She straightened, then paused, as though considering adding something more to her statement. Something along the lines of "but don't say I didn't warn you when it all goes horribly wrong" perhaps?

"Thank you." Bryony's icy politeness probably would have extinguished my forge fires. Fen and Liam and I stayed deathly silent by mutual unspoken agreement as the Seneschal led the way across to the far door.

"Before you can go through, I need to check your belongings."

"We don't have anything illegal," Bryony said.

"No?" The Seneschal tilted her head, then pointed at Fen. "That one carries iron."

"Merely a chain around his wrist."

"That can be enough." The Seneschal's mouth set in a stubborn line.

"He needs the iron," Bryony said.

"Why?"

It was Bryony's turn to look stubborn.

"Either you tell me, sa'Eleniel, or you will not enter."

Bryony looked back at Fen. He grimaced.

I nudged him. "Fen, you have to."

I knew how he felt about the Fae knowing about his powers, but really, I doubted it was a secret that there was a half-breed seer in the City. "Fen."

He scowled. "The iron blocks my visions."

The Seneschal's eyebrows shot upward. "You have the Sight?"

"I have something," he agreed.

"You need iron to control it? How is it that you have remained untrained for so long?"

"Because I chose not to turn my life over to either the Beasts or your kind," he said bluntly.

"You would rather wear iron?" She sounded appalled.

"Yes."

Her mouth flattened again, her eyes narrowed as if she was trying to determine whether there was something more to the story, more that she wasn't being told. She held a hand toward Fen for a moment, then snapped it shut. "You are part Beast?"

"My grandmother was *immuable*."

"Is your power from her?"

Fen shrugged. "No one seems to know." He held out his wrist, pushing his cuff back roughly to bare the chain. The Seneschal fell back two steps as if worried that he might try to touch her with the iron.

"Do you want me to take this off?" he asked.

"It is a burden on the land, to have iron inside the court," the Seneschal said.

"It's a burden on him not to have it," Bryony replied. "It is not a weapon. I will pledge my word that it will not be used against any of the Fae."

The Seneschal looked as though she didn't particularly think that was enough. "I will allow it. Under one condition. Once inside, the *hai'salai* will present himself to one of our healers. They may be able to bind him a different way. Then the iron may be removed from the court."

Bryony looked at Fen. "Is that acceptable to you, Fen?"

Would he refuse? And if so, what then? Would Bryony go on without us? And what did that mean for the agreement we'd made?

We couldn't turn back. Not with everything that was at stake. I could feel the hours slipping by, each one ticking away like a gear winding down, propelling us toward the moment when Ignatius would be free to carry out his threat and dissolve the treaty.

Before the war started.

The queen had to change her mind. We had to make her change her mind.

I watched as Fen studied Bryony and the Seneschal. He touched the chain on his wrist, twisted it against his skin, then pushed his sleeve back down. "Yes. I agree with your conditions."

Beside me, Liam made a noise that might just have been a stifled sigh of relief. His hand uncurled, the red of the Templar sigil muted against his dark skin but comforting somehow. I knew that he, for one, wouldn't break his word or abandon us.

The Seneschal nodded. "An agreement, then. I will let your party pass, sa'Eleniel."

She bowed again as she produced an ornate metal key from beneath her robes and unlocked the door.

Beyond the doorway I caught a glimpse of a stormy sky

and couldn't help glancing back over my shoulder. The weather outside the Gate had been a perfect summer's day. But we were apparently stepping into stormier climes. The queen's connection to the Veiled Court and the Fae lands was an intimate one and what the lands showed spoke to her mood and our likely reception.

An ironmage in the Fae courts. I couldn't help feeling as though such a thing might act somewhat like a lightning rod, drawing trouble and fire and destruction.

But it was too late to turn back now, so I took deep breaths while the Seneschal examined our luggage. It didn't take long. She gave us permission to pick up our bags and then she walked back to the trio of doors and pressed her hand to the central one. It swung open. My curiosity surged and it was only my endless hours of protocol training that made me remember to bow politely to the Seneschal as I walked past her and stepped into another world.

Fen

Summerdale.

I wanted nothing to do with the Fae. Yet here I was, trooping across the threshold to the Veiled World on a fool's errand like it was just a trip to a borough across the City.

Perhaps that was the key to surviving here. I had to tell myself it wasn't a big deal to be here—and then it wouldn't be a big deal.

I almost snorted. If I believed that particular bit of chicanery then I might as well sell myself a bridge or two as well.

Still, whatever I thought of the matter, I was here now and we had a task to complete. Like it or not, we needed the queen to return to the negotiations. Or else the City could fall.

The door closed behind us with a quiet click. I couldn't stop myself from looking back over my shoulder. The door had vanished.

The hairs on the back of my neck stood on end.

Perfect. No way out without someone who knew how to reveal the door again. I was truly screwed.

Better to look forward than back. I turned my attention to our surroundings. That was hardly less unsettling. We stood in a large garden—or a courtyard perhaps. There were smooth stone tiles underfoot and garden beds filled with tall and spiky blooms. It may have been pretty in sunshine, but under the suddenly sullen sky that loomed above our heads, it merely looked gloomy and quietly menacing.

"Now what?" I asked Bryony. "How do we get to see the queen?"

"The Seneschal will have told her we're here already," Bryony replied. "So we may be summoned."

That sounded less than pleasant. "And if we're not?"

"Then we will attend the court."

"How long do we wait to decide which?"

Bryony frowned at me. "Patience, Fen. Time runs differently here."

Was that supposed to make me feel better somehow? If so, it failed.

"Guess I'll make myself comfortable, then." I walked toward one of the low stone benches set in front of the nearest garden beds. There was a statue of a woman beside the bench and as I passed it, its head turned to watch me. I jumped half a foot, then caught myself as Saskia giggled.

Damned Fae tricks. I was half tempted to brush my chain against the statue to see if that had any effect on it, but that wouldn't exactly be in keeping with the promise that Bryony had made.

Instead I frowned at the stone face, only to see the lips curve slowly into a smile. Which was somehow even more disturbing. Statues shouldn't watch you or smile while they were doing it. I couldn't help feeling that someone was inside the stone, looking out.

Hells, in this place that could well be true. I decided I didn't need to sit down after all and walked back to where the rest of the party stood.

Saskia gazed around the courtyard with wary fascination. Liam stood next to Bryony, body poised for action. You could take a knight's hand, but it seemed that it didn't change his instincts to protect those he'd been charged to protect. I needed to remember that. Liam didn't entirely approve of me. I doubted his opinion would improve any if he found out I was bedding his brother knight's little sister.

Bryony looked composed, but her chain was as gray and dull as the overcast skies. I didn't think she was as sanguine about being home as she pretended.

"How long is it since you've been here?" I asked.

"Not that long." She looked around the courtyard with a frown. "A half dozen years or so."

"Six years?" I blurted, then remembered that she was Fae. To a Fae six years was a drop in the bucket of their lifetime. Six years away from the Veiled World for a Fae was probably like a two-week trip to the country for a human.

I guessed we would find out. There was a soft rumble from the sky. Thunder. Perfect. Was it going to rain? Standing around waiting for the queen of the bloody Fae to summon us was one thing. Doing so while getting soaked was another entirely.

But no drops followed the thunder and Bryony made no move to leave. I wondered exactly what form a summons to the Veiled Court might take. Saskia had wandered over to the statue, who had now tilted her head to study Saskia. Saskia looked more fascinated than appalled. Of course, she'd known what to expect.

She reached out a hand, holding it a few inches from the surface of the marble. I wondered if she was using her powers.

Perhaps. A small spark leapt from the statue to Saskia and she yelped softly and drew her hand back quickly, shaking her fingers as if they burned.

I laughed, and she turned to glare at me. Given the choice of stilted small talk with Bryony and teasing Saskia, I chose the latter. I walked back over to her, skirting the statue warily. "What did you do?" I asked.

"I was trying to see what she's made of," Saskia said.

"Apparently she doesn't appreciate snooping."

"I wasn't snooping," she said indignantly. "It's not snooping to be curious." One side of her mouth curled up. "This place is . . ."

Her voice drifted off.

"What?" I prompted.

She curled her fingers back against her chest, then stretched her arm again, gesturing around the garden. "It feels . . . Don't you feel it, Fen? The power? The earth fairly sings with it here."

Sings? Was that how it seemed to her? It didn't feel like a song to me; it felt like a vast weight pressing on me, trying to hold me down. The ache in my wrist was worse than usual, the iron a solid band of burning pain against my skin.

But I couldn't tell Saskia that. She would just worry.

"I hadn't really thought about it," I said. "Maybe the iron stops me from noticing."

Her eyes flicked to my wrist, her expression guilt-stricken for a moment. "Maybe the Seneschal was right and the Fae healers can help."

"Maybe." I wasn't looking forward to being examined by any healer, let alone one of the Fae. Nor did I fancy them working magic on me, which was the only way I could think of that they would possibly be able to help me.

Saskia smiled. "That would be something good out of this." She moved a few steps farther, bending down to look at one of the strange plants. "I wonder what these are." She didn't try to touch one of the blooms, though—the odd purple-gray flowers had a spiky surface that looked potentially painful. Instead she bent closer still to inspect it and then sniffed one of the black roses that grew alongside it.

"Perhaps Bryony can tell you," I said. But as Saskia turned to look behind us there was a clatter of hooves and her expression turned guarded. I twisted too.

A large carriage drawn by two black horses had pulled up at the far end of the courtyard. Was this the queen's summons?

The carriage door opened and Saskia and I stood watching as a Fae man descended, dressed in robes as black as the roses. He had dark hair too—as dark as Bryony's—and pale skin, and he carried a shining black cane, though he didn't move as if he needed assistance.

Bryony's back went stiff as he walked across the tiles toward her and stopped a few paces away from where she and Liam stood.

"Bryony sa'Eleniel," the man said with a shallow bow. He extended his hand and I saw the flash of a Family ring. Blue and purple. The same colors as the ring on Bryony's hand.

Bryony took the hand and bowed over it. "Father," she said with equal politeness. "It is good to see you."

SASKIA

There was a long silence in the coach after Bryony's father had directed us into its depths. While I was glad to leave the eerie courtyard, I would have liked to know where we were going. But if Bryony and her father weren't going to speak, then none of us seemed willing to risk offending a Fae lord by breaching some unknown rule of etiquette.

Beside me, Fen was particularly still, as though he thought that unmoving, he would remain unseen. But he would need Lily's powers to pass beneath the notice of the Fae, and those he didn't have.

He was closest to the window, blocking the view so that I caught only glimpses of the country we passed through as the coach rolled smoothly along. What I could see intrigued me. The sky stayed the same uncertain gray, but the landscape itself seemed to alter at will. Whose will, I wasn't sure. Perhaps the changes marked the boundaries of Fae territories, but it was both intriguing and disconcerting to see rolling hills give way to ancient-looking forests and those, in turn, dissolve into fields of long grasses.

It only brought home the fact that we were definitely not in the City anymore and that the rules of this land were very, very different.

And Bryony was the one who was meant to guide us through them. I turned back to her. She was watching her father with an expression that I would have called almost wary, but I had never actually seen Bryony look daunted by anything in all the years that I'd known her, so perhaps I was mistaken.

I looked across to her father, who was watching her in turn. His face was perfectly calm. A little too calm. He hadn't seen his daughter for six years. Surely he felt something?

"So, Father," Bryony said suddenly. "To what do we owe the honor of your regard?"

Lord sa'Eleniel cocked his head slightly, long pale fingers curling around the curved head of his cane. "The Seneschal did me the kindness of informing me that my daughter had seen fit to return to the Veiled World. It is only proper that I come to greet her."

"You could have greeted me anytime in the last six years. You have known where I was."

His eyes darkened a little. I had seen that look on Bryony's face many times and almost snorted. Like father, like daughter, apparently.

"I have too many concerns here in the courts to waste time in the world outside."

"That world outside is somewhat disrupted right now, thanks to—"

"Be careful," he warned. "Now is not the time to draw the attention of the queen in the wrong way."

"That's unfortunate when I am seeking an audience with her."

"So I am told." He rubbed his chin, the ring on his hand, twice as large as Bryony's, flashing suddenly. "What confuses me is the reason for that request."

"Don't be coy, Father. You must know what happened at the negotiations."

"Indeed I do. Our Speaker was murdered." His face twisted with the first sign of genuine emotion he'd displayed. "A sign of the perfidy of the outer worlds."

"The humans had nothing to do with the killing," Bryony said.

"How do you know?"

"Because they have nothing to gain by the negotiations' failing. In fact, they have the most to lose."

"Perhaps."

"No, not perhaps. They are the ones who risk being overrun by the Beasts and the Blood."

"If that happens, then perhaps it is meant to be."

"Father!"

"Don't be naive, child. The queen has held this peace through her will and power for a very long time now. If it fails, then it is the will of something greater than all of us."

"It is the will of Ignatius Grey," Bryony snapped. "And he is not greater than me."

Lord sa'Eleniel frowned. "Do you know that for sure?"

"No. Nothing is certain. But Ignatius is the one who is determined to be the next Lord of the Blood. And he seems to share Lord Lucius' ambition. Lucius grew bolder these last few years. He was building to something. I think that Ignatius is following in his footsteps. No good will come of that."

Lord sa'Eleniel leaned back against the seat, the cane tapping the floor for a moment. "Regardless, it is the queen's will that will determine the outcome."

"Which is why I am here. Someone has to make her see reason."

"Dangerous words."

"The queen is giving in to grief and affection. But she cannot afford to. Not now."

"Nobody tells the queen what to do." His tone suggested that he meant nobody sane at least.

"I am not telling her. I have a case to make."

"If you are given an audience."

"Why wouldn't I be?"

Her father shrugged.

"Father. Please. Do not interfere in this."

His brows drew together. There had been a plot against the queen in the Fae Courts. Guy and Holly had helped uncover it, but I hadn't heard that the queen had successfully hunted down all those who may have been involved. If Bryony's father was counseling her against going to the queen, was it out of concern for her safety or was it because he was one of those who might desire a change in power in the Veiled World?

The collapse of the treaty might be enough impetus to power a strike against the queen. I didn't know enough about Fae law, but maybe it would even give a reason for the court to bring a genuine grievance against the queen. If there were those who wanted someone else to rule the Fae, then this was an opportunity for them too.

I rubbed my forehead as my head began to ache. The whole thing was a mess and I didn't see how anyone could find a solution to it. Maybe Fen's visions were right and we were all doomed. Perhaps I should just stay here in the Veiled World, sheltered from whatever might come in the world outside. Even if the Blood did wrest power in the City, they would never be allowed to cross the borders of Summerdale. The Fae magics were too strong for that. The Blood could defeat the humans with sheer strength and viciousness, and they could probably sway the Beasts to their will as well, but the Fae had always been safe from them.

Then I remembered what Fen had said he had seen. Both Fae and humans kneeling to Ignatius. My stomach turned over again as the implications of that struck home for the first time. Could a Blood Lord rise that high?

No.

I had to believe it wasn't true. Maybe there would be a few Fae—those who'd made their lives with the humans, like Bryony—those who might fight and lose with us, who could be defeated, but the Fae as a race were too powerful to fall. Which was why we needed them. Needed the queen to come back and keep the peace that she'd defended all these years.

Grief, Bryony had said. I knew about grief. Knew the rage and pain that came from losing someone you cared about. I didn't know if the queen had loved the Speaker, but it didn't really matter. What mattered was that she moved past pain to see reason again. It had taken me years to get over Edwina's death, not that I was reconciled to the fact even now.

We didn't have years to convince the queen, and she had known the Speaker for far longer than the sixteen years of my sister's life.

How much worse might the grief of centuries be?

And how the hell could we overcome it?

FEN

The journey continued through the disconcerting, ever-changing landscape of the Veiled Lands. Bryony and her father lapsed back into silence after their somewhat heated conversation. Heated for them, at least. Nothing seemed to have been decided, but perhaps there was some other deeper thread of dialogue being carried beneath their words that the rest of us just wouldn't recognize.

I had no idea where we were going or what we were supposed to do when we got there. I'd assumed that we would go straight to the Veiled Court when we arrived in Summerdale, but I should have known that things were never quite that simple when dealing with the Fae.

Just as I was deciding that I'd had enough and I was going to ask Bryony to explain what the hell was happening—protocol be damned—the coach made a swinging turn and the landscape around us changed again from a high and barren-looking moor to a leafy green avenue of trees that lined either side of the smooth white stone path beneath our wheels.

"Where are we?" I asked as the coach began to slow. I couldn't quite see what lay ahead through the window, not without poking my head out, and I was reluctant to do that in a place so obviously steeped in magic. Who knew what might happen if I did? I might get turned into a frog, or something might just decide to lop it off altogether.

"This is the boundary to the sa'Eleniel territory," Bryony said.

The coach halted and Lord sa'Eleniel opened the door and climbed down without a backward glance.

I stayed where I was. "I thought we were going to the court."

"My father thinks it best if he presents me. Which means we are stopping here for a while first."

"A while? How long is a while?" Saskia said, with an anxious flick of her hands, which I suspected was as close to disapproval as she was willing to show this deep in Fae territory.

"I know," Bryony said. "Don't worry," she added as she gathered her skirts and prepared to climb down after her father.

"That's easy for you to say," Saskia muttered as Bryony left the coach.

She looked across at me. I shook my head at her. There was nothing that we could do, other than follow Bryony and see what happened. If we were no closer to the queen after another few hours, then it would be time to come up with another plan.

Chapter Twenty-one

FEN

The coach had halted in a courtyard similar to the one we had left. This one was semicircular, the cobbled drive a dark gray sweep against the grass on either side. The flat side of the semicircle was a house. Though "house" seemed too tame a word. It was massive. Bigger than the DuCaine mansion—and that was saying something.

We followed Bryony into the house, where a bevy of servants—I assumed that's what they were—appeared and started fussing around her. Liam and Saskia and I stood in an awkward group watching the commotion.

Eventually Bryony extricated herself from the gaggle and joined us.

"Our rooms will be ready soon."

"Rooms? How long are we going to be here?"

She gave me a quelling look. "Patience, Fen." She made a little gesture when I started to protest, as though to say, "We can't talk here."

I held my tongue, deciding that waiting a little bit longer wouldn't hurt. But I was determined to get the full story as soon as we were somewhere private.

The servants ushered us down long corridors, the walls painted with twining plants and flowers, and into a suite of rooms that had several bedrooms situated around a central living area. There was no ceiling on the central room, though it was richly furnished.

Was the sky that showed clearly above us just an illusion or did some other magic protect the furniture from the elements? I couldn't feel a ward overhead but the general background level of magic here in the Veiled World was so strong, I didn't know if I could sense a ward if there was one.

The servants left us at Bryony's command. She closed the door and pressed her palm against it. I felt a flare of power and her hand twitched before she straightened and turned back to us.

"Are you going to tell us what's going on now?" Liam said.

I turned to him in surprise. He'd stayed silent up until this point, stoically following orders. I hadn't expected him to be the one demanding information. Even Templars had limits of patience, it seemed.

"Come sit down," Bryony said. She pulled out a chair from the round table near the glass doors that led out to yet another garden.

We all obeyed, positioning ourselves around the table, watching Bryony expectantly.

There was a knock at the door and one of the ubiquitous servers entered after Bryony released the wards.

"My lady, there are healers here to see to your guest." The servant didn't look at me.

Beside me, Saskia stiffened and I moved my hand over hers briefly, ignoring the churn in my gut.

Bryony nodded. "Fen? Are you ready?"

I rose from my seat. I didn't like it, but I wasn't going to let the Fae see that. I made myself shrug. "No point putting it off."

Bryony looked almost sympathetic but she nodded. "I'll come with you." She looked at Liam, sitting across from me. "Liam, do you wish to come too?"

Surprise flashed in Liam's green eyes. "Me? There's nothing wrong with me."

"I know your arm has been treated at St. Giles," Bryony said gently, "but the Fae here can sometimes do things that we can't achieve in the City. If you wish, they will examine you."

"Unless they can make my hand grow back, I'm not sure what good they can do." Liam's tone was light, but it held a thread of sudden hope that was almost painful to listen to.

"They can't do that," Bryony said. "But they can ease some of that other pain that you refuse to admit to." She fixed him with a stern look. "Your missing hand hurts sometimes, doesn't it?"

Liam's expression turned stubborn. "I said I was fine."

I was surprised at his defiance. I suspected that Liam had a slight crush on Bryony—he was unfailingly deferential to her and even more quiet than usual when he was in her company. A High Family Fae and a Templar was not a relationship fated to succeed, so I thought him wise to keep his feelings to himself. But for him to be refusing what Bryony offered now meant that he felt very strongly about it.

"Beside," Liam added, "I'd rather not leave Miss Saskia alone in this place."

"She's perfectly safe here," Bryony said.

"All the same." Liam folded his arms across his chest, making it clear that he wasn't going anywhere. "Thank you, but no. I have no need of the healers."

Bryony sighed. "Very well. But remember, you only have to ask while we are here. Fen, we should go."

I looked down at Saskia, wishing I could think of something to say to ease the worry in her eyes. "As you wish, Lady Bryony."

"We shouldn't be overly long," Bryony said. "I'll reseal the wards when I go. Please don't go anywhere until I return."

I wondered where she thought Saskia and Liam were likely to go, then wondered if she was actually worried about someone trying to take them while she was gone. Not the most cheerful thought I'd had.

Liam nodded. "We'll be here."

Bryony led the way through another confusing series of hallways. I tried to memorize our route, but there was something about the angles of the corridors that didn't entirely make sense, as though the house itself was located in more than one place. Which may well have been possible here in Summerdale.

I stuck close to Bryony, who didn't seem at all concerned by the house's odd geography.

Another Fae woman was waiting for us when we finally reached our destination. Her nearly white blond hair was caught back from her face and piled high. It contrasted with the deep gold of her skin and ice blue eyes. From her coloring, I assumed she was no relation of Bryony's.

Bryony halted at the sight of her and I nearly bumped into her from behind.

"Saffron sa'Namiel." The words were almost a hiss.

The blonde smiled, but the expression in her eyes remained as icy as their color. "Lady Bryony."

I saw Bryony stiffen slightly. "You are the healer the Seneschal has sent to us?"

"Yes," Saffron said. Her eyes met mine for a second, then moved back to Bryony. I felt as though I'd been effectively dismissed. "This is the *hai'salai* I am to treat?"

"Examine," Bryony corrected coolly. "He isn't unwell."

The blonde looked pained. "That remains to be seen. If you could ask him to remove the iron and place it in the receptacle provided"—she pointed at a box made of some dull gray metal that had been set just inside the doorway—"I will begin once it is not interfering with my power."

Bryony made a soft noise that I thought was a stifled snort. But she didn't say anything other than to ask me to remove the chain.

Did the iron really interfere as the blonde claimed or was this all just some sort of power game? After all, the Fae healers at St. Giles managed to work around iron. And to live in the City.

But maybe they had become acclimated to its presence. I was a half-breed and it took prolonged direct contact with my skin for iron to affect me. But all half-breeds are different. Holly, for example, had no problem with iron whatsoever. Lucky girl. Though if I had been completely immune to it, Lady only knew what I might use to control my visions, so perhaps my weakness was a good thing.

I took my time as I unfastened the chain and unwound it from my wrist. My skin burned and stung as it was laid bare. For once I couldn't ignore the bruised and raw-looking state of it. The deep bruises staining my skin made me vaguely ill. I took a deep breath then another as I carried the chain across to the box. It was large enough for ten of my chains, but I simply placed it inside and closed the lid.

Almost immediately images flared to life around the blonde's head, though they were more indistinct than usual.

I stared at her, trying to work out what they were, as if I could focus them by mere concentration.

But as I focused, pain spiked into my head savagely. I winced and looked away.

"Fen?" Bryony said.

"Leave him," Saffron said sharply. "This is what I need to see."

I groped my way to a chair and sat abruptly as pain flared again. Gods, it was worse here than it had been back in the City. It felt as though someone was pressing a fiery knife through my right eyeball and up into my brain. The room swam greasily around me and I fought to breathe.

"Fen." I felt Bryony's hand on my shoulder. "You need to concentrate."

"Get Saskia," I grunted, gritting my teeth. If I couldn't have my chain, then I needed something to control the pain. Or else I doubted I was going to stay conscious long enough for anyone to examine me.

"Who is Saskia?"

Saffron's voice sounded closer now.

"The human metalmage," Bryony said.

"And why does he want her? Are they lovers?"

Don't answer that, I thought desperately. Then I relaxed when I realized that Bryony didn't know about Saskia and me.

"No," Bryony said. "But her power somehow damps his."

"That is . . . unusual for a human."

That gave me pause. Did they mean that amongst the Fae there were those who could do what Saskia did?

"She is from an unusual family," Bryony said dryly. "But perhaps you should attend to your patient rather than talking to me."

Saffron made a skeptical noise. "I'm going to put my hands on you now, *hai'salai*," she said. "Stay still."

Easier said than done. The pain was still pulsating through me. I wanted to scream, but I clenched my teeth instead, digging my fingers into my thigh.

Cool hands touched my forehead. The pain didn't recede, but it didn't get any worse at least. "Interesting," Saffron murmured. "Such a tangle. I—"

Whatever she had been about to say was cut off by a brisk knock at the door.

"Lady Bryony," a voice said, "you have been summoned to attend the queen."

Bryony at least allowed me to put my chain on before she hurried me back to the chamber where we'd left the others. The iron tamped the pain down to a bearable level, but still, I made a beeline for Saskia and took her hand.

"What's wrong?" she asked, looking alarmed, her fingers tightening around mine. The rapid disappearance of the pain almost made me gasp.

"Nothing," I managed.

"The queen has summoned us," Bryony said. "We need to act quickly." She looked us over critically. We'd all worn formal clothing for the trip to Summerdale, on the expectation of being able to see the queen as soon as we arrived, but after the hours of travel and waiting we were all a little rumpled.

Apparently Bryony didn't think we had time to change; she frowned, then came over to each of us in turn and gestured sharply. The wrinkles fell out of our clothing.

I wished she could do the same for my brain. Saskia's touched helped soothe me, but I was still drained after the pain and was not looking forward to this next stage of our journey. Plus, part of me was wondering exactly what Saffron had meant by "a tangle" and whether or not she might be able to cure me.

I'd resisted coming to Summerdale, but now that I was finally here, the idea of a cure for the pain of my visions was enticing. A normal life . . . one where I didn't have to cripple myself with iron and alcohol. What might that be like?

I looked at Saskia, at the fingers twined through mine, and caught my breath again at just how much I wanted to believe that it might be a possibility. That maybe, just maybe, I could be whole. That I could be good enough for her.

Bryony finished with Liam and gestured for us to follow her. I expected that we would be going back to the courtyard and the carriage, but I should have known that things in the Veiled World wouldn't work that way. Instead we went through the house and out into a formal garden, with rows of neat hedges that formed intricate patterns lining garden beds full of more odd flowers in a hundred shades of white.

In the center of the garden, bordered by four square knots of hedge, was a narrow gate that gleamed dull gold in the still, sullen light of the overcast sky.

Bryony led us up to the gate and then paused before it. "Once we pass through the gate we will be in the court," she said, voice serious. "You will follow my lead and not speak unless the queen or I request you to, understand me? A wrong word might damage our case permanently. The queen's mood is dark."

I didn't know how she knew this, but as if to underscore her point, a low rumble of thunder rolled around us. Saskia moved a little closer to me. I wasn't going to argue with that. Bryony sighed as she inspected us one last time and then we went through the gate.

I held Saskia's hand as I stepped underneath the metal gate, but as my foot hit the white marble beyond, I was alone. I whirled, but there was no gate to be seen behind me. Just a vast square of marble that stretched for what had to be a mile or more, fading into different landscapes on each of its four sides.

Where the hell were the others?

Damn the Fae and their tricks.

Maybe it was an illusion—a test.

Think, Fen.

I lifted my right hand to reach into my pocket, where I'd tucked some charms, but as I did so I noticed that my chain had vanished.

Shit.

I braced myself for the wave of pain, but it didn't come.

"I am blocking your pain."

I whirled again. The owner of the voice was standing behind me, gray, gray veils covering her face and floating around her body, though there was not a breath of wind to move them. The only color came from the jewels on her hands, rings covering the first knuckle on each of her fingers. Except for her left ring finger. That one was bare.

Or was it?

I blinked as one of the veils swept across her fingers, reminding me exactly who this woman was. The Veiled Queen.

I bowed deeply. "Your Majesty."

"Pretty manners, for a *hai'salai*." Her voice was somehow gray too. Gray like granite or storm clouds or the depths of a winter ocean. Full of power and the potential for pain.

I straightened, cautiously. "Might I ask where my companions are, Your Majesty?"

"They are safe enough. I wanted to see you for myself." She walked a few steps closer and I fought the distinct desire to move backward in response.

"Brave, aren't you?" the queen said. "Don't you know the tales about me?" Her veils darkened a little and I fought a shudder. I knew enough to understand that if those veils turned black I probably wasn't going to leave this place alive.

"I know that you are a great queen," I said through a mouth gone horribly dry. "That you have worked for the peace we all value so highly and helped the City greatly."

Her head tilted. "Value? Value so much that someone killed my Speaker?"

"That wasn't me," I said hastily. "Or anyone that I know."

"How do you know?" she said. "Have you seen?" She stretched out a hand toward me, not quite touching me. "Such a muddle inside that head of yours. How did those powers get so twisted? Yet they are strong. Tell me, *hai'salai*, have you seen?"

The visions roared around me then, driving me to my knees with a shuddering gasp. Blood. Fire. And the faces of the Du-Caines whirling around me. Saskia. Guy. Simon. The City blackened and burning. The Treaty Hall exploding and the Speaker falling. Me with my head in my hands and a bottle of brandy, alone in an empty room, tears rolling down my face. And Ignatius smiling through it all. The images speared through my head like shards of jagged glass and I cried out.

Then they vanished, taking the pain with them.

"What did you see?" the queen asked.

I swallowed hard, willing my heart to slow, not certain that the memory of the pain wouldn't yet make me retch. Then I told her.

"Ignatius Grey," she said, veils shading darker still. "This one troubles me."

"Then you should return to the negotiations, Your Majesty. Because otherwise there is little to stop Ignatius Grey from seizing the power he wants."

She sighed then. A dusty sound like wind across stone. "Why should I care? What has this treaty gained me? Other than death and care and trouble."

"You lost someone close to you," I said. "And that is a grief—" More of a grief to a Fae perhaps, who would live many, many years longer than any human. Perhaps the losses eventually grew too hard to bear. "But there will be more losses if you do not return to the negotiations."

"Not my losses."

"There are Fae in the City, Your Majesty. Fae who may die." Or worse. Saskia had told me what Adeline had said about Ignatius taking Fae women. That couldn't be for any good purpose. But looking at the queen and the deepening gray of her veils, I didn't feel like raising the subject.

"True. Though your visions are a tangle. Who knows if you even see truly?"

"I may not see the whole truth but I have seen my visions come to pass often enough to know that I see at least a part."

"Perhaps." Her head tilted. "And you insist on looking despite the pain. That is interesting."

"I don't have a lot of choice in the matter."

"You wear iron. And you chase them away using other methods. That is a choice of sorts."

"It doesn't always work," I said.

"The question is, what choice would you make if there was no pain? If you had control?"

For a second her veils lightened and I thought I caught a glimpse of greenish eyes, the color reminding me of Holly's. But it was gone in a flash, the veils turning to writhing dark again.

"I don't know," I said honestly. If I could choose whether or not to see? Part of me thought I would never look again. But what if control meant clarity . . . a way to be able to truly see—to be able to trust my power? Then my life could be very different.

Or it could drive me mad.

Knowing the future was very overrated.

"Perhaps we will find out." The queen snapped her fingers and suddenly I was no longer alone. Bryony and Liam and Saskia stood with us.

"Fen!" Saskia hurried to my side. "Where did you go?" She threw her arms around me. "I thought you were lost."

"Not lost." The queen's voice sounded almost amused.

Saskia let me go, stepping back abruptly as though she suddenly remembered where we were. She dropped into a deep curtsy, bowing her head. Bryony did the same and Liam bowed. I stayed straight. The queen had already had me on my knees. She didn't need any more obeisance from me just now.

"Bryony sa'Eleniel," the queen said. "Why have you sought my counsel?"

Bryony came out of the curtsy with the grace that only a Fae can muster. "My Queen," she said. "I bring a petition from the human delegation. A plea for you to recommence the negotiations."

"Have they found the proof I need?"

"No, Your Majesty. But as you will not allow them access to the Treaty Hall, I'm not sure how you expect them to uncover the true culprit behind the explosion."

The queen's veils swirled faster. "Your time outside our realm has made you bold, sa'Eleniel."

Bryony lifted her chin. "My time in the City has taught me to value the humans. They want the treaty and the peace. They need it. They would not put it in jeopardy."

"No? Even when some of them are pursuing avenues that might be unlawful?"

Fuck. The queen knew about Simon and the cure. My stomach dropped and I glanced at Saskia, who had turned pale.

Bryony, however, seemed unsurprised. "That need not destroy the peace. It may require some . . . adjustment, but the humans do not wish to destroy the Blood."

Just Ignatius and his cronies.

"Be that as it may, why should I return when those who caused my Speaker's death go unpunished?"

"Without the treaty there will be more deaths. And little chance of bringing anyone to justice," Bryony said. "You know this, Your Majesty. Ignatius Grey is grasping for

power. He is killing those who oppose him in the Blood
Court. Even now there are Blood under Haven in the Templar Brother House. The City needs you. Needs your protection."

"And what about what I need?"

The words came like a whiplash, raw with pain. Grief
again. Deeper, perhaps, than affection for her Speaker
would explain. Love might be closer to the truth.

"The humans are willing to assist you in finding justice
for your loss. They will do whatever it takes."

The veils stilled, holding motionless in the air. "Are you
asking me to name a price?"

"No, I am telling you that the humans hold true to the
bonds of friendship between our races."

"But what if I do have a price?"

Bryony blinked. "My Queen?"

"If I want something in return for my cooperation?"

"We will of course endeavor to do what is in our
power—," Bryony began.

"What I want is not in your power to grant," the queen
snapped. Her head turned slowly and dread swept over me
as her veiled gaze settled on me. "I have need of a seer. My
Speaker is lost to me and I need someone who sees truly. I
do not trust my court right now."

"Your Majesty—" Bryony tried again.

"This one." The queen nodded at me. "If this one will
swear service to me, stay with me here in Summerdale, then
I will rejoin the negotiations."

"No!" Saskia's cry was as pained as the queen's had been
earlier. I met her eyes and then suddenly another vision
rolled over me. I saw myself refusing, saw myself leaving
with the others. Saw the queen's veils turning black. And
saw the death that would result if I didn't agree to what she
wanted.

Saskia's death.

The queen had decided she wanted me, for whatever
purpose. She would brook no rivals for my loyalty.

Saskia.

Grief closed my throat. She wouldn't give up on me. And
if she tried, then she would die. I saw it a hundred ways.
Knew that there was only one way to stop it.

I had to break her heart. Make her hate me.

Had to lose the hope of a future I had let myself believe in.

There was no other way.

The visions left me in a rush and I knew what I had to do. The smile I summoned made my face hurt, as though my body fought me.

"Of course I will stay, Your Majesty," I said. "It would be my pleasure."

"Fen. No!" Saskia's voice choked and Liam flung an arm around her to hold her back as she lunged toward me.

I stepped back.

Away from her. Toward the queen.

It hurt like walking on broken glass.

"You misunderstand," I said. "It's not a case of having to. I want to. Why do you think I came here?" I made the words lazy, careless. "The queen can cure me. Free me." I made myself smile at the veiled figure with some approximation of pleasure. It was an expression I had practiced many times on the women who flocked to the Swallow. It came easily enough, despite the loathing I felt.

"Besides, she can keep me safe. It's not a question of choice, Prentice DuCaine. It's a question of what's best for me. And what's best for me is right here. What, did you think I came here out of that same misguided need to save the world that you DuCaines seem to harbor?"

"You—" Saskia spat and Liam pulled her against him, turning her head into his chest so that she didn't finish the sentence. His face was contemptuous as he stared at me. Bryony's expression was equally disgusted.

I felt a small sense of victory—they believed me. Which meant Saskia would be safe. Lost to me. But safe. It had to be enough.

I turned back to the queen. "I offer you service, Your Majesty," I said and dropped to my knees, bowing my head because I couldn't bear to see Saskia any longer.

"Very well," the queen said. "You may tell the humans to be ready in three days, sa'Eleniel. I will return then."

"My Queen, I—" Bryony faltered. I heard her take a single breath. "Very well, Your Majesty. I will tell them."

"Good. Now leave us."

There was a sudden tingling of power and I somehow

knew that they were gone. I didn't look up. Couldn't bear to see the empty space where Saskia had been.

Instead I waited, head bowed. The queen's footsteps were soft taps on the marble.

"So, *hai'salai*," she said. "Let us see what you are truly capable of." Her hands came down on either side of my head and the world went white around me.

Chapter Twenty-two

SASKIA

⚡

"Saskia? Is it true?" Holly's voice came from the doorway of Bryony's office, where Bryony had left me when I'd refused to go back to my family's rooms. I wasn't ready to face anyone just yet. Not until I was sure I could do more than breathe without dissolving in tears.

It had taken all my will during our journey back to the City to do just that. Each breath in and out was an effort when all I wanted to do was stop. To not be. To not *feel*.

Fen.

I couldn't stop hearing his words in my head, seeing the pleased smile as he'd turned to the queen. Had I really been such a fool?

And now here was Holly, wanting to know all about it. I hugged my arms tighter around my knees. "It's true," I said dully. "Fen stayed in Summerdale."

"I don't believe it."

I lifted my head, saw the expression of shock and disbelief on her face, mirror to what I felt. "Believe it. He wanted safety."

Holly shook her head. "That's not Fen."

"Isn't it?"

"She must have done something to him."

"She didn't even *touch* him." My words sounded bitter. They tasted bitter. I swallowed.

"She's the Veiled Queen. She doesn't need to touch him. Maybe she bound him somehow."

"No." I shook my head. I had heard the truth in Fen's words, seen the look he'd given the queen. "He wanted to stay. Guy was right about him."

Holly's expression was stony. "I don't believe it. She must have done something. You've been gone for three days—"

"What?" I straightened, the shock of this information enough to burn through the fog of pain. "We weren't even there a day."

We stared at each other.

"Shit," I breathed. "Bloody Fae." We'd forgotten that time could move differently in the Veiled World. Nothing had appeared different when we'd exited the Gate and we'd hardly had a chance to check the date anywhere since returning less than half an hour ago. "What day is it?"

"Sunday," Holly said. "Ignatius' deadline is up in three more days."

"The queen said she'd come back in three days. That's cutting it fine."

"She's coming back?"

"Yes. So she says." I was reluctant to place any faith in the bloody Veiled Queen at this point. She had Fen. My Fen.

I wanted to claw her eyes out.

Which was going to make the negotiations interesting. But even more than her, I wanted to hurt Fen. Hurt him like he'd hurt me. Grief rolled over me again, and I dropped my head back down to my knees.

"He chose her," I whispered.

"Oh, Sass," Holly said. "I didn't realize. I swear, if I get my hands on him, I'll skin him."

"You can't skin him," I said. "He's the queen's pet now."

"Pet or not, I'm going to—" She broke off as a sob escaped my throat. "I'm sorry. This is my fault."

"I think it's Fen's fault." My throat burned with his betrayal.

Holly sighed. "He never did know how to show any restraint."

No. He didn't. I remembered those unrestrained kisses and the passion of him in my bed all too well.

Stupid, stupid, stupid.

"All right," Holly said. "But you can't mope up here. There's no time for moping. You can mope after the negotiations. I promise I'll bring you all the chocolate and champagne a girl could want and help you curse his name. But you have to be strong just now." She squatted beside me, took my hand in hers. "Can you do that?"

I thought of Fen. And the queen. Thought how they would be amused by my weeping. "Yes," I said. "I can."

"Good," Holly said. "Because I want to show you something."

"In here," Holly said. She pressed her hand against the door of the hospital ward she'd practically dragged me to and I felt the buzz of the other kind of ward shimmer over me. We were still in St. Giles, though in one of the lesser-used wings. Why was the door warded?

The answer was sitting on a chair by the bed, one elbow resting on the sill of the window as she looked out of it.

Reggie.

Her expression was faintly puzzled as she turned toward us.

"Hello," Holly said. "Do you remember Saskia?"

Reggie frowned, her blue eyes distant. "I . . . maybe. Did I make you a dress? Holly tells me I make dresses." Her words were slow, her voice lazy, like someone slightly drunk.

I looked at Holly questioningly. She nodded at me. "Reggie's been ill. She's lost her memory. But the healers say she'll get it back." She crossed the room and leaned down to hug Reggie. "Isn't that right, sweetie?"

Reggie smiled slowly. "I guess so."

"Saskia wanted to come and say hello. She's been worried about you, like all of us. She's glad you're getting better. Aren't you, Saskia?"

"Yes, very glad." I forced the smile into my voice, my mind whirring with questions. "And you did make me a dress. A beautiful pink dress. You have to get better so you can make lots more."

"Pink," Reggie said, with another slight frown. "With your coloring?"

"Pale pink," I said. "It was lovely." The ache in my throat

burned more fiercely. I remembered how Reggie had tried to dissuade my mother from the pink. Mother, as usual, had insisted. Would Reggie ever make me another? I made myself smile, the expression stiff on my face.

Holly nodded approval at me over Reggie's head. "It's time for you to take a nap," she said to Reggie. "Simon will come and see you soon, with your medicine. I'll be back later on."

"All right," Reggie said placidly. She turned back to the window and I wasn't entirely sure that she hadn't completely forgotten that we were in the room with her.

Holly put her finger to her mouth and we left silently.

She shut the door behind us and reactivated the wards. I waited until we were a little way down the corridor before I dragged her into the first vacant room we passed.

"Care to explain what in hell's name is going on?" I said.

Holly grinned at me. "Just a second." She waved a hand and I felt an aural ward spring to life. "There."

"Tell me!" Had Simon found the cure? After all this time?

"I did what Fen wanted," Holly said. "Asked Simon to talk to Adeline about blood-locking and turning. Apparently something she said gave him an idea."

"Which was?"

"Adeline said that any of the Trusted being turned are fed blood from only one vampire. Otherwise the ritual usually fails."

"I don't understand."

Holly shrugged. "Neither do I, not entirely. But we know that the Blood become possessive, so by the time somebody is locked, they've usually been claimed by a single vampire and would only be consuming that vampire's blood. Simon wanted to see what would happen if we gave the locked blood from more than one source. Not just Atherton's blood but the blood of several vampires. Somehow he talked Adeline and some of the others into letting him take some of their blood. And when he gave some to Reggie . . ."

"She woke up? Is she better?"

"She's improving," Holly said. "She still needs the blood—less often, but she still gets shaky—but you saw her. She knows who we are and she eats and she's . . . aware."

I rather thought that "aware" was too strong a term for

the vague girl we'd left back in the ward, but I didn't want to burst Holly's bubble. And Reggie definitely seemed better compared to the last time I'd seen her. "What does Simon say?"

"He and Atherton think it has to be something magical. Competing magics weakening whatever has the hold over those who get locked. Simon's been going mad waiting for Bryony to get back. He wants to see what she thinks. Maybe you can help too."

"Me?"

"Simon said something about changes in Reggie's blood. You can sense blood, can't you?"

"I can sense iron in the blood—at least that's what Simon says I'm feeling," I corrected. "He says that's how I know where my family is, but I'm not sure that's all there is to it."

Holly's face fell and I hurried on. "But of course I can help. I'll try to do whatever Simon needs." It would give me something to do other than go crazy.

Holly laughed. "Wonderful. How about we go find him now?"

The next forty-eight hours passed in a blur of helping the delegates prepare a new venue for the negotiations—the Treaty Hall being out of consideration—and spending time with Simon in the hidden ward.

I didn't entirely understand the medical jargon he threw at me, but I obediently bent my senses to vial after vial of blood, trying to determine if there was anything unusual I could sense about them. Turned out I could sense the difference between human and vampire blood and also the difference between the blood-locked and an unaddicted human. Reggie's blood definitely felt different again to me, but I couldn't tell him why.

Still, it was enough to convince him he was on the right path.

I was glad to be helpful. Because no matter what I did, there was a constant background of pain. Whenever I was alone, the tears came and I was unable to stop them. I didn't know if I was crying because I'd lost Fen or because I'd been stupid enough to fall for him in the first place, but it hardly mattered.

What mattered was that he was gone.

I worked long into the night with Simon, needing exhaustion to find sleep.

When I finally crawled into bed, I was sure that I'd only been asleep for seconds when my door slammed open. I bolted upright, my heart hammering, fumbling for the lamp on the table beside me.

"Miss Saskia, it's Liam."

I saw his face as the lamp flared to life. Saw the sword in his hand. My pulse redoubled. "What's wrong?"

"I'm here to take you to the Brother House."

"Why?" I was already scrambling out of bed, grabbing for the first pieces of clothing that came to hand. I pulled pants on, then threw a tunic over my nightgown, not caring what I looked like. "Why?" I repeated, realizing that Liam hadn't answered me.

"The hospital is under attack," he said bluntly. "Hurry now."

"What about my parents and Hannah?" I panted, jogging after Liam as he led the way down back stairs and into the tunnels.

"Others are fetching them. The attack is only on the main building for now. But we're defending it."

"But who?"

"Beast Kind," Liam said shortly. "We think they're after the Blood who came here."

"Shouldn't they be attacking the Brother House, then?"

"They're not all in the Brother House. It was overcrowded . . . some of the Blood were put into some of the disused wards. But no one knew about that." Liam spoke easily as though our pace didn't bother him.

Bloody Templars.

I was growing soft away from my forge and the rigors of my studies. I hadn't even had time to pick up a weapon to exercise since I'd joined the delegation. I carried weapons, of course, but I hadn't needed to use them. Though I was glad enough of the pistol in my hand and the sword at my hip now. I'd forged the sword myself, and it was high in silver content. Any Beast wouldn't find its bite pleasant.

Liam led me down another flight of stairs and I glanced out of the window—the last chance to do so before we would be belowground. Sure enough, I saw fires around the

courtyard and dark figures moving on the grounds. I paused,
frozen, not believing it. Why now, so close to the negotiations recommencing?

"Miss Saskia." Liam's hand tugged on my arm and I
started to turn, but then I saw another flicker of flame out
of the corner of my eye.

That wasn't the main building. That was one of the other
wings. I gasped as I suddenly got my bearings. Not just any
wing.

"Reggie," I said. "There's a fire in Reggie's wing."

Liam protested as I turned and started to flee back up
the corridor, pounding after me, calling my name, demanding that I come back.

"You said they were defending the main building," I
yelled over my shoulder. "They might not have noticed this
yet. We have to get Reggie."

My heart clutched, thinking of the wards on Reggie's
room. They probably meant that no one could get to her,
but neither could she get out if there was a fire. If she was
even capable of realizing she was in danger.

Liam caught up with me. "Saskia, Guy will kill me if anything happens to you."

"Then you'd better make sure that nothing happens to
me," I retorted. I stopped as I reached one of the exit doors,
trying to work out the quickest path across the grounds to
the other ward. It wasn't far. A few hundred feet. I had an
invisibility charm, the one I used to get to the hidden wards.
And, I realized with a sudden surge of relief, I had a second
charm, a fresh one that Bryony had pressed into my hands
earlier that evening, to replace the one I'd been using, which
was nearing the end of its life span.

I grabbed the charms out of my pocket and thrust one of
them at Liam. I had no idea which was which. "Do you
know how to use that?" I asked.

"I'm a sunmage," he said. "I can manage."

"Good."

I triggered my charm, wrenched open the door, and ran
out into the night.

The air smelled like smoke and something acrid and oily
that made me cough as I drew in a breath. I almost blun-
dered straight into the path of a Beast racing across the

courtyard. I pulled up and held my breath, but he was obviously intent on whatever he was pursuing and didn't falter in his path. I ran on, my heart hammering, hoping that Liam was somewhere behind me.

It seemed to take an hour to cross the short distance, as though I ran through honey or toffee, each step an effort, but that was just the panic, I knew.

I reached the side door I'd been aiming for and sent a burst of power at the lock. The tumblers clicked into position obediently. I slipped inside, gasping for breath. There was a quick rush of footsteps and then Liam's voice said, "Shut the door."

I didn't need to be told twice. I sent another shot of power that would lock the door to anyone else but me and looked around. "Reggie's room is upstairs," I said. The air was smoky in here too. I couldn't catch my breath. I coughed, and then covered my mouth with my hand.

"Turn off your charm," Liam said.

I did as he asked. I'd no sooner seen myself blink back into existence than I felt a hand at my knee and Liam reappeared too, dagger between his teeth. I realized what he was going to do and bent. "Let me." I took the dagger and cut two strips from my nightgown.

I tied one over my mouth and handed the other to Liam. Sunmages and metalmages are well schooled in how to deal with fire. The cotton masks would help with the smoke, though it would have been better if we could have damped them. No time to get to water, though.

"Can you put the fire out?" Liam said.

"Maybe." I would need to be closer to the source and the fire would need to be not well established. Controlling a fire that I hadn't started was a Master-level skill.

"Let's get to Reggie," I said.

Liam nodded, his expression stern. "As soon as we get her, we go down into the tunnels and straight to the Brother House."

No argument from me about that.

We ran again, our pace even faster, sprinting as though a whole pack of Beasts was at our heels. Liam's hand closed over mine, and he half pulled me along, his longer strides propelling us faster than I could have managed alone.

We climbed the stairs at the same pace and I felt as though my heart was going to burst as we turned into the corridor where Reggie's room was. From below us, I heard a crash of glass and knew that the fire was worsening.

I pushed harder, calling on the earth for strength as we ran toward Reggie's door. A gleam of light shone into the corridor and I bit back a cry when I realized it was Reggie's door, partly open.

Not caring what might be waiting for me inside, I crashed through, Liam tumbling after me.

Holly was sitting on the bed, Reggie cradled in her arms. The room reeked of smoke and gunpowder and, I realized, the stench of the Beast lying dead at the foot of the bed.

My throat closed as I turned back to Holly and noticed the horrible angle of Reggie's head.

"Holly," I breathed. "Oh no."

Holly's eyes were bright, her face stained with soot and blood. "I came to get her," she said. "But I was too late. He broke her neck as I came through the door. He *laughed*. He said 'Let this be a lesson' and then he just . . . killed her."

Liam sucked in a ragged breath. His eyes held a vast sorrow. And an equally vast fury. "Holly, we need to go. Saskia and I will help you with Reggie."

"I was too late," Holly repeated. "But I shot him. Even when he tried to get to me. I just kept shooting."

"Yes, You did." I spoke carefully. "But Liam's right. We have to go now. Let us take Reggie. We'll take care of her."

"All right." Holly's expression was strange as Liam bent over her and slipped his arm around Reggie's too still form, lifting her away from Holly. His face twisted with what I recognized as pure frustration that he couldn't carry Reggie on his own. I stepped forward to help him, but as I did so, I saw Holly press her hand to her side, saw the dampness on her dark shirt.

"Holly? Are you hurt?" I demanded.

"A little," she said with an odd smile. Her eyes tipped back in her head and she toppled over.

"Liam!" I yelled as I lunged for Holly.

He twisted and we looked at each other helplessly.

"We can't leave Reggie," he said.

Nausea rose in my throat as I looked down at Reggie's face. She looked peaceful, at least. "We have to," I whispered. "Reggie is dead. Holly's still alive. We have to take Holly." My voice cracked and I bit back a sob, eyes stinging with more than smoke now.

Liam looked sick but he nodded once and then eased Reggie back onto the bed. He traced a cross on her forehead as I bent to Holly, trying to see where she was hurt. Her left side was wet and my hand came away red. Too red.

"She's bleeding. A lot. I don't suppose you're a healer?"

Liam shook his head. "I've never had that talent."

"All right." I squared my shoulders. I could cauterize the wound, but that would leave Holly with scars that would never be healed. And wouldn't do a damn bit of good if the damage was internal. I thought fast, trying to remember the lessons Simon had given me in first aid. Stop the bleeding. Get help.

"All right. I'll bind the wound and then we carry her. Down into the tunnels. As fast as we can."

I only hoped we would be fast enough.

We made it to the tunnels and I frantically stretched out my senses, trying to work out where Simon was. There was a whirl of sensation as I found first Mother and Hannah and Father, deep within the boundaries of the Brother House. I didn't have the breath to spare to sigh with relief, but I closed my eyes and muttered a quick prayer of thanks, not caring what god might be listening to me. Then tried for Simon again.

I found him at last. Not in the hidden ward as I'd hoped, but in the Brother House, though not with the rest of the family. I tightened my grip, looked down at Holly's pale face, thought of Reggie, back there in her room, with fire all around her. And then I did the only thing I could. I kept running.

There was no sleep for any of us for the rest of the night. I helped Simon with Holly, waiting with my heart in my mouth until he pronounced her out of danger. And then I did anything anyone told me would be useful.

The Templars beat back the Beasts, but there was a steady stream of wounded, amongst both the Templars and the hospital patients and staff.

And, as the sun rose and the grim task of finding bodies began, we realized that several of the Fae healers were missing. Or dead, maybe. There were some parts of several buildings where the fire had taken hold and it would take a long time to determine if there were bodies within.

The morning brought rain, unusual for the City at this time of year, but it felt right somehow, as though the weather itself was mourning with us.

It took until midday before anyone had time to remember that the negotiations were due to start that night. Several of the delegates suggested calling the whole thing off and going after the Blood and the Beasts with all our strength.

Surprisingly, it was Guy who talked them back around. Amongst the dead Beasts was Henri Favreau. The other Beast Kind corpses that the Templars could identify belonged to the same group of rogues as him. Which meant there was no way to prove a connection to any particular pack. Wholesale slaughter wasn't the answer.

We had to do what we could to try and rebuild a peace, even if that looked like a near impossible task just now. Guy was rumpled and a bruise blossomed around his eye, and all of us knew that Holly had almost died during the attack. Perhaps it was that—that he could still speak of peace when he had ample right to want revenge—which let cooler heads prevail.

Father Cho and the Guilds sent people to secure the area chosen for the negotiations—a plain outside the City limits that offered no cover for any ambushes and didn't have any structures for follow-up explosions. Much like the place where the treaty had first been forged. Makeshift stands would hold the rows of chairs and the metalmages would conjure a speaker's circle up from the earth. If it rained we would all get wet, but other than that we would be in a location difficult to sabotage. The delegations would use some of the Templars' field headquarters tents to retire and discuss and privacy would come from wards.

It was as good as we could manage.

All that remained to be seen was whether or not the queen would keep her word and come to negotiate.

By late afternoon I was exhausted and snatched a few hours' sleep. It was nearly six by the time I awoke, which gave me just enough time to eat and change and drink several cups of one of Bryony's teas that scalded the fatigue from my body but left me feeling somewhat strange, as though I couldn't quite feel my feet on the floor.

I assumed it wouldn't impair me in any real way or else Bryony wouldn't be feeding it to half the delegation. Unless of course, Bryony was the mastermind behind the attacks and she was taking us out in one fell swoop. The unlikeliness of this scenario made me want to giggle and I bit my lip hard, not looking at anyone as I climbed into one of the carriages waiting to take us to the negotiation field.

The tea did nothing to soothe the nerves that churned my stomach and made my palms damp. This night had the potential to shape the rest of my life. The rest of all our lives.

And Fen would be there, a small voice in my head chimed in. I shoved it away. I didn't care about Fen, I told myself.

I nearly believed the lie.

Chapter Twenty-three

FEN

I watched the queen warily as we stepped into the carriage that would take us back to the City. I'd been watching her warily for the last three days—had it been only three? I was losing track of time here in the Veiled World—trying to learn anything I could from her that might help me survive her mercurial moods.

She had kept me by her side every waking moment. There had been no sleeping moments. I should have been exhausted, but whatever the queen had done to me, it had apparently allowed me to connect to the source of power that gave the Fae their stamina, as I was still wide awake.

Of course, it might also have been the never-ending adrenaline-inducing tightrope of trying not to provoke the queen. In my days with her I had seen her weep and rage and fall into frozen silence.

She also spent hours asking me to see for her, sending my mind down countless possible futures. The fact that I could now do so without pain and that I could also turn the ability off when I needed to was a joy. I should have been grateful to her.

And maybe I would have been, if she had taken the

memory of Saskia from me at the same time she'd burned away whatever had been tangling my control of my powers.

But she hadn't and I couldn't forget. No more than I could forget Holly and Reggie. Nor could I forgive.

But I would accept the price the queen had demanded if she managed to hold the treaty together. I had promised to serve and I would do so for as long as she required. Of course, I risked being assassinated by one of her other courtiers, none of whom seemed particularly happy with my presence in the court. I was thankful that the Fae could not kill with just a look or I would have been dead many times over since I'd come to Summerdale. Lord sa'Eleniel was amongst those who disapproved of me. He tapped his cane and turned his back on me whenever our paths crossed.

Being the queen's new favorite was an uneasy position.

As the queen settled back against the cushioned seats of the carriage, I cleared my throat.

"Do you have any final instructions for me, Your Majesty?" I asked.

"You will know what is required of you." Her voice was distant and I took it as a sign that I should be silent. I was happy enough to comply. The queen had not been impressed when one of her court had pointed out that I was a named delegate in the human delegation and would therefore, to fulfill the requirements of treaty law, need to sit with them. I could only be with the queen during the breaks when the humans spared me.

Personally I thought it unlikely that the humans would welcome me back, but they couldn't gainsay treaty law any more than the queen could. So they would have to let me be with them, even if they didn't acknowledge me.

Which meant I could at least see Saskia. Not speak to her—that would be too cruel—but see her for a little while longer and store away a few more memories to take with me back to Summerdale.

As I had anticipated, Guy almost exploded when I appeared by the humans' allocated seats and presented myself to Father Cho. Only Father Cho's restraint saved me from a fist to the face or worse. The Abbott General's eyes were cool though, as he instructed me where to sit—next to

Brother Anthony in one of the front rows. Just as I turned to leave, he called my name.

"Yes, Father?" I said.

"There are things you should know," Father Cho said. "After the ceremony, find me."

"Yes, Father. I will."

I thanked him again and went to find my seat, wondering what it was that he wanted to tell me.

I'd been hoping to be dismissed to the back row, where I would be able to watch Saskia. Now I wouldn't be able to see her without turning and that would not win me any favor with the queen.

Still, I couldn't help searching the crowd for Saskia's face. Eventually I spotted her standing with Bryony. At first she didn't see me but all too quickly, her eyes found mine. They went wide, then she blanched and turned away.

I hadn't expected the rejection to hurt quite as much as it did.

Still, I had only myself to blame. As the sun drifted lower in the sky, the Beasts arrived and took their assigned places. Martin also sent a vicious look in my direction, reminding me that he and I had unfinished business too. Ah well, he could apply to the queen in Summerdale if he wanted a piece of me.

The thought of his face when he found out my new position was almost cheering.

As was the fact that I was still free from the visions. I'd been half afraid that once I left Summerdale, I would lose my newly gained control, but apparently the queen had done a thorough job. I opened my mind a crack to test the theory and then slammed it shut again when the press of so many people's futures sprang up around me with the fury of a thunderstorm. It didn't hurt, but it was overwhelming.

Time enough for that later on. I would use my sight as I could to help the Fae and the humans, but it would be easier during the negotiations, when I could focus on the one person in the speakers' circle as the queen had taught me to do.

I looked back at the delegates only to find Bryony's father—who had joined the Fae delegates to replace one of the dead—regarding me with displeasure. Wonderful. I had made myself persona non grata with all four races. Quite the accomplishment.

I focused my attention on the shining gold circle that looked so out of place amidst the green of the grass. As far as I could tell, the metalmages had called the metal up out of the earth. It seemed part of the field rather than being laid on top of the grass. It wasn't as impressive as the circle at the Treaty Hall and the four platforms that marked the compass points were plain polished wood. They didn't hold the chests and the stones—those would have been destroyed in the explosions—but they would serve as places for the leaders of the delegations to stand while they swore themselves to the service of the negotiations.

Lady only knew if those oaths would hold this time.

The field itself was so ringed and overlaid with wards that the magic shimmered like an ocean. Roared like one too, the rolling buzz of the spells ringing in the back of my head. Far more wards than the Treaty Hall. Or maybe they were just less subtle, having been hastily laid. I wondered what they felt like to the Fae and the mages who were more sensitive than I. Maybe something like the visions felt to me.

As the night turned to true dark, the first of the Blood arrived.

Lady Adeline and her contingent, accompanied by a squad of well-armed Templars..

The Blood's seats had been divided into two sections with a barrier of wood that gleamed with wards, which I guessed was the best solution possible to the split in the Blood Court, given the tradition that each race's delegates must sit together. Even if Ignatius had gained control over the rest of the Court, with Adeline here he couldn't claim all their votes, and that was some small comfort.

Then Ignatius arrived, followed by a retinue of silent and subdued-looking Blood. I saw Adeline studying faces and frowning. Not good. My wrist ached suddenly and I rubbed it absently.

The Fae healers had mended the damage my chain had done to my wrist as best they could—the skin looked perfectly healthy now—but it still twinged occasionally. The iron would take some time to loose its hold on my body, it seemed. The pain was almost comforting in a strange way. A familiar thing in my new life.

When everyone was finally settled, a silence fell across

the assembled delegates. The night sounds of wind and the buzzing snap of the lamps hung from poles around the square to light the proceedings were suddenly very loud.

Without the Speaker—the queen had refused to name a replacement—it seemed everyone was uncertain as to how things were to begin.

Though I was unsurprised when it was the queen herself who rose to step into the circle.

The silence deepened as she rotated to face each of the races in turn. "These negotiations have been disrupted once," she said. "To the pain and cost of many of you. I will not tolerate further disruptions. Heed my words well." Her veils shifted a few shades closer to gray, then lightened again.

"We will begin with the naming of the delegates, as there are changes in some delegations. We will begin with the Beasts, then the humans, then the Blood. I continue to speak for the Fae."

She turned once more, nodded her head at Pierre Rousselline. He rose hastily and moved to the east platform to recite the names of the delegates, speaking the names with as much speed as he could muster and still remain coherent. The Beasts, it seemed, were not of a mind to challenge the queen in her current mood. At least, not openly.

The human leaders, Father Cho and the Masters of the Guilds and Barnabas Stoke, were slightly more dignified in their recitations, but they too did not linger at the south platform.

As Ignatius moved to take his place on the west platform, I straightened, preparing myself to let the visions free and see what I could see.

Ignatius nodded at the queen and then drew a folded parchment from inside his jacket and held it out to her. "Your Majesty, these delegates have ceded their votes to my control."

The queen's veils fluttered. She unfolded the parchment slowly and bent her head to read.

"You'll find it is in order. You can question those assembled here." Ignatius said.

The queen's head lifted. "This is not the full complement of Blood delegates." She turned to Adeline. "Lady Adeline, do you not join Lord Ignatius?"

Adeline rose in her seat. "Your Majesty, I do not. Neither do those here with me. We will cast our own votes."

"Very well." The queen folded the parchment. "Thank you, Lord Ignatius." She held the paper out to him and as he reached for it, I let the sight rise, curious what I might see from the queen and Ignatius in such close proximity.

The sensation was something like time fracturing. A rain of sparks clouded my eyes, and then I saw the future roll out before me, like a series of moving pictures, clear as day.

I saw Ignatius take the parchment, saw him turn and nod at someone within the Fae delegation. Saw a rising figure and the spark of gunpowder. Saw myself throw myself forward and somehow . . . somehow manage to push the queen out of the bullet's path. Saw myself rise to my feet and tackle Ignatius and then time fractured again.

Time sped, moving faster. There was the uproar of the negotiations, Ignatius being carried off, saw the queen rise to her feet and regain control. Then the negotiations faded and even my excitement turned to a chill. Because then the flood of images became a torrent and they were as I had seen all along. Death. War. Destruction. The City in flames.

I shook my head, feeling the movement in slow motion. How could that be true? If I saved the queen, how could it bring ruin upon us anyway?

But the vision clamped down around me, insistent, tearing my mind with vicious certainty.

I couldn't interfere.

I blinked, swallowed, saw Ignatius' fingers close around the parchment. He smiled at the queen, fangs very white in the flickering lamplight. I sat frozen as he turned and nodded to the Fae delegation.

I sprang to my feet, unable to accept that I was meant to stand idly by and watch someone die. Calling on any speck of my Beast heritage, I flung myself into motion, sprinting across the circle. The queen rose, her veils a shifting gleam of color. Behind me I heard shouts, but I was focused on the Fae behind the queen. Who had I seen? Who?

Gods. I needed Saskia's power to sense the metal of the gun. If it was even metal . . .

There. Several rows behind the queen, one of the Fae men had half risen.

From behind me, I heard someone—Saskia, perhaps—

shout my name but there was no time to pay it any heed. The Fae man was nearly on his feet.

"Stop him!" I yelled, trying to run even faster. So close now. I sprang through the suddenly confused crowd of Fae and tackled the man, throwing him to the ground.

My pulse roared in my ears as I saw fury and fear roll over his face. I tightened my grip, knowing that if he chose to use his powers on me, I was a dead man.

But still, I had stopped him. Victory flooded through me.

And then I heard the gunshot. A thunderclap of hate echoing across the field.

Sweet Lady, *no*.

I let go of my captive and thrust myself to my feet, but I was slow. Too slow. As I twisted toward the queen, she fell, a red stain flooding across her veils. Ignatius smiled as he watched her fall.

Pandemonium erupted.

I was the first to reach the queen, managing a solid punch to Ignatius' face as I passed him. Luckily for me, he couldn't retaliate as a tide of Templars and enraged Fae quickly encircled me.

I pressed my fingers against the queen's wrist, hoping desperately to find a pulse. Somebody put their hands on my shoulders, yanking me backward. I snarled a protest, then subsided as I saw Guy. One of the Fae healers bent to the queen, put her hand on her chest, face intent. I felt a surge of power.

Lady, please. Gods. *Anyone.*

The healer's face twisted with sudden grief. She shook her head and straightened. "There is nothing I can do. We will take her back to Summerdale."

I swallowed against the nausea rising. This was my fault. I hadn't seen this future. I should have saved her. We needed her.

I rose as one of the queen's guard lifted her, readying myself to follow them back to Summerdale, but somebody stepped into my path. I recognized Lord sa'Eleniel.

"Where do you think you are going, *hai'salai*?" he said coldly.

"The queen . . . I swore to serve her."

"The queen has no more need of service," he said. "If

you wish to live, I suggest you remain here amongst your own kind."

His cane hit the earth with a thump and he turned and followed those carrying the queen.

I watched him, my mouth open, not entirely believing him. The queen . . . how could she be dead? It was only a bullet. Surely the Fae could heal such a wound.

I turned and stumbled away, leaning over the nearest vacant seat to retch onto the grass.

The queen was dead.

Lady help us all.

For the second time, the delegates streamed away from the negotiations as fast as possible. I caught a fleeting glimpse of Simon hurrying Saskia toward a carriage, but I didn't go after them. Instead I followed Brother Anthony and found myself in a wagon with six armed Templar knights. They were too busy watching the night around us, weapons at the ready, to bother about me and I didn't press the issue.

I locked my powers down tightly. I didn't dare look. Not yet. I didn't want to see that I had ruined everything.

I just wanted to go home.

Not that I had a home to go to.

When the wagon passed through the gates of the Brother House, my first thought was to find Holly. She, at least, might still speak to me.

I nearly bumped into Liam as I walked into the Brother House.

"Fen." He frowned. "What are you doing here?" His tone was distinctly unwelcoming.

"I wanted to see Holly and Reggie," I said. "Then I'll go."

His expression turned odd. "I see. You should come with me."

I didn't like the sudden studied neutrality of his voice. But I wasn't going to ask questions. I wasn't sure I was ready for the answers. Liam hurried me through the hallways to one of the guest chambers. He knocked once, then opened the door, gesturing me through.

Holly was lying on the bed propped up on pillows. She wore loose trousers and a looser shirt, her hair roughly piled up on her head. She looked too pale and too thin.

Her eyes lit at the sight of me and I had to take a deep breath.

"Fen!"

I crossed the room without thinking, dropping to my knees and hugging her. She made a soft noise of protest and I let her go. "Gods. Are you hurt? Holly? What's wrong?"

I searched her face and was horrified to see her look of pleasure had turned to sadness, tears welling in her eyes. "I'm fine," she gulped. "I was hurt but I'll be all right. But, Fen . . ."

She didn't need to tell me. I saw it suddenly, clear as day. Saw Reggie with no light in those pretty blue eyes. Saw Holly screaming as she defended her.

I swallowed hard. Reggie. My little sister. Gone. I didn't know what to say, so I just hugged Holly to me again and let her cry.

SASKIA

It was Liam who told me where to find Fen. In the craziness at the negotiations I had lost sight of him as Simon dragged me away and shoved me into a carriage headed for the Brother House.

I'd seen him spring to his feet just before the queen had been shot, had seen his desperate sprint across the field, but then he'd vanished behind a wall of Fae and Templars and I didn't know whether he was hurt or even still alive.

But I knew I wanted to find out.

Stupid stupid stupid.

Was there anything stupider than love?

I'd half expected to hear that he had returned to Summerdale, following his precious queen, but then Liam had passed me in the corridor and, with a grimace that expressed clearly how unhappy he was with the situation, stopped to tell me that Fen was with Holly.

I'd almost kissed him. Sweet, serious Liam. Who'd been very quiet since Reggie had died. Quiet and deeply angry.

Those who choose to be Templars don't contemplate

failure. Nor do they accept it easily. I knew that well enough from my brother.

And I understood that particular sentiment. I didn't like failure either and carried my own burden of guilt and grief that we'd arrived too late to save Reggie. And now, tonight, I hadn't felt the weapon that had killed the queen. None of the mages had. Not soon enough anyway.

The field had been awash with magic and the earthsong was so much stronger away from the City that it had been hard to feel anything at all. I had felt a strange surge of power before the shot, had screamed Fen's name as though that might help but I hadn't stopped anything. Once again, too late. Yet here I was, unable to stop myself from walking toward my biggest failure of all.

The door to the room where Holly was recuperating from her wound was half ajar and I heard the sound of her crying before I reached it.

She had been nearly inconsolable since Reggie had died. Simon had been worried that between Fen's defection and Reggie's loss, she wouldn't want to recover from her wounds, but she had pulled through. Now she just had to deal with the grief.

I hoped I could help her with that, as she had comforted me after Fen had left.

I pushed the door open quietly and saw Fen sitting on the bed, his arms around Holly.

He looked so lost my heart cracked all over again.

Stupid stupid stupid.

"Fen." His name left my tongue on a breath before I could stop myself.

Green, green eyes met mine. He smiled sadly. "Hello, Saskia."

Holly lifted her head from his shoulder, made a gulping effort to stop her tears. I pulled a handkerchief from my sleeve and passed it to her. She blew her nose noisily, then blinked up at me. "Thanks," she said. It was a familiar exchange. I'd spent too many hours with Holly as she'd cried these last few days. And shedding tears of my own. Though those weren't all for Reggie.

"You told him about Reggie, then?" I asked, not knowing what else to say.

Holly nodded, gulped again.

I made myself look at Fen. "I'm sorry for your loss." That was the truth, at least. No matter what pain lay between us, the loss of a loved one was something nobody deserved.

"Thank you," he said, equally formal.

"Are you—"

"Are you—"

We both started, stopped, fell back into awkward silence. Beside Fen, Holly snorted, the glimmer of a smile on her face.

"You two need to talk," she said. "Go on. I have to take another dose of Bryony's disgusting tonic now and it makes me fall asleep."

"Are you sure?" I said. "I don't like leaving you alone."

She rolled her eyes. "You sound like Guy. Go on. Come back in an hour or two." She gave Fen's arm a little shove. "Don't even think about arguing with me."

He kissed her cheek quickly and I tamped down the flare of envy that sparked in my chest. "I won't be far."

Outside in the corridor, we looked at each other in another awkward silence. Part of me wanted to stay with him, part of me wanted to flee before he could hurt me all over again.

I pointed down the hall. "There are a few empty chambers that way."

He nodded and we walked. I could feel the gap between our bodies like a wall of ice. But I didn't move closer. I wasn't quite that foolish.

Another silence descended as we entered the room. It held a bed and a table and chair, as did most of the guest chambers. There was no way I was going to sit on the bed, so I crossed the room and perched myself on the table, hands gripping its edges.

"Are you staying long?" I asked in a rush before he could say something.

He nodded. "The queen is dead."

I sucked in a breath. "Dead? But she—"

His mouth thinned. "Dead."

My mind went blank for a moment, then a thousand questions sprang to mind. I started with the most obvious. "What does that mean?"

Fen shrugged. "For the negotiations? I don't know. But

it does mean that I'm not going back to Summerdale. I didn't exactly endear myself to the court while I was there."

"Really? You annoying people? Who would have thought it?" I said, unable to stop myself.

His mouth quirked and I hated the fact that my heart warmed a little when it did.

"The Fae are immune to my charms, it seems."

"Lucky them," I muttered. Then I squared my shoulders. "So are you leaving the City? Going somewhere *safe*?" The last word cracked more sharply than I intended and he winced.

"Ah," he said. "I guess I deserved that."

All at once all the hurt and anger boiled over me. "You have the fact that I don't want to inflict any further hurt on Holly to thank for me not showing you exactly what you deserve," I snarled, hands biting harder into the wood.

"Am I allowed to defend myself?"

"Can you?"

"I don't expect you to believe me, but I did it to protect you."

That was the last thing I had expected him to say. "What?"

"I had a vision, back in Summerdale, when she asked me to stay. The queen was going to kill you if I didn't agree."

"What? Are you insane? Why in earth's name would she do that?"

"I don't know." He shrugged, the gesture studiously casual, but his eyes were very intent on my face. "Maybe it wasn't a true vision. But I couldn't take the risk."

"But that's crazy."

"No. But I'm not entirely sure she wasn't. The last few days have been . . . odd, to say the least. I think she loved the Speaker and I think she was very tired of ruling the court alone."

"But she was the Veiled Queen. All that power . . ." I faded off. Power, I knew, was little consolation for grief.

"Power doesn't mean that much, in the end. Not if you're alone." He looked away for a moment. "She seemed very lonely to me."

"I didn't get that impression."

"Maybe it was a case of like recognizing like." He

stopped, rubbed at his eyes for a moment. "She helped me, after all. And look how I repaid her."

Now I was honestly confused. "I don't understand."

He held out his right arm, pushed his sleeve back. No chain. No bruising on his wrist. No raw red skin.

"She cured you?"

"She did something. Fixed whatever it was in me that fought the power. My visions are under my control now. Much good that it did her."

"What's that supposed to mean?"

He looked away again. His shoulders were tense, stretching the black velvet of his elaborate coat. I got the feeling he was trying not to break down.

"Fen?" I slid down from the table, moved closer to him. "What's wrong?"

"I saw what was going to happen." He lifted his head, green eyes bleak. "Just before. I saw it, Saskia. Saw someone shooting the queen."

"And you tried to stop it."

He shook his head. "But I failed. I didn't see the second man—whoever it was who fired the shot—in my vision. Maybe I wasn't looking hard enough. Because I saw what came after if I did save her. There wasn't going to be a peace, not if the queen lived. The City was going to fall."

"But—"

"You don't have to believe me. I wouldn't, if I were you." Despair cracked his voice and I somehow knew that I did believe him. Knew that the man before me was true, as clearly as I knew the lines of metal threading the earth beneath me. Knew what he'd done and what it had cost him.

And I knew that I loved him for it. He'd risked everything he'd had. Given up those he'd loved to save us. Stood alone to face what might come.

Brave. Braver than me with my family always standing at my back. He'd been willing to give up his entire life for the City. To save all of us.

"I do believe you," I said.

"Why?"

"Because you're you," I said and I reached up to kiss him and show him he wasn't alone any longer.

Epilogue

FEN

The night of the first curfew, we gathered on the roof of the Brother House to watch the sun set. All six of us, standing silent watch as the sky darkened.

Below us, we saw the line of sentry lamps wink into life along the edges of the human boroughs. Ignatius had declared the peace broken, and though he hadn't yet made any moves other than stating that the Night World boroughs were subject to Night World law and no others, no one believed he would be content with that for long.

The human council had declared a curfew. No one other than Templars would be allowed to cross from the human boroughs into the border boroughs—those that hadn't petitioned to belong to the humans and thereby declared themselves truly no-man's-land—after sunset.

Tonight that decree would be put to the test. Beside me, Guy stared down at the line of lights. He would be patrolling later and I imagined that had something to do with the whiteness of Holly's knuckles as she held his hand.

I tightened my arm around Saskia. I didn't know exactly what she—and Holly perhaps—had said to her brothers, but they hadn't tried to beat me up yet and they were talking to me, so whatever it was had worked.

Which brought us to where we now stood. Six of us, united against a common enemy. There had been no word from Summerdale about the state of the Court. Bryony refused to talk about it or go home, and the rest of the Fae in the City—the few who remained—were equally tight-lipped.

"What now?" Lily asked, breaking the silence.

"We have the day," Guy said, his free hand flexing, the cross tattooed there rippling like blood. "We'll hold the night."

I felt a shiver run through Saskia and pulled her closer. She smiled up at me.

"What do you see?" she said softly.

I shook my head. "I—" But then I stopped, flames springing up around me and spreading out across the City. And through them, an army came riding to meet the Blood. I blinked and the vision disappeared as quickly as it had come. "I think we're going to need some help," I said.

Guy grunted. "Already working on it. Might take a while."

Simon shifted, and a ball of light sprang to life in his hand. I felt the warmth of it, warm as Saskia's body against mine. Sunlight. *Hope*.

"All right," Simon said. "We hold."

ABOUT THE AUTHOR

M. J. Scott is an unrepentant bookworm. Luckily she grew up in a family that fed her a properly varied diet of books and these days is surrounded by people who are understanding of her story addiction. When not wrestling one of her own stories to the ground, she can generally be found reading someone else's. Her other distractions include yarn, cat butlering, dark chocolate, and fabric. She lives in Melbourne, Australia.

CONNECT ONLINE

www.mjscott.net
twitter.com/melscott
facebook.com/authormjscott

Want to connect with fellow science fiction and fantasy fans?

For news on all your favorite Ace and Roc authors, sneak peeks into the newest releases, book giveaways, and much more—

"Like" Ace and Roc Books on Facebook!

facebook.com/AceRocBooks